SINGING TO THE SUN

SINGING TO THE SUN

A Novel

REGINA RODRÍGUEZ SIRVENT

TRANSLATED BY BETH FOWLER

Previously published as *Les calces al sol* by Penguin Random House Grupo Editorial in Spain in 2022. Translated from Spanish by Beth Fowler. First published in English by Amazon Crossing in 2026.

Published by Amazon Crossing, Seattle

www.apub.com

EU product safety contact:
Amazon Media EU S. à r.l.
38, avenue John F. Kennedy, L-1855 Luxembourg
amazonpublishing-gpsr@amazon.com

ISBN-13: 9781662532443 (paperback)
ISBN-13: 9781662532436 (digital)

Cover illustration and design by Philip Pascuzzo
Cover image: © AdrianHillman / Getty

Printed in the United States of America

To my father, for believing in dreams.
To my mother, for holding us all together.
To my brother, for everything in life.
To Koeman, for existing.
To Guillem, for the magic.
To Nord, for infinity.
To Bruc, the explosion of light.

To my host family, for becoming family.
To Aksel, Eva, and Bini, because
I could never do them justice.
To Lídia, for the great adventure.
To Clari, for coming: We'll always have
the Grand Canyon.
To Britt Dean, for seeing me.

AUTHOR'S NOTE

Any resemblance between fictional characters and real people is no coincidence. You'll never know what is true and what isn't. But the truth doesn't really matter anyway.

Part One

The Neon Sign

"So, how did you know you wanted to be a . . . a waxtress?"

Pam concentrates. Molten wax drips onto my thigh. I'm anticipating second-degree burns.

"Well, I became an *aesthetician*"—she emphasizes the word "aesthetician"—"because I was always the best out of all the cousins at doing my auntie Paquita's hair." She blows on the wax. "Is it still scalding?"

"Yes, Pam, it's torture . . . You know, I've got a very important date tomorrow night, so the appearance of my inner thigh is going to be crucial . . ."

(I don't actually know for sure whether I have a date; I've been waiting two days for him to text, but nothing.)

"*Okay*, quit complaining—it's barely a burn at all; I'll give you a one-euro discount."

"One day you should do it for free, as compensation for all the epidermis I've left on this bed."

"Hey, don't get all technical on me with your 'epidermis.' Shall I do your arms?"

"Pam, no! Isn't the rest of my body enough? Anyway, they're not too bad."

"What do you mean, not too bad? This shaggy coat wouldn't be acceptable in the zoo."

"So, you figured out your vocation in life because you did Auntie Asunción's hair nicely?"

"Auntie Paquita."

"Paquita. And that's it?"

"God, Rita, you're such a pain. Yes, when I was little, I liked doing my dolls' hair, my sisters' hair, and Auntie Paquita's hair."

"Uh-huh . . ."

"And, as an adult, I don't know—I just saw it clearly. One day I realized this had always been my vocation. It lit up in my head like a neon sign. I've been into beauty design since I used to put conditioner in swimmer Barbie's hair and give Ken hair-follicle transplants."

"Ken was bald? I always thought he had a good head of hair."

"In my house, he was bald. No more questions, please. Why do you want to know, anyway? Aren't you about to finish your degree?"

"Look, see that piece of paper where you've put that blob of wax full of my crotch hair?"

"Yes."

"Well, that's the slip I need to take in to find out my grade for English, the last of my marks for the year. If I pass, I'll be a graduate."

"Wow! A graduate! A lawyer!"

"Psychologist."

"Damn! A shrink! Don't go analyzing me, huh? My nails have always been like this, you know. Well, actually, no, my mom—"

"Pam, relax. That's not how it works. Anyway, I have no intention of practicing. I studied psychology just to get a degree, because I didn't know what to do with my life, and . . . that's it."

"And?"

"And now that I'm about to graduate, I still don't know."

"And so?"

"So nothing, no vocation. I'll have to look for that neon sign you were talking about."

Pam gives one last agonizing tug and removes three layers of skin in the process; my eyes swim with tears, but she doesn't bat an eyelid.

"Honestly, Pam, are you sure your name isn't Dolores?"

I venture outside, trying to minimize the dry graze of my pants against my skin. It stings like hell. The Barcelona sun dips behind a fluffy cloud as I make my way across the main square outside the Universitat Autònoma, which is erupting into the euphoria of the last week of school, June 2007: cries and laughter and class photos tucked under arms. I look at the sky, close my eyes, and allow myself a luxury I haven't yet earned: the feel of summer on my face.

I check my reflection in the glass wall of the newspaper library and decide that I don't look too bad—toned body with no superfluous curves, a dark mane of straight but untamed hair, scorched quads beneath my jeans. I've got two weeks before the hair grows back.

I check my phone: still no messages.

I leave the square behind me and walk toward campus. The others have been waiting for me a while, and I suspect we'll be a sizable group today. I pause at the main door of the language school and take a deep breath before striding in decisively, my flip-flops slapping noisily down the corridor.

I'm sure I've passed. For the first time ever, I checked over all my assignments. Filled in the blanks in the sentences. Searched for quality synonyms, and watched and rewatched the tape where Stephanie goes out for fish-and-chips. Impossible to fail.

My hand lingers on the doorknob, and, just as I'm about to enter, my phone rings: Manolo Escobar, pride of Andalusia, singing "*Mi carro me lo robaron*" embarrassingly loudly.

I turn it off—I'll call her later; I'm too nervous to talk to anyone right now. Summer is waiting for me. My degree. The future. Life.

I take another deep breath and, forcing a smile, knock on the door. Every little thing helps.

"Come in." A sharp voice greets me, although its owner doesn't even look up from her papers. Typical British warmth.

"Good morning, Soooz—"

"Ah, Rita. It's you." Her disappointment couldn't be plainer.

Oh, Susan! "Sooozan," as she makes us call her, in an attempt to neutralize our Spanish pronunciation. She's the perfect representative of the expat community here in Catalonia: Originally from a small walled town near Newcastle, she must be in her sixties, slim and pale, and she compensates for the thinness of her hair by blasting it with a hair dryer every morning. Her teeth are uneven and stained the hippie yellow of someone who lived in London through the 1970s. Perhaps she and her husband have a lot of sex, but you wouldn't know it. She must have been good-looking in her youth; I picture her strong and svelte, with one of those bodies full of promise. That's why she doesn't think she should be here, teaching in this state-run university in southern Europe, closer to Africa than Yorkshire, and resents the sight of the girl in front of her now, forty years younger and totally clueless.

"I've come to get my slip signed and find out my grade . . ." A blob of wax is obscuring the file number. I try to peel it off.

"Just give it to me. It doesn't matter . . ."

"Just a second, it's . . ." I can't hand it to her with hair on it. Damn it, Pam!

"Rita."

"It's almost there . . ."

"Rita."

"One second."

"Rita, you failed."

"Wh-what?"

"You failed English."

Shit.

"But . . . I can't have! I know how to order fish-and-chips and . . ."

"How can you know an English word like 'clumsy' and yet be incapable of producing a simple phrase in the conditional tense?"

"But, I do . . . I know the conditional just fine . . ." I've always struggled with the conditional, although I know I was taught it, starting in third grade.

"Listen." Susan leans her skinny torso over the desk. "If you can translate, right here, right now, the phrase '*Hoy podría acabar la carrera*,' I'll pass you."

"Just like that?"

"Just like that."

"One second, one second, let me think . . ."

"Now."

"Tudei . . ." Five words and I'll get my degree. But what are they? "Tudei, ai . . . will . . ." Shit! "Ai will could . . . finish . . . de digrí."

"I'll see you next year."

As the door closes behind me, I screw up the exam paper in my hand, having left my dignity and dream summer on Sooozan's gray desk. My flip-flops dragging now, I retrace my steps down the corridor, wondering how to tell my parents I won't graduate because I don't know how to speak a language I've been learning since the age of eight. Shit.

I choose the path heading away from the language school, noticing the red roses climbing the warm cement walls across the street. I take out my phone, which has been playing in my mind, and listen to the message Yaya left me after Manolo stopped singing.

She wants me to bring her some salt cod from La Boqueria market, from Carme's stand, because her friends are coming to the restaurant tomorrow, and she wants to make them a good *esqueixada* salad. She also tells me she doesn't want to go on the Social Services outing to see the barnacle farms in Galicia because she doesn't give a damn about barnacles, but mainly because Social Services trips are for old people. She's eighty-four. She moans that it's so cold that the geraniums won't have grown in time for San Pedro's day, plus another thirteen minutes twenty-eight seconds of other disappointments. And, of course, that it's been too long since I visited.

I absentmindedly drop the exam paper that has ruined my day. I bend down to pick it up and toss it in a trash can.

A gentle sun warms my face, lighting up the expanse of greens and browns of the garden of Vila Universitària, Barcelona's student village. I catch sight of Bombo, a twentysomething guy who's been "about to finish geography" ever since I arrived. He's performing one of his songs for an audience of four soon-to-be freshmen who've come to visit the campus. Bombo and the new arrivals sing the chorus enthusiastically, feeling they're part of that clichéd dream where the shaggy-haired senior sings a song he wrote bare chested and with ink-stained fingers, on a guitar plastered with antiestablishment stickers.

A red car pulls up, and a couple of parents get out, somewhat reluctantly, as if attending a distant cousin's wedding. The father adjusts his pants and stares at Bombo with open disgust, the repugnance common in parents about to leave their perfect, virginal daughters in what looks to them more like the Playboy Mansion than an esteemed college.

Bombo's audience has grown. Now he's oversinging the chorus as though he's in AC/DC, but the lyrics are something like "I like you more than Gram-Gram's macaroni. Yeah, yeaaah . . ."

The mother from the red car smiles with wistful joy, seeming to drift into a dream, or perhaps a memory, in which she would have liked to have played the lead role all those years ago, when she still thought in the first person. Finally, from the back of the car, between suitcases and two bags of oranges, the daughter emerges—a child of eighteen who gazes at her surroundings as if she's just landed on the moon, or even farther away, her open mouth betraying both excitement and terror.

It's half past one. The sun is beating down, and the smell coming from Tupperware containers being opened simultaneously in the hundreds of kitchens around me is a reminder that I'm running late. What a drag having to tell my friends I failed English. And I'm so hungry.

But, suddenly, without warning, the world stops.

My throat goes dry. The brief double beep of my phone surges into a ripple of hope, the simultaneous vibration holds the potential to open the doors to heaven. "Beep-beep, beep-beep."

I slip my hand into my pocket as though trying to deactivate a letter bomb and notice that the scene around me is now playing out in slow motion.

The mouths of Bombo's fans are moving slowly, silently. The red-car family stands stock-still as the bulldog-faced father trips and oranges tumble across the asphalt. My hands are cold, and I can no longer feel the heat of the sun.

I close my eyes and grab my Nokia.

1 NEW MESSAGE.

Let it be him; please, let it be him.

Gonçal: Hey sexy! What's new? I arrive tomorrow night. Come to my place at 9. I have a surprise.

Boom.

My throat reanimates and emits a kind of voiceless cry that might be recognized by a member of the dolphin family. In a matter of seconds, the student village has transformed into a garden of delights, as though a cold shadow has moved away and allowed a mass of wildflowers to grow in its wake. I'm so happy that I picture Bombo wearing mossy underwear.

I reread the message six, seven, thirty-eight times. I conjure an image of tomorrow night as a collage of the nights we've already spent together . . . until a hysterical shout tears me from my daydream.

"Ritaaaaa!" Astrid jumps up with open arms, as though her crazy voice hasn't already alarmed everybody from here to Marrakech.

Thirty-one hours until I see him. I walk over to my friends, looking at the sky and smiling.

"Rita, you're drooling." Demura glances at me over the top of her sunglasses with a slightly disgusted expression.

"Shut up, idiot. Jeez."

"Rita, you have a drop of saliva on your chin. It's glistening in the sun. It's a fact." She lights a joint.

She's right, but luckily the others in the group don't notice the droplet, because they're too busy basking in the inevitable joy of having finished their degrees, of knowing where they'll be working next year, of having a life plan that I don't have, of being able to go to their respective homes in triumph, where their families will cook paella and break open the good cava to celebrate the end of an era.

"*Bono*, *bono*, happy lady, have you finally passed English?" asks Nofre in his sexy Mallorcan accent.

Here we go.

"No." And before I can continue, my friends' officially qualified gazes crush me.

"Shiiiit!" shouts Astrid.

"What do you mean?" asks Demura. "You . . . failed? But it was level one, Rita; it was mandatory for—"

"Yes, I know . . . It doesn't matter, and to be honest, it's no surprise. I'll get there someday."

"But why are you so calm about it?" Astrid still hasn't gotten over the shock.

"What do you want me to do? Don't worry. One day I'll learn English, and I'll see Susan again and chat to her for hours about Yorkshire villages."

"For Christ's sake, Rita, how can you joke at a time like this?"

Perhaps she's right. With my degree in hand, I would have had a plan, whatever that might have been, a provisional neon sign, but now, suddenly, I have nothing. An existential void in every way. Well, no, I have tomorrow and the rest of eternity with Gonçal.

"So, I think the moment has come to open our graduation souvenir," says Nofre with pride, unusual in the modest guy we're used to. "I, Onofre Torres Mulet, a native of Son Macià, grandson, great-grandson, great-great-grandson, and blood relative of the first hominid to set foot on the most glorious island in the Mediterranean . . ." He takes out an octagonal box wrapped in tinfoil and holds it like an offering to the heavens. "I present to you the *ensaïmada verda*, prepared with marijuana I saw sprout from the earth and that today, June 29, 2007, has sacrificed its leafy fruits to become the Hulk of *ensaïmadas*, the missing link between botany and patisserie."

With a single tug, he removes the foil and reveals his masterpiece, tracing a semicircle with his arm, like a bullfighter. Everyone's face lights up.

"But, but, but . . . That's six pounds of marijuana in a pastry spiral!" I shout.

"You can laugh, but you have to try it first." Nofre speaks as though in possession of an absolute truth. He takes out a knife and cuts the green-flecked pastry into overly generous portions.

Thirty hours until I see him.

Wa Yeah!

I wake up draped over the arm of the kitchen chair, my head dangling.

On the table are two packages of Bimbo bread, mashed potato, and an empty pack of Nevados doughnuts. We never buy Nevados doughnuts. Someone must have been here.

"Have you finally regained consciousness?" asks Astrid, lighting a joint at the kitchen counter.

Suddenly, I get a sequence of flashbacks: *The Simpsons*. The American flag. *Mary Poppins*. Three children destroying a stuffed panda I had when I was tiny and haven't thought about since.

"Shit . . . my mouth is dry as anything. My God, I feel like I've been stuffed with sawdust. What happened? What time is it? And who brought those Nevados?"

"You've been sleeping on that chair for ten and a half hours."

"What?"

Astrid bursts out laughing and chokes on the smoke.

"Man, I'm not surprised you've got a dry mouth—you wolfed a whole box of shortbread cookies."

"Shortbread cookies? We had shortbread?"

"Yes, they were out of date. Someone must have brought them to a party at some point. Afterward, of course, your lips started to feel dry, so you decided to eat pâté to make them better."

"Pâté?"

"Pâté, Rita, pâté. And when the pâté didn't help, you gulped down half a carton of juice."

"I don't believe it. You're making it up."

"Ha! Man, what a trip. Fucking Nofre. That was some weed! I woke up at six o'clock because your phone was ringing. You have forty missed calls."

"Gonçal?"

"No, not Gonçal." Astrid takes a drag. "I was pretty far gone, but you . . . I made you some coffee and added a couple of teaspoons of salt, to see if you would react."

"Bitch."

"But you didn't. We were talking for ages. Don't you remember?" Astrid hands me an ibuprofen. "About my trip to America, about whether you're going to walk the Camino de Santiago . . ."

"Me? Walk the Camino de Santiago?"

"That's what you were saying. After that, I have no idea how we got to these chairs. Or how those Nevados doughnuts got here."

On this strange morning, the sun is floating in an ocean of blue sky, its rays filtering through the filthy dining room windows to land on Astrid's ash-colored hair in a kind of visual poem. Astrid, whose innate beauty allows her to handle even a hangover like this with dignity, stretches out lazily on the recliner, which has only a few hours left before being removed from our apartment and returned to the edge of the swimming pool where we found it, four years ago, on the first day of college.

These are the last hours we'll spend together here, just the two of us. The melancholy has already started to gnaw, but we're hiding it well. I'm doing better than her. We hug and reminisce with lumps in our throats.

It isn't long before Astrid starts crying. She's crying at the vertigo of leaving college, at the whirlwind of adult life, the advent of slack skin, and the clothes that, according to her, we can no longer wear. I comfort her and laugh to myself. I find it hard to cry. I find it hard because goodbyes are a bummer, because I have amazing skin, and because I have no intention of changing my wardrobe . . . But mainly, I don't cry, because I'm looking forward to the best date in history.

Once I'm through the Cadí Tunnel, the final frontier before entering the Cerdanya region, high in the Pyrenees, I start singing. I can't help it. Going home, that "home" being the high valley of Cerdanya, is enough to make anyone sing. But today I'm mostly singing to steady my voice, because I'm thinking about him, and my voice is trembling, my knees are trembling, and my life in general is trembling.

As I draw out the final *a* of Cerdanyaaa, made even longer by the brain fog resulting from the ingestion of Mallorcan weed, I start seeing sparks and hyperventilating slightly. I'll stop. Yes, best to stop. I pull up at the side of the road. The pickup smells slightly of cod, even though Carme wrapped it up carefully; what a sight La Boqueria market was today!

The sun is starting to set, and the sky glows in gradients of pink. In the center of the scene, where sky and land meet, the mist melts into droplets that light up the valley.

The mountains, adorned with thousands of pines, frame the picture like a crown—a dense green cape that thins as it progresses down the slope, until it turns into villages of stone houses with black-tiled roofs and pointed bell towers.

Just below me are the fields belonging to our neighbors, the Flotats, Moxó, and Oliu families. Each field sewn into the next with a row of poplars and dirt roads; velvety waves that change color when the wind gets up.

From this height, the cows are miniature toys. They're grazing at the edge of the straightaway where I always used to do my final sprint after running ten miles in training for the ski season.

I used to go as far as the meadow with a long stone wall that reminds me of the one where Morgan Freeman finds the box hidden by Tim Robbins in *The Shawshank Redemption:* "If you've come this far, maybe you're willing to come a little further."

Little by little, the weak evening light starts to stain everything pink. As I get up to leave, I notice the Barcelona train progressing like a zipper closing in slow motion, before disappearing toward Puigcerdà, the closest town with a train station. Everyone will be on that train this weekend—I can almost hear my friends' cries, see Riqui and Riesgo smoking between the carriages—and suddenly I want to party along with them so much, it's killing me.

Up here, there's nothing but silence and tranquility. I take a deep breath and steel myself to continue with my journey.

Gonçal's house lies at the end of an unpaved road that no one ever ventures down. The turnoff is marked by the ruins of a stone building once used by peasants to store their tools, but now no more than an echo of a bygone time, when Cerdanya was more earth than asphalt. But even when you reach the end of the road, you could still mistake the house for the ruins of an ancient church with a huge cherry tree growing up inside it.

I smooth down my white dress and tip out the sample of Coco Mademoiselle perfume that came with *Vogue*, most of it on my neck and chest, and I wipe what's left on my panties.

Breathe in; breathe out. Breathe in; breathe out. The air is filled with thyme and the unmistakable freshness of a summer evening in the mountains. I reach up and grab a handful of cherries, eating them slowly and deliberately, as though this were the start of a porn movie—I can only hope so—swaying my hips exaggeratedly as I walk.

I duck under the branches and finally reach the low stone wall hidden beneath the tree. Pausing again, I take another deep breath before entering the patio; my quavering shadow falls on the wall.

I knock on the door.

"Hello? Gonçal? Gon . . ."

The door opens on its own. On the dining table, there's a note with a freshly plucked oxeye daisy.

I've finished the tree house. I'll wait for you there.

The fact that he's asked me to go to the tree house means that he's decided to deploy all his weapons today. Apparently, it's not enough for us to be in a beautiful stone house built when people still lived in caves. It isn't sufficiently magical that, from the living room, the only sound is the trickle of water in the stream that runs across the yard (I mean, hippies could record it to use as background music for massages!). The bastard has also decided to fix up the tree house, to wait for me there, and to notify me with a handwritten letter and a freshly picked oxeye daisy. I bet he's bought the cheese I like and everything. He's a pro.

To be honest, I'm kind of indignant because just when it seemed impossible to improve him, when it felt like I couldn't fall any deeper in love, I discover that's not true.

I set off toward the tree and inevitably start reminiscing about the first day, when we shared the most romantic walk in the history of walks.

I remember the kisses. The cool water in the pool. The breeze that ruffled our hair just the right amount, as though we were hair models standing in front of a fan at a photo shoot. The birds cartwheeled overhead and seemed to be laughing, their feathers ruffled in the same calculated way by the wind.

We sang "*Wa Yeah!*," by our favorite Mallorcan band, Antònia Font—*Jo cant sa Lluna i s'estrella, sa jungla i es bosc animat*—while life went on somewhere else and the world only existed for him and me. The truth is that shit could have started raining down from the sky, and I still would have thought it the most romantic walk in history.

I remember that when we reached the tree, his face lit up. "It's one of only three redwoods in Cerdanya, and it's all mine! No one ever comes here, Rita!" he said. In fact, there are plenty more redwoods in Cerdanya, and this tree isn't one of them, but who the hell cares?

"I'll do up the house and make a window in the roof so we can watch the stars." And even though I knew I shouldn't fall for it, I believed him.

That day, the tree house was no more than four boards wedged precariously between the branches and some bits of wood nailed into the trunk to serve as footholds. I have a clear memory of the protruding nails, because when he pushed against me to lift my skirt, I felt one digging gently into the base of my spine. But I didn't say anything and let his hands continue their journey between my thighs. The spell only broke for a second, when he said the name of that waitress from El Raval, and I noticed another, invisible, much more painful nail digging in. Even then, I stayed quiet.

Today, I'm venturing down the same little path through the underbrush and feeling both terror and happiness riding on my shoulders.

I come out where the path is intercepted by a pool in the stream. The waterfall is more impressive than I remember it, the crashing water only regaining its velvety texture several yards farther down. But if I want to get there, I have no choice but to cross. Breathe in; breathe out. I feel the solitude. The prelude, the silence, the dramatic noise of the white water sweeping the melted memories of winter along with it.

I plant a foot firmly on one of the largest stepping stones and push forward. One, two, three steps up. I climb to the last rock and, with my hands wet and free, I reach the other side. I continue down a faint path until I reach the last trick of this hideaway: The path seems to disappear behind the brambles, but if you push through, paying the toll of a couple of scratches, the light falls on a flat area that opens up to present the grand finale.

The tree house.

A soft, dark blue has taken over the entire sky. An elegant Pantone shade that contrasts with the freshly painted wood and the candles flickering in the frames of the two windows. Goddamn candles. What a photo it would make. Anger tries to worm its way into the torrent of love, but it's no good. It's too late. Gonçal's silhouette appears in the doorway.

Birdsong merges with the notes of a tune that's just starting. A gentle, but unmistakable drumbeat. A guitar launches into the melody, marking the rhythm of this beautiful night. Summer is truly here now.

A rope shoots out from inside the house and drops to a calculated distance from the ground, suitable only for the daring. I grasp the end with both hands, determined to scale it, and I run my gaze up the rope until I meet his eyes.

The first words of the song, in a Mallorcan accent, rise through the branches: *"Jo cant sa Lluna i s'estrella, sa jungla i es bosc animat . . ."*

At the other end of the rope, Gonçal is smiling, and I see how he's starting to devour me with his eyes: He's standing still, waiting for the right moment to sing me the words that will be seared into my mind forever: "So sexy, so sweet, and so cold, *wa yeah* . . ."

Ripe Tomatoes

Some days are so beautiful they'd make a unicorn vomit. This is one of them.

I'm driving toward my hometown, Alp, with a glorious smile on my face, closing my eyes every few seconds to relive last night. I sniff my lips. I clamp a lock of damp hair between my mouth and nose and inhale the scent of the shampoo I used this morning.

I had to drag myself away after the third call from my mother; they were waiting for me before they started eating, and I couldn't make any more excuses; I told her I was stuck in traffic at the Cadí Tunnel, but we both know it's Sunday and that was a lie.

I pass the village bench; no one is sitting there today. There's not a soul on the street. I pull up outside, touch up the concealer over the hickey on my neck, and let my hair down.

The church bells tell me it's one thirty. I go into the yard and peer through the windows: there's hardly anyone in the restaurant. Good thing, too, because I'm a half hour late.

I decide to go in through the back door to the kitchen and see that the TV is tuned into Channel One. Anne Igartiburu is announcing the day's upcoming features on *Corazón, corazón.*

I see her from behind, talking loudly as she washes tomatoes. She's wearing her usual cleaning tunic, so worn I couldn't tell you what the original colors were, but now a light gray with a faint sprinkling of pink squares and years of history. Her slippers bear traces of soil from the yard.

"Yaya!" I shout too loudly, and a tomato goes flying.

"Jeeeezus!" she says, stretching out the *e* as far as it will go. "*Mi arma*, what a fright ya gave me, honestly!" She spins around with her eyes closed, her back up against the counter.

When she recovers and I'm about to hand her the salt cod, she widens her eyes like saucers and shouts even louder than usual, which is saying a lot.

"Ohohohoh!" Her hand on her chest, her back arched. "Mother of God, jus' look at your face, my girl! You're head over heels, yes you are!"

I stand stock-still; I'm not sure whether I'm more taken aback by the shout or the speed with which she's able to read me. I smooth down my hair and turn to look at myself and make sure I haven't forgotten something.

"Don't go checkin' the mirror. I see it in your eyes—they're the window to the soul, yes they are. And your soul is caught—hook, line, an' sinker, my girl . . ."

I hug her. She smells of bleach and the yard.

"What's going on? What's all the shouting?" My mother rushes in.

"Rita gave me a fright, an' I almost pissed myself, yes I did."

"So, there was traffic, huh?" asks my father, wrapping me in a hug that makes me creak before he sits down to watch the news.

"Yeah, in the tunnel . . ."

"Wow, is that right? A Sunday lunchtime in Cerdanya, you know, big delays can happen . . ." he continues sarcastically.

Now my mother hugs me.

"Hmm, new perfume?"

"Shampoo," I reply.

"Shampoo."

She pretends not to notice that my hair is still wet. She kisses my cheek and tells me it's about time I showed up. She says I'm looking well. I smile, and I'm happy to be home. Especially because no one seems to have remembered that I just got my English results, which determine my immediate, not to mention long-term future. Good thing too; I'm ravenous.

For lunch, we have zucchini soup, a charcuterie board that could halt a train, and soft, homemade *sobrassada* sausage smeared on bread. It's been a month since I last visited, and it feels like an eternity.

I pick up the tomatoes, and I'm assaulted by the image of Gonçal, last night, at the chopping board with his shirt buttoned up askew after we made love for the first time, and me wondering whether it might actually be possible to stop time.

"Rita, Rita!" Every face in my family is turned toward me. "Rita!" My brother shouts again from the kitchen door. "Jeez, you're spaced, huh?"

"Albert!" He picks me up as though I weigh ten pounds. When he lowers me to the ground, he notices the hickey.

"About time you visited, eh?"

"C'mon, let's go! Everyone to the table!" shouts Yaya as she removes the lamb shoulder from the oven.

I think about when I crossed the threshold of the little tree house, a jump up from the topmost foothold. When we didn't say another word. When we started to take each other's clothes off, very slowly. His hands tracing my thighs under the white dress, the song in my ear, his lips on my breasts. The smell of his breath. The clean sheets, the cheeses laid out on a cloth on the floor. A bottle of red wine.

I'm counting the minutes until we go to Girona together. There's something fluttering wildly in my stomach.

"By the way, do you need me in the restaurant on Friday?" I ask. "I'd like to go to Girona."

"To Girona?" says my mother. It's been years since she herself went to the city, just two hours' drive from home.

"Yes, I've arranged to meet Astrid and some others from college. And Santi and his friend"—I try to control the magnitude of my smile before I utter his name—"Gonçal." I wrinkle my nose, trying to repress the dream that one day we'll all be one giant family and get together in this very dining room on Christmas morning.

"I don't need your help on Friday," says my father, without shifting his gaze from the TV, celebrating the replay of Ronaldinho's goal yesterday. "We're quiet this week. You go and have fun."

The wine has notes of almonds and orange peel. I can taste the alcohol, but it isn't harsh. It makes me think of the scent of autumn and Yaya's bony, wrinkled hands working the marzipan to make *panellets* and spending whole afternoons regaling us with tales of smugglers.

"Delicious!" I exclaim wildly, stretching out my dress over my bloated stomach.

"It makes me happy to see you eatin', yes it does, *mi arma*." Yaya gives me a proud kiss.

"So, you failed English?" Albert and I have come outside to kick a ball around.

"Yes, Albert, I did . . ." I warm up with some low passes. "But don't say anything to Mom and Dad. They're a bit worried because things were quiet in the restaurant this June."

"June wasn't any quieter than usual. They say the same every year, and then the *pixapins* start flocking in, and we don't have enough food for them. But Rita"—twenty passes—"how can that be?"

I'm distracted, thinking of that annual influx of city dwellers to our little mountain town, so ill-prepared for the long drives around here that they literally have to "piss on pines" at the roadside.

"How can what be?"

"That you failed! You didn't get your degree!"

"English and me are just incompatible."

"Come off it. You've already passed harder subjects, and not so long ago you got an 'excellent' in a writing assignment, didn't you?"

"True." Forty passes.

"You see?"

"That was lucky. I came up with a good story. But it doesn't matter now. The thing is I don't have a degree." I shoot the ball and recover it with surprising control.

"So, what are you going to do? When will you finish it?"

"Oh, I don't know. I studied psychology, but I could just as easily have studied taxidermy or bagpiping. I would have done it with the same lack of enthusiasm." Sixty-five passes. "The thing is getting a degree, you know?"

"You could sign up for a course in something you like, that you really want to do, and take it from there . . ."

"Yeah, like it's that easy to know what I want to do."

"So, what's going to happen next year?"

"Don't be such a downer, Albert! I don't know. Don't stress me out. I have no idea! Do I have to have my life all figured out at the age of twenty-three or something?"

"Sure, sorry." Albert allows himself a bit of fancy footwork that puts my counting at risk, but he manages to regain control. He returns the ball to me. Eighty.

"For the moment, all I know is that I'm going to Girona this Friday with Gonçal!"

"Uh-huh."

"Life can be wonderful when you have no fucking idea where you'll go after the party, you know?"

"If you say so . . ."

"Ninety-nine, one hundred!"

Dawn

I can't sleep. For the last six nights, I haven't slept a wink. All I can think about is him, his back, his mouth, the cheeses, "*Wa Yeah!*" Today's the day: we're finally going to Girona.

After turning over in bed at least eighty times, I finally give in just after six o'clock. I go down to the kitchen to be met with that unique silence of early morning, when there's a kind of static order to the world, everything poised, ready to burst into action.

There are still a few crickets chirping, but aside from that, the gentle clunk of the bread bin feels like the first sound of this Friday morning. I set the milk on the stove and go to the vegetable patch in search of tomatoes.

A rooster is crowing, and Antònia is milking the first cow. I sit for a while among the tomato plants, imagining how the day will unfold. Gonçal and me, in the streets of Girona; Gonçal and me, eating ice cream; Gonçal and me, going to . . .

"The milk's boilin' overrrrr!" The voice ripples through the window like a shock wave.

I run to the kitchen.

"Yaya! Shhh! Don't shout, damn it! You'll wake the whole village!"

"*Mi arma*, you always do this with milk, yes you do . . . Why you up so early? Are you ill or somethin'?" She nudges a glass of just-squeezed orange juice across the counter toward me.

"I couldn't sleep . . ."

"Of course, you could see it from China, my love. It's because of that Punsá," she says with conviction, rinsing out the milky cloth.

Juice spurts out of my nose.

"Watch, dear. You'll drown yourself."

"Yaya, his name is Gonçal, not Punsá."

"Gunsá, Punsá, what difference does it make? Long as he isn't an assho—"

"Yaya, what are you saying! You don't even know him . . ."

"Belief me, I don' need to."

"Pass me the olive oil, please."

The rest of the house is on the move now. Antoni Bassas is reading the morning news on the radio. Yaya is wearing some kind of mesh on her head and pouring coffee into a huge mug as she hums one of her favorite songs from Radio Teletaxi: "Like a beaver, my girlfriend enjoys a log in her river . . ."

I dunk the bread in the remaining oil on my plate as if my life depends on it and cut myself another slice of my favorite cured sausage, *llonganissa*. Just as I'm about to ask Yaya what the hell the mesh thing is, she turns around, holding a tray bearing a smorgasbord that would exceed the recommended calorie intake for any NBA player: a couple of fried eggs, a glistening *xistorra* sausage, a blood pudding with onion so plump it looks ready to burst, two thick slices of bread soaked in oil, and a mug of coffee with milk.

"But . . . but isn't that your birthday breakfast?"

"Ha! How you think I stay in such good shape? Eatin' lettuce?" She adjusts the mesh on her head. "I'm eighty-four with the cholestrohol of a twelve-year-old boy who goes to confession, yes I am." She dips the blood pudding into the molten egg yolk and continues, "And how you think I keep my skin wrinkle-free, hmm? Nivea isn' *that* good, no it's not, *mi arma*!"

If we're being honest, her face has more wrinkles than a hundred-year-old Basque woodsman.

I run upstairs to dress; it's getting late. For the first time ever, I laid my clothes out before I went to bed last night: ripped jeans, black sweater with a white neckline, and black patent leather shoes. A bold but elegant ensemble. Girona will appreciate my style.

"I'm off!" I shout loudly so everyone can hear me. "I'll be back tonight!"

And just as I'm about to close the door, my brother stomps into the kitchen, swimming trunks in hand, looking very annoyed:

"Yaya! You've pulled the lining out of my trunks again! These ones were new, damn it!" Then Albert realizes that the lining he's looking for is being worn by his grandmother on her head, and his ill humor evaporates in an instant.

I blow a kiss into the air—"Bye!"—and go out to the yard.

Santi's pickup is waiting for me at the gate.

The Most Romantic Restaurant on Earth

Whenever I've been to Girona before, it's been nighttime and I've never ventured any farther than the drink stands at the Sant Narcis festival, sticking to the well-trampled bar areas where it was obligatory to hold a beer in one hand and a joint in the other. Once, with my friend Koeman, I remember we saw someone with a monkey on his shoulder, and we just exchanged a glance and carried on like it was no big deal. So, you could say that I'm visiting the city for the first time today.

I'm also on a special mission. For anyone raised among dish towels and cooking pots, for those whose parents calculated their children's heights according to their potential for serving tables, going to eat in the original restaurant belonging to the Roca family is like going to see the Beatles live.

I peer through the window from outside and catch a glimpse of Mother Roca. Wow, it's like spotting Paul McCartney. I scan the menu and waver between the cod with *samfaina*, pig's feet, or the classic Catalan beef stew, *fricandó*. I still have time. It's so hard to choose.

Astrid is already here but pretends to be just arriving. She's looking gorgeous.

"We can go in now. I reserved a table for four," she announces, seeming simultaneously self-conscious and excited.

"You guys go in. I need to make a call," says Gonçal, moving away with his phone clamped to his ear.

"Gonçal's acting strange. What if he's talking to another woman?" I ask Astrid, panicked and despondent, as we troop into the restaurant.

"Don't overreact," she replies, just to say something, following Santi like a lapdog. "Don't get all paranoid now. He was the one who invited you here, and it's barely a week since you two last screwed!"

The tables fill up with diners and employees of the sons' restaurant next door. The employees eat lunch here every day before returning to face the daily battle in defense of two Michelin stars; one day I would love to eat there with Gonçal and try the langoustine with mugwort.

Eventually, I opt for the *fricandó*. And on my third mouthful, I spill it on myself. All over my lap. Once everyone has finished laughing at me for just a tad too long, Gonçal suggests we go somewhere else for coffee.

We lose ourselves among the flower-decked stone alleyways and see ivy growing up columns in abandoned courtyards. We stroll through the pretty, historic center as Astrid and Santi fool around in a darkened doorway. Gonçal is smiling, distant, and if I didn't know him better, I would say he is embarrassed by them. Then I remember our last night together and that we were the ones acting like idiots then, less than a week ago. I decide to make a move. With my heart pounding in my throat, I'm only a couple of feet away when I see something at the last second and pull back. An epic goddamn pullback.

"There she is!" he shouts, and shoots off down the next street, only to return moments later with a girl. "Rita, allow me to introduce Sònia. She's a childhood friend—I've known her all my life." *Friend, childhood, all my life*. Great. Wonderful. Let's rejoice in our hearts; glory, hallelujah!

"Hi, nice to meet you!" I lie automatically, her patchouli scent washing over me. I take a step back and check out her ass and hands and teeth.

Sònia is one of those clichéd rock chicks like you see in Levi's commercials: jeans, white T-shirt, and leather jacket. She has a blond Afro that stands inches above the top of Gonçal's head; her eyes are lined with a deep black that brings out their darkness. This girl is so cool that suddenly I feel like I'm wearing Antònia's Sunday frock.

"By the way," I add jokily, pointing at my lap, to break my own ice, "this stain isn't just any old *fricandó.* It's Can Roca *fricandó*!"

"Great, nice to meet you too," she replies, friendly, with a local accent. I can't tell whether she gets the joke.

Then Santi and Astrid catch up, hair tousled and lips swollen. After the requisite introductions, we turn a corner and, in a few steps, come out into Cathedral Square. We sit on the terrace of Café L'Arc, at the foot of a long staircase up to the cathedral doors. The bells are ringing, the sun staining the facades orange.

Now it's nearly six o'clock, and Sònia and Gonçal have spent ages recalling anecdotes that, I have to admit, are quite funny. But what makes me very, very happy is that Sònia mentions something about her partner. She has a partner. Best news all day.

The evening progresses with G&Ts until night falls, and we finally abandon our childish recollections of having to perform in the Christmas pageant wearing tights that showed off our junk, and we move onto politics and conspiracy theories. Just when I'm thinking we should be getting back to Cerdanya, it suddenly appears that everyone has a desperate need for dinner.

As we arrive on the terrace outside Le Bistrot, I realize I've seen this place on a postcard. This archway, this staircase. The whole scene is a trip through time, a movie.

The restaurant has old wooden doors that open beneath ivy dangling from the roof, four stories up. Gonçal opens the door, giving us each a cute little bow as we pass, starting with Sònia and culminating with me. And I blush. Idiot.

I end up at the head of the table, next to Gonçal. Santi and Astrid are still in their own little world, and Gonçal and Sònia are still laughing at the fucking pageant costumes.

"I'll have the grilled-vegetable tart," I say. "And a gin and tonic, please."

"Would you like the gin now or afterward?"

"Now. Right now."

I look pointedly at Astrid and get up to go to the bathroom. When she finally arrives, I'm soaping my hands for the third time.

"So, is it just my imagination or . . . are they really into each other?"

"What?" Astrid reacts as though she's just woken up after a drugged sleep.

"Can't you see how that girl looks at him? And he does nothing! Shit, we were in bed together less than a week ago!"

"Huh? What are you saying? She has a partner, she said so. Look, they haven't seen each other for centuries—they're childhood friends . . ."

"Maybe you're right . . . but I really like him . . ." I reply, to myself, because Astrid is already on her way back to the table.

Back in my seat, I watch the room with my chin resting on my interlaced hands, waiting for my grilled-vegetable tart. I enjoy the tickling in my cheeks from the second—or is it my twelfth?—gin and tonic. I check out the plates on the neighboring tables and wonder if I should have ordered the cannelloni. I bring my focus back to my own table, rather unwillingly, and then something close by catches my eye.

Suddenly, time takes on a new dimension: The seconds stretch out like molten glass, my pupils dilate, and I feel like I could itemize an entire world within this moment. My fingers come apart under my chin, and my eyes come into a gaze sharper than ever before. My memory has just flicked on the lights to record it all.

I watch carefully as Gonçal's nose slots itself into Sònia's face. I think that if I stretched out my arms, I could touch them. She closes her eyes and opens her mouth slowly and delicately; her lips seem to experience an absolute, familiar pleasure. This isn't the first time. The kiss lasts a million years. Slowly, with the dance of those hypnotic tongues, I feel like the world is starting to turn black and little by little annihilating any hope of ever feeling love again, of ever feeling again. And, with a fatal stabbing pain, I notice two ghostly hands pass through my skin, reach into my soul, and take hold of my heart to mercilessly wring it out.

Bile

"Rita . . ." A tinny voice is shouting at me from a distance, at the other end of a black tunnel. "Rita." Little by little, the words become clearer; then the volume suddenly turns up, and I see Astrid's distorted face.

"Rita!" she repeats, concerned. "The vegetable tart was yours, wasn't it?"

The waiter puts the plate down in front of me as Sònia rolls up a sliver of veal carpaccio, oblivious to everything. Santi tucks into his steak, and Gonçal glances at me for a millisecond before turning away to gaze at Sònia's lips again.

I can't believe what just happened. Did I dream it? I stare at my gin and tonic in search of explanation, and then I look at Astrid, who is watching me out of the corner of her eye with a mixture of embarrassment and shock. I down my gin in one.

The smell of *fricandó* from my lap seems stronger than ever. Suddenly, as though the vegetable tart had jumped off the plate and slapped me square in the face, I am roused by a pain that takes my breath away. I literally can't breathe.

"Be right back!" I shout. I grab my phone and walk out.

Outside, I sit on the movie-set staircase and start phoning everyone. I call Pol, who's closest. He doesn't answer. I switch to Koeman, who doesn't answer. I try Marta, Gemma, Clara. No one is answering me! Where the hell is everyone? Breathe in; breathe out. Astrid doesn't come to find me.

Did it really just happen? Suddenly, without any kind of logical explanation, a burst of laughter wriggles out from my guts. Did it really just happen? I bring my hand to my mouth and yank down hard on my face.

"Fuck," I say out loud. "Fuck, what just happened?"

I peer back into the restaurant, but Astrid isn't coming out. On the door, I notice a little sign: "This restaurant has been voted one of the ten most romantic restaurants on Earth." Fantastic. I have to get away from here.

I go down the steps and start walking. My brain is numb; I can't think about anything. My clothes, shoes, and hands feel too heavy.

I turn into alleyways that are no longer pretty but a stone labyrinth that won't let me see a goddamn thing. At one turn to the left, I think I see water; I go that way. My ears are buzzing. I cross a street where I come across a group of drunk teenagers who point at my pants and ask if I've shit myself. I'd like to think that any other day I would have come up with a witty riposte, but I only have the strength to walk. I reach a bridge formed in a red iron crisscross pattern and stagger halfway across, exhausted, floating, and sit on the ground with my legs dangling over the edge. I close my eyes. My head is spinning. I think I'm in shock.

My phone rings. It's Pol.

"Baaaaabe!" he shouts crazily, loud music playing in the background.

"Hi, Pol, listen . . ." I'm surprised by how calm my voice is. "Could I borrow the car?"

"Right now? Wait, I can't hear you . . . The car, right now? But aren't you with Astrid?" He moves away from the noise. "Hey, we're in Palamós, and it's eleven o'clock at night. Where are you?"

"I'm in Girona. Please . . ." I leave a long silence, and my tone is so unlike me, I'm scared.

"Rita, are you okay? What's happened?"

"Yes, yes . . . I'm fine—I can't talk now. But come, please. I'm on a bridge over the river in Girona. It's red with these crisscrosses . . ."

"I know the one. I'm on my way."

I can't move. I open my eyes again and see Girona reflected in my patent leather shoes.

Little by little, silence falls. Clothes are hanging out to dry along the row of overhanging facades that reflect in the river. I fix on a pale beige house with damp stains; a mother with her child in her arms is saying good night to the city from behind the window. The streetlights draw steamy haloes on the water. The bulbs on the bridge reflecting in the water look like a necklace of white lights; then the breeze stretches them and turns them into teardrops. Tears. I haven't cried yet. The cathedral pokes its head out too. I remember the imposing staircase, back when I was enjoying my first gin and tonic and still thought it was a lovely day, but I can't summon the strength to look at it. Astrid calls me repeatedly. Santi too. No word from Gonçal. I switch off my phone. What I want more than anything is for no one to find me.

I drop my head and look at my reflection in the river again. I look down at the sweater and pants that I laid out last night, especially for this trip. "Last night" seems like a lifetime ago. It strikes me that the fact that the *fricandó* didn't soak through to my panties is the best thing that's happened all day.

I close my eyes again. But only for a moment, because before I know it, I'm throwing up the whole day over my shoes; as I wipe my mouth with my sleeve, an old woman tuts behind me. "Young people these days . . . shameful, young lady."

I've been an idiot. Ever since I got into Santi's truck this morning, I've been an idiot. Since I climbed up to the tree house. Since I saw him for the first time, behind that bar, and I fell for him entirely.

I'm an idiot to have thought that when this moment came, I could control him. I wish it were a thousand years from now.

Pol arrives after a half hour, slightly anxious. When he sees me, he calms down and realizes that I'm not going to tell him anything just now, and he doesn't dare ask what the stain on my pants is.

"Pol, if I had shit myself, the stain wouldn't be at the front, for fuck's sake—it would be behind."

He hands me a bottle of water and twenty euros, and covers my shoulders with a fleece he only wears when he goes fishing. It stinks of sardines. I thank him with the serenity of someone receiving condolences and ask him to call Astrid to tell her I'm going with him and not to call me.

Panties on the Line

Yaya clambers up the last step onto the roof and, like a royal guard announcing the arrival of a pesky commoner, hands me the phone.

"It's Atri."

"Astrid?"

"Yes, damn it, what did I just say? She says to put you on the line." She covers the mouthpiece with her hand and adds, in a shout, "She doesn' belief you horse ridin' anymore."

"Horse riding?"

In the morning, I took my breakfast up to the roof and told Yaya that if Astrid called, she should tell her I'd gone out. "Out" in general, but clearly, she's decided to embellish the lie.

"You can't spend five hours in the shower, Rita, no you can't," she grumbled. "But if you don' wanna talk to her, then don' talk to her."

I couldn't agree more, but equally, I can't avoid Astrid forever. I'm aware that I'm probably overreacting, but the fact that she saw me on the verge of collapse and decided to stay with Santi hit me like a fall from the fifth floor.

Astrid greets me with a timid, groveling hello, then starts to apologize: She thought it was just a peck on the cheek; she was kissing Santi at the same time (bravo, Astrid!); she thought I'd gone outside to make a call and that I'd come back, and she sent a thousand messages . . . and other excuses that I'm sure are true, but I couldn't care less.

"It doesn't matter now," I reply.

There's a long, unfamiliar silence. Then she says that, actually, everyone knows that Gonçal sleeps around—I feel an icy prickle down my back—and she just keeps on talking, filling my silences, until she manages to bring the conversation around to Santi: How much she loves him (I'm about to hang up) and how she doesn't want to go traveling because she can't bear the idea of being apart from him . . .

"So don't go. Problem solved."

"I can't. It's all paid for and arranged. If I don't go, I'll lose the money. I'm leaving in less than a week . . ." she continues, sounding as though she's only containing her romantic weeping out of compassion. After a dramatic pause, she adds casually, as though recommending a restaurant, "Why don't you go in my place?"

"I'm sorry?"

"It would be good for you to get a bit of distance, a change of scene . . . And it would be perfect—you'd learn English once and for all!"

"And who the hell said I had any interest in learning English?"

"Well, if you don't, you won't graduate."

"As I'm sure you can imagine, I don't give a flying fuck about my degree right now. I never wanted to be a psychologist, anyway."

"But you always said it's a first step, a start, an opportunity to find out what you really want to do."

"Well, I've changed my mind." Silence. I'm thinking about America. "Anyway, you know I wouldn't survive a day with the Yanks . . . I can't even hail a taxi . . ."

"Actually, you can. It's the same word in both languages."

Ha, ha.

Then I lie and tell her I have to go because I'm needed in the restaurant. She pretends to believe me, and we agree to speak later. We hang up, saddened because, although we both know that one day in the not-too-distant future we'll laugh about this, we also know that a crack has appeared in the shatterproof bond that's united us for four years.

I check my cell phone in the hope of finding a missed call from Gonçal, a message of apology, a sign. I fantasize about the possibility that, at some point, without realizing, I ate the slice of Mallorcan hash cake I stashed in the freezer and that this has been nothing more than a bad trip. But the sadness and rage are too real. I check the screen again: There are a bunch of older missed calls from Astrid, a couple from Santi, and the now-useless replies from all the people I called last night, mid-shipwreck.

I close my eyes and feel the heat of the sun filtering between the sheets fluttering dry in the breeze. Yaya's voluminous panties ripple against the sunlight. I think I could stay up here forever: I would sleep in the open and ask my family to put food in a basket I would hoist up with the pulley once a day. I would watch the night sky over Cerdanya and trace the constellations with my eyes. It would be perfect: I'd have the best views in the world, and I wouldn't have to deal with anyone ever again. Well, hardly anyone . . .

"Yaya, you can come out. I can see your slippers under the curtain."

Her reflex reaction is to hide, as though I haven't just said exactly what I said. Then she grumbles and, with a "son of a bitch," comes out to the roof terrace, acting offended. She grabs a wooden chair, dusts it down vigorously with a cloth as though beating it, and then lays the cloth carefully over the seat so as not to dirty her tunic.

"What did she say . . . hmm . . . that girl?"

"Nothing. Nonsense, excuses. And she has the nerve to drone on about how she's so in love with her boyfriend that she doesn't want to go traveling anymore."

"Pah, she's not very tactful, that one."

"She says I should go to the States in her place."

"What states?"

"America."

"America . . ."

"Yes, Yaya, where they make cowboy movies."

"Ah."

She doesn't have the vaguest idea. We sit in silence for a while, listening to Antònia whistling as she opens the gate to let the cows through: "Cowwwws coming." In the meantime, a family from Barcelona gives a very enthusiastic running commentary. "Kids! Look at the cows—their thighs are covered in poop!" "Stiiiinky!"

Yaya closes her eyes, takes a deep breath, and expels the air. She smiles and blurts out, "So, why dontcha go?"

I look at her, wondering whether she's gone crazy.

"Yaya, you don't know what you're saying . . ." We fall silent again. The only image in my head right now is the episode of *Sex and the City* where a Russian woman waxes Carrie's entire pussy because she doesn't speak any English. I would be that Russian. Every day, waxing pussies by mistake. "What would I do there? It's the other side of the world—they speak English and . . ."

"An' what? You think I knew Catalan when I moved here from Andalusia, do you?"

"Of course not . . . And you still don't." I laugh, lacking any better response.

She's sitting back with her hands wedged beneath her breasts, nose to the sun and smiling broadly.

"So, whatcha gonna do, Rita? You gonna stay sittin' here waitin' for Punsá to call?" She knows I have no answer and continues, grateful to the sun for warming her bones. "That isn't love, no it isn't. True love, the kind that blinds you and burns you, it's like a tidal wave that takes everythin' in its path, which is what happen' to me when I left behind my family, my friends . . . my life."

I've never heard her talk like this. Speaking about her past without joking. We fall silent again; she's still smiling mysteriously . . . I stay quiet, not wanting to squander this rare moment. Then suddenly Yaya's body goes rigid; she's recalling a former self she hasn't seen or spoken to for years: Natalia.

She loves Natalia because she's the life and soul of every party, the voice and star of the stage in Andalusia. The young woman who lit a spark in everyone who went to see her sing and dance, behind her mother's back.

She rubs her hands very carefully, but for the first time, she doesn't look at them with melancholy or tears of rage as she does so often when she thinks no one is looking.

"They tried to marry me off to Granaíno, but I didn' want to, no I didn' . . . I just wanted to get away from my mother. And I loved your grandfather, yes I did, I had eyes for no one else . . . And he . . . well, you can imagine how it drove him crazy when he saw me on that stage in my sequin dress singin' along to my Carlos Gardel.

"Oh, my poor boy . . ." A tear slips from the corner of her eye and makes its way down her velvety cheek. "I was jus' a girl. Not even twenty when I ran away from home with the mule, scared to death, yes I was. I took the few pesetas I had and left my keys in the door. If my mother had caught me . . ." she continues quietly, and I notice the hair standing on end from her arm to the back of her neck, "she would have kill' me, my mother would have beat' me to death, yes she would.

"But that night, when I saw your grandfather curled up in María la Tuerta's doorway, waitin' for me, I knew that was my only chance. Comin' to Catalonia with your gramps was the best decision of my life, yes it was. Leavin' my songs behind was the hardes' thing I ever had to do, because I wanted to be a singer! I *was* a singer! But a life at the stove seemed like paradise if it meant I could be far away from my mother. You know we had a bad time of it, yes we did. We were hungry and cold, an' other hardships that no one should have to bear. But I've lived life on my own terms, an' I swear on San Benito I would do the same again." She turns her head. "Well . . . almost the same."

She opens her eyes and kisses the locket hanging around her neck, which still holds a black-and-white wedding photo. She pulls her handkerchief from her bra, inadvertently bringing with it five euros, a sachet of sugar, and a lottery ticket, and she dries her tears brusquely. She returns to the present moment and looks at me.

"You and your brother are my joy, yes you are. You know I would do anythin' for you two, but there are some things you can only do for yasself. You don't know it yet, because nowadays young people don't know what it means to suffer. Life is wonderful, yes, wonderful! But it's not all parties and *xistorres, mi arma*. Life can also be a complete bastard, an' it hurts. But you mustn't let someone else take the reins in your life. Especially not a shameless bastard like that one, oh no." She leans on one leg, clenches her fist tightly, and fixes her eyes on me. "I don't have many years left, no I don't, but when I look back, I'm proud o' what I've done." A lump seems to form in her throat, and for a moment it looks like she won't be able to continue. "Make the most of your lot in life! You have to grab it with both hands! Drink it all down! And you can't do that sittin' here on a roof terrace, watchin' panties on the line!" She clutches my hands firmly. "Go and see. Go and look for life, find what makes you truly happy, and when you want to come back, we'll be here waitin' for you, yes we will."

The opaque blue sky sends a gentle breeze through the oxeye daisies, riffling through the napkins on the tables below us. Yaya gets up and walks to the railing, leaning her arms on it with a slight wince, and gazes at the horizon.

She's alone. Far away from me, far away from everything.

Gradually, her rusty, stubborn old body slips into a dance retrieved from some remote part of her muscle memory. From when she was an artiste. When life fizzed in her veins. An ancient aura clings to her body and elevates her soul. I don't recognize her.

She stretches out her fingers, which have forgotten their pain for the moment, and she looks at her hands as though reuniting with two old friends. Suddenly she returns to the days of spotlights and success. Natalia is back on the stage.

She lifts her hands in the air and rotates her wrists, as though waking them up. She lifts her head, offering a broad grin to the sun, and for the first time in my life, I hear her sing, with a voice as deep as a storm, "*Volver*," the tango by Carlos Gardel.

Yo adivino el parpadeo
de las luces que a lo lejos
van marcando mi retorno.
Son las mismas que alumbraron
con sus pálidos reflejos
hondas horas de dolor.
[. . .]
Volver con la frente marchita,
las nieves del tiempo platearon mi sien.
Sentir que es un soplo la vida,
que veinte años no es nada,
que febril la mirada, errante en las sombras
te busca y te nombra.
Vivir con el alma aferrada
a un dulce recuerdo
que lloro otra vez.
[. . .]
Pero el viajero que huye
tarde o temprano detiene su andar,
y aunque el olvido, que todo destruye,
haya matado mi vieja ilusión,
guardo escondida una esperanza humilde
que es toda la fortuna de mi corazón . . .

An eagle soars above the poppy field. It's getting close to midday; the light is reaching the cornices of the village houses and the treetops and the neighbors' clotheslines. It's a beautiful scene . . . But I don't see any of it.

I don't see the eagle or the poppies, or the cornices, or the neighbors' clotheslines. Because all I see is her.

Who is this woman who talks about traveling with new eyes, walking paths to a new me?

Where has she been all this time?

I'm watching her, and I could swear I see her levitate as she sings. Still at the railing of the roof terrace, she performs to the sun the moves borrowed from her youth and expresses her thanks with a final smile.

Yaya returns to the here and now, dressed in her tattered gray tunic and her garden espadrilles. And the pain. And the surrender.

She turns and looks at me. An incredible serenity has transcended the nostalgia and bitterness; she has made her peace, perhaps with the past, perhaps with herself. She ignores the fact that my face is flooded with tears. She ignores the terrific connection between us—words, art, and her voice. She just looks at me and, backlit by the summer sun, says,

"You don't go travelin' to escape. You go travelin' to find yourself."

Where Did You Say You Were Going, Crazy Girl?

"All right, Rita." Yaya's head, covered in curlers, is barely visible above a mountain of Tupperware. "I packed cold cuts, *paparajota* fritters, a bottle of olive oil—the good stuff, of course—penne, and cod in *samfaina*. An' some fritters for the airplane."

Then she looks up and wipes her hands on her apron. And with the certainty of someone who doesn't entirely understand what it means to go on a plane or exactly what the United States might entail, she asks, "Will it be enough?"

I'm thinking that two months in America might turn out to be nothing at all, but right now it feels like an eternity.

"Yaya, I think it's perfect." I hug her again.

She pulls away from me and adds, "And don' forget to check all the pockets in your backpack!"

I go out to the patio and look through the window at the restaurant tables; the light filters through the windows and picks out the folds in the cloth napkins and five "Reserved" signs. The *pixapins* are on their way.

Shit! I pause for a moment in a fit of panic and open my backpack. Yes, there it is. The dolphin-shaped vibrator and the pig keychain with the extendible penis that my friends gave me as a parting gift are packed. Yesterday we had an improvised goodbye meal, and it ended very late. I've had forty minutes' sleep.

"Where did you say you were going, my dear?"

A string of neighbors is waiting for me at the gate as if I were a bride leaving for the church. They've come to say goodbye, and the general feeling is one of profound incomprehension.

"I'm going to America." It feels odd to say it out loud.

"Almería, did you say?" Antònia doesn't get it at all.

"To the United States, to New York, where they make all the Woody Alle—I mean, cowboy movies." Antònia gives me a couple of *llonganisses*.

She blows her nose with an ironed handkerchief. "Ay, ay, ay, Rita! That bad head of yours, you failed your degree, and now you're going to the back of beyond. Lord, have mercy on us!"

Sometimes I forget the supersonic speed at which news travels in a village. It turns out that my parents haven't forgotten about my English exam. Luckily, we talked about it before service started in the restaurant, in a bit of a hurry, but their disappointed faces around the kitchen table were no less harrowing. "But, Rita, you could have had a wonderful summer, free of obligations, and all because of one simple subject, English . . . What a pity, honey, what a pity. What are you going to do now?"

"What city did you say you were going to?" Lluís shouts from a distance. For some reason, he's decided to remain in the middle of the street.

"To New York." The two words sound ridiculous.

"Where are you going, crazy girl?" shouts Pere, who's peeling an apple on his balcony. "Who's going to help your parents in the restaurant?"

"You must be crazy!" Isidro looks at me like I'm a yeti come down from the high Pyrenees.

I would like to tell them that yes, I am crazy. But I just accept the final cured sausage with a smile.

"Shut up, all of you, damn it!" Trini hugs me. "Have a good trip, dear, and take care! Don't let them trick you. It's chaos over there, and some of them are real assholes!"

In the car, I do my best to stay awake so that I can say my goodbyes to Cerdanya. We leave Alp through the same landscape as the other day, the same as ever. *Two months,* I think. *It's no big deal* . . . but the truth is that I've never been so far away from home, or for so long. Will it be enough to find a real vocation?

It's around eight o'clock in the morning, and the valley seems to be still asleep. The church in Alp strikes the hour, and the bells echo until they fade into the fields and the black roofs of the houses. My roof terrace. And Yaya.

In the background, Puigcerdà becomes a tiny speck at the top of the hill.

I turn to face forward again, feeling melancholy, intending to close my eyes and not open them until the airport, when suddenly, like a ghost in black emerging from the morning mist, I see him.

Gonçal's truck is stopped at the end of his road. An old, yet all-too-recent reflex makes me sit up straight—a powerful reflex that destroys any shred of dignity and forces me to raise my hand to greet him. From my seat, my face embalmed by my hangover and with one hand frozen in the air, time switches into slow motion once again: I see Gonçal's face, as surprised as mine, his gaze following me. And I can't look away. For a few seconds, I feel like I could still go back, that we could go back to being who we were just days earlier, at the other end of this road, in the little tree house . . .

Then the sun catches the passenger seat, and I see her. Sònia and her perfect-as-fuck Afro. Once again, I feel the long shadow that overwhelmed me four days ago in Girona, and I realize that any scrap of hope I might have held inside me has just died. My hand is still raised. And yet, despite the possibilities offered by this infinite moment, he doesn't wave back. Gonçal, his indicator flashing, remains stock-still, following me with his eyes. Sònia, oblivious to the moment, leans forward to turn up the radio. She smiles and looks at him. But he is still staring at me, without lifting his hands from the wheel. The moment ends, and Gonçal disappears behind the bend. He, and my entire life until now.

Teenage Mutant Ninja Turtles

I sit in the only empty row of seats at gate B34, Terminal 2, Barcelona–El Prat Airport, and carefully unwrap the iPod my brother has just given me. The clean lines of the box make me want to handle it with a delicacy that I don't recognize in myself.

Since I said goodbye to my parents and Albert on the other side of the security gate, all of us waving like contestants on a game show, I've had a lump in my throat. I tried distracting myself by daubing my skin with duty-free cosmetics, but it didn't really help. And now, when I see that Albert has loaded up the iPod with my favorites as a surprise—he's even included "*Turistas heridos*" by Cyan—the lump has grown to the size of a lychee.

I open my eyes at prudent intervals to make sure they haven't started boarding. At the same time, I enjoy the multiple perfumes mingling on my skin. Magnolia, green tea. Then, suddenly, an unidentified object enters my field of vision: a curly tress.

My row of seats fills up with a crowd of backpackers. Around thirty rumpled figures, dressed in hemp and hiking boots, all in black, sit obnoxiously in the chairs around me. I picture the image from above, my white jersey standing out as though I were plain yogurt at a chocolate buffet, Snow White at a family meal.

They don't talk. You don't need a refined sense of smell to realize that they haven't showered during their visit to Barcelona. Which can't have been short. Did they have to leave early and unwashed from a silent retreat? My neighbor looks at me and says something I don't understand. He's speaking English. He points at the iPod. I hand it to him, and he shows me how to change songs and adjust the volume by rotating my finger over the circle.

"Thank you," I say in English, grateful, although I already knew. It appears I'll have the pleasure of losing my transatlantic virginity with this very friendly group of crusties. I hope, at least, that I won't be sitting in the same row on the plane.

I think the last time I wore headphones, they must have been covered in black foam. I almost feel bad choosing a song after spinning the circle round a thousand times. I don't want to have to think: Queen.

I get up unceremoniously, mid-takeoff, and shuffle across to the window to the beat of "I Want to Break Free." I need to say goodbye to Barcelona from the air. The city that became a part of me five years ago is shrinking beneath my feet. Goodbye, beers on Plaza del Sol and shawarmas in El Raval . . . Goodbye, goodbye, friends.

Evening is drawing in, draping a purple cloak across the sky. The mauve light enters through the windows of this giant plane like a lightning bolt searching for the exit and spatters the seat backs and matted hair of my traveling companions. Little by little, the city fades beneath a layer of vaporous clouds, until it disappears entirely in an immaculate sky, a no-man's-land. It vanishes just as the roof terrace, and my mountains, and Yaya and her apron vanished this morning. Like Gonçal did. Like I'm doing. The void in my stomach feels all too tangible, and I close my eyes to control a sudden nausea. I fall asleep.

I don't know how long I've been sleeping, but judging by my swollen ankles, it must have been a few hours.

I peel the cover off the food tray I find on the unfolded table with high hopes. It's overcooked sea bream fillets with potatoes and, after one bite, I realize its appearance doesn't do justice to the taste. My neighbor is devouring a fistful of almonds as he reads *On the Road*, his torso swaying slightly, and with each movement he releases wafts of sweat and mothballs. Despite the rancid odor, I chew on a slice of brioche with butter, then settle down with the pillow to close my eyes again, but suddenly all the lights inside the cabin go off as if a show were about to begin.

We're starting the descent.

The pilot's voice on the intercom wakes the passengers with unexpected enthusiasm. He issues an unintelligible but cheerful message, ending with a half shout that turns into the first notes of a song I've usually only heard in nightclubs at six o'clock in the morning, and which now stirs up a murmur of emotion among my fellow passengers. My neighbor, who has given up trying to communicate with me using onomatopoeia—I told him I don't speak English hours ago—reaches across me and raises the window blind.

And it appears.

Whoa. We tell the stories of our lives through the moments that paralyze our brains. We know we're truly alive during those instants that shoot us out beyond the here and now, light years from ordinary life. Out of time. A sight like this.

A black screen full of lights. The city stretches out on the other side of the window like a big pool of night with rivulets of fluorescent fog. Buildings and buildings. I can't see where it ends. I draw closer to the glass. It seems impossible. Frank Sinatra's voice singing "New York, New York" carves its way slowly and deeply into my consciousness.

I think the entire plane is singing along to Frank in such a range of accents that I'm amazed and terrified at the same time. Hundreds of voices from every corner of the cabin singing in full voice without shame.

I see the Empire State Building. The Empire State! I think of Meg Ryan and Tom Hanks, and the taxi driver outside the building, who says to Jonah, "What are you gonna do when you get up there, spit off the top?"

I join in, humming along as best I can in a state of sudden ecstasy, until, to the astonishment of my pestilent curly-haired flight companion, I sing out with a shout that rises from my guts,

"New Iorccc!"

I'm in America.

The airport was wall-to-wall carpet and patriotic, eagle-themed insignias. I stood in line for more than an hour to reach the desk, and had to hide my surprise at the sight of so many nationalities, so many turbans, all the makeup, tunics, and hairstyles of the world.

And after getting through passport control without incident, I had an experience I've always dreamed of: seeing my name written on a piece of paper at the exit.

Holding it was a guy who couldn't have been more than twenty and who, from the way he kept compulsively folding over the corners of the sign, must have been very nervous. I walked up and pointed at the paper to show that it was me.

"Welcome!"

Outside, I was met by a blast of city air and a row of yellow taxis; I was so excited that I took out my camera for a photo, but the boy scolded me. We were late.

The postadolescent ushered me toward a minivan that had no logo advertising a language school, or anything at all for that matter, and from its appearance, I could only imagine an exotic load: pigs, chickens, cocaine. In that order.

The boy threw my bags into the back between a dozen other pieces of luggage and tugged open the old sliding door. As I stepped inside, I took a quick glance around, and the lights from the arches of the airport building picked out a pale, skeletal face, slotted in between two seats, that frightened me half to death.

"Renata," she introduced herself. She extended her hand, theatrically, between the two headrests. And repeated, "Renata." The other seats were full, except one; tired eyes stared at me.

"Rita," I replied.

The sliding door shut behind me with a clunk.

"We're running very late," the boy announced, overenunciating, his hands now grasping the steering wheel; his tone seemed inoffensive enough for me to curl up in the seat and watch New York unfold on the other side of the window at two o'clock in the morning.

"I'm in New York," I repeated, in the hope of convincing myself.

An hour later, we reach the city center. My traveling companions wake up when the interior lights turn on in the van, and I soon figure out that none of them know each other. (They're all girls! What kind of language school did Astrid sign up for?) I get out and stand on terra firma, happy that, for the moment anyway, this doesn't appear to be a human-trafficking situation. I look around, and the soul of the city floods through me in an instant, the scene punctuated by the undefined noises of suitcases, coats, and monosyllabic logistical communications: "yes," "no," "ah."

The underground world rises in dense columns of steam that hover around the traffic lights, store signs, car headlights. I can think of only one thing: *Teenage Mutant Ninja Turtles*. I see a woman dressed as a clown, a limo driver pulling away, and a homeless guy transporting a whole dining room suite in a shopping cart. Inhabitants of a labyrinth of smoke and neon lights. The general fog drifts up the facades, caressing the brown bricks before reaching the top, where old water tanks stand like consummate watchmen.

Behind me, I notice an orangey concrete building that looks like it dates from the 1950s, climbing skyward in towers of different heights.

Right at the top, those red letters I've seen countless times, cutting through that vanilla sky . . .

"Miss! What are you doing?" the postadolescent scolds me again. "We're all inside the hotel—we're just waiting for you!"

Those red letters spell out The New Yorker.

A commanding, middle-aged woman is waiting for us at the top of a flight of stairs, at the far end of the white marble entrance hall. Elevator music is playing, and it smells of worn carpet.

It's just us and the woman, who has shiny skin and short blond hair, like an army captain. She's wearing elasticized jeans and a long slogan T-shirt. She receives us in silence and with open arms. Her smile widens in slow motion, her chin pulling inward and her jowls jutting out. When we're all there, standing in an improvised, but surprisingly symmetrical line, the woman bursts out in an exclamation of euphoria that, although she's obviously repeated it hundreds of times, doesn't seem to have lost one iota of enthusiasm. Her voice is strikingly raspy. I don't understand a word, but from the tone and exaggerated arm gestures—we seem more like lab monkeys than students, but I can't deny it's appreciated—I interpret that she's going to split us into groups.

I've been allocated a room with Renata and Ana, who's Argentinian. Ana takes only seventeen of the forty floors in the elevator to tell me in excruciating detail that she's spent the last three years doing odd jobs—from driving questionable passengers to shearing llamas—to save enough money to come here, to experience this moment.

"Could you show me a euro? I've never seen one!" She's so happy and fascinated that I envy her.

All settled in, we introduce ourselves, gesticulating in an entirely unnecessary manner:

Meee (hand on chest).

Rita (double thump on chest).

Barcelona (both hands open in the air).

"Idiot," says my new best friend Ana. "I can't believe it. Have you really come all this way with that level of English?"

"I might be exaggerating it"—I am very tired—"but yes, it's true, I've come here with this level of English."

We're in bed already; even Ana, who keeps gabbling away with her eyes closed and the lights off. When she falls silent, I open the curtains and reacquaint myself with the city from behind the reinforced glass window. I get into bed and fall asleep under what seems like a mirage: The Empire State Building is no longer just a poster in my room in Vila Universitària.

Just a Liiiiittle Surprise

"Shiiiit!" I say out loud, the *i* lasting as long as it takes me to notice that the other beds in the room are empty.

I take the elevator down to the first floor, forty stories with my hands over my ears. The foyer is empty. The receptionist, alone, with the telephone wedged against her shoulder as she unwraps a candy, sees me and points the transparent wrapper toward the doorway to my right. On the door, a poster says "Au Pair in the States." I turn back and shake my head at her. But she insists.

I go in. It smells of Play-Doh.

Two hundred faces turn in unison, and the shock wave makes my sphincter tense. Two hundred female faces. What the hell is this?

Presiding over the ceremony—because this clearly must be a ceremony—is the raspy-voiced woman from last night. She says good morning with another jowly smile and, with a theatrical gesture, invites me to sit. In the distance, I see Ana sitting next to two wide-eyed girls. She's trying to tell me something with her hands; she winks at me and laughs and tries again.

The walls are covered in posters of children. Posters of children in idyllic families of all possible ethnicities, interspersed with short slogans written in colorful letters. On the stage there are soft toys, scooters, dolls, and a mountain of children's games. All that's missing is Chucky.

Is this a cult? I know that Astrid's aunt is a believer but . . . Are they going to shave our hair off?

A volunteer goes up onstage. Raspy, her serious expression inverting the position of her jaw—lips out, jowls sucked in now—hands her a plastic baby that the volunteer accepts with equal gravitas and places on a metal table. The volunteer starts to touch the baby, in front of the expectant audience, who are taking notes as urgently as if they had to decipher a bomb code in the final few seconds before it blows. The volunteer pumps the plastic chest with two fingers and does mouth-to-mouth, breathing air into the doll's face. Impressive. Disturbing.

When the volunteer feels she has finished the exercise, she moves her mouth away from the faded doll—multiple mouths have sucked the paint from that flesh-colored face—and sits down to effusive applause from the room. As though she has just saved the baby for real. Raspy waits for the applause to die down before she grabs the doll by the foot and shakes it brusquely. The effort brings droplets of sweat to her brow.

Finally, she stops shaking it and says, *"No!"* And as if we're monkeys in a cage eating each other's fleas, she repeats, loudly and emphatically, *"No, No!"*

The audience makes a note of this. *"No."*

I'm watching the scene around me, searching for a complicit smile that I don't find. Ana is concentrating intently. As the woman changes the baby's diaper, my catatonic state gives way to silent amusement. Besides, I'm curious about a word she keeps repeating. What the hell does "au pair" mean?

It's break time. Ana comes up, smiling, satisfied, and helps herself to a Styrofoam cup of coffee.

"Hey, you're a heavy sleeper! I tried to wake you three times!" And giving me no time to reply, she continues, "It's amazing for the first day, isn't it? But God almighty, it's intense! I liked the bit about American history. You would have loved it!" she informs me as though we had exchanged more than five minutes of conversation in our entire lives.

"Ana, sorry!" I'm aware that when I ask the question, I'll look like the dumbest person in the world, so I decide to test the waters. "Do you know when the English classes start?"

"English classes? No, these three days are to teach us the basic rules. You know, what's expected of us, the relationship with the parents, what we should do when it's raining so they don't get bored, taking temperatures . . ."

"When it's raining? Whose parents?" I ask, dropping any kind of filter that might make me appear to be a coherent woman who crossed the Atlantic with a known objective.

"What do you mean, 'whose parents'? The kids' parents. My family's in San Francisco. They've got two kids: One's three and the other's five. What about you?"

At this point, I break out in a cold sweat, with a slight hum of panic in my ears and a metallic taste in my mouth. Like when I left the gas on in the kitchen for a whole morning in my apartment in Vila. Or when I saw my phone dancing round inside the washing machine. Or when I left the radiator on for the entire Christmas vacation. Or . . . so many other times. Although I would never admit it to my family, it's true: I'm kind of a scatterbrain.

I run back into the room that smells of Play-Doh to speak to Raspy, who sees me and smiles, but, when she starts to welcome me, I realize that once I've said hello, I don't know how to continue. I don't know how to express any of what I want to say. So I smile back and run off to look for Ana.

"Ana, tell her there's been a mistake. I came here to learn English. In a language school. Two months in New York. Not to look after children. I should be in another room in this hotel, not this one."

"Whaaat?" exclaims Ana. "You're fucking ki—"

"I'll explain it all later. You tell her, tell her. Get her to check the list: Rita. Rita Racons."

Ana agrees, her pupils dilating madly with the stress, and she explains the situation in the English she learned during her master's in comparative literature at Princeton, New Jersey.

Raspy listens carefully, and I give a frozen smile as my eyes flick from one to the other as though I'm at a tennis match. As Ana's little speech progresses, the woman's face transforms, moving from curiosity to incomprehension, until it reaches an expression of terror that makes her eyes shine and she lifts her hand to her mouth. Her ears are sweating. This is serious.

She turns and runs out. What's going on?

She comes back promptly with a list. She finds my name, picks up the sheet and shows me, just inches from my face. She's waiting for a reply, a reaction, something. I shrug, lost, and hope to make it clear that it doesn't matter what they say. I haven't come to America to babysit anyone.

"She says you enrolled at the last minute," Ana informs me. "That you were a replacement for a . . . an Astrid Casanova."

When I hear Astrid's name, my heart flips and I go pale, the reflection of my face in their eyes revealing that I am indeed in the correct clay-scented room. But the bad news isn't over yet. After a solid silence, Ana continues:

"Your family is in . . ." She looks up and shakes her head sadly, as though notifying me of the death of my husband in the war. "Rita, your family is in Atlanta." The woman purses her lips, controlling a reaction I can't figure out. "They have three children: a boy of five, a girl of eight, and another boy of ten."

My body temperature drops two degrees all of a sudden.

"I have to make an international call."

"Astrid, can you hear me?"

"Rita!" she replies with the enthusiasm of a Mediterranean summer and beers at sunset by the sea, a million miles from the smell of vanilla air freshener in this carpeted foyer. "How are you? How's New York?"

"Well, I couldn't tell you, because since I arrived, I've spent the whole fucking day shut up in the hotel watching someone perform mouth-to-mouth on a plastic baby."

"What?"

"So, what's this about me having to go to Atlanta to look after three kids?"

"What do you mean, 'what's this about'?" she answers in a severe tone as she moves away from the background din. "I don't understand."

"I'm the one who doesn't understand. I've come to New York to study English for two months over the summer . . . haven't I?"

"Ri . . . Rita . . ." She contains a giggle she knows is dangerous. "You're shitting me. The documents I sent you had all the details, even a photo of the family . . . I explained it all to you on the last day in Vila. The company's called Au Pair in the Sta—"

"But you told me you were coming to learn English!"

"Yes, and . . ."

"What does 'au pair' mean, anyway?"

"An au pair is someone who looks af—"

"Yes, yes, I know that now, because I have to go and be a fucking au pair!"

"And Rita . . . the contract isn't for two months."

"What?"

"The contract . . ." Silence. "The contract is for a year."

My body temperature drops another two degrees.

"Rita?"

"A year?"

"But, Rita—"

"Astrid, that last day in Vila I scarfed an *ensaïmada* laced with marijuana that gave me worse paranoia than Lou Reed and David Bowie combined."

Then Astrid starts listing all the times when she explained it to me and when I, for some reason that I can't pinpoint right now, had my mind elsewhere. That's something that happens to me. I get distracted by random things, like wondering why young guys seem so naturally at ease on motorbikes. Or the smell of fabric softener on people who go running outside. But young guys and fabric softener don't matter now. Because it turns out I've come to America to babysit in Atlanta (where the hell is Atlanta, anyway?) for a whole goddamn year.

A song is playing somewhere—it's everywhere this summer, high notes and an upbeat rhythm. The receptionist smiles at me from across the desk.

I look through the revolving door of the hotel and see a girl my age, alone, stunningly beautiful, getting out of a red convertible with a coffee in her hand. She's holding a magazine with a beautiful drawing on the cover. She's laughing. You can tell she knows where she's going. How I long to be her. To know what to do. To know where to go. And I think that, if she found her way here, perhaps I can do it too. I return the receptionist's smile.

"Rita . . . ?"

"Yes, yes, I'm here," I reply in a calm and friendly tone that surprises her. "Are you in Palamós?" I can visualize her in the magnificent town, the blue-green bay below.

I hear Santi's voice laughing in the distance and an uncertain, almost imperceptible monotone, which confirms that Gonçal is there too . . . and Sònia.

"Yeah . . . we've come down to Palamós. There was an olive-pit-spitting contest in s'Alguer . . ."

S'Alguer bay and its colorful houses. Big-bellied men serving burned rum that evaporates with the bluish haze of nightfall. Grilled sardines, *fuet* sausage, and bread with tomato. The incessant lapping of little waves against the stones.

Summer nights in the Mediterranean would extend anyone's lifespan; every word in that phrase weighs a ton of magic. Those nights are like home to me. I lived them for many years, and I'll live them again next year, and all the years to come . . . What I'll never have again is this moment, this leap into the void, the uncertainty of that revolving door . . . The opportunity to discover what Yaya was talking about on the roof terrace.

The bombshell of realizing everything I'll miss over the next year is overwhelming: the lake party, La Mercè festival, Palamós Carnival, Christmas (Christmas!), springtime in the plazas of Girona, snow on the roof terrace, my friends, 365 nights surrounded by a life I love.

I have a split second to decide whether to spend my twenty-third year far away from everything I like and all the people I love.

The red convertible pulls away in slow motion. The decisive girl with clear plans exits the scene with an elegant tilt of the head.

"Shit, Astrid . . . The Palamós pit-spitting contest . . . I won the last time, do you remember?" I reply happily.

"Man, how could I forget!" Astrid laughs, disconcerted. "But hey . . . are you going to Atlanta, or are you coming home?"

"I have to go now, Astrid. There's a plastic baby waiting for me. Bye."

Atlanta

Compared to New York, Atlanta from the air is a patch of cement with a dozen prominent buildings claiming the status of state capital. Beyond that high-rise core, the city is an infinite, leafy expanse of green nature. Miles and miles of trees punctuated by what look like small scars or hundreds of centipedes from above. Each laceration is a street, and at the end of each one—or at each centipede foot—there's a house on either side. This isn't how I imagined it. It looks as though everyone lives in the woods. If that's true, it'll be awesome.

As I learned from the fact sheet that my future host family included in the lovely welcome basket they sent to the hotel, in among all these trees live five million inhabitants who make Atlanta the third largest city in the country. I also learned that Atlanta has the busiest airport in the world and that, apart from being home to the headquarters of Coca-Cola, CNN, and Delta Airlines, this is where the first Black millionaire in the country achieved that feat. I've never known so much about a city. Even if this experience ends up being a complete disaster, at least I will have acquainted myself with some US anthropology and geography.

Not to mention the fact that if I find some kid at death's door on the streets of Atlanta, no one needs to worry, because I now know roughly twenty-four different methods of resuscitation.

We're coming in to land. I try to relax and psych myself up for arrival. I'm going to be an au pair, for fuck's sake. An au pair! In Atlanta!

The airport is ultramodern. After waiting for my luggage, I have to take a train (with no driver!) that crosses the entire airport. Unheard of. The future.

At the final security check, a pleasant woman with hair teased and gelled within an inch of its life says some brief, friendly words, of which I understand only one: "Elena."

Seconds later, an equally pleasant, equally gelled man says something about this Elena. Who is she? The patron saint of Atlanta?

I go through the exit door. There aren't too many people, and I spot him quickly.

The father is waiting alone, wearing a Hawaiian shirt open over a T-shirt that reads *I'm Not Just Perfect; I'm Also American.*

Wonderful.

He shakes my hand and says, "We're all dying to get to know you. We have cockles."

Or at least I think that's what he said.

Although we both know it's been a few days since I arrived in the country and I've gotten used to the time difference, the excuse of jet lag grants me a bit of leeway and excuses the Catalanisms I've been blurting out since the airport. Among others, instead of saying "door," I said "port." One of the few words I know, and I say it wrong.

When he introduced himself, he used the words "Fulbright" and "Fahrenheit" in the same sentence, and now I don't know whether he has the same name as the scholarship or the temperature.

He must be six feet two and somewhere between forty and fifty. A few gray hairs give way to a decent dark-brown thatch; he has blue eyes. He doesn't look very athletic, or like he's ever played sports. There's something funny about him, something that makes me laugh. And it isn't the shirt.

We're in a spotless BMW all-terrain vehicle with beige upholstery that smells brand new. The radio is set to a station playing classical music. The car is showing ninety-four degrees Fahrenheit—I have no idea what that is in Celsius, but it's very hot—and the air-conditioning blows the hair off my face. He's slightly nervous, but he knows how to make small talk; not just because he's American, but also because I can't be the first au pair he's picked up from the airport.

He tells me he wore this shirt specially to pick me up and that he's worn it for every au pair he's come to meet. See? I find it funny, because the serene, intellectual tone of his voice couldn't be more different from the clothes he wears. He tells me he's a physical therapist or a psychologist; I'm not sure which. Please let it be PT, please.

I understand him a little better than the other Americans I've met so far, which makes me think he must have a slight British accent. But I ask him if he knows who this Elena is, and he can't give me an answer. He's wearing a classic, slightly old-fashioned cologne, Acqua di Giò, and he says a lot of things I don't understand.

It must be twenty minutes since we left the airport. It's nighttime, and we're traveling down a highway with very little traffic, until we turn at a fluorescent green sign announcing our destination: Decatur.

Soon after we leave the highway, we reach our neighborhood. I notice the strip of infinite grass that surrounds each house with no boundary fences. Most of the houses are vast. I see one that looks like a castle, oh my God, but the rest are pretty and colorful.

"Our house is right at the end," he informs me with a note of pride, "in the cul-de-sac."

"Cul-de-sac? 'Cul-de-sac' is a Catalan word!" I exclaim.

"Yes, and French, Occitan, Sardinian, and Romani."

It must be the scholarship. The man gives me the same polite smile he did after "port." And then I see it. The house at the end of the cul-de-sac, blue, with all the lights on.

"This is where the Bookland family lives, Rita. Welcome home."

Home, I think, my throat constricting. My only response is a smile.

He parks up in the driveway, and I get out to discover a bucolic silence filled only by the whispering of tall trees and the murmur of a nearby stream. I make an attempt to ask him where the sound of water is coming from, but I don't even know where to begin. What comes out is "Be water, my friend."

The smell of grass intensifies in the humid atmosphere bathing my arms. The place gives off a mysterious warm air that makes you want to sit on the sidewalk and take in the silence. I take a couple of steps back to look at the facade, and he gestures for me to follow him to the backyard.

"We designed the house ourselves. The only one of the three kids to have been born here is Bini." Bini? Who calls their child Bini and expects them to get the most out of life? "We call him Bini, but his name is Xavier."

"Xavier?" What's going on? Why does everything sound Catalan?

The house is crowned by three triangles, the one in the middle larger than the other two. To the right is a kind of rectangular annex with square garage doors, also blue, with two white beams forming a cross.

But the best part is to the rear of the house: a flight of stone steps climbing up the center of the facade, guarded on either side by two symmetrical bushes, leads to the porch. A porch wide enough to fit a fifteen-seat table. A ficus is hanging from the ceiling, and right at the end, there's a swinging bench hanging from two ropes.

Compared to the two-feet-thick stone walls of my house, these look like they might blow away the moment the wind changes.

"Shall we go in?" he asks as he opens the garage doors.

"We go in," I reply, with a tremble in my voice.

"Welcome, welcome, welcome!" The high-pitched cries merge with the clunk of broad heels. "Weeelcome!"

The mother of the family is waiting on the landing between the garage and the living room. She has dirty-blond hair—it looks natural—she's plump, pretty, and smiling, and half a head taller than me.

"This is Hanne," says the father with a genuine smile.

The walls are filled with children's drawings, and the house smells of detergent and lemon. The mother hugs me. She seems nice. She isn't wearing perfume, but she smells clean.

At the top, the stairs open onto the living room. The height of the ceiling and the white walls make the space seem a little cold, but the brown sofa and rug save it. At the back, there's a grand piano! Mr. and Mrs. Bookland sit down and offer me a glass of wine.

Good start.

Because she keeps calling him "honey," I still don't know whether his name is Fahrenheit or Fulbright. So, although it sounds overly formal, the only way I can address him is to call him "sir." I hope "sir" doesn't relate exclusively to the British aristocracy.

Sir puts his arm around his wife, and the couple sits in an everyday position, neither amorous nor forced. I get through the first polite questions as best I can: an "of course" here, a "great" there, and "amazing" wherever I can manage it.

"The kids are asleep." They anticipate my question. "It's really important that they're in bed by eight."

Hanne keeps explaining something about the yard—I think—when suddenly she realizes that, while they have barely wet their lips, I only have a half inch of wine left in my glass. She slows down her explanation—perhaps this was a test for alcoholism and I've failed already—and her husband asks if I'd like some more. *Say no, of course not, noooo!*

"Yes, thank you . . . sir."

"Por siertoh," she says, and continues in what I assume to be classic Spanglish: *amigoh/fiesta/servesa*. "*Mi maridoh y yo hablamos español*, or at least what we can remember from school, which was about three centuries ago . . ." They laugh. She continues her explanation in a hokey accent, but with perfect grammar. "So, to begin with, if you're struggling, we can speak Spanish."

"No, no! Don't worry." I want them to see how motivated I am. "I've come here to learn English. And to take care of the children, of course. I'm quick to adapt. I'm tired today, but I understand about eighty percent"—that's good, introduce data, percentages—"of what you say in English."

So they start to speak English. From their faces, they're clearly explaining concepts that are relevant to my job, important things, damn it. I nod very slowly, with my head slightly tilted, and focus my gaze, concentrating. I even lift a finger to my lips for dramatic effect. But all I hear is "hakuna matata, hakuna matata" on a loop.

"Sorry . . . could you possibly repeat that in Spanish? Just for today, I want to be sure I'm absolutely clear on the basic pillars." Very good, that: "absolutely clear," "basic pillars."

"Yes, of course," answers Hanne, who's laughing, but I catch a flicker of indignation. "We were just saying that one of the main reasons for us to hire, well, initially Astrid, and then you"—another flash of indignation—"is so that whenever you're around, the children must speak Spanish, all the time. Even if they try to convince you otherwise. And they will try."

"No problem," I reply emphatically.

Her husband refills all three glasses without asking.

"How were your first days in New York?" asks Hanne in slow English.

Before telling her anything about it, however, I take the opportunity to do a little investigating.

"Well, it was very hot . . ." I stare at them and pause dramatically. "Many . . . many degrees Fahrenheit . . ."

They gaze at me in bemusement. No reaction to Fahrenheit. Yes, it must be the scholarship.

"We were asking," clarifies Hanne, "about your first days in New York . . ."

"Yes, yes . . . Well, they were amazings." I let myself go here; I've prepared this. "As well as the city, which is amazing, the best thing was to meet the other au pairs."

"Sorry, I didn't catch that. What did you say?" he asks.

I repeat it again, slower. Shit, surely he can understand this perfectly!

"Mm-hmm, mm-hmm . . ." He takes a sip. He doesn't understand me at all.

"And are they happy with the families they got?" asks Hanne.

"Yes, yes, although some of them had to talk to some very strange families before they found a good one." I pretend I haven't noticed that I've slipped back into Spanish. "There was one who only offered vegan food, others who demanded that their au pairs went to Mass every day, and even some who didn't have a television in the house! It's like, guys, this is America!"

They laugh without showing their teeth. They exchange a look. Then they gesture at the wall on the other side of the living room. Where the television should be, there's a fish tank.

"We don't watch television," she says.

"Wow."

Just great. Ten minutes of conversation and they think I'm an alcoholic, illiterate TV addict.

"We do have one, though. Downstairs, in the games room, but it's only tuned into the History Channel and National Geographic, which are the only worthwhile ones." I take a drink; there's no more wine in my glass. "The thing is, we don't really have time to watch it, you know? We always find better things to do, which is what we hope you'll do, too, of course." She drinks.

"We listen to a lot of music. We do have that to offer, right, honey?" Sir looks at Hanne with honest pride, and she responds with a look of contained sweetness. "Chopin, Beethoven . . . Melody, emotion, and memory in the most evolved art form. Music, tribal origin, a mother's beating heart, music is ecstasy!" I'm about to burst out laughing because I think he's joking, but he isn't. And to be honest, he doesn't look much like a physiotherapist. "The composer Alexander Scriabin considered music to be the most complete artistic discipline, and ecstasy, the most evolved human emotion." I pick up my glass. "Dissonant harmonies can hurt the ear with the tension they create, but they culminate . . ."

He picks up his glass, raises it in the air, and sways it back and forth as though conducting an orchestra. I'm about to do the same, but I stop myself in time. "But they culminate in ecstasy! And not just with sound but above all with silence . . ." He looks at me, as though I should recite what comes next along with him. I'm completely lost.

"Cheers!" I raise my glass. They do the same.

Next, the husband leans forward to pick up what looks like an album from the coffee table.

I spot a medallion hanging round his neck with a letter on it. Shit, it's an *F*, of course. I didn't get much response with the Fahrenheit attempt, but who's called Fulbright nowadays?

"Fulbright," I say at last.

The two of them look up expectantly. He nods.

Now what do I say?

"It's a very . . . academic name."

The smile becomes even stiffer.

"Thanks," he replies, confused. And then he continues: "Of all the au pairs we've had, this is by far the best introductory album. Well done, Rita."

Album?

"Yes, you're right," adds Hanne. "Although Daniela's was very good, too, do you remember?"

"Oh, yes . . ." They're clearly infatuated with this Daniela.

"And in between the pages," continues Hanne, "there were dried cedar leaves that she gathered for the children in Chingaza National Natural Park." Both of them nod with a smile.

"Perhaps the thing we liked best about you," says Fulbright, "was that unconditional love of children and the fact that, thanks to your studies in developmental psychology, you handle your goals and emotions through the values of sports." Gosh, Astrid really pushed the boat out to make sure they accepted me. "Sports, after all, are an extraordinary vehicle through which to explore the world. Of course, it's all based on the sense of security forged during childhood, don't you think? Bowlby and Ainsworth's attachment theory. But it all starts much earlier than that: Hobbes and Rousseau. Who do you think we are, the wolf-man or the noble savage? And I won't mention Margaret Mead's example of Samoa, because the study is full of holes . . ."

Shit, why couldn't he have been a physical therapist?

Was it a rhetorical question?

I sit for a few seconds without talking. They're looking at me. It wasn't a rhetorical question. I have to reply. Four years! Four years of studying and I can't answer the first goddamn question I'm asked about psychology.

I try to keep smiling as though I didn't realize it was a direct question. And he asked me in Spanish, as well. Fulbright, the man with the name of a scholarship, hands me the album, a lifesaver, to prompt me to tell them something. I see around twenty photos of my pupils over the last three ski seasons—and some other kids, I don't know who they are. The memories set my teeth on edge, and perhaps my face is betraying the fact that this is the first time I've seen this album. The photos are accompanied by lengthy explanations of psychological jargon in bold type that, except for the odd bit of classical conditioning, I don't recall having ever studied.

Astrid even included my class photo! Even I don't have that one! The main thing is that I look good in it.

"So, Hobbes or Rousseau?"

"Rousseau?"

"Oh! Are you sure?"

"Hmm." I pretend I'm pondering. "Yesss." I extend my *s* decisively.

"Okay, okay . . . you can explain that to us tomorrow—you must be very tired now," says Hanne. But what's the deal with Rousseau? "Come on, then, we'll show you the surprise the kids have prepared in your room."

Downstairs, next to the door through which we entered from the garage, they point out the games room. It's vast. On the floor, occupying the entirety of the beige carpet, a battalion of soldiers is laid out in formation.

"See? There it is!" says Fulbright, pointing at a newish TV set. "And this is the room where the children spend most of their time . . . imagining and creating. If we don't provide an environment in which creators and inventors can let their minds run wild, we'll never have any new ideas, don't you agree? It's that simple. And you'll see, you'll be spending a lot of time here too. Without turning on the television!"

"And this is your room." Hanne looks at me with a playful smile, gripping the handle of the door next to the games room. "Ready?"

The first thing I see is a simple assembly of ropes that activates a radio and starts a song.

The hymn "*Els Segadors*" rings out loudly in this cul-de-sac in the state of Georgia. Hanne and Fulbright move their arms contentedly, as though conducting an orchestra.

"We couldn't decide between '*Els Segadors*,' '*La Santa Espina*,' or '*Muntanyes del Canigó*.'"

"*Muntanyes del Canigó*"? How do they know these Catalan songs?

"What do you think of the room?" he asks proudly. "The kids spent all afternoon getting it ready."

I open my eyes wide, frozen in the doorway.

On one wall, there's a series of cartoons relating the legend of La Moreneta, the Black Virgin of Montserrat, starting in the year 880.

Arranged round the headboard are some traditional Catalan recipes. From *escalivada*, smoky vegetables, to *carn d'olla*, a potful of meat. And next to them, *brandada de bacallà*, the miracle pairing of cod and potatoes. It can't be; it isn't possible: the cover of the Xuriguera dictionary and a vertical diagram of the diacritic accents used in Catalan.

Who are these people?

"The cookies in the colors of the Catalan flag are tomato and banana. Eva made them. She ran out of strawberries." Hanne laughs.

"It'll be a job to take it all down!" says he, "but leave it up until tomorrow. They'll want to explain the rope system, and they weren't sure how weak pronouns work." (Who is?) "Do you like it?"

"I'm speechless."

"We'll leave you to rest," she says. "Oh, and another thing . . . we go to church on Wednesdays. And we'd really like it if you came too."

River Bitches and a Sicilian Nose

With the exception of one final drawing taped to the ceiling, showing the Sagrada Familia with some prawns on one of its spires, there are no more Catalan surprises in store. So . . . here we are. This bed, next to this closet with a mirror on the door, is where I'll be waking up for the next 365 days.

It's 9 a.m. on the dot. I try one of the cookies, spit it out, and flush the rest down the toilet.

It's the biggest room I've ever had to myself. In the daylight, it looks very different from the way I saw it yesterday. The light filters through the slats of the blind, and it's very pleasant. The quiet is broken only by the singing of American birds.

I don't know if it's a hierarchy thing that means the nanny has to inhabit the lowest part of the house, next to the garage, and whether that's why I have the only window with a bush pushing up against the glass . . . But I'm not complaining. I have a double bed, a lounge chair on which Fulbright must have enlightened several hundred of his patients, and, get this: In my bathroom, I have the same shower curtain as Joey and Chandler (the transparent one with the multicolored world map). This is America!

I go upstairs without changing. I'm wearing basketball shorts, a flesh-colored Lycra T-shirt, and, halfway up the stairs, I realize that

I'm not wearing a bra, but I'm so hungry I can't be bothered turning back. I go into the kitchen with the singular goal of investigating the refrigerator (will there be peanut butter? milk in bottles?) when I hear two South American voices chatting and laughing, with bachata music playing in the background.

I find two women, moving their arms and asses to the beat. One is eating a carrot and the other, what looks like a Kit Kat ice cream bar.

"There she is! You're Rita, right?" exclaims the younger of the two, the one with the carrot, still dancing, and she kisses me on the cheek. "*Mi amor*, I'm Daniela, the au pair."

"The au pair?" Aren't I the au pair?

"Well, the outgoing au pair!"

The outgoing au pair is a stunning brunette whose curves, if she hasn't already had work done from top to toe, must have been a source of inspiration to every plastic surgeon in South America. I'm replacing Miss Universe.

"Nice to meet you," says the other woman, extending her hand and gripping the Kit Kat between her teeth; less courteous, less happy to see me and exchange Miss U for me. "My name's Conchi. Con-chi, not Concha," she stresses with a note of rebuke. "It's short for Conchita. And this"—she holds up the Kit Kat ice cream that she's wolfing at nine o'clock in the morning—"this is fucking menopause."

"Nice to meet you too," I reply, friendly and holding my body entirely rigid so that it won't occur to them to get me to join in the dancing.

"What would you like for breakfast?" Conchi asks.

"To be honest, I don't care . . . I'm starving."

"I'll fix you some pancakes. I'll do it today because it's your first day, but don't get used to it, all right? I've got enough to do already—it's my job to keep this place clean."

"She's a doll really, you'll see. She's just a bit sad that I'm leaving . . . We've become good friends," explains Daniela, taking me by the hand. "Come on, honey, we've got lots to do before the kids get home."

Daniela, who in addition to being stunning is also superfriendly, takes some time to show me the house and give me some gossip.

In general, the decor is how I imagine Indiana Jones's university study, if Indiana Jones had kids. I see colorful Mexican plates, Moroccan hats, a miniature Taj Mahal, a silver-plated kiwi from New Zealand . . . Diverse and brightly colored souvenirs from all around the world. There's even a photo of Fulbright and Hanne sitting on the edge of the fountain in Plaza Sant Felip Neri in Barcelona. That said, most of the walls display a disproportionate—and unnecessary—number of photos of the children, as well as pictures drawn by them and even oil paintings by the budding little artists. The only place I don't find any is the huge bookshelf that occupies an entire wall behind the grand piano.

The room I like best is the parents' study. Two of the walls are floor-to-ceiling glass, a kind of glass box with the feel of a greenhouse, and the main feature is two old wooden desks with two iMacs! Two! I've only ever seen one iMac, at college, but never up close.

And look at that: Just as I'm checking out that wonder of a screen, I notice a photo on the desk showing Hanne hugging Bush! George Fucking W. Bush!

"Yes," laughs Daniela, as proud of the anecdote as if she'd experienced it herself, "that was during Hurricane Katrina. Hanne's a doctor, and she went to New Orleans to volunteer, but no, she's not in government . . ."

"So, how come she's posing with Bill Clinton"—Clinton!—"in that photo up there, behind the ficus?"

"Oh, sure . . . Hanne's father is a Democratic congressman." And she adds, lowering her voice, as if confiding in me, "He's a big fish, very big."

Big enough to allow her to put Bill Clinton behind a ficus.

In the study, away from the shade of any trees and hanging on the wall in a frame several inches thick, are two Harvard diplomas. One is in her name with "cum laude" written in gold, and next to it an identical one—also cum laude—in his name.

I realize that my armpits are damp. It turns out that Fulbright isn't a psychologist or a physical therapist but a professor of history—cum laude—and director of the History Department at Emory University. And that she, as well as being a doctor, is in charge of the American team researching I don't know what kind of vaccine to take to Africa. These guys certainly aren't the Simpsons.

"They're a very good family. Worth their weight in gold," Daniela says, back in the kitchen, elbows resting on the counter, before taking an extremely elegant sip of her detox tea (detox from what?). "With the kids, you just have to do cultural activities that keep their brains active, and that's it. But not just anything. They love going to the Fernbank Museum—that's the natural history one—especially when there are exhibitions on the planets, minerals, or dinosaurs. I've been noting it all down on the list of Important Things that I'm just finishing off. By the way, perhaps they've already mentioned: They don't like the kids watching television."

"But why not?" I sound a little too outraged.

"Because they believe there are many more interesting things to do. And I agree with them," she continues, clearly unhinged by this year of disconnection and misery. "But it's not a total prohibition, you know? They're allowed to watch the odd documentary . . . Although, now that I think about it, I don't think they've watched any this year. No . . . they haven't."

I take one last bite from my fifth pancake, adding a scrape of butter and a final squirt of maple syrup. I think about my childhood in front of the television. The hours of Disney, Spielberg, and 1980s classics straight into my veins. Perhaps without that exposure, I would now be less of a dreamer and idealist . . . I'm sure I wouldn't have thought for a second that Gonçal might have been my Prince Charming. Who can say. It's also true that I wouldn't know things like how dinosaurs are born from a mosquito stuck in a ball of resin, or how to answer the all-too-frequent question of what the Universal globe is.

"Come on," says Daniela as she removes the plate I was about to scrape clean. "I'll show you the neighborhood and, if I can, a bit of Elena."

"Elena? But who is this Elena?"

"Elena?"

"You just said you'd show me Elena."

"No!" She laughs. "Atlanta! That's how they say it here. I suppose I've picked up more of a southern accent than I realized."

Incredible. Apparently, they don't pronounce the letters *a* or *t* here in Atlanta. This year is going to be tough.

I have no time to change my top before we leave. And, in the absence of my bra, I think a nipple hair has forced its way through the Lycra.

The garage is spotless. There are bicycles, shelves holding files and (more) books, but . . . where are the balls? The skateboards? All I see is a huge American flag hanging from one wall.

"Allow me to introduce you to . . . your car!" announces Daniela, opening her arms in a way she must have learned at the Miss Universe final.

"What? Seriously?" I reply with all the elegance of Antònia among her cows.

"Yes, honey, seriously." Then she starts grumbling, cursing everything: "Son of a bitch, what a drag going back to Colombia, I love my car so much . . ."

Yes, indeed, ladies and gentlemen: The all-terrain BMW that came to pick me up from the airport, the one that smells new and has beige upholstery, is my new car. But I can't drive it yet. When did she say she was leaving?

There are only seven houses on our street. All elegant, all beautiful, and each in a different color, none of them garish. A row of majestic trees follows us right along the road and behind each house. They must be thirty feet tall, and I can't figure out what species they are.

"First of all, you have to see the club, which is where everyone goes and where you'll spend most of your time." She takes the first turn we come to. If the car weren't an automatic, she would have stalled fifteen times.

The club is basically an empty house where it seems that all kinds of events are celebrated, from birthdays to Halloween and Sunday afternoons. At the back of the house, down a slope, are four tennis courts, a swimming pool, and a basketball court. All outdoor.

It's eleven o'clock in the morning on a working Wednesday, and four men are playing doubles tennis. Two lose their point as they nod at us and confirm that, despite their prayers, the Booklands' new au pair isn't going to be another Miss Universe.

After the next point, Daniela shouts, "This is Rita!" gesturing at me. I raise my arm—only slightly, because I can't remember whether my underarm hair has grown back—and everyone says hello; well, all except one.

"Look, honey," says Daniela in a confidential tone, "that one there, in green, is Bleh, the other is Bloh, and that one is Prrr. Oh my God, they're so friendly! Especially Prrr!" I've always had a terrible problem with people's names. It's as though, when it hears the word "name," my brain issues a "biiiiiip" that makes it impossible for me to retain it. It's always the same. Well, almost always. "And that one there," she continues, "the one who's a bit more reserved . . . that's John."

We've skirted the court and are walking toward the pool. It doesn't take me long to notice that most of the women here are twice my age, with twice the abs, and the traditional bikini must be blasphemous because most of them seem to be wearing a kind of curtain-like wrap that covers their belly and ass.

"Yes, honey," Daniela informs me, "forget about cute little two-pieces. The South is conservative territory; in fact, I've had to moderate my wardrobe," she says, pushing her breast back into a bra so aggressive, her chest almost obscures her vision.

On the way back to the car, as her dark mane shimmers wonderfully under the blazing sun, Daniela pauses to say goodbye to an older lady dressed in American flags up to her ears—quite literally.

"Let me introduce Mrs. Gee." Mrs. Gee takes my hand and gives it an unexpectedly strong shake. "She's the tennis club founder and a coach and all-round Leafmore legend."

Mrs. Gee looks like she could be one of the Golden Girls. She has a smooth and healthily pink face, covered in freckles, a stark contrast to the rest of her body, which reveals her true age: a million years.

But Mrs. Gee is one of those cheerful, unworried people who retain their good health thanks to plenty of sleep, good digestion, and an obvious innate tendency not to worry too much about the inescapable blows of life.

I squeeze her hand back, with moderate force, then give her and Daniela a moment alone. I feign interest in something I've seen and stroll away, toward the trees, giving them space to fall into a theatrical farewell embrace. The humidity is brutal, and I realize I have crescent-moon sweat marks under my tits.

"They're river bitches." A velvety voice makes me jump.

"I'm sorry?"

"The trees. They're river bitches."

"Uh-huh . . ." I reply. What did he say? It's John. The reserved one. He has a towel draped round his neck and is pointing his racket at the trees.

I don't think the trees can be called "river bitches." My serious lack of knowledge of the English language has just opened up a parallel reality.

"Bill Gates plants them because they're quick growers. In the spring, I wear skirts, in white, like a Sicilian nose."

This can't be right. I need to learn English, and fast.

John must be around thirty-five, and he has the air of a classic gentleman, the magnetic kind, the kind who makes you feel special just by shaking your hand and listening to you as though everything you say is Shakespearean verse.

His skin is tanned but surprisingly smooth, the same color as his hair; his eyes are a disconcerting implacable grayish green.

He smells of wood and earth, and from the hypnotic effect of his aura, I'd be willing to bet he has all the answers in the universe. This fleeting moment is all I need to distinguish a hidden promise in his words, as though this encounter were written somewhere, as though he and I just had to meet to discover a world of possibilities.

"Hello, Rita. My name is John, John Lapton . . . Welcome to Elena."

And, instead of replying with a profound and intelligent comment, instead of borrowing a line from some movie or song he'd recognize and find witty, I come out with "Nais tu mit yu" in a strong Catalan accent.

NASA HQ

When I saw a yellow bus, I froze. It's not as though I had pictured any particular form of transport, but, jeez, that yellow bus is such a cliché, I didn't think they used them anymore.

Now the three children are playing downstairs, in the games room. I'm in the kitchen with Daniela, who's adding to the list of Important Things as she dips carrot sticks into a kind of mousse made from chickpeas. "Hummus," she tells me.

Meanwhile, I go to poke around the little yard outside the kitchen. It's small and tidy; there's a glass-topped table coated with an inch of pollen, in which I can't resist writing "Hello" with my finger.

I go back inside to be talked through the mountain of membership cards and, as we get to the children's math club, Bini, the little one—he must be just over three feet tall—enters the kitchen. He opens the refrigerator and takes out a bottle of skim milk and a box of cereal.

Unlike his siblings, Bini has brown hair and olive skin, but his most prominent feature are his huge eyes, with long, curled lashes, that accentuate his extreme curiosity about everything.

Bini sits at the little table, painted in the colors of a ludo board, and fills a bowl with milk and cereal, spilling an equal amount on the table.

"He wants to serve himself," says Daniela, with a doting smile.

The five-year-old fetches a paper towel and lays it across the mess he made. Then, like an executive analyzing the day's stock market, except irresistibly endearing, Bini reads the back of the cereal box, on which various bits of paper have been stuck.

"What are those papers?" Daniela asks him.

"A game," he replies, his Spanish wavering between an Argentinian and a Colombian accent.

"Doesn't the box have a game in it?" she asks.

"Yes, but it's ridiculous." He takes his time, slurps from the Jupiter spoon, and continues, "I asked Eva to invent some new games that are more fun. More difficult."

Aksel enters the kitchen barefoot and shy, the imminence of puberty making him feel intimidated by so many women. He takes a look in the refrigerator and slams it shut, feigning indifference to hide his embarrassment. On the way to the table, he runs his hands through the tangle of thick, dry curls that tumble messily over his head. He sits next to Bini, in a yellow chair that will be too small for him within a few months, and looks at the box from a distance. Daniela adds another couple of points to the list of Important Things, and I open a drawer, pretending to look for something.

"In Spanish, okay?" Daniela warns them.

The children don't answer, but they obey.

"Is this the game Eva made you?" asks Aksel, pouring some of the colorful cereal into an MIT bowl.

"Yes . . ." replies Bini. "Hey, give me back the box—I'm nearly finished."

"Oh my God," groans Aksel, who has just seen the original game on the packet.

"I know—it's terrible," answers Bini.

"But it makes no sense! How can a *T. rex* and a bunch of eoraptors fight a stegosaurus? Some are from the Late Cretaceous and the other is Jurassic. Everyone knows that! And not just that—look at the trees!" He shows the picture to Bini, who is so attentive to his older brother that he spills milk down his T-shirt.

"What's wrong with the trees?"

"Well, this is a variant of the Paraná pine!"

"Ahhh . . ." Bini doesn't get it.

"The Paraná pine only grows in Argentina, and they've never found *T. rex* fossils there. My gosh . . . Just wait till Dad sees it." They both laugh, and Aksel adds, "They say kids don't pay attention in school . . . but then they make us start the day with these incongruities!"

I don't know whether my eyes widen more at the word "Cretaceous" or "incongruities." I look at Daniela, expecting her to share my indignation, but she doesn't. She's too busy turning the list of Important Things into an animated flow chart. Damn it! What is this place? NASA?

I take a gulp of coffee.

Bini notes down the answer to Eva's game on the back of the box while Aksel checks the nutritional values of the cereal. I stay quiet until suddenly, through the kitchen window, I see a squirrel climbing a tree.

"A squirrel, a squirrel!" I come out from behind the counter to get a better view. "Look, look! A squirrel!"

The children exchange uncomprehending and embarrassed glances.

"Rita"—Daniela clears her throat—"Atlanta is full of squirrels. You'll see them all over the country. In fact, they're the equivalent of pigeons in Europe."

The children laugh through their teeth, and I go over to their table, trying to control the last traces of exaltation that my body is still emitting, as though it had been Beyoncé herself climbing that trunk.

"May I?" I point at the cereal box and make the most of the only intimidating weapon I have available to me at this point, which is, who would have thought it, my stature of five feet two inches.

"Yeah, sure . . ." replies Aksel, lowering his head and looking at his brother.

I pour myself a bowl of cereal, unhurriedly and with a note of insolence I'm not sure they even pick up on. The milk is horrible; it's essentially white water, the worst I've ever tasted. And the cereal, which looks like unicorn shit, is a shot of sugar that I'm convinced must be bordering on illegal.

"Do you want to come downstairs?" Bini asks. "I'll show you what we're building."

I try to repress my joy at, even just momentarily, being asked before Daniela.

"You too, Daniela," adds Bini.

She jumps off her stool with a "Well, suuuurre!" followed by a phrase in English that I don't understand but which makes them burst out laughing. The children get up and run into her arms, crying with laughter. I move away from the scene, allowing the three of them to join hands and descend the stairs in front of me to the games room.

Eva's blond hair has been left in the same ponytail for more than ten hours, which gives her the look of a bohemian genius. Sitting on a stool at the back of the room, the girl holds her bony back straight, her gaze fixed on the tip of her paintbrush. She spreads the paint with an adult calm that contrasts with the size of her hands, which are small and soft. On her face, the freckles spread across her nose.

Her stool is sitting in the center of a raft of newspaper sheets that have saved the beige carpet. Eva is putting the final touches to a shining moon of yellows: the moon from Van Gogh's *The Starry Night.*

"Oh, Eva! It's turned out wonderfully!" exclaims Daniela, clearly impressed, as she strokes her hair.

"Really? Thanks . . . But to be honest, there's not much merit to it . . . I just followed the steps in the book. Gauguin's self-portrait was harder, because I did the whole thing from the photo, without references, but since you like Van Gogh so much . . . I had to be sure it was perfect."

"What? This is for me?" asks Daniela, as if being given an original Van Gogh.

"Yes!" Eva opens her arms, and, when she sees me, she smiles, seemingly with a touch of embarrassment as she sinks into the arms and perfect (fake?) breasts of her old au pair.

Daniela, who's crying now, lifts the girl in a triumphant embrace.

I give them some space to play out this moment of extreme emotion that has precious little to do with me and go over to the two boys, who are concentrating on loading a cannon.

"What are you playing? Soldiers?"

Aksel looks at me askance, as though "soldiers" doesn't go halfway to defining the historical and military strategy before them. He kneels down and starts to describe the scene.

"It's the first day of the Battle of Gettysburg."

"July 1, 1863," adds Bini.

"I already said that," clarifies Aksel, the smart-ass. "So, it's the first day. These guys here are the Army of the Potomac, with General George Meade, who, of course, was born in Spain, and these are the Confederates, with General Robert E. Lee. Well, that's clear from the flags they're carrying." Bini illustrates the speech by pointing a finger at what his older brother is saying, his mouth lolling open. "It was the bloodiest battle of the American Civil War, and, since we can't recreate the fifty-one thousand deaths, we've made a proportionate calculation based on the area of the room, and we've got two hundred and eighty-seven." He shows me a mound of strips of foil painted blue and red scattered over an area of a couple of square feet.

Bini has been listening with a slight buildup of saliva on his lower lip. He adds, "And now she's finally finished the Van Gogh, Eva can build us the Shenandoah Valley to make the escape on July 3 more realistic. In the meantime, I'll be working on the small mound where Lincoln will give his famous speech, you know?" He looks at me. "'Four score and seven years ago, our fathers brought forth on this continent, a new nation . . .'"

I leave the boy with milk teeth reciting historic speeches and return my attention to Eva and Daniela. They've left the Van Gogh to dry and are now flicking through a book about lesser-known surrealist women artists from the 1940s.

I watch the scene with the same distance and curiosity with which I might watch an evening class in cross-stitch; that is, with disinterest and a touch of sadness. But then, from the doorway, I find a scrap of joy. A friend.

In between a botanical atlas and an old edition of Schopenhauer's *The Art of Survival*, I spot a half-deflated ball. I grab it and, to the complete indifference of everyone else, go out to the street and kick it against the garage door until night falls.

"I Will Always Love You"

I wake at six in the morning to the clumping of Hanne's chunky shoes, which triggers a series of noises relating to the scene playing out upstairs: Daniela's send-off.

I hear the children whimper and melt once again into the Colombian's embrace. I admit I'm feeling jealous; those kids will never love me the way they love her.

The last thing I needed was to hear her sing after the farewell dinner last night.

She spent all afternoon cooking typical Colombian dishes—categorically refusing to let Fulbright and Hanne pay for the ingredients—and served up a delicious farewell feast.

First, she made *ajiaco santadereño*, a magnificent chicken soup. I thought she had invented the name, but no, not only did she choose that dish because it's an emblem of Colombia, but also because, and I quote literally here: "The ingredients represent the transition of Colombian culture to Spanish culture on an organoleptic level."

Here you get a free history lesson with your soup.

I have to say, though, it was delicious. She rounded off the meal serving a *tres leches*, a kind of sponge cake (I felt this was an opportune moment to explain that in Catalan, we call it *pa de pessic*, or "pinch bread") soaked in condensed milk and cream and, as if the threat of lactose-induced flatulence was in any doubt, she added a final slug of whole milk.

And, just as I was wolfing down that *pa de pessic* as if the world would end after coffee, Daniela decided to sing, baring her glowing white teeth and straightening her back.

I thought that, for this goodbye scene, she might sing something from *The Sound of Music* or, even better, one from *Mary Poppins*, before flying off with her umbrella and shapewear leggings.

But no.

She sang "I Will Always Love You" by Whitney Houston. And it was incredible.

It's no exaggeration to say that I've never heard such a beautiful voice up close. She sang it better than Whitney did; yes, I know that's impossible . . . but at that moment, I would have sworn she did. When she launched into an ultra-epic crescendo, a chill ran down my spine. The rest of the diners' too. Well, everyone except Bini, who was again collecting saliva on his lower lip, his mouth hanging open as if all the tendons in his jaw had snapped. He was dazed, so surrendered to the moment that, if a breeze had blown into the room, it would have knocked him off his chair.

Daniela finished the song with her eyes closed. And with those incredible high notes, she impregnated her voice forever into the walls of the room and onto our skin. As if she needed to. After the final notes, soaring and then soft, I almost had to get up to reanimate Conchi, who claimed that Daniela was the daughter she never had.

So, yes, the au pair I'm replacing is also a professional singer and future coach—so she announced over dinner—on *Operación Triunfo Colombia*, her home country's premiere TV talent contest.

Whereas I, on my very first day, knocked back half a bottle of wine and complained about the lack of TV.

So, when I hear the children whimpering and hugging her, I'm jealous, but I get where they're coming from. In fact, I'm tempted to get up and climb the stairs to kneel before her and beg her not to leave.

To tell her I don't know how to do this. That I only came to America to learn English and find my vocation in two months, which have turned into a year!

I hear a door slam. And the sound of an engine moving away.

Then silence.

The whole family seems to be taking her to the airport. I traipse up to the kitchen, happy to have the house and its full-to-bursting refrigerator to myself. I open my new white MacBook Pro, barely two weeks old, which I inherited from Daniela and don't know how to use. On it, she's left me the animated flow chart of Important Things and a photo of herself with the kids in the pool, all brimming with joy. I change the snapshot for a scene of snowy mountains.

I run through the list and see that every day except Wednesday they have extracurricular activities: piano, violin, Mandarin, and algebra. It's enough to make you want to put a bullet in your brain. Oh, and tennis with the old lady with the dangly earrings and American flags. The problem is that none of these places are near the school, so they can't walk; I'll have to be the one to ferry them from one place to the next. Starting today, with piano in a Greek Orthodox church.

The computer won't connect to the internet, and I don't know where the router is, so it's now two days since I checked my email. And I have to reach my family, as soon as possible. I start drafting emails to my friends and family to let them know what I'm doing here. I even copy in María's sister, my ski instructor, Antònia, and other important people. The phone they gave me is a flip phone, and, as Hanne made clear, it isn't set up to make international calls, so, even if I wanted to pay a thousand dollars to call home, I couldn't. The possibility simply doesn't exist. So right now, I'm alone in a huge house, but entirely disconnected.

I take my coffee and go for the obligatory nose-around I've been itching to do since I arrived.

My first stop is a no-brainer: I head straight for Hanne and Fulbright's study. I go in cautiously, glancing furtively into the corners of the ceiling to make sure there are no cameras, and I sit on his chair. On the rather messy desk, there are two checkbooks: One is more formal, bordered in silver gray, showing the address of the house and his full name, Fulbright H. Bookland—some people are just born to win the Nobel Prize for Literature—and the other, also in his name, is decorated with dinosaurs, on which I see my name and the amount $198.05.

Is that how much they're paying me per month?

Am I here on an intern basis and no one's told me?

And why did he choose the dinosaur checkbook and not the silver one?

As I flick through the names on the files in one of the drawers, I unintentionally knock the mouse, and the computer springs to life with a photo of the five Booklands lighting up the screen. They're wearing matching Hawaiian shirts. Palm trees, bare feet, and smiles that grant me access to the computer without asking for a password.

I glance out of the window to make sure that, yes, it's true, people don't live their lives in the streets here. Not a soul in sight, except for another squirrel in the yard. I go online.

I check the browser history: a Falcons game, the battle of something or other, words I don't understand, more words I don't understand, Greek poetry, Esperanto poetry, more words I don't understand, and then suddenly one I understand perfectly: HunkPorn.

Well, a man of his age watching porn seems normal to me, even recommendable, you might say. I don't know whether the inhabitants of Atlanta would agree, given the covered bellies and asses around here.

What I notice is that, when I click on HunkPorn—yes, I go into the HunkPorn account of the father of the family I've been with for all of a day—I find more than twenty searches for a certain Federico Chitawas.

Federico Chitawas is a short, muscular Latino, with a prick that could knock Nacho Vidal from the podium. He has a tattoo of a cute dog with, odd as it might seem, the words "Mother's love." The last video watched is a trailer in which the doorbell rings and Chitawas goes to answer it, wearing nothing but a thong; surprise, surprise, it's the woman next door, who lifts a finger to her lips and says, "I was just wondering whether you have any salt?" and Chitawas, as eloquent as they come, replies, "I don't have any salt, neighbor, but I have a cock like a rock." Bravo! Now that script deserves the Nobel Prize in Literature!

The sound of an engine approaching pulls me out of Fulbright's viewings of Federico Chitawas. I close the browser history, run to the kitchen, and pick up a book of Cajun recipes from New Orleans, feigning innocence.

Shit, the cup! I left my cup on his desk!

The vehicle is at the garage door, and someone has already gotten out. I run back to grab the cup and see that the screen is still on.

I run out of the study with my heart pounding in my ears. They'll catch me, for sure. I pick up the book again, and, although I'm still alone in the house, I shake my head as though I don't agree with one of the recipes.

They're about to come in. The screen is still on. Shit, I think I might faint.

But then the engine moves away. I wait for a few minutes and go to peer out of the windows on either side of the front door.

I see the recycling truck pausing outside the house next door and picking up the blue bin they've left by the side of the road—just as, I realize, we and all the other houses on the street have done too.

Phew.

Toto, I Have a Feeling We're Not in Georgia Anymore . . .

After my first day on the job, during which I discovered that the father of the family is gay or at least into gay porn—as first days go, it's not bad—I decided to go and find some Wi-Fi in a café. But I got lost.

Atlanta and its affluent suburbs are a constant déjà vu of micro-neighborhoods, big trees, and shopping malls all with the same stores and restaurants. McDonald's, Starbucks, Dunkin' Donuts, Target, Kroger. Repeat.

By two o'clock in the afternoon, I had asked four cars stopped at the traffic lights how to get to Decatur, but that didn't help me any. I didn't understand what they were saying, and the kids had been waiting for five minutes already (five whole minutes!).

An hour later, I came to the third gas station, trying to hide my despair as best I could: "Decatur!" I said clearly to the man at the gas station. "Day-cah-turrr." In the end—I don't know why it took me so long—I wrote it on a receipt, and he and the employees at the cash register all responded with the classic "aaaaah," and pronounced the word light-years from the way I said it: "Duh-kay-tuh," they said. "Duh-kay-tuh" in "Elena."

I felt like crying, but I held it in. It was when they explained to me for the third time how to get there, friendly but scratching their heads and sighing, that I just gave in and said yes. This accent is impossible to understand. And the car has no maps. I left the gas station, munching on M&M's and crying with rage, and called Fulbright for the umpteenth time.

"Reeda?" he replied finally, scared, and after confirming that I was still alive, he mentioned that the algebra tutor had called him, concerned, because no one had come to pick up the children. "And that's never happened to the Booklands before."

End dat's nehvuh happened to the Booklaynds before, nya nya nya.

When I told him where I was (about to cross the border into Alabama, it would seem), the man had to cancel his weekly tutorial at the last minute to go fetch his children. Conchi was at tae kwon do and didn't answer. "That's what you're there for, dear," added Hanne, during the next call.

Despite my tears of frustration, I must say that when I heard I was so close to Alabama, I was excited. I've always liked the idea of Alabama. *Forrest Gump*, *Big Fish* . . .

In the end, Fulbright had to come and fetch me that night, on who knows which highway, giving me explicit orders not to move. "Rita, don't move an inch."

I decided to wait for him and de-stress in a Chinese restaurant with Styrofoam dishware. I started writing dirty postcards to my friends—the card selection in American supermarkets is generally a treasure trove—and I had bought several of one showing a fat man with a hairy ass wearing a thong in front of the Eiffel Tower. I made up a story about getting lost and ending up in Paris, having had a sex change. My friends would be pleased; not only did I send them emails about my life now, but hairy-ass postcards too.

Fulbright arrived, utterly flummoxed. He didn't ask me how I had ended up there because he knew that whatever I said wouldn't explain why I was at the Alabama border. Or perhaps he was too scared to hear my answer.

When I got home, the children had already showered and were going over their piano lesson.

"What happened to you? Why didn't you come for us?" asked Eva, on behalf of all three, who were gazing at me, excited by the sudden change of routine.

"Children, I've already told you: She got lost," explained Hanne as she dressed the lettuce with lemon. "It's normal. Atlanta can be very confusing." She gave a little laugh.

"Daniela never got lost," said Bini, with the implacable truthfulness of a five-year-old. It was as though he'd plunged a dart right into my forehead.

I suppose that, really, they have good reason to be pissed at me, but when Hanne saw my bereft face, she couldn't help but burst out laughing. She came and hugged me.

And as I rested my face on her shoulder, noticing her patting my back and the space between our bodies, I thought, *You can laugh, Hanne . . . but your husband gets off to Federico Chitawas.*

My Name Is Rita

This week, the sky has turned a leaden gray, a metallic cape that won't allow even a whisper of breeze to pass through, and for us terrestrial beings, the air is unbreathable. The air quality in Atlanta today is worse than in Vietnam.

After following a squirrel into the spotless yard of a private property—I wanted to take a photo but didn't succeed—I come back to shelter myself from the stifling atmosphere in the air-conditioning blasted out by this car of mine that ought to belong to a bougie fifty-year-old.

I didn't have to pick up the kids from school today. It turns out that, once a month, we go to a church for dinner, and the teachers take the children there themselves. A dinner at five o'clock in the afternoon in a Methodist church (it's the fifth religion that's been mentioned here). To me, that's an afternoon snack.

I'm the only car in the parking lot, waiting for the rest of the family to show up. I've arrived a half hour early to make sure I don't screw it up again and that I remain in the state of Georgia. I've been reading *The New Yorker*. The magazine's covers always show beautiful drawings, and the style of writing—which I still don't understand a whole lot—is creative rather than journalistic, and that makes it much more interesting, in my opinion. The best thing is that the articles are interspersed with black-and-white cartoons with witty captions that aren't too difficult to understand. Ever since Hanne gave me my first copy, I've been carrying a dictionary in my purse.

Today's best illustration shows a girl introducing her boyfriend to her parents; the "boyfriend" is a penguin lovingly holding the daughter's hand and saying to the parents, "Actually, I prefer the term 'Arctic American.'"

The church hall has no pews. It looks more like a multipurpose games hall, with stained-glass windows and hardwood floors, than a church. Around the room, there are tables laden with food that, as Hanne explains to me, is all cooked by the same old ladies who are serving it. You pay three dollars and eat all you want.

At the first table, they're offering a kind of boiled semolina that, as unlikely as it might seem, looks pretty good.

"This is called grits," Eva informs me. "I don't like it, but Mom and Dad sometimes have it for breakfast. It's the official dish of Georgia—you should probably try it."

So, it turns out that Americans have their own recipes too; I help myself.

The second table is the vegetables. And the main event is something that looks like a miniature green pepper oozing an intriguing mucous.

"That's okra," continues Eva, dolloping a clumsy spoonful on her plate.

"Ah, like the television presenter!"

"Nooo!" she laughs. "That's Oprah!"

"Ah, right . . . Sorry . . ."

"Okra is one of the most typical Southern dishes, although the plant comes from Ethiopia." She picks up a piece in her fingers to show me. "If you cut it crossways, it's like a perfect star. See?"

Eva continues her dissertation on the nutritional properties of okra, but my attention is caught by the elderly woman serving it.

Except for the baguette-cut diamond ring, her hands look a lot like my Yaya's: long, bony fingers, covered in thin, transparent skin with lots of darker patches, and you can see the veins climbing up the muscles like naked branches in the fall.

I get a dry lump in my throat, and suddenly I can't talk. I look around me; this place is full of people, but I can't see anyone I know. My eyes cloud over, and the old woman notices. She shoots me a wise, calm look, as though reading my thoughts, as though she knows it's all going to turn out okay, and serves me a generous portion. I nod as best I can, biting my lips, and thank her with the least trembly smile I can muster.

"Shall we go get some mac 'n' cheese?" asks Eva.

I stick a large piece of okra in my mouth. It's crunchy and sweet, reminding me of the taste of sweetened asparagus. I notice how it slides down my throat and soothes the horrible dryness.

The tables, covered with stars-and-stripes tablecloths—surprise!—fill up with an army of calories on plates and blue and red napkins. Apart from the okra, there's no trace of green in any of the other dishes. Most have cheese or barbecue sauce or glisten with a thick sticky glaze, like the ribs.

On the adult side of the Bookland family, Hanne and Fulbright keep raising their hands and emitting monosyllables to greet other parents from a distance: "Hey," "Hi," "Yeah," "Ha, ha!" Occasionally, a neighbor comes to gossip, perhaps to see with their own eyes that, yes indeed, Miss Universe has left the building. I stand up with a smile and shake hands with the classic "Nais tu mit yu."

A tall man wearing an expensive-looking sport coat (we call them *americanes* back home, but I guess that would sound dumb here in the States) comes up to the table. Seeing that he provokes gestures and reactions wherever he passes, particularly in Hanne and Fulbright, I'm guessing that this guy is someone important.

The man shakes the kids' hands. He asks them a question and listens attentively to the answer. Then he goes through the same procedure with the parents, and then it's my turn. Hanne makes the introductions (she seems to think it relevant to mention that I won the Spanish slalom championships when I was seventeen).

"Hello, Rita. Welcome to Atlanta and to our church." The hand is warm and soft, but not overly so. "My name is Paul and I eat figs, figs from *Mary Poppins.* What about you? Dolphins from Versailles?"

"Yes."

"And pigeons with sideburns?"

"Yes."

"Fantastic, I've always preferred chickpeas to sing jazz."

If you say so, dude!

"Nais tu mit yu, Paul."

Paul moves away, and the elderly women start to clear away the buffet. The room looks like it's set up for a wedding, but with informal diners who all get along well, eating food that isn't remotely organic, at round tables covered in patriotic tablecloths.

As I'm taking the last bite of my third rib, there's a hubbub of scraping of chairs, children, and cutlery, which echoes round the white walls of the church.

Everyone gets up. Silence falls.

Paul stands in the middle of the carpeted area to welcome us. Shit, Paul is the pastor.

My eyes rove around the room, utterly oblivious to what Paul is saying, and I see Prrr and Bleh, who nod at me. I analyze my romantic prospects, which don't look very hopeful at all, until I hear the sound of an oiled door opening at the other side of the room.

A man appears; he's suave and sexy in equal measure. It's a perfect balance, a fascinating harmony. He takes off his hat and apologizes for the interruption with a bow of his head and his hand slightly raised. A potent elegance. Then he moves his hand to his hair to smooth it down. When he walks, he seems to levitate. It's John. A dandy among dandies. I follow him with my gaze, but I lose him among the hundreds of heads.

I go back to the table to wipe my fingers with a paper napkin that disintegrates with the remains of the caramel glaze from the ribs. I'm staring down at my fingers, covered in stars and stripes, when suddenly I notice the weight of the whole room upon me.

I look up. My adoptive family is watching me with an urgent smile and willing me to move, to walk.

"Come on!" exclaims Hanne. "You're the only new person in the room, and new people have to be introduced to the community!"

Huh? What's happened? Where do I go?

"Come on!" insists Hanne, gesturing at Paul. "I told you earlier that you'd have to say a few words. That you live with us and that you ski and say thank you and blah, blah, blah, and the okra and blah, blah, blah . . ." Hanne's voice fades as I advance toward the center of the room, where I'm engulfed in a massive round of applause.

I find John's face again; he's looking at me now and nods in satisfaction. I stand alone in front of Pastor Paul, who's waiting for me with open arms in the middle of the floor, saying something unintelligible. I hide my sticky-papered hands, balling them into fists.

The pastor is waiting for me to speak. I see John widen his eyes and nod, encouraging me to speak. The children are wincing. Aksel has clamped his hand over his mouth, dying of embarrassment. Fulbright's and Hanne's smiles are frozen on their faces.

Finally, I speak. I speak with the clarity and intensity of a newly qualified kindergarten teacher introducing herself on her first day in the turtle class, in front of her three-year-old pupils:

"My name is Rita." Loud and clear.

The audience nods calmly, after confirming that I'm not in fact an orangutan, affirming that Rita is, in fact, my name. That I am able to speak. But they want a speech. I turn to face them all, clearing my throat. In my mind, I run through my entire knowledge of English, from my high school diploma and subtitled TV shows to Sooozan and fish-and-chips. But I can't remember a thing. Nothing! I have a total mental blank. All I can remember is one phrase, one phrase . . . Finally, before the attentive gaze of my audience, I declare, "Actually, I prefer the term 'Arctic American.'" And I round it off with, *"Thank you."*

The audience doesn't seem to have realized that that's it. That I won't say any more because I can't think of a single thing.

I make a timid retreat to my table and cross a desert of hardwood and silence with the torn American flag still clinging to my fingers. Finally, after a million years, someone dares to start a hesitant clap in the distance: clap . . . clap . . . clap.

I reach the table to intermittent and pitying applause, and I find the children, laughing with their hands over their mouths. A generous droplet of sweat slips down the side of my cheek. My damp hands are making confetti of the flag. So I take the opportunity to sit down and stuff my mouth with okra.

Back in the parking lot, a million years later, Paul greets me from a distance with a sincere smile and a thumbs-up. I return the gesture. I want to leave this place.

"Rita," says Fulbright, squeezing his key in the air, trying to locate his car in the crowd, "you can go for a drive or whatever you like. You have the morning off tomorrow!" Technically, I've done barely any work at all yet. "We'll look after the kids for the rest of today—getting them to shower every now and then won't do us any harm!"

He winks at me, and I feel the scorching in my throat again. I can't swallow. My chin starts to wobble at supersonic speed. I've never felt so homesick in my entire life.

Ovaries

This is surreal: It's only six o'clock, and I've eaten dinner already. When real dinnertime comes around, I'll be dying of hunger.

I stop off at the first Starbucks I find, in a building with a fake brick frontage, like all the other restaurants on the block. As I hold the door open to allow an elderly woman on a motorized scooter to leave, I notice an arm sticking out of a window round the corner, serving coffee to go, which people collect without leaving their car.

The first person I see inside is Black. I've heard that Atlanta has one of the highest African American populations in the South, but I've seen no evidence of that since the airport. Certainly not in that goddamn church, where every person was white. Every single one. No Asians or Latinos either—what a boring neighborhood.

It's a small café, six tables and two armchairs. There's a large window offering views of the parking lot and the Dunkin' on the other side of the street. Hey, it's just like Cerdanya.

"Good evening! How are you today?" An extremely friendly barista greets me from behind the counter. I seem to have sparked some degree of curiosity in him. "My name is Left Ovary, and I have a hamster and a rat. What can I get you today?" The guy and his rounded belly are waiting for a response with a paper cup and a marker pen hovering over it.

"A coffee with milk."

"Large?"

"Yes." I don't know how to ask for decaffeinated, so I just won't sleep tonight.

"Okay. Today's special is a school of rabbits flying over Mississippi." He punctuates the explanation with gesticulations at the menu and then points at the cup. "We'll dye your ankles a camel and you'll get a beetle with bangs. Methusaleh, too, all right?"

"All right."

The guy marks a cross on four of the five little boxes on the side of the paper cup.

"What's your name?"

"Rita."

The marker pauses.

"Sorry?"

"Reeda," I repeat with as much of an American accent as I can manage, thankful that I don't know anyone within a four-thousand-mile radius.

"Oh! What a lovely name! Where are you from?"

"Barcelona . . ."

"Oh! Barça, Barça! Ronaldinho! I've always cooked faucets from Olympic trampolines . . . Ha, ha, ha! Do you paint your nails?"

"Pardon?" I say as the other baristas laugh and pull faces to tell me not to pay any attention.

"Nothing, nothing!" He laughs, still friendly. "That'll be five dollars thirty-five cents."

"Fuck . . ." I mutter under my breath as I hold up my card and ask with my eyes if I can use it.

"Yes, just put it here . . . Thank you very much!" he concludes, satisfied, and points at the other end of the counter to tell me to wait there.

I look for a table and turn on my laptop. I enter the Wi-Fi password, and, in less than a minute, I hear my name: "Reeda!"

My coffee with milk is waiting for me at the end of the counter. I take the cup, on which I see he has written, literally, *Reeda*, and find that the coffee with milk I ordered—or so I thought—has become a six-inch-tall mug full of caramel, pumpkin syrup, and pink chocolate swirls on top of two inches of whipped cream.

"Do you like it?" Left Ovary asks me excitedly, raising his thumbs at me.

"Yes! Thanks . . ." I take a sip, tensing my cheeks and squinting.

I sit down and open my email to find around twenty juicy messages from friends in response to the last one I sent, describing my fleeting visit to the Alabama border. But I'll read them later. I open Skype in the hope that my family will have the computer on and my brother will hear it from the kitchen.

I call and . . . *Bingo!*

"Rita?"

"Albert?"

"Ritaaaaa!"

My eyes brim with tears. It's only been two weeks since I saw them, but I'm so excited, you'd think I'd been shipwrecked for four years, living on a desert island and eating nothing but leaves and worms, my eyebrows grown so unruly, they'd joined in the middle. The café is fairly full, and there's a lot of noise, so I'm well camouflaged to be able to enjoy the call.

"Dad! Mom! Come here—it's Rita! Yayaaaa! Yaya, come here!"

I hear my parents hurrying down the stairs and a chair being knocked over in the kitchen: "Shiiiit! Tell her not to hang up, put another euro in!"

My parents lean into the camera, and my brother complains because they're pushing his head up against the screen. We've spoken a couple of times since I left, but only very briefly. They ask the predictable questions, delighted to see me, and I answer enthusiastically, grateful for the slightly shaky connection that hides my quivering voice. But it only takes a couple of minutes of talking to them for the lump in my throat to iron itself out.

I see Yaya in the background, staring at the screen with the same surprise and incomprehension she must have felt when she heard Manolo Escobar singing from inside a box, behind glass, in black and white. I don't know if she's more amazed at seeing me or seeing me speak directly through a screen.

I hear her ask my brother, "Is that Rita talking?"

"Yes, of course, Yaya, say hello! She's in a café, in America."

"But can she see us? How many people are watchin'?" she asks, one hand on her chest, horrified.

"Of course she can see you—say hello!"

"Ay, ay, ay! No, no, no! I'm wearin' my gardenin' overalls!" She gets up and leaves, scandalized, trying to hide the curlers in her hair with her hands.

"Rita!" she yells, interrupting my conversation with my parents. "I'm here, okay? I'm here, even if you can't see me!"

My parents have to leave for a moment to attend to some customers in the restaurant, and I'm left alone with her and Albert.

"Can they see me now?" Yaya asks Albert, her head filling half the screen—I can even see the stains on her teeth from the lipstick she has just hastily applied.

"No, Yaya, no one can see anything."

"Listen, *mi arma* . . ." She lowers her voice, adopting a confidential tone, moving so close, she must be about an inch from the screen. "There, where you are . . . Are there people with guns?"

"Yaya! What a question to ask!"

"But are there? I'm interested, my dear, yes I am."

"I have no idea, Yaya. I mean, I suppose I'm just not thinking about guns, for God's sake!"

"Oh, Mother of heaven!" she exclaims, looking up and crossing herself. "Just get one yourself! A big one, just in case!"

"What? Yaya, please, don't be ridiculous! Let's talk about ham, please, oh gosh, I miss ham so much."

She thinks I can't hear her, but her grumbling is clear in the background.

Meanwhile, my brother is trying not to get irritated when, after he informs me that "people" were asking after me on Saturday night, I ask for specific details of who they were, what time they asked, in what tone, and with which exact words. And he moans, as always, because I won't relent on the subject.

And it dawns on me that confirming that everything at home is just the same as ever is exactly what I needed.

Albert changes the subject and tells me he hooked up with a girl in the bathroom at El Refugi. Meanwhile, Yaya, who has been listening from the armchair with her hands clasped across her chest, starts to tilt her head, as though trying to figure out something puzzling, and approaches the screen, slowly and progressively, in the light reflected by my image.

Then I see her mouth and eyes suddenly widen, and she shouts, "Ritaaaaa! Rita, I see a man coming up behind you! Maybe he has a gun!"

The barista, who, as I understand it, is still called Left Ovary, has come up to my table and is very kindly offering me a sample of a chai latte. As I turn to take the tea, I notice Yaya gesticulating nervously.

I accept the cup with a smile and the sincere hope that he doesn't understand a word of Spanish.

"Do you like thumbtacks?"

"Pardon, I don't understand."

"Family?" he asks sweetly and politely, gesturing at the screen.

"Family, family . . ."

When I hang up, it feels as though I've just had a cold shower after crossing the Sahara wearing neoprene. A reset.

And now, feeling calmer, I think how strange it is to be sitting here, alone, not waiting for anyone.

I gaze around me as I take a sip of caramelly cream and realize that no one here knows me. No one in the parking lot, or Dunkin' Donuts, or the whole of the United States.

No one knows my name, who my parents are, or that I ran away from school at the age of twelve with a cigarette in my mouth and three aspirins in my pocket and the fire service found me in the woods with a friend at eleven o'clock at night. Here there's no need to cross the street if I see a teacher I don't want to speak to, nor do I have to worry about what I'm wearing to leave the house. Nor do I have to pretend that I'm indifferent to Gonçal while in truth I'm melting inside.

Here, no one will ask me whether I've finished my degree, or what I plan to do with my life, because "it's about time, you know?" and I won't have to recite a rehearsed speech full of excuses to explain that, actually, it isn't all that unusual to have no idea what you're going to do with your life when you're twenty-three. That the strange ones are those who never have any doubts and want to be doctors from the age of fifteen.

Here no one cares who I am or what I do. They don't care if I'm lost, that I came to Atlanta by mistake, that I'm here to find myself, to try and work out what will truly make me happy. And that I don't have the faintest idea what that will be. They don't give a shit about any of that.

And it feels wonderful. It's absolute freedom.

I get into the car and set off down the first highway I see.

After twenty minutes driving through neighborhoods showing a bit more life than mine, I reach the district of Little Five Points. One of the first things I see is a bar where the door is the open mouth of a huge skull.

I park under a weeping willow, and, as I walk away, I think how the tree's drooping branches make my bougie BMW look even more out of place in this neighborhood.

The leaden sky is breaking up into gentle purples that offer increasingly long respites from the brutal humidity. On the way to the skull bar, I flick through my pocket dictionary where I hope to find the English for "gin and tonic."

A juggler with gray dreadlocks watches me crossing the street. Behind him, there's a secondhand clothes store that looks like it's got a bit of style. I alter my course and head for the door.

It smells of leather and Windex; the store is full of old wheelchairs and posters of Jesus with witty captions.

"Hello, how are you?" The assistant is wearing a sky-blue air hostess cap. "Has Buddha burned your toast today?"

She's waiting for an answer. I look at her and don't know what to say, so I smile, pick up the first item of clothing I see, and go into the fitting rooms.

In no time at all, the assistant's shadow appears on the other side of the curtain.

I stay stock-still, praying I haven't chosen anything too obscene. But the woman doesn't leave, so I'm obliged to try on the shiny green swimsuit I grabbed without looking. I look like the intern on a 1970s variety show, presenting a pool episode. The swimsuit is all cleavage, and the straps cover not much more than my nipples. The flight attendant won't shut up, and I say yes to everything . . . then she suddenly swipes open the curtain.

"Wow!" She seems surprised at the daring of my ensemble for early evening on a Wednesday.

She doesn't ask me to, but I give her a 360-degree turn, and, when she sees the curtain of hair sticking out from my bikini line, fading down my thighs, she looks at me with renewed respect, as though I've just become her new heroine.

"Me lo quedo," I say very slowly in Spanish, as though if I speak clearly, she'll be able to understand that I want to buy it.

I look at the air hostess with a smile and give her the four dollars scrawled on the tag, but she says no, it's on her; she puts it in a bag and seals it with a sticker. Next to the cash register there are some Bibles "signed by the author." I take one.

I leave the store and find the atmosphere has lifted slightly outside. In the time it took me to become a presenter of kitsch pool shows, a line seems to have formed in front of what looks like an old movie theater.

I head toward it, grateful for the first fresh breeze to tickle my arms since I arrived in Atlanta. It's called 7 Stages Theater, and it smells of dust and marijuana. It has only one screen, and I reckon it must date from the 1970s. The board announcing the movies is one of those old-fashioned panels, where the background lights up and the letters are positioned by hand, always with one that's slightly off-kilter.

Its faded, shabby aura echoes all along the street: It's in the tank tops, the tarnished silver jewelry, and the extreme hairstyles of the passersby; damn it, it's cool. The general neglect is mostly calculated, giving the area a certain charisma and personality and making the giant panel of Jim Morrison hanging from a facade seem to fit in perfectly.

Across the street, a group of very stoned young men is drinking apple juice and rapping next to a boom box straight out of the 1980s Bronx. Just twenty minutes away from my very staid neighborhood; Atlanta is a city of strong contrasts.

I join the line. Going to the movies is the best idea I can think of. I realize that I haven't been around people my own age for weeks. Compared to the world of children, snobs, and pastors I've just come from, this street is the closest I've been to myself. It's hard to tell whether the women's clothes are from when their grandmothers were protesting against the Vietnam War, or whether they've just spent three hundred bucks on cropped jeans.

Speaking of jeans, mine are about to burst. I'm getting fatter by the minute. I decide to unbutton them—who's going to say anything?

In front of me is a group of loud young women who can't stop laughing. They aren't loud in the hysterical American way, but like they're having a good time, a really good time. I'm jealous. They say something funny that I would love to understand, so that I could join the conversation and contribute some witty and intelligent comment that might allow me to make a friend—particularly because at some point I think they mentioned *Showgirls* and "extinguisher"—but instead, I pretend I'm looking something up in the dictionary.

I think about the spectacle in the church and cringe. I don't think I'll ever go there again. I'll limit myself to taking the children here and there, without ever speaking to or looking at anyone else from the neighborhood. I'll be a robot. My God, what a disaster.

After another burst of laughter, one of the young women leaves the line to order a beer. Her lips are painted a beautiful matte red, and she's holding a cigarette with the ease of someone who has smoked a million, but with an innate flair on top of that. She also has colossal tits.

I watch her quite openly, but she doesn't seem annoyed. And when the pump spits out the last bit of foam on the top of her artisanal IPA, the girl glances at one of the friends she left behind in line and, with a gluttonous smile, utters the most beautiful phrase I've heard in my life:

"Damn it, Monica, I'd take you right now and fuck you in the middle of the street . . ."

Catalan has never sounded so sweet.

"Excuse me, excuse me!" I say. She turns, almost as surprised as I am, and, as though her response could win me the lottery, I ask, "Are you Catalan?"

"Shit! You heard what I just said?"

"Yes, and it was wonderful."

"You must think I'm depraved!" she says with a hint of embarrassment. "My name's Six." She holds out her hand.

"Did you say 'Sex'?"

"No, you idiot." Did she just call me an idiot? Already? "My name is Six, like the number, like . . . like Blossom's friend, you know, on TV."

"I'm Rita." I kiss her on both cheeks.

"Gosh, yeah, sorry. I've been here nearly a year—I've lost the two-kiss habit. What are you doing here? Do you live in Atlanta?"

"Yes, I arrived two weeks ago."

"Oh, great! Are you doing a master's? Or at college? Or do you work?"

"I'm not doing a master's or studying at any college. I'm working as an au pair."

"An au pair? A babysitter?"

"Yes . . ."

"Ah, great. So, were you coming to watch a movie?"

"Yes, well, the truth is I was just looking around, and I joined the line for something to do. I don't even know what they're showing."

"If you really want to invest three hours of your precious life watching a Polish woman talking about her periods and eventually killing herself, go right ahead. If not, I'll buy you a beer."

We're on the balcony of a bar next to the highway, at a wooden table that sticks to our elbows and smells of damp cloth. Nothing has ever seemed so luxurious. There must be a hundred people around us, most of them in their twenties and early thirties, and they don't look like they're worrying about getting up at eight tomorrow to go to work. Through the balcony railings, I see cars below pausing at a traffic light, which is hanging from the same cable as three pairs of shoes. The street names are shown in clinical green letters; the walls of the buildings painted with stunning graffiti: multicolored trees, Martin Luther King, Lincoln wearing sunglasses . . . Six calls it "street art."

Anyone who saw us would think we've been friends for a lifetime. Six hides it beneath a veneer of well-founded braggadocio, but she's as happy to have met me as I am her.

The crowd on the terrace laughs and drinks and sings. Bloated English words echo in every corner, like a poorly tuned radio, but here, in front of me, Six's voice cuts through clean and clear, like a stream of crystalline water.

"Don't worry, no stress. Finding your path in life isn't easy. I have a degree in journalism, and I'm here selling luxury faucets. But we all have to start somewhere, right? And at least you've left your home and your country, so you're part of the vast minority. Congratulations!"

"I suppose so. Thanks."

"Do you have a plan for working out what you'd like to do?" she asks.

"A plan? Me? For the moment, survive. And learn English."

"Well, you have a year. Keep your eyes open, and one day it will become clear."

Six is more or less my height; she has beautiful hands and uneven teeth. She's from the Hospitalet area of Barcelona, she has a piercing on her lower lip, and when she eats tacos, she licks her fingers.

After two watery Budweisers, we decide to switch to some local artisanal brews and order another round of nachos with a thick layer of melted cheddar.

"Man, getting it on with another girl in front of you, he sounds like a real jerk. But it seems pretty clear he was screwing around, no? In the end, he did you a favor, you'll see . . ." She takes a gulp of beer, and I clear my throat. "Hey, what's that? Not a single fucking tear, okay, not for that guy . . ."

"No, no . . . I'm not crying because of him . . . I'm crying because it's been weeks since I understood so much of a conversation."

I call Fulbright to notify them I'll be back late. I tell him I have keys and not to worry. He thanks me for calling and takes the opportunity to mention that Eva can't find her piano score—I left it in the trunk of my car—and that Bini did badly in his homework the other day because I hadn't supervised properly. "Which is okay, since it's early days, but don't let it happen again," and he reminds me, with a half laugh, that tomorrow at half past two I have to be at school to pick up Bini.

"For God's sake, they're kids," Six says. "Okay, the oldest is ten, but they have to do what you say and that's it. Fucking snobs, they go to Harvard, and it turns them into robots. And they don't watch TV? Come on, at least *Chucky*, that'll really teach them what fear is!" Six gets distracted by a bra-less waitress's tits. "By the way, is this Daniela coming back to visit?"

The guys at the next table toss us their phone number, written on a paper napkin screwed into a ball, and the waiter informs us that they paid for our first round.

"Look, Rita, the best thing you can do right now is to come to an orgy."

I choke on my drink. I'm interested. What?

"I'm serious—it's the best way to socialize. In fact . . ." Six checks the time and makes a calculation, looking at the sky.

"In fact what?" I spill half my beer down my front. "In fact nothing! I'm not going to any orgy! It's Wednesday, and my pants are too tight!"

"Yes, it would be best if you came one day in the right size of pants . . ." She laughs, glancing at my protruding belly.

"You're crazy," I say, taking a drag of menthol cigarette, and add, with more curiosity than intention, "But . . . there would be men, too, right?"

"Yes . . . There will be mennnn . . ." she replies sardonically, "but what do you want a man for? Enough of men! And enough of traditional, predictable, patriarchal sex. Enough! Enough of dicks! I mean, there are even men in this country with that name!"

"What? What do you mean?"

"Dick is short for Richard, Rita! And there are loads of men here who go by the name Dick! Mothers call their sons Dick! Oh, what a beautiful baby . . . What shall we call him? Dick!"

"It can't be . . ."

"Taxi drivers called Dick. 'Good morning, to the station please, Mr. Dick!' And grocers! 'How much for two pounds of bananas, Mr. Dick?'"

"Ha, imagine if your partner was called Dick. 'I love you, Dick.' Or worse, your father! Freud must have written something about it. Did Freud have children? Perhaps he was the first to call his son Dick!"

"The patriarchy tries to beat us in the face with its dick, and we thank it with a smile just to get a ride to the station."

"Harsh."

"Anyway, back to the orgy . . . Men. Have you ever thought about what a woman has to go through to give a man a blow job?" I look around me, and for once I'm glad of Catalan's limited diffusion around the world. "It's so uncomfortable! You have to watch your teeth don't get in the way, your jaw gets tired, it makes you retch as you go up and down trying to breathe through your nose . . ."

"Maybe you're out of practice."

"Ugh, for sure!" She laughs. "But I have no intention of getting any."

Six rounds off her phallic discourse with a theatrical but no less heartfelt shake of her head, and asks, "So, what exactly do we know about this John guy?"

Do You Think the Police Sometimes Turn the Siren on Because They're Hungry and They're Actually on Their Way to Rock 'n' Taco?

I've managed to tune into other channels apart from National Geographic, and I feel like even the TV is grateful for it.

Well, if I'm being honest, David the mail carrier tuned into the channels.

It all came about because I was shoveling down my second bowl of breakfast cereal when I noticed that Hanne hadn't collected the newspaper from the drive. I went out barefoot, still in my pajamas and with mug in hand, and picked up the *Atlanta Journal-Constitution* rolled up in its plastic bag. (And I thought newspapers being tossed into the yard only happened in movies.)

Then a little square blue-and-white-and-red mail truck pulled up outside. David slipped the letters into next door's mailbox and, as any American would, decided to say hello.

"Good morning!" he called from the side of the street.

"Good morning!" I replied, raising the newspaper.

"Are you the nude au pair?" Shit, I don't know whether I understood him or not. Is he referring to the flesh-colored top from the other day? In any case . . .

"Yes! Good morning!"

Then David switched to a robotic but intelligible Spanish and told me that he had lived in Mexico when he was ten, and that now he was fifty. Then he mentioned that a short time ago he had been on an episode of Oprah talking about how he had twelve siblings, and his older brother, who's now dead, had been the first African American in the neighborhood to go to the University of Georgia. I told him I'd never watched Oprah and explained the situation with National Geographic and the History Channel.

And that truly shocked him. He shouted, *"What?"* loud and tremulously, and came over to take my hand. And, given our instant camaraderie, I allowed him in—his car was outside with the door open and the engine running, so it didn't strike me as too dangerous—and in a flash, David the mail carrier accessed some channels that were, in his words, "required viewing."

One of those required channels was showing reruns of a program named after its presenter, Jerry Springer.

Initially, I thought it would be a kind of talk show like *El Diario de Patricia*, which I used to watch back home, but a bit more serious (the presenter wears a sport coat, after all), but after watching a couple of cases, this show makes Patricia look like a renowned scientist.

It has a simple structure: A guest comes on the show to complain about something someone else has done. And by "guests," we're talking about the worst kinds of people. For example, one episode featured a girl who wanted to get her boyfriend's attention, and, in order to do that, she had screwed his best friend and his cousin, and now she had decided to come on the show to tell him that she had also slept with his twin brother.

Then the boyfriend comes on, kicking off as expected—egged on by Springer, who's throwing wood on the fire (he's the worst of all)—until the third participant appears, in this case the twin brother. This moment is always fascinating: Two bodyguards position themselves between the brothers, waiting, well practiced after more than three thousand episodes, for the fight. There's always a fight. Meanwhile the audience is shouting "whore" and "slut" at the girl and encouraging the boyfriend to lay into his twin brother. The human race, what a wonder. I told David to put on the most recent episode.

I spent two hours watching *Jerry Springer*.

I was almost late going to fetch Bini.

Bini's school is called Oak Grove, and it fits the architectural pattern of the majority of American schools: a low, horizontal, orangey building. At the entrance, there's a sign similar to the one at the movie theater in Little Five Points that says "Reading Will Set You Free and God Bless You."

And I ponder how nice it would have been if, apart from repeating the second part of the message for the entirety of my sixteen years at the nuns' school—"God bless you, Rita"—they had presented me with some vaguely passable book (apart from dusty medieval classics) to persuade me that reading could not only educate me but set me free.

It's been years since I read a book. In fact, I'm not sure if I've ever finished one. Saying that out loud makes it sound blasphemous. But it's true; I think it's true to say that I've never finished a book.

The school corridor smells of tangerines and dirty socks.

Bini is in the Penguins, a detail that, recalling the scene in church yesterday—*I prefer the term "Arctic American"*—seems like a joke in bad taste. I stand in line behind two mothers who have come to pick up their kids with the same joy as if they had just left the delivery room and were setting eyes on them for the first time.

"Good morning, I'm here for Bini," I say.

"Pardon?" The teacher, who must be genetically endowed with infinite patience and a keen ability to decipher the words of small children, can't understand me.

"Bini, Bini Bookland."

"Ah! Bini!" And she pronounces it exactly the way I just did. "So, you must be Rita?"

"Yes."

"Delighted to meet you." She shakes my hand and fixes her sky-blue eyes on me, making sure I get the message as clearly as if I were another penguin. "They're a wonderful family . . . especially the kids. Be patient with the kids. They're very smart, the smartest in class, and also the baldest in Oklahoma. I've taught all three of them."

Bini approaches, dragging his feet, head bowed, resigned, as though every time he feels more than two eyes on him, he goes through the worst torment of his short life.

"Bye, then, Bini."

Bini gazes at her respectfully and offers a sweet and practiced goodbye.

"Goodbye, Miss Moore. Have a nice day."

"Goodbye, Rita." She takes my hand, as if about to say something momentous. "And remember, Jesus Christ was vegetarian and Bini has glass pasta for dinner."

"Thanks," I reply.

We walk down the corridor, unsure of what to say to one another, and get into the car. Bini fastens the belt across his booster seat.

"Bini, could you repeat what Miss Moore said, please? I'm not sure I entirely understood . . ."

"Hmm . . ." He's hiding a smile—let's see if he lies to me. "She said she wrote a note in my agenda for Mom and Dad." He's chewing a candy he found between the seats; I think he's telling the truth. "But I already know what the note says—they want to move me up a grade. They did the same with Eva and Aksel. I don't mind . . . Deep down, in my heart, I know I'll still be a kid."

I let his answer sink in, wondering whether it's genius or depression, and slow down to let a police car whiz past.

Bini asks, "Do you think the police sometimes turn the siren on because they're hungry and they're actually on their way to Rock 'n' Taco?"

A genius.

"No doubt about it, Bini, they're going for tacos."

"Well, since they're going anyway, couldn't they offer rides to people who want to go to Rock 'n' Taco too? It would cause less pollution, right?"

I think that when I get home, I'll start a section in my notebook to write down Bini's genius ideas.

"And what else did Miss Moore say?"

Bini laughs and doesn't answer.

An Icon Comes Home

Bini is munching on a snack and entertaining himself with the game on the cereal box. At three o'clock on the dot, Eva's bus arrives, as it does every day.

The official protocol states that I have to wait for Eva at the front door and issue a visible greeting, with my arm well raised, "as a sign of adult authorization," before the driver can open the door and release the precious child, safe and sound.

I remember when my brother and I were her age, how we would wait for two or three hours inside a cash machine vestibule, at night, watching the snow, until our parents or grandparents could get away from work to come fetch us. In all that lost time, I could have read an entire canon of literature or become a lawyer by the age of fourteen, if only someone had suggested it to me.

The worst was when the stores closed, which meant it was after eight, and my friends would wave goodbye from their cars, heading for home.

We never complained. Not like these three, who are up in arms if you arrive so much as five minutes late.

A half hour later, I have to repeat the ritual with Aksel. I go to the door to wait. For the love of God, he's ten years old!

The Atlantic is so much more than an ocean.

"Will you help me with my division, Eva?" After trying his best to solve it himself, Bini finally gives up.

The sudden spotlight on Eva makes her slam her agenda shut and blush. Her forehead breaks out in salty microdroplets. She's hiding something.

"I'll help, if you like," I offer, making an effort toward family inclusion, without stopping to think that it's a thousand years since I've done division.

"Okay!" Eva grabs her agenda and runs to her room.

3,987 divided by 16.

Not a clue.

I try for a good five minutes, and Bini, who explains the steps I have to follow, looks at me, surprised that an adult isn't capable of solving a five-year-old's math exercise. I guess he's got a point.

"At your age, shouldn't you be adding instead of dividing? Or painting tomatoes?" I ask.

"They give me division to see if I'm ready to move up a grade," he replies, an open book, not really understanding the question.

I tell him I'm going to the bathroom, and I run to my room. Google.

But it's no help. I come back upstairs in the hope that Aksel might have come to the rescue, with his characteristic cockiness and indignation. And he doesn't fail me.

"Ah, suuuure . . ." I say, looking at the paper, as though I've just seen the light. "See, back home, we did it another way . . ."

"Oh yeah?" says Aksel. "And what way was that, Hairy?"

"Hairy?" I ask.

Bini and Aksel exchange an awkward smile.

"'Hairy' means . . ." starts Aksel.

"I know what 'hairy' means, Aksel. My English isn't that bad." I pretend to be insulted, but to be honest I'm just glad we're not talking about division anymore.

"We called Daniela 'Shiny,'" adds Bini, to make the peace.

"'Shiny' means . . ." continues Aksel.

"I know what 'shiny' means, Aksel. But I prefer Hairy to Shiny—it's funnier." They exchange another glance; they obviously weren't expecting me to take it so well. "After all, I'm hairier than I am shiny, right? Hair doesn't reflect the light. And which part of my body is it that makes you call me Hairy . . . if I might ask?"

Aksel's and Bini's faces turn competing shades of red. Until Bini ventures, "The other day, I went into the bathroom while you were having a shower . . ."

Now I'm the one trying to contain my blushes. After all these weeks without waxing, it's a miracle they didn't name me Chewbacca. Hairy almost makes me sound like royalty.

My God, given that the only body hair Bini will have seen in his life is on his blond, Vikingesque, mustache-free mother, I'm surprised he didn't faint on seeing me.

I go to Eva's room and find her listening to Hannah Montana (she's human!) as she completes the electric circuit on a world map she's made out of recycled materials.

She's wearing pants that must belong to her brother and a T-shirt with the name of the local church, also Aksel's. In this house, fashion and the classic model of childhood exist at polar extremes to the rest of humankind.

"How's it going, Eva?"

"Good . . ." And she adds a long, garbled phrase in English.

"Eva, you know you're supposed to speak to me in Spanish . . ."

She says nothing. She tries the switch after applying a final layer of insulating tape to the cable. The map doesn't light up.

"Eva . . ." I smile, friendly. "Will you let me see your agenda?"

Her neck goes rigid. She's trying to hide her fright, but luckily, she's only eight and as yet unable to smooth over the cracks in her lies.

"Why?"

"I want to see if the teacher wrote something; you know, she usually does, doesn't she?"

Eva pauses, considering her words.

"Do you want to read it? You wouldn't understand the first word, anyway . . ." She laughs.

I take a deep breath.

I'm being bullied by an eight-year-old.

"Will you let me see it, please?"

"No."

"Well then, I'll have to tell your parents." Let's see who's the bigger bitch.

The girl shoots daggers at me and gives a defiant smile, as though she's just realized that I do have the balls to play in her league after all. Her face becomes a mirror of the series of thoughts running through her head:

1. I have to act quick; this woman knows I'm hiding something.
2. Daniela, come back!
3. Shit, my agenda is right there on my desk—it's too late to hide it. And I've just seen her looking at it. Shit.
4. Hmm . . . I really like this song by Hannah . . . There's a syntactic inconsistency, but if Hannah can let it go, so can I.
5. Can I negotiate with this postadolescent? I don't know if I can trust her . . . She seems kinda dumb, not really with it . . . she doesn't seem to understand anything. I'm sure she still thinks Edison invented the light bulb and that Earth is flat. And, she can't say "Wi-Fi" properly; she pronounces it "wiffy." I think I can play her.
6. Daniela, come back!
7. Shit. I think I have to give in. I have no viable strategy.
8. Okay, I have to do it; I have to explain myself to this Neanderthal who was raised by goats in some mountains no one's heard of.

"I'm failing phys. ed."

"What?" A wave of joy floods every corner of my being.

"If I don't learn to play soccer or at least to perform the basic exercises accurately, I'll fail . . ." The rage and catastrophe inherent in the word "fail," coming from a Bookland, make her raise her head and add, "Do you hear me? Fail!"

I bite my lips and try to hide my delight. And, aware that this is an incendiary question, I add, "And so?"

"I'm sorry? Are you saying it's no big deal?" She puts down the screwdriver. "How many Harvard students do you know who have the word 'fail' anywhere in their file?"

I remember that spring afternoon in Puigcerdà when Alba and I decided to buy some spray paints. And, just for the hell of it, we painted some walls in the village, and then we painted our hair green. We were about the same age as Eva is now.

She continues, outraged, "Last year, I collected six thousand dollars for my Girl Scout troop, and this year I have the class record for hours devoted to charitable causes. I have an impeccable résumé. I can't fail!"

The girl truly believes she's a disgrace.

"Eva, failing will teach you much more than passing all the time." She gazes at me uncomprehendingly. "For example, Van Gogh failed too."

"What? Did Van Gogh even go to school? And how do you know he failed?"

"Well, because anyone remotely interesting has screwed up at least once in their life. Failed, fallen. How boring it would be otherwise!"

"You're just saying that to convince yourself." Wow.

"Perhaps." She might be right. "Perhaps I've screwed up because I'm on the other side of the world from where I should be right now, where I should have a job related to what I studied. Perhaps I am a screwup. I don't know. All I can say is that I've come here to find out. So at least I've taken the first step. I have no idea, but I'm not complaining."

"You have a degree?" She looks surprised and grumpy.

"Yes, Eva. I have a degree. And I can inform you, from the future, that it isn't the answer to anything."

Eva comes to her senses and lowers her head and her tone.

"I need you not to tell my parents." Bingo! "I have a strategy to resolve it."

"Oh yeah?"

She sighs, showing the early symptoms of boredom at having to lower herself to my intellectual level.

"I've analyzed the strategy of the best soccer teams in the world." I raise an eyebrow. "Yes, Barça too, of course. Three-four-three and the false nine . . . And I've chosen the best moves to apply to our team. I'll be the coach."

I pretend that her idea hasn't impressed me at all.

"All right." I draw out the moment, as though forgiving her for her entire life. "But keep me updated."

The doorbell rings. The fun never stops.

"Oh! It's Mike!" shouts Bini, banging his head on the corner of the table. "Mike!"

I pass Aksel's room on the way to the door, and, if I didn't know any better, I'd swear I hear him singing. Rapping, in fact.

Bini grabs me by the thigh, and we open the door together. We find a boy with round, plastic-framed glasses and his two front teeth missing, holding a hand out to me.

"Oh-la, Riza! I'm Mike, and I'm Bini's best friend, from Mrs. Sweet's class. I've been dying to meet you."

"Ah! Hello! Nice to meet you, Mike." One of his eyes is already drifting away from me.

Then I raise my head and see his mother; with the boy's incisive introduction, I hadn't noticed her.

For a beat, I feel the strange nostalgia of having met her on some other occasion, many years ago.

I used to see her on weekends when I went to Lauri's house. We would do her hair and dress her—I used to get nervous because I wasn't sure what I was supposed to do—and we would sit her next to her perfect husband who, like her, always seemed to be up for anything. Once they were dressed and brushed, we would put them in a pink Jeep, covered in glow-in-the-dark stickers, and make them fly to planets where Lauri was in charge.

It's her; I have no doubt: This woman is Barbie.

She holds out her perfectly manicured and moisturized hand that—like all the women I've seen—bears a diamond the size of her son's two missing teeth. Her jacket is Chanel, and her purse would have paid for both my and my brother's degrees at a private university. Finally, an American woman with style.

Her blond hair, which seems to exist in a slow-motion breeze, falls in soft waves down to her breasts, firm and round like a couple of French melons. Her slightly stretched eyes are an intense sky blue, broken by flecks of navy. She's wearing jeggings, molded to her long, firm legs down to the ankles and sculpting an ass that makes mine look like a goose barnacle. The motion of her arm, when she stretches her hand toward me, releases a perfume of roses and clouds that would make Vladimir Putin close his eyes in bliss. She's surrounded by a celestial halo, like a commercial for sanitary napkins or shampoos that give you an orgasm in the shower.

"Hello?" she says tentatively.

She's looking at me with a strangely naive expression, as though she's not aware of the impact she causes, as though every day she gets up like this, as Barbie, and it's the most normal thing in the world. As if all the women she meets are like her: tall, slim, smooth-armed, impossible.

"Reeda?"

"Yes!" I realize that I'm shaking her hand too effusively. In fact, she's holding it completely still, as though, instead of shaking it, I should have kissed it. Royalty.

"Delighted to meet you. My name is Samantha." Samantha! "Welcome. I'm sure you'll do photosynthesis in dust just as well as Daniela." My God . . . How old is she? Fifteen? Fifty-eight? Such symmetry. Not a blemish or a wrinkle—she seems to glow. She glows in the dark!

I smile and nod as she explains important things about her son. I can't make out a word of what she's saying. She points delicately at her eye as she says "cheese," "platypus," "glass," and "Theresa of Calcutta."

"Very good, perfect, all under control . . ." I reply.

"Thank you very, very much, Reeda. You're so kind. Now I'm going to fry some asparagus with an air freshener," Barbie informs me as she bends down on supple knees in her stiletto heels, confirming, once again, the divine touch.

Having reached the height of her toothless son, she squeezes his shoulders and plants a noisy kiss on his cheek. Mike allows himself to be kissed, but immediately runs off into the games room hand in hand with Bini. Barbie follows her son with her gaze and, with an exaggeratedly sad expression, heads for the porch and, as she leaves, says, "The battered eggplant always makes me limp. We'll heat it up another day."

She waves her glittering hand and winks, slightly naughtily, at me.

I could swear I hear a click as she winks. She's Claudia Schiffer, Jessica Rabbit, and the Virgin Mary rolled into one.

Mike Has Decided to Cut His Penis Off

I return to the living room and see a red light blinking on the front of my cell phone.

> 1 MESSAGE RECEIVED.
>
> Rita, I've left you 2 voice messages: Listen to them! Have you got new pants yet? Because there's a party tonight at my apartment (8 p.m., because this is America). Yes, there will be men too. And dogs. And a giant bottle of Jäger, I sold a fucking gold faucet today! Oh, and I have *llonganissa*!

Of the entire message, out of all of Six's words, there's one that changes everything. It isn't "party" or "men." She said the most magical word of all: "*llonganissa*." I'd pay my entire month's pay just for a bite of my favorite Spanish sausage.

Yes, that's right, the $198.05 I saw written on the dinosaur checkbook before discovering that Fulbright is gay is my weekly pay. That means I earn about a thousand dollars a month. That is to say, much more than I'd earn in any HR department as a trainee (or untrained) psychologist. Tomorrow morning, I'll have another sniff around on Fulbright's computer to see if he's visited Chitawas again.

But back to more important things: the *llonganissa.* I'm salivating just thinking about it. I committed the serious error of giving one of the prized lengths I brought from home to Fulbright and Hanne as a thank-you gift. And a Catalan liver terrine, a *morcón xoriço* with egg, and ten ounces of good ham.

"Oh . . ." Hanne exclaimed. "Delicious . . ." she said as she swallowed down the ham. "I like it even more than prosciutto!" And I wanted to shout, *"Ignoramuses! This is* jamón! *The finest* jamón de bellota*!"* Prosciutto . . . If I didn't know they could speak impressive Italian, I'd think they said "prosciutto" just to sound sophisticated. "We eat salami here."

Salami.

Heathens! By salami, you mean a basketball compacted into a tube shape, right? Because it isn't even an Italian charcuterie salami—no, no, I've seen it in the fridge. It's supermarket salami, the pink, plastic stuff.

What a waste of a good palate!

Luckily for me, and for them, over the last couple of weeks, I've been able to enjoy the cold cuts that they weren't able to appreciate. In the absence of decent bread and olive oil, I've been munching away at the liver terrine and the *morcón* on my own, slice by slice, chunk by chunk, savoring them as much as possible in front of the children's horrified gazes. They watched me in silence from their ludo table, pale, as though instead of biting a slice of liver terrine, I was ripping out a goat's eyes. I almost enjoyed the terror sparked by every mouthful as much as I did the garlic hit.

But it's all gone now. So long, supplies. Goodbye, my beloved high-quality, free-range, well-fed pork. Who knows when the package of reinforcements I asked my mother to send will arrive. So, I'm not ruling out the idea of going to this orgy just to eat a good piece of *llonganissa.*

What an unexpected yet opportune analogy.

"Eeeeeek!" A screech rouses me from my porcine dreams. It's Hanne.

I look around and realize that I haven't heard any noise from the children for some time. And that's with four of them in the house.

I rush downstairs, imagining electrocuted tongues, cut fingers, blood everywhere.

But when I enter the games room, I realize that it's much worse. In fact, it's the worst that could have happened.

The four kids are sitting on the sofa in a state of absolute ecstasy at the most Dantesque spectacle they've seen in their—until now—pure and immaculate lives.

On the television screen, Jerry Springer is laughing as two of his bruisers hold back a hysterical father.

The story is that this father has just been told that his son has decided to marry his own mother (what's more, the mother said yes and turned up on set in a wedding dress). In a fit of rage, the father ripped off his wife's prosthetic leg, calling her "pig" and "whore" over and over, and claiming that he won't return the leg until they listen to reason. Mother and son start making out, and the father beats them over the head with the prosthetic leg. Meanwhile, a banner running along the top of the screen announces the next guest: "Mike has decided to cut his penis off. He's coming on the show to tell us why."

"Oh, his name is Mike, like me!" exclaims the toothless boy, looking at Hanne in search of some kind of answer. "But . . . why does Mike want to cut his penis off?"

"Aksellllllll!" Hanne is beside herself. "Where is the remote?"

Aksel is about to pass out. He's fighting between laughter and the impossibility of absorbing what his eyes are telling him. Eva is watching intently, analyzing the scene between giggles and asking out loud:

"But why does that man want to marry his mother? And why has the father come on the show, if he doesn't want them to marry?"

At the other end of the sofa, his lower lip glistening with saliva, captivated by what his privileged brain codifies as a poltergeist, Bini has abandoned reality to devote all his cognitive capacities to what he's seeing.

And I watch as the figures on the screen tattoo themselves onto the child's hypothalamus as one of his indelible memories: the memory of a father beating his son with his wife's prosthetic leg—or will Mike, the man who wants to cut off his penis, make more of an impression?

Hanne is glaring at me furiously, red and sweating, and I feel like I'm shrinking ten inches every second. She doesn't stop shouting.

"Aksel! Give me the remote right now!" She's desperate.

In the tussle with the bruisers, one of the bride's breasts falls out of her dress. The son tries to cover her up, and the father starts shrieking like he's possessed.

Aksel is losing his mind; he's writhing on the floor in laughter.

Hanne can't find the remote, so as soon as I'm capable of reacting, I run to the TV and turn it off. The image of the parent-bride's tit disappears with that sort of electronic fart noise that takes me back to the 1980s.

Hanne sends all the children to their rooms. Mike clambers off the sofa as though he has just watched *Sesame Street* and holds out his hand to Hanne, as he did to me earlier, waiting for her to squeeze it with more kindness than he receives.

Hanne, at the peak of her anger, turns to me and says, "We're going out now. We have a dinner, but we'll be speaking about this. When we're back, we'll talk. Let it be clear that this must never happen again."

And she disappears upstairs, muttering between snorts of anger.

What did she mean, "this" must never happen again? They're not going to deport me, are they? Yesterday I dreamed I was meeting Gonçal on Plaza del Campanar, and I turned into dust and got swept up.

And what does she mean, they have a dinner?

I have an orgy to go to!

Machu Dicchu

An hour after the television fiasco, Fulbright came home and beeped the car horn to warn Hanne that they'd be late for dinner. She came out of her room with her hair dripping over a black polka-dot dress that showed the outline of her underwear. Before opening the door, she shot me a deliberately forced smile and repeated, "We'll talk later." It didn't sound good at all. It felt like I'd been sent out of class. Then she turned and left behind her a scented trail of moisturizer and Trésor perfume. Her forced smile had its effect. It made me sad.

The slam of the door releases the four children from their respective rooms, and they gather around the ludo table to discuss the episode in low voices. They avoid making eye contact with me and huddle in a circle, arms around one another, making it clear they don't want my participation.

From the looks on their faces, this show was the best thing that's happened in their lives. From Aksel, flustered by the multiple incongruities, to Mike, who doesn't appear to have received an answer as to why his namesake wanted to cut off his penis.

I serve dinner and go out to the porch to call Six.

Beeeep.

I sit at the top of the stairs and breathe deeply: the scent of lavender.

Beeeep.

It's seven in the evening, and there's no sign of human life on the cul-de-sac. I'm living in a theater set.

Beeeep.

I stretch out on the floor of the porch. It goes to Six's voicemail, and I listen to her American accent with admiration and hope. "People actually use voicemail here," she told me, "so if I don't answer, speak after the tone."

"Hey, Six . . . I don't know if I can make it . . . The parents have gone out for dinner, and who knows when they'll be back. And I've screwed up letting the kids watch *Jerry Springer*. Do you know this Springer guy? Anyway, call me when you can and let me know how crazy it's getting."

I shut my phone with a dry snap. From the floor, I see the treetops quivering, but in general the scene is a wave of elegant harmony. The warmth of the wood at my back transports me to the warm poolside back home in Alp, where I used to lie when I was small and feeling cold. I open my arms in a cross and close my eyes in search of some peace. The scent of the warm wood, the humidity on my skin, the night starting to fall. The sound of these tall, tall trees and the voices of the children laughing as they wash the dishes and fill glasses of milk.

After today's roller coaster, they'll take a while to fall asleep. I hope Six's party goes on until late and I can get there before it ends. I've never needed a piece of *llonganissa* so badly.

"Hi, Rita."

I snap my legs shut.

It's a man's voice, inches from my feet. From the calm tone, I'm guessing he's been there for a while and didn't bother to make his presence known.

"Oh!" I sit up on my elbows for a provocative moment, focus my eyes under the shade of my palm, and get to my feet with all the feminine wiles I can muster, which isn't saying much: "Hi, John."

From the dust clinging to his ankles, I figure he must have been playing tennis for about three hours, and despite a slight whiff of sweat, he's maintained the impeccable appearance of a period-drama gentleman. His voice is low, young, and sexy.

"Siesta?" he asks, laughing as he lets the weight of his back fall against one of the porch columns. Don't Americans know any other Spanish words? *Siesta, servesa, amigoh.* I laugh and shake my lowered head; it's not like my English is much better. John continues, "Are Fulbright and Hanne at home?"

"No. They're out. Dinner."

"Okay, no problem. Could you tell them I came round to invite them to the fluorescent pickled unicorn we're holding at the club?"

"Pardon, what?"

"The olive cactus . . ." The expression on my face stops him in his tracks. "Don't worry, I'll send them an email. But please tell them I came by. It's important." He rubs the tips of the lavender flowers, sniffs his fingers, and adds, "You're invited too."

To a pickled unicorn party? What an honor!

"Ah, thank you very much," I reply. John runs his fingers through his hair, and I realize I'm salivating. "I'll come."

The conversation seems to be over, but John doesn't leave. I haven't heard the children for a while. I suppose that, when you're between ages five and ten, the topics of mother-son incest and penis amputation are only interesting for so long. I take a quick glance inside and see that both Eva and Aksel, lying on the sofa, are reading a volume of the encyclopedia. Outside, the silence continues, broken only by the song of the crickets.

"What about you, Rita? How are you?"

The question catches me off-guard.

"Fine . . ." I answer automatically. "Fine."

But he insists, as though we're close friends.

"Sure?"

Do I look that bad?

Today is Friday. My parents will have prepared the weekend menu while Yaya does the rounds of the vegetable patch. Tomatoes, nectarines, peaches, and melons spread out over the kitchen counter. My brother will have come downstairs, already in his pajamas, his hair wet after a basketball game (or soccer or tennis), and they will have had dinner and served the tables in the restaurant on a glorious Catalan summer night. Yaya will have fallen asleep with her hands slotted beneath her breasts, and when they wake her to go to bed, she'll indignantly claim, "I wasn't asleep."

The weekend is starting.

A few hours later—that is to say, right now—all my friends will sit on the terrace of Plaza del Campanar with beers, showing off their summer tans. Some will have eaten at home; others will order something to nibble on: some olives and a charcuterie board, *patates braves*, and *pa amb tomàquet* and Arbequina olive oil. The conversation won't be particularly momentous, but it will be in my mother tongue, and they'll be able to express exactly what they're thinking, what they want, and what they've done; and they can make jokes that everyone understands.

They'll talk about the latest guy they've met on Messenger or their new roommate in Barcelona; their first experiences as shiny new interns with promise. Others will announce that they've been hired as respectable workers in jobs that barely pay enough to live; that this might be the first day of several decades with the same company; or perhaps the first bounce on a trampoline in a life full of professional zigzags. They'll drink the first gin and tonic. When they finish, they'll walk to the usual bars and bump into the usual people with an enthusiasm that never diminishes. They'll drink shots with unrequited loves and discover new ones, perhaps visiting from Barcelona, but only for tonight.

In one of those bars, camouflaged in the fug of a hundred cigarettes and the hazy light of a corner lamp, Gonçal is drinking in silence. Alone. He looks shy, but he isn't; it's that combination of mystery man and lone wolf that makes him irresistible. As he sips his gin and tonic and greets people from a distance, the lone wolf casts an eye over the girls at the bar, throws out the first looks of a hunting strategy that he'll deploy very slowly. Perhaps it will come to a head this winter, perhaps next summer. It will come, though; that much is certain. For the moment, a girl with an Afro and a leather jacket appears through the door and greets him with a kiss, to the general envy of the crowd.

My friends will wave to him from the other side of the bar and drink a shot to my good health, unaware of how lucky they are to have each other and to be able to talk in their mother tongue. The vodka will leach into their blood and their words; they'll dance to the usual repertoire and slur sweet and silly truths that the next day they won't remember, or they'll pretend not to. They'll end up at a nightclub, probably Trànsit. Some will make an Irish exit while others go out to chat under the porch, but most will make their way to the Palau bakery. There, they'll sweet-talk the baker, who's sick and tired of them all, and they'll eat chocolate croissants bought for extortionate prices as the sun starts to rise over Cerdanya.

The mauve light will seek out the damp backs of the couple from the bar, Gonçal and Sònia, making love for the second time that night on a kitchen table.

There will be no more police officers on the roads at this time. My friends will reach home with their mascara melting down their faces and smell the herbs in the garden, completely oblivious as to how wonderful it is to live another same-old weekend.

Meanwhile, four and a half thousand miles away, I'm taking care of three brats who talk to me as though I were an anteater and pray every night to the rings of Saturn and the Late Cretaceous for Daniela to return. I'll clear the table and wipe up the milk and spaghetti on the floor, and when their parents return, I'll have to swallow their anger at me for having corrupted their children's pre-Harvard brains.

And, bearing in mind Hanne's last look, perhaps I should be begging them not to deport me. (What I should really say is that, actually, it's entirely David's fault for having tuned into mentally disturbing channels; but perhaps it's best not to admit I let the mail carrier into the house.) All of this as I imagine the man I love wrapped in the body of another woman on the same table where we made love for the first time . . . when he told me I was everything he had dreamed of and he broke me forever.

"Yes, I'm fine," I reply finally.

"Well, you don't look it." I'm not sure why, but I seem to have caught John's attention.

"I'll be better once I can communicate in English."

"Have you signed up for classes?"

"No."

"Do you play tennis?"

I don't know how to say that it's been years since I played, but that I like all sports. Goddamn English.

"Yes." I gesture backward with my hands to imply the past. "Well, no, well, yes . . ."

"Yes or no?" He's laughing.

"Yes."

"Well, then, I'll tell Mrs. Gee to give you the test for warm mummies from Albacete."

"Mum . . . what? Albacete?"

"The test to join the club. Albacete."

"All right. By the way," I venture hopefully, "what was the name of the trees again? Those ones there?"

"They're the same as at the club. They're called 'river bitches.'"

Still the same.

"Mm-hmm, mm-hmm . . . river bitches. Thanks."

John says goodbye and hops on a bike that looks like it's from the 1970s. I watch him. I think that every time he enters a scene, the world suddenly feels like a novel. A novel full of slicked-back hair, hand-cut crystal glasses, the first breezes of spring in a gallery with high windows. Paris. All my dreams.

His muscular calves, speckled in coppery dust, disappear round the bend in the cul-de-sac. I get up and, with a final sigh, go back inside, close the door behind me, and start wiping up spaghetti.

Aksel and Eva have finally disappeared into their rooms, so I go downstairs to send the other two to bed.

I can hear that they've turned the television back on.

I peer through the crack in the door and see that it's only commercials, but they're staring as though they were watching the moon landing. I retreat a couple of steps to come down them again noisily and give them time to react.

"What are you up to?" I go in, slow and shrill.

"Nothing!" they reply in unison.

The two boys run to Bini's room and shut themselves in the bathroom to brush their teeth.

They're taking a long time. I don't want to rush them—I remember that the list of rules for au pairs specifies that you shouldn't be alone in the bathroom with a child who isn't yours; the last thing I need right now is a harassment charge—but after a few minutes, when they still haven't emerged, I tap on the door.

"Bini?"

No response.

"Bini? Bini? Is everything okay?"

Finally, he answers with a quiet, inexpressive yes—a yes that means, actually, something's up.

"Can I come in?"

After a few seconds, he replies with the same lifeless yes as before.

When I enter the room, I see Bini sitting on the toilet with a buildup of saliva on his lower lip that suggests he's been watching his friend the entire time they've been in here. Mike is looking at his reflection very closely in a tiny section of mirror. He seems to have something in his eye. He doesn't stop talking, which keeps steaming up the mirror.

"Come on, Mike!" yells Bini, who's just woken up from wherever he was.

"I can't!" replies Mike, tired. Then he turns and says to me, "Rita, can you help me?"

Mike looks at me brimming with joy for life. But . . . but he's only looking at me with one eye . . . because the other . . . the other eye is in his hand!

I don't react. Mike continues to gaze at me with his hand outstretched. Now I understand Barbie's preoccupied gestures and the confiding tone of all the words I didn't understand, to which I replied, "No problem!" overwhelmed by her impossible beauty.

"One moment!" I say calmly to Mike. "Bini, tell Mike I'm going to look something up on the computer." And I run to Fulbright's desk.

Google: "Replacing a child's glass eye."

But I can't resist: twenty-three searches for Federico Chitawas. I run through the list and see that he's not just on HunkPorn but also Punish and Moans. Each search is better than the last: from "the spiciest taco" to "Machu Dicchu." This Federico is a fucking ace. And at that very moment, the iMac informs me that a new email has just arrived. Sender: Federico Chitawas.

"Rita?"

I jump so hard, I bang my knee against the desk, and it feels like I've displaced the kneecap. Bini is calling me from the doorway.

"Coming, coming, coming . . ." I close the search history and go to Google to open a screen showing a hundred gleaming eyes. I click on a video that should come with a warning not to view it while eating and focus all my energy on trying to understand how it works. Why didn't Raspy explain this to us in her military classes?

"That's it!" Mike and his ever-present smile appear behind Bini. One eye is looking toward Ohio, but at least both of them are where they should be. Bini adjusts the iris to center it, and they run off into the bedroom.

I stop the video and return to the search history. And what with the children's ruckus and the bang on the knee (I'm still seeing stars), I don't notice that Fulbright and Hanne are watching me from the study door.

"Rita, what are you doing in here?" he asks, evidently concerned.

I try to come up with a decent response, but the only image in my mind is Chitawas saying, "Machu Dicchu."

"Well, see, Mike couldn't get his eye back in." I'm aware of what I've just said, but I keep my cool.

Hanne laughs and disappears, not wanting to get involved. She's drunk. What did I say? Do they know about Mike's eye?

But Fulbright's not laughing. And nor am I. He follows his wife with his eyes and, when he's sure she can't hear him, adds, "All right, Rita. But next time use your own computer. I have some very important documents here that can't get messed up."

I stand up with an apology and cede the chair to Fulbright. He sits down anxiously, and apparently today it doesn't matter that it's 9:30 p.m. and the kids are still up and about.

I walk down the hall and find Hanne face down on the bed, snoring away with her jacket and purse still on. I take the opportunity to send all the kids to bed and announce that I'm going to a party. Which, in this case, is a euphemism for an orgy and a good piece of *llonganissa.*

Crossing to the Other Side

Six lives in a refurbished high school that stands proud at the top of a grassy knoll in the middle of Little Five Points. She pointed it out to me the night we met. The night we ended by chatting at the edge of—and in—a swimming pool all night, until the sun came up.

I park the car in front of a surprised local who's lugging a basket of dirty clothes. As if it's abundantly clear that this car isn't mine, that I must be one of two things: either an au pair or a high-class prostitute.

I cross the street. It's so humid that the glow from the streetlights seems to wrap them in a pale pink gauze.

Traces of old rust are starting to show through the recent brushstrokes around the lock on the front door. I look up to admire the windows on the main facade, and inside I can make out kitchens and beds and staircases, and two hands dangling from an open window, holding cigarettes that jiggle with every burst of laughter. The damp grass wets my toes, and I run my hand along the iron railing to the gate into the yard.

Is it normal to be fixating more on the *llonganissa* than anything else? Am I really going to take part in an orgy in a matter of minutes? The mere possibility makes me feel like the journey was worthwhile.

Inside, the hallways are tall and elegant, retaining their old-fashioned feel in the metal lockers where pupils used to keep their ink and crumpled papers in the 1920s. The classist, racist, and segregated legacy of those years shines through explicitly in a couple of display cases of scholarly souvenirs: a newspaper cutting, a lacrosse mask, photos of white children wearing tennis uniforms (also white). And these people must still be alive outside these walls. In the neighborhood. In the country clubs and the movies and the Starbucks.

From the yard, there's a door directly into the laundry room, where years ago the sports equipment was kept. At the back of the room, now full of washing machines, there are gymnastics rings hanging from the ceiling and a worn brown leather vaulting horse that the wealthy and modern young residents of the apartments use to fold their clothes. The hallways have an airy smell of clean, which contrasts with the metallic note of varnish.

Every floor is a journey to the past. An old classroom, former storerooms, teachers' offices. In the dining room of some of the apartments, there are still green chalkboards hanging up, and on the floor, the worn lines of a basketball court skirt the bathrooms and bedrooms, continuing from one apartment to the next. Apparently, there's also a theater hall with wooden seats, but when Six wanted to show me, we heard noises like footsteps and, after exchanging a look of fleeting panic based on nothing, we ran for the main door. Like idiots. We'd had too many beers, but it was also an early moment of closeness in our incipient friendship. We sprinted until we were able to clear our minds in the yard: "What do they feed you in the mountains? Man, you can run!" she said, on the verge of throwing up.

Six lives on the first floor in a high-ceilinged apartment, ideal for one or two people, with windows stretching across the entire main wall. The views over the communal pool are reminiscent of an episode of *Melrose Place*. That's where I find her, by the pool, smoking like a postwork prostitute.

Her compact, curvy figure is leaning against a hidden wall. I go around the back of the bushes, avoiding the party, and watch how the cigarette smoke creeps up the wall to the outside lights. Six's face is very shiny.

"Can I ask why your face is so shiny?"

Six tosses the cigarette. I can see the lights reflected on her cheeks.

"I put foot cream on." She laughs nervously, appearing less sure of herself than I know she is. "I thought my skin felt very dry." Six is wearing a very tight dress, tighter than usual, and I'm willing to bet she's not wearing panties.

"Hey, dirty girl, is it possible that you're not wearing—"

"No, I'm not wearing panties, because if I were, you'd be able to see them." She slaps her thigh. "Oh my God . . . I'm really nervous because Monica's here! Oh man, Monica!" She stuffs her tits into the narrow space allowed by her bra and twists the piercing in her lower lip. "How do I look?"

"Fine."

"Fine?"

"Very fine, gorgeous."

"Thanks, you . . . you too." She doesn't say anything, but she's noticed that the button on my skirt might fly off at any moment.

"Hey, so where's the *llonganissa*?"

"What? The *llonganissa*? Are you serious?"

"Deadly."

"Speaking of sausages, I suppose you know that Atlanta is the gay capital of the South?"

"I had no idea . . . What does that have to do with anything?"

"I want to take my time, make Monica suffer a bit. Have you ever been to a gay nightclub?"

"Hmm . . . I'm going to say no, not that I recall."

"Well, I'm not surprised. Chances are that while I was seeing my first girl-on-girl action in Arena, you were at Euro Disney."

"What do you mean? There're only two years between us, you drama queen. Anyway . . . you haven't seen me in party mode." I take a swig of beer. "Don't underestimate me, m'dear."

"That's perfect, then. I can't wait to see this other side of you. And as luck would have it, my client, who's an idiot but very generous, has given me passes for that new nightclub, Whatchamacallit, and we have to use them. Maybe tomorrow. Chances are we'll spend the whole night surrounded by short, boring macho types with hyperdeveloped muscles. But it's a free bar, so, you know."

"Did your parents take you to Euro Disney?" I ask.

"What?" Suddenly Six gets nervous. She grabs my beer abruptly and takes a long gulp. And another, and another.

"I asked whether . . . whether your parents took you to Euro Disney . . ."

"Oh. No, no, no . . ." Silence, more fretting—I don't get it at all.

"Everything okay? Did Donald Duck assault you or something?"

"What are you saying, freak!" If I've learned anything about her, it's that when she's nervous, she issues more insults than usual. "Come on, idiot! Let's go inside!"

We go in to the party. It's a party in an apartment, just like in the movies. With red plastic cups, people from around the world, and Americans wearing baseball caps, dressed as though they've come to watch some kind of sports game. Cyndi Lauper is playing—classy—and of the fifty or so people crammed into the room, I fix on the three guys at the bar. One is blond, small eyes, French looking. The other is gay. And next to the gay guy is my perfect type: dark, shy, a beard, no flab, a Mediterranean vibe. I walk in front of him, trying to appear interesting, but to no avail.

"Jägermeisteeeeeer!" Six fills a long row of cups and plies her audience with them, waiting eagerly behind the kitchen counter. "Rita! Come here! Jäger-fucking-meister!"

This obsession with Jägermeister and the extermination of memory. I had no idea that in this country, gin and tonic is for grannies who play bridge. I look for the *llonganissa*, but I don't see it. Two shots. The prickle of the anise-flavored alcohol climbs behind my ears, and I hurry to the bathroom to apply my eyeliner before it's too late.

I enter the bathroom with the clear aim of a basic but effective paint job. But the slight sway of a bathrobe when I close the door reminds me I still haven't had the chance to properly poke around in Six's home.

A subtle aroma of bleach informs me that she took the trouble to clean the apartment before the party. I pull back the shower curtain and continue with my analysis: Six has her shampoos, shower gels, and conditioners—two of each—lined up in order of size and color along the edge of the bathtub. The general tidiness of the bathroom is impressive. The toothbrush, the hand soap, the symmetry of the towel.

I open the top drawer in search of makeup, but I find monothematic spaces arranged with clinical precision: washcloths, sanitary pads, erotic massage oils, brushes . . . which could suggest incipient, or perhaps fully blown, obsessive-compulsive disorder.

The door swings open. The intruder is a Russian girl who comes in clutching an electric-blue shot in each hand and makes a beeline for me, as though she knows exactly what I was doing; we say cheers, we drink, and she sits down to pee, only after making sure I've seen her fully waxed pubic area. I lean into the mirror, which is giving off the same smell of dampness as the sink, and I paint my eyes.

We go out. One gin and tonic. Two gin and tonics.

I strut past the three guys again, intent on doing a better job of it and attempting a more appealing, dare I say attractive, dance. I stand next to the Mediterranean guy, proactively feigning ignorance, but, as I accidentally stick my elbow in a puddle of orangey liquid, my ideal man sticks his tongue into the mouth of the dumb Frenchman. Hand on his package.

Why can I never figure out when a guy is gay? I'm clearly not going to score today.

Six says she's been searching for me all night—I'm puzzled as the apartment can't be more than 130 square feet—and she introduces me to Monica with exaggerated excitement that only highlights the complete lack of interest with which she introduces me to her other friend. I ask her again where the *llonganissa* is, but she stares at me furiously.

"Really?" she insists.

"It's not that big of a deal, is it? Just tell me where it is and I'll leave you in peace!"

I chat to Monica's friend and ask if her name is Rachel—my God, what a level we've sunk to—and I don't know if she gets the *Friends* joke, but she laughs. After about four words, she seems to find everything I say funny; perhaps I've impressed her with my Alp accent.

The room is jammed. The music is pumping. The people are very friendly. A big woman perched on a window ledge shouts out, and the crowd shouts in reply. We all jump at the same time. I hug complete strangers. Complete strangers hug me. I see faces in the throng smiling in slow motion, drinks swooshing from red cups in slo-mo liquid forms. Here, people sing in English, and they know the words and they understand them. Everyone seems incredibly cool. And I feel incredibly cool for being right here, right now.

I think about my friends, but I don't miss them as much as usual. I'm happy to be here. Three gin and tonics. The Strokes are playing, and I go wild.

Rachel pours me a shot of unidentified liquor—this one is green and gelatinous, disgusting—rolls a joint, and tells me that three years ago she studied chemical engineering at Georgia Tech but that she's never been to Little Five Points before. She talks a lot and says she adores this neighborhood and what a party and how lucky I am to live in Europe—she wishes she were from Barcelona! And could I show her the rest of the school?

We skirt the pool, cross the yard, and walk to the main door. But . . . I pause. For an instant, I think I see the last person I would have expected to see here, and, if it weren't for the effects of the liquor I've just drunk, I would swear that, yes, the hazy glow of the outside lights is falling on Samantha, hand in hand with a guy young enough to be her son. I recognize her divine aura—yes, it's definitely her. But I can't process that information right now. Tomorrow.

I turn the handle of the front door again and run my finger round the rusty keyhole. Rachel and I advance, stumbling like drunken teenagers, as I tell her the history of the place, the lights, the lockers. I'm impressed by how fluent my English sounds.

I show her the display cases with black-and-white photographs of the pupils in their tennis uniforms; we laugh at the lacrosse masks. I try to follow the lines of the old basketball court drawn on the floorboards, but it's impossible. We come up with a speech to recite to the neighbors and knock on a couple of doors that no one opens, so we decide to continue and, without knowing how, come out in the laundry room. This girl is good fun.

It smells of fabric softener. There are T-shirts folded over the leather horses, a denim jacket with safety pins hanging from a hula hoop, and a dryer in motion. I grab one of the gymnastics rings and start playing the fool, Cirque du Soleil style. Rachel applauds, and during one of my tricks, I notice an old broken trampoline parked in a corner.

And behind the trampoline, a door. I wedge my foot between the springs that a hundred years ago sent white kids in their gym shorts flying, and I turn the doorknob.

The old theater opens out before us, empty and backlit.

I brush away the hair that stuck to the corner of my lips from all the exertion of my calisthenics. The frenetic rhythm of the multicolored alcohol in my body has now transformed into a swelling tide that pulls me slowly toward the center of the stage. The spirit of the room, in eternal waiting, has taken hold of us.

Rachel sits in the middle of the stage, lights two cigarettes, and hands one to me. Our legs dangle over the edge of the wooden platform, and we examine the room in silence, drag by drag. The night creeps in through the windows in cylinders of light and dust, picking out one row of this invisible audience. Rachel's lips are painted purple, and she has her hair in a bun, much more elegant than mine.

She lights another cigarette.

I decide to back up, looking for something to lean against, and I move with my drunken body weight on my wrists, like a crab, until I let myself fall against the plentiful fabric of the long, heavy velvet curtain. I look at her: The emergency light runs down the line of fuzz that climbs her back to her neck in a bottle-green contrast.

Rachel has smoked half her cigarette, but, with a gesture both delicate and self-conscious, aware that I'm watching her, she decides to stub it out on the wooden floor where she's sitting. She scoots over, telling me an anecdote about her childhood, about a dog or her neighbor, I'm not sure; she gesticulates with her arms and points at the last row; she doesn't seem to mind that I barely understand what she's saying.

She reaches the curtain and sits next to me; I would say she's nervous, but even so, she grabs my finger and runs it, faintly and tremblingly, over the tattoo on her right ankle. It says "coffee and cigarettes." I ask if it's because of the movie, and she replies that she wants to go and live in Europe, in Paris. I tell her Barcelona is better.

She talks about the surrealists; she even mentions Buñuel, but gets sidetracked and loses the thread. And I tell her I've been to Paris three times, that I spent three weeks staying with a distant cousin in the Marais quarter; that when I went Interrailing with Alba, I saw the sun rise from the steps of the Sacré Coeur after a night on the town; and that my favorite place in the city is the armchair upstairs in the Shakespeare & Co. bookstore.

My words seem to astound her. Suddenly she's looking at me as though I were Madonna or the Dalai Lama.

The music from the party pounds against the thin glass of this old room, and I gaze at the hundred or so wooden chairs in front of us. Outside, someone laughs and shouts and jumps into the pool. Rachel is still watching me, but I pretend I don't notice. She tugs her T-shirt from her denim skirt and ties it in a knot at her navel. It seems like an inoffensive gesture. It's a Pink Floyd shirt.

I count the chairs in the sixth row, but out of the corner of my eye, I see her lighting another cigarette, detaching it from her lips in the sweetest of movements, and bringing her purple lips close to my mouth. I turn, acting surprised, take a drag so long it makes me dizzy, and close my eyes.

Rachel's cold hand grasps my face.

She kisses me. A short but tender kiss.

I pull back and breathe out the smoke in my lungs with a nervous laugh, but she doesn't move away.

I touch the unfastened button of my skirt and lament all the pancakes I've been wolfing down. I wonder whether I'm showered and stubble-free (I only shaved with a razor, so the countdown has already started). I can't remember what panties I'm wearing, but I hope they're decent. And she's only kissed me, for God's sake!

Distance, adventure, panic, none of it has ever felt so tangible.

I think about my last kiss. Gonçal, in the tree house, his eyes, Antònia Font. That's another world; I'm another Rita. Rachel's a girl!

I gaze at her, the fuzz on the back of her neck, her very short skirt. I think her tongue will taste of Jägermeister and menthol Marlboro. That I won't regret it, that suddenly nothing exists other than what I'm about to do on this stage.

Act Two

A girl's lips are softer. The nose gets in the way much less, the skin is more delicate . . . Rachel smells of watermelon. Our tongues move in a surprisingly easy dance; I can't believe what I'm doing.

I run my fingers through her hair, and the bun uncoils like a shot of silk; it's longer than I expected. She covers my lips with nervous breath, and I'm surprised again by her small mouth, soft chin, and, for an instant, I almost feel like I'm doing this to myself in the mirror. We stroke each other's arms with our fingertips, goose bumps; our bodies continue their hypnotic dance—hips, hands, bellies moving together; her legs intertwine with mine, and we fall back against the curtain; I notice the rough, spongy feel of the velvet against my back.

I look into her eyes and realize they're an unreal shade of blue; I've never seen eyes that color, as dark as tonight's sky.

The fingers of this unknown girl make their way beneath my T-shirt, the contact prompting a shiver that shoots to my forehead, and, in a fit of lucidity, as though it were suddenly three o'clock on a Tuesday afternoon, I pull back.

She smiles, as though she expected my reaction, then kisses me again.

We resume. We resume and then some. I'm so horny. My thoughts stutter and then stop.

She takes off my top, and her hands travel down my bra straps with a confidence that no man will ever achieve. She caresses my tits, squeezing them gently, and I feel dizzy. She lowers the zipper of my skirt; I hear the metallic crack of each tooth. My heart pounds; it's imminent.

Rachel's hand inches its way into my panties with a slow, long, wet caress that makes me shudder. She lingers there, and I tremble. I tremble; I tremble all over.

The sensation is strange but familiar at the same time. I know exactly where to find all the nooks and crannies of pleasure, the angle, the pressure.

I hesitate for a moment; then I do it: I raise my hands to her breasts; I stroke them and squeeze the fragile nipple, urgently. The chemistry is strong; I'm not self-conscious; I have no perception of time; I want to do it all. I run my hand down her belly and under her skirt, along the hem of her panties. With my eyes closed, I caress her lips, clitoris, the damp heat . . . I've crossed to the other side.

She repeats my name in a distant voice; she says, "Baby." I'm in a movie. Rachel is about to cry out; she's agitated; her breathing is irregular, and her cheeks crumple as though she's about to cry. But she holds off her orgasm, suddenly stopping, ripping off my skirt, opening my legs, and disappearing down there.

The precision is formidable; the touch, the rhythm, the licking are unbearable. I'm scared I'm going to faint. My head is spinning. Her long, thin fingers inside me. Her tongue. I can't take any more. I let out a shout that echoes off the wooden sides of the stage and gets trapped in the waves of velvet.

For what feels like hours, we levitate before an invisible auditorium in a spectacle of moans and fading lesbian virginity until the final scene, the end of a path of delightful agonies. My orgasm breaks out in a spasm that spills over my entire body; it arches my back and contorts my face.

I picture a horse made of ice that shatters into a cloud of bright pink dust.

Rachel's body—is Rachel even her name?—naked and white, collapses weakly on top of mine, in the middle of the stage. We look at each other and laugh. I feel life fizzing inside me. I might tattoo the words "carpe diem" on my ankle.

We stay there for a long time. I look at the invisible audience and imagine the last performance that took place on this stage; perhaps a nativity scene or a prize-giving for lacrosse.

Who would have thought that, in a high school in the conservative Deep South, the show would ever be this?

I look up at the spotlights on the ceiling as Rachel leans her head and its watermelon aroma on my shoulder. Perfect, I'm not just a lesbian, but I'm the man of the couple.

I think I've just experienced one of the most extraordinary moments of my life, the kind that flashes before your eyes when you die. And I'm only twenty-three. I don't know what my life will bring, whether it will be uphill or downhill from here. Looking at the lives of most adults, I'm struck that it easily becomes boring and redundant; from about the age of thirty, people stop feeling and enter a kind of loop that repeats year on year. But my life won't be like that, I know; nights like this raise the bar in terms of what I'll demand from life. I want my years to be filled with stages like this.

Rachel lights another menthol cigarette. And I think how ironic it is that I only came to the party for a bit of *llonganissa*.

The First Book

My phone beeps. Six has called forty times, left I don't know how many voice messages, and now, finally, texted me:

> Welcome to the club! Please tell me it wasn't just a one-night thing and that you felt the true call of the pussy. You'll be a great addition to the lesbian community.

I brush my teeth as I examine my eyes, slightly more swollen than usual. The hangover. And Rachel, Rachel, Rachel. My God.

I need coffee.

I climb the stairs, remembering last night's magnificent sexual experience, and I can't help but feel immensely proud. For having tried it. For having let myself go like that. For having enjoyed it so much.

I imagine the sight of the two of us from the point of view of a spectator sitting in the wooden seats. I feel disbelieving and defiant in equal measure.

I might send her a message. It's strange, because I don't feel like it's the same dynamic as it would be with a man. Who texts first? Perhaps that's sexist, and I just haven't realized? For sure. After all, I was raised on 1990s Disney. Yes, I'll text her.

I arrive upstairs, grinning from ear to ear, and see Conchi's ass appear in the kitchen door shaking to the rhythm of Shakira.

"Oof! Honey, you look like shit. Didn't you sleep? And . . . you're looking a little chubby, *chancha*!" She looks at me with horror, as though I've actually turned into a pig.

"Thanks very much, Conchita. You're so kind . . . Is it that obvious?"

"Yes, and you should probably take a look at those zits on your chin," she adds.

Don't they have any social filters in Colombia?

It's true—I have a small row of four pus-filled zits on my chin that, like my slight weight gain, I've never experienced before. But, given that I'm driving everywhere, eating pancakes with maple syrup for breakfast every day, and my only walk is along the supermarket aisles—although the other day I did try one of those motorized carts and ended up doing the whole shop on wheels—perhaps nine or ten pounds isn't too bad. I knew it was happening; I've been wearing nothing but dresses for a week.

I open the refrigerator. I see pancakes. I take out the pineapple.

"It's because this city makes it impossible to walk anywhere."

"It's because you're bored. Apart from last night . . ." Touché. Conchi launches that dart of truth from the laundry room. "When I was your age, I had no time to get bored. In fact, I haven't had time to get bored since I was thirteen. First to survive, and then with my son . . ."

"What?" She straightens up and falls silent. She didn't mean to say that. "What?"

"Yes, *chancha*," she says, lowering her voice, "I have a son . . ."

"And?"

"And it's complicated. We weren't all lucky enough to grow up in Europe and be able to choose the future we want. To be with our families." She wipes away a tear. "But we take the life we're given, don't we?" She shoots out of the laundry room, her energy and smile restored. "Anyway, don't distract me—I've got work to do!"

I hear the garage door and the children huffing and puffing up the stairs. Eva calls out hello to the air and sits down next to Aksel, who's reading volume C–D of the encyclopedia, slumped on the sofa, his feet black. She gets up to grab Kennedy's biography, which has a bookmark halfway through, and drops into the chaise longue. Bini follows them with an illustrated version of Stephen Hawking's black hole theory (it's the theme of this Saturday night's dinner, and he's presenting). Fulbright and Hanne greet me happily. "How was last night? Good?" "Good, good . . ."

They go to their room and return with a book each.

Within minutes, silence has fallen. The whole Bookland family is reading in every corner of the living room as Saturday continues outside in dazzling sunshine.

I wonder how best to escape. I want to go to my room to think about Rachel. First, I stay perfectly still; I don't move a muscle; I make no sound; I barely breathe. I decide to slink ninja-style and shut myself in my bedroom as soon as I can. To prevent them saying anything to me. I move with light, completely soundless steps.

"Rita?" Shit.

It's Hanne's voice, and she doesn't even look up from her book.

"Hmm?" I tread on the third step without turning around. I'm scouring my mind for an excuse, but all I can think of is that episode of *The Simpsons* where Homer gets so fat, he makes himself clothes from the living room drapes.

"Come on, join in. It will be good for you. Grab something in English."

When I return to the living room, I see Bini has gotten out of the armchair for me, and he's now studying gravitational collapse with his head on his father's lap. He seems to have given me the seat of his own volition. Touching. I settle into the chair.

As I flick through the first few pages of my magazine, a trace of Mon Paris by Yves Saint Laurent clings to my hands. In the fashion photographs, I notice the models' arms, necks, ankles.

I can't stop thinking about Rachel. This morning, I opened my eyes abruptly, looked out of the window, and couldn't get back to sleep. Rachel on a loop. The velvet curtains on the stage, her purple lipstick.

Come on, relax. I think back on the sexual pleasure, that incredible sex. I stroke my lips with my fingertips; I squirm on the armchair. (Does what we did count as fucking?)

To be honest, it's no big deal . . . In fact, physically, anatomically, it's the same kissing a man or a woman. If we were in a room in the dark and the smell was neutral and there were no beards and you couldn't touch the other person's body, the kiss would feel the same, impossible to tell the difference. The tongue, saliva, breath—all that is asexual. And the pheromones too . . . aren't they? Do they activate regardless or only with the gender you like? I studied all this. See? College is almost useless. In any case, I had an amazing time.

"What does 'vogue' mean, Mommy?" Bini's eyes are watching me from his small jowly face.

The question doesn't seem to have disturbed the general concentration.

"Vogue?" replies Hanne, still reading. "In what context does it appear, my love?"

"Vogue means fashion, with an emphasis on its temporary nature," adds Eva, from memory.

"It's what Rita's reading," Bini points out.

Now, yes. The Harvard pack comes back to tangible reality and stares at my August issue of *Vogue*. Fulbright represses a smile.

"Oh!" exclaims Hanne, covering up her surprise at such frivolity intruding into Bookland Land. "Have you found any interesting articles, Rita?"

"Hmm . . . Yes . . ." Well, yes, actually, it's not just advertising in *Vogue*. I flick through the first pages of ads. "One moment . . . One mooooment . . ." Ten, fifteen, twenty-five, thirty-two pages of advertisements. "It was here . . ." I skip the four-page interview about Choupette, Karl Lagerfeld's Siamese cat, which details its daily bowel movements. I skip the couples special: Penélope Cruz and Javier Bardem are an item! The spotlight on me is intensifying by the second. I have to say something right away or invent something that suggests some kind of popular wisdom. "Here it is!" The whole family is looking at me; even Conchi has peeked out from behind the fish tank to see what's going on. "Yes . . . hmm . . . it's about the sister of the queen of England."

"What period?" asks Aksel.

"I don't know, in general."

Conchi leaves the room. Silence.

Eva and Aksel go back to their reading.

"Interesting." Hanne returns to her novel.

"What kind of books do you like?" Fulbright asks me.

Here we go.

"Hmm . . ."

"What's the last book you read?" asks Ful. I decide he needs a nickname. This conversation might make us friends.

The question was inevitable. It had to come at some point.

I feel as though I have the power to induce a family heart attack. If I tell them the truth, if I say that at the age of twenty-three, I could honestly say that I've never finished a book in my life, I'll smite them all and be left without a home.

"One for my degree."

"Yes, of course, I can imagine. But what about novels? Fiction? What genre?"

"One by a Catalan author—you wouldn't know him—it's an indie publisher."

"I might; try me."

"It's called *The Passing Weather*, by Francesc Mauri."

"And what's it about?"

"Well, it's about everyday life, personal growth, landscapes . . . and the weather." I'm not lying here—the guy's actually a TV weatherman.

I think he knows I'm making it up, but he pretends to believe me.

Fulbright gets up and stands in front of the old wooden bookcase that stretches out behind the grand piano. Shelf after shelf of hundreds, possibly a thousand, books fitted into a solid oak wall. His eyes flick from side to side for some time, and while he's occupied, I take the opportunity to glance at the *Vogue* feature on hats. I think I'd go for the turban-style one with the vertical feather.

I turn back to him and find him stroking the spines of the oldest volumes, delicately and emotionally. Dreaming of Federico, no doubt. He moves up to the third step on the ladder and inspects an extensive collection with matching spines. He stretches out his left arm so far that the effort makes him lift his right foot. He picks one.

"I'm sure you will have read this at fourteen or fifteen, but for learning English, it's worth reacquainting yourself with scenes you already know." He comes down the ladder, making the wood creak with every step. "Besides, books, like us, grow with time. Hemingway used to say that the writer should show the world to his readers, not explain it, that way we discover more about ourselves than about the character. I'm sure the world Mr. Caulfield showed you all those years ago"—Caulfield? I get ready with my smile—"will be nothing like the one you discover now. They will be new lessons." He hands me the book.

The Catcher in the Rye.

"Thanks." At least it's a slim one.

Fulbright returns to his own book, and I'm left alone with an unexpected story in my hands.

A gesture as simple as that. A seemingly insignificant moment. It's the first time anyone's ever recommended a book to me.

At home, there was always too much work for anyone to be reading. We had books, sure, but I never saw any of them open. I suppose we could have read, but the little time my parents had to themselves, they used to take a nap or watch movies. Although, looking at the Booklands' happy faces, I think I might have enjoyed a Saturday afternoon like this.

I make sure I mark the interview about Choupette the cat, and the hats feature, and I put *Vogue* down on the floor.

I read the first page. I'm sure I'm not picking up on absolutely everything, but I'm enjoying it. I turn a page. Then another, and another. After what seems like an awful lot of words, I raise my head and observe my new family. A happy silence spun between five immobile bodies in wildly separate worlds . . . and for the first time since I arrived in this house, I feel like I'm in good company.

PART TWO

The Shadow

Ignoring the unexpected twists and turns that caused me to travel halfway around the globe to look after three impertinent children, I generally regard myself as a fairly stable person. Happy, positive. But on the odd, extremely rare occasion, I've been overwhelmed by a strange, destructive feeling. Like shame, disgust, and misery rolled into one.

It's like a toxic blend of boredom and apathy, but it makes me want to throw up more than it makes me want to cry. Like when my driving instructor put his hand on my thigh and I didn't know how to react, so I didn't say anything and kept going to his classes and tolerating the stench of cigars and his stories about the prostitutes he'd been with that week. I had the same feeling when I didn't want to continue seeing Pol, my boyfriend that summer, but did nothing about breaking up with him. It gives me the worst taste in my mouth.

In all the long hours I've spent alone in Atlanta, in the house, wearing pajamas and sweating from my armpits, I've often worried about falling back into that well, but in general, the boredom and the weight of solitude have been rather more instructive here.

I've stood for hours in front of the bathroom mirror, where I've discovered parts of my body I never stopped to think about before: veins that are too blue and raised, the uneven angle of my eyebrows, or incipient wrinkles on my chest caused by sleeping on my side. The silicone gel I ordered to rub between my breasts should be coming next Tuesday (and a waist trainer as a little extra).

The other day I sat for ages, wondering whether it was normal to breathe only through your nose or only through your mouth, and I was concentrating so hard that suddenly I didn't know how to breathe normally, and I started coughing. Solitude and hypochondria always go hand in hand. I've also noticed that the central axis of my teeth is more deviated than I thought. I even phoned a Spanish-language emergency line to discuss the symptoms of a cleft tongue, but, after studying the photos I emailed them, they told me I had a "completely normal" tongue. I gorge on salty crackers and multicolored cereals and bagels with Nutella. I've lost all notion of when it's normal to feel full or when it's normal to be sleepy.

In my efforts to find my vocation, I've tagged along to the kids' various extracurricular classes, in case I find some spark of enlightenment or, at least, of hope. I've been to piano, singing, algebra, ballet. I've read essays on nuclear physics, quantum physics, and astrophysics. On opera and the Paleolithic era. I've listened attentively to all the Harvard friends who come to the house for dinner and talk about philosophy, artificial intelligence, Voltaire, and the antiracist policies of Lincoln and Kennedy. I've shown an interest in a thousand different topics, but so far nothing's had the slightest impact. I've also confirmed my strange fixation with mundane but slightly odd traits: Professor Morales's prominent earlobe or the vertical angle at which Dr. Forte holds his knife to cut his meat.

I do all this, and yet I'm supposed to be an adult now. I thought that when you reached adulthood, you got a kind of pill that suddenly put you in control of everything. Knowing how to behave, enjoy opera, understand the fundamentals of politics, and having a grasp of when the Paleolithic period began. But seemingly the pill is more like a hard slap with an open hand.

Perhaps the problem is that I still don't particularly want to step through the glorious golden gates of adulthood. That I'm too happy in this sweet intermediate state, the prelude to the big show, my comfortable status as a "girl." Old enough to take care of children, but still too young to master the important things in life. Every time someone says, "You're still too young for this or that," my day gets a little bit brighter. Hope. An excuse. I'm still in the back seat of the car, with my parents at the wheel, but no one has noticed I'm not wearing my seat belt.

I laugh when my friends phone me drunk, but I don't return the call when they hang up. Sometimes I want to be there with them. Sometimes I don't. I occupy myself in the mornings wandering around the supermarket aisles, the ones with loaves of bread and postcards—my favorites—and I ensconce myself in the local Starbucks to write them. I must have sent two hundred. I write a lot.

One of my greatest everyday pleasures is composing emails about my latest Atlanta adventures. Sometimes they're long anecdotes (Machu Dicchu), sometimes brief (squirrels). I enjoy it. I dream. I laugh. It's therapeutic. The keyboard with the apostrophe in the wrong place and no accents encourages me to write in torrents. It makes me happy to send a text before I go to sleep and wake up to read my friends' replies. These emails are my diary and my preferred isolation pod.

The other day, however, I woke up to find no replies. I went up to the kitchen and started reading an article about analyzing your personality according to the angle of your toes. That's when the alarm bells started to ring. That's when I thought I'd hit rock bottom. The terrible shadow of depression was approaching.

My body could no longer tolerate my inactivity. My reticence to do something of substance, other than being a chauffeur to three children with vital purposes of their own.

For a moment, I wanted to stop thinking. To prolong my inertia. I wanted to be one of those women from the 1950s with no options. I wanted a tiny waist and to be kept by a husband; pleasing him would be my daily, vital labor. I wanted that with all my being. A clear objective. Everything would be easier if that was my life, if I put curlers in my hair and cleaned the kitchen and the house. Everything would be perfect if someone told me exactly what the hell I'm supposed to be doing. But no. I happen to be living here, in 2007, where women are free (freer than they used to be, anyway) and the world has so many possibilities that it could make you agoraphobic. And I alone can choose my path. So there's nothing for it but to act: I have to sign up for English classes.

Back to School

Eight! Eight lanes in each direction on the highway leading from the house to the city center. As Daniela mentioned, Atlanta appears to have some of the worst traffic in the country, but it's nine o'clock in the morning, and I'm making swift progress toward the campus of the Georgia Institute of Technology, Georgia Tech to its friends.

Yes, I've done it; I've signed up for English classes.

I tested the waters at a couple of churches offering free lessons, but the smell of communion wafers in the "classroom" was too far removed from my image of an American college. So, I scraped together my savings and asked my parents to give me my birthday, saint's day, and Christmas presents in advance so that, for the sake of my mental and social health, I could pay for a decent course.

To start, I'm doing a test to determine my level. It's a drag just thinking about it. The formal letter, the fill-in-the-gaps, the list of irregular verbs . . . The same nightmare that has pursued me since the age of ten.

I go into a Starbucks to grab a quick coffee—I won't be more than ten minutes—and I realize that the café is inside a giant store that sells all kinds of items customized with a bee wearing sunglasses, which is the university's mascot. I go to the counter and launch into my well-worn procedure for ordering: "Coffee with milk." Cofi whiz meelc! Jeez, cofi-whiz-meelc, it isn't that hard.

After repeating myself only twice, the first question from the hyperactive barista—she asks me, very quickly, if I want "towel or intermittent"—catches me off-guard, and I say yes, but manage to say no to the rest. Emphatic and clear. And when she asks my name, I say, "Reeda."

As I wait for my drink, I notice that the extra pounds I'm carrying have made my dress a bit shorter than before, and I'm showing the top of my thighs, which are unshaven.

"Dreeda? Breeda?"

I go to the end of the counter in the hope of finding a simple coffee with milk, but I'm met with a large cup of frothy milk that smells of vanilla, with a cinnamon stick and my name on the side: *Burrita.*

I leave the café and toss the cup in the first trash can I see. I don't even take a sip. Pah.

The language school is in the O'Keefe Building: According to Fulbright's explanation—which he insisted on giving in English—O'Keefe is a well-known American florist. I'm surprised they've named a building after a florist.

"Are you here to test your level?" The secretary is a pleasant, plumpish, gray-haired woman who, from her imperious gestures, must have been working here for a thousand years.

"Inglish?" I get straight to the point.

"Yes, honey, this is the language school—we teach English . . . Fill out this form and go to the door at the end. Donald Trump is about to arrive."

"What? Donald Trump is coming?"

"Donald Trump is coming?" Her eyes widen like saucers. "Where did you read that? In the winter inauguration program?" She pushes her chair back urgently. "Jennifer!"

"No, no, I . . ."

"Jennifer! Jennyyyy! Do you know anything about Donald Trump coming for the inauguration of the winter boogers?" She turns back to me. "She's an intern, and she doesn't know how to peel a papaya. The same in the summer! You see? I can't delegate! Jenny!"

"No, no, I . . ." How do I explain that it's my fault?

Jennifer arrives sweating.

"I'm checking over the winter boogers"—she sweats some more—"and I'm not seeing Trump, but I don't have the papayas updated."

"Well, run along and update them—we can't allow another trampoline!"

"I . . . I . . . I said it wrong." I raise my voice. Both women look up. *"Mea culpa! Mea culpa!"* Apparently I speak Latin, too, now.

"Sure? Are you sure you didn't read it in the boogers? Papayas?" insists the secretary.

"Sure, sure."

My God, let's hope this language school is good.

Finally, I get to class. The teacher is speaking in a low voice to a colleague. In front of me is a Venezuelan woman with thinning but well-styled hair and a huge rock on her finger, who blatantly looks me up and down. I glance at the athletic-looking Asian man next to me to say hello, but I catch him looking at my thighs, and we both avert our eyes quickly. It's no surprise; chances are he's never seen this density of hair in his life.

"Hello, my name is Tek Soo. I'm from Seoul." His face is burning, but he holds out his hand with a degree of enthusiasm and a hint of apology.

"Hello, my name is Rita. I'm from Barcelona."

"Roma?" Rome? Seriously?

"Bar-ce-lo-na."

I take three tests in two hours, and they seem easier than the last ones Sooozan gave me. And I don't have to use the structure of a formal letter. We're asked to write something on any topic we like, and since it was fresh in my mind from the last time I wrote, I described how our family restaurant came about. Let's see what happens. Writing in

English is much easier than speaking it. And speaking it in Atlanta, of course.

Meanwhile, the program says that one of the senior students will give us a tour of the campus, so we all go out together and sit on the stairs as he introduces himself. There must be a hundred of us, and everyone seems to understand him . . . But isn't everyone here to learn English?

The guide's name is William Hernandes, and his patter is loaded with useful and anecdotal information about college life.

Our first stop is outside Alpha Epsilon Phi, a sorority house. Two cheerleaders wearing white and gold park in front of the house and disappear inside. William speaks for a long time, but I only seem to understand the phrases containing insults.

"Don't think that frat and sorority houses are clubs for snobs, you dumbasses. Remember that the first American woman astronaut lived in a sorority, and all the astronauts on Apollo 11 were frat boys!"

We continue down the road. We skirt fraternity and sorority houses that make me think of an avenue in Tibidabo built from papier-mâché, until we stop at the foot of a brown brick staircase with rampant ivy that a gardener has just started taming.

The stairs climb to an old building with a tower that, right at the top, in white capital letters, announces TECH. The guide pauses, looks up at the tower as though seeing it for the first time, and makes a solemn gesture.

"And this building, ladies and gentlemen, is one of the best loved, most venerated of this university. Better than the *Harvard Crimson*, better than the *Yale Daily News*, comparable only to the *New York Times*! The journal gives a voice to the most restless minds, the voice of the South, the leaders of the future . . . the journal that delves 'even deeper between the lines.'" He does a drumroll: "*The Georgian*!"

Then the Venezuelan with thinning but well-styled hair tells her group of fellow Venezuelans, "I've heard that Jimmy Carter wrote for it several times."

"*The Georgian* has a little brother," continues the guide. "Well, more like the pothead cousin who fails everything, way more irreverent, but lots of fun . . . It's called *North Avenue Review*. It's thinner and driven by students with literary aspirations . . . This is the way in."

Pothead cousin piques my interest. I must pick up a copy.

On the other side of the revolving door into the offices of *The Georgian*, I see an elderly man, stooped and friendly, wearing a college cap. His main function seems to be to greet visitors. Since we arrived, he's said hello and goodbye to about thirty people, and each one—each one—he greets with enthusiasm and sincerity, as though this were his first day. It isn't the first time I've seen a retiree doing this. I feel like hugging him.

The door keeps on spinning. Emerging now is the classic group of sporty girls, with giant shirts and tiny shorts clutching files under their arms. And behind them appears an elegant man in a beige suit and wide-brimmed hat, who, in contrast with the students, looks like a fashion model from the 1920s. The man looks up.

Even from this distance, I know he has green eyes and that his tan is the result of hours of clay-court tennis. I can even smell the Tom Ford perfume from here . . . John is walking toward the kindly doorman, giving him the customary American embrace, more genuine than most of them.

But what is John doing here? Should I say hello?

Man, I really should; it's obvious we've all seen him come out. It's impossible not to see him. I glance down at my hairy thighs and think that if I just stay still, perhaps he won't notice . . .

"Rita?" Shit, how did he come over so quickly? My back is half turned as I'm pretending not to see him, so I spin around. "Rita!"

"Oh! John! What a surprise! What are you doing here?" Out of habit, I kiss him on both cheeks, which discomfits not just him but the entire group, who are waiting in expectant silence.

"A flag and a lion," he says. "Will you have the tuna ready tonight?"

I laugh.

The Venezuelan woman shows a sudden interest in me and takes a step forward like a peacock.

"He's asking if you're going to the charity event he's organized at the club tonight. In your neighborhood, your local club."

"Ah, yes, yes, sure."

"Very good, Rita," John says goodbye in a low voice. "I'll see you tonight. Tuna. Albacete."

I say bye and watch him walking down the stairs, imagining his calves and muscular ass moving beneath his linen pants. Perhaps I'm not entirely lesbian after all. Could I be bisexual? Does it make any difference?

I turn around, anticipating the scene: The Venezuelan women look at me confused, they're doing all kinds of mental calculations to figure out how someone like me, with less English than the neighbor's parakeet and thighs covered in fuzz, could know someone like John.

The cafeteria in the O'Keefe Building is a gray-carpeted room that smells of curry and fish, with three microwaves that don't stop running all day. I still have time before I go to pick up Bini, so I sit at one of the tables, against the wall, in the hope of finding a potential friend. To kill time, I take out the birthday cards I bought to send to Marta and Clara. Tek Soo immediately appears and sits three tables away. A few other young men join him at a long table. I start writing to Marta, reminding her of that time we scammed those arrogant assholes at the Santa Tecla festival in Tarragona, and how we planned to pass ourselves off as the kids at the top of the human tower in the Xiquets de Valls.

"Hello?" Tek Soo gestures at his busy table and invites me to sit with them.

The youngest-looking boy at his table—he must be about fourteen—starts eating and points a finger at me.

"Spain, yes?" His finger is inches from my face. "Madrid or Barça?" The guy is waiting for a response, but I can't utter a word in light of what I'm seeing. He chews violently, moving his mouth as if trying to kill whatever is between his teeth, like how I imagine a Tyrannosaurus having lunch. "Huh? Madrid or Barça?" I notice the first tingle of a cold sore on my lip.

"Barça! Barça!" I come out of my stupor.

"Oh! Barça! Ronaldinho! Messi! Baaarça!" All five boys erupt with joy, as if they've been waiting their whole lives for that answer. "*Tot el camp*! *Éééés un clam*!" I can't believe my ears. I've awoken a monster. "*Som laaa la la laaaa*." They beat on the table with their fists like brainless trolls. Soups are being spilled. The entire cafeteria is watching us. "*Blaaaugraana veeee*!" I can't take my eyes off the sight of those mouths as the Barça club anthem bursts out. "*Teeeenim un plo plo plo plooooo*!" Shit, they know the whole thing. They're all staring at me, as though I were the president of Barça and they were looking for phonetic approval. I nod. It seems impossible, but without pausing in their indecipherable song, they manage to put another spoonful in their mouths. And they're gearing up for the finale. Before my eyes, they round it off with *"Barça! Barça! BAAARÇA!"*

I can't remember the last time I laughed so hard.

I say goodbye to these guys who seem to have become my new friends; I have to go pick up Bini. On the way, I call Hanne to ask whether I can go to John's party tonight, but she doesn't answer.

Homo sapiens and Sports

"Rita!" Bini shouts indignantly from upstairs. "Riiitaaa! Would you kindly come here?"

He's five and he's just said, "Would you kindly come here."

It's two thirty in the afternoon. Aksel and Eva are about to get home, and I go upstairs in no particular hurry; on the landing, the parenthesis between the two floors, the sun is creeping through the colored-glass panels that flank the front door. Outside, the street is deserted as usual.

"Ritaaaaa!"

When I reach the bathroom, I find him talking to one of the wall tiles, his legs dangling from the toilet. He sees me, puffs, and puts his head between his knees. He wants me to wipe his ass.

Four years of college down the drain. That eight-hundred-page book on the physiology of behavior, Erikson, Vygotsky, classical conditioning, all for nothing.

"Rita." Bini is studying an invisible diagram he's drawn on the tile.

"Yep."

"Can you imagine . . . can you imagine having a little TV where, when you watch a cooking show, the smells of the dishes come through like air freshener?"

"Don't talk about smells right now . . ." He finds that funny. "But actually, that's a very good idea."

"And the TV could have a camera and a telephone."

"Mm-hmm."

"And, and, and a calculator too. And a piano."

"A TV and a piano? But . . ."

"And it would fit in your schoolbag or pocket!"

I hear the rumble of Eva's bus—I need to run down and raise my arm.

"Okay, down you get!" He's about to shoot off down the hall. "Bini, wait a moment. Next time you need help, just 'please' is fine, all right? No more 'would you kindly.'"

Bini lowers his head like a puppy and moves off with his next business idea on the tip of his tongue.

"And wash your hands! Pig!"

"Aksel, have you taken my Hannah Montana CD?" Eva comes out of her room to ask the most mundane question I've ever heard her utter.

"Your Hannah Mont—me?" Aksel blushes at the very idea of someone thinking he'd been looking at the photo on the case.

"Yes, and it wouldn't be the first time, don't try to hide it."

"Look, Eva"—he couldn't get any redder—"you want to know how much I care about your Hinni Mintini CD?"

Oof. With this scathing change in the dialectical register, I sit back on the sofa to enjoy the anomaly of the two Bookland siblings fighting like normal, everyday kids.

"The universe is more than thirteen trillion years old, you know that, Eva?"

Here we go.

"I think you'll find it's thirteen point eight billion, to be precise. Although some figures suggest it could be less, but for the moment, the official figure is thirteen point eight billion years."

They just can't help themselves.

"Well, if we use a cosmic calendar to illustrate the evolution of the cosmos and of humankind, that is, imagining the three hundred and sixty-five days in the year in relation to the whole of evolution, gravity wouldn't appear until January 10."

"On what scale?"

"On a scale where each month represents a billion years and each day represents almost forty million years."

"And what does the evolution of the cosmos have to do with the Hannah Montana CD you stole from me?"

"I didn't . . . Wait and you'll understand."

"So, January 1 is when the universe begins?" Bini appears on the scene. It runs in the blood in this family. They're unbearable.

"Indeed, Bini, I see you've grasped it before Eva has—January 1 is the Big Bang."

Eva doesn't rise to her brother's bait.

"From January 1 to 13," continues Aksel, "after the Big Bang, we are in darkness for around two hundred million years."

"In darkness?" Bini is clearly worried.

"Yes, cosmic darkness, Bini, nothing."

"Therefore, the sun would be born on August 30." Eva has done her calculations.

"August 31, to be precise," Aksel corrects her.

"Come on, speed it up."

"Now I want you to look at this." Aksel shows her his pinky.

"What's wrong with your finger, Aksel?" Bini has gotten very serious.

"I want you to remember this measurement."

"Aksel, tell me where the Hannah Montana CD is, and I won't say another word."

"We're getting there, Eva, don't you worry. Life on Earth won't start until September 21. It hasn't yet been established exactly where it started. There's a suspicion that it was some remote part of the Milky Way—"

"Aksel."

"Cool it. I'm getting to December. On December 17, the tiktaalik was one of the first animals to risk coming out of the water to step on land . . . The same week that forests, dinosaurs, birds, and insects all evolved.

"Now, do you remember the measurement?" Aksel shows them his pinky again. "That's the approximate measurement, about an inch, that caused two asteroids to collide, and one came to land on the earth and—"

"The dinosaurs!" shouts Bini.

This is very educational; I should have taken notes from the start.

"Very good, Bini, bye, bye, dinosaurs."

"Stegosaurus, Albertosaurus . . ." Bini starts listing.

"Either you get to the point, or I'll tell Mom and Dad that—"

"I'm just about to! The universe is thirteen point eight billion years old, and there's still no trace of humans . . . Because humankind, ladies and gentlemen, doesn't appear until the last day of this cosmic year! In fact . . ."

"In fact, it's only the last fourteen seconds," adds Eva, arms folded.

"Fourteen . . ." Aksel tries to hide his surprise at the accuracy of his sister's calculation. "Exactly . . . fourteen seconds."

"And?" asks Eva.

"Do you know . . . ?" says Aksel sarcastically. "Do you know, Eva . . . within those fourteen cosmic seconds, *where your Hannah Montana CD comes in*?"

"You're an idiot."

"Do you see the absolute insignificance; how utterly inconsequential it is?"

"When you decide to give it back, leave it on my desk."

The doorbell rings, and all three of them look at me.

"What's up?"

"The doorbell rang," Eva says pointedly.

"And?"

"We don't have any playdates or visitors on the chalkboard."

"Mother of God."

We go to the door and see that David the mail carrier is waiting with his usual beaming smile at the edge of the yard. It's the closest I've felt to Alp since I've been in this country.

"Good afternoon, Rita!"

"Hi, David! Come on, kids, let me introduce you to the mail carrier . . ." The children are frozen in the doorway. "What are you doing? Come!"

The Bookland trident advances behind me with heads bowed, in silent single file.

"But what are you doing? Can you please say hello to David? I've already told you, he has twelve siblings and only the eldest was able to go to college and . . ."

David starts talking nonstop. Slang and multisyllabic words all mixed together; he couldn't be friendlier. But the children remain paralyzed.

"Aksel, David asked you a question . . ."

I watch as the cosmic arrogance of moments earlier turns into stardust and comes to land in the gutter. Where is this embarrassment coming from? Where are the thirteen point eight billion years of the universe? That tiki-taka animal that came out of the water? Finally, Bini speaks.

"I . . . I . . . years ago I had a little toy car like yours."

David is grateful for the comment and launches into another stream of speech. It's incredible; this man could talk for days without stopping. Finally, after a few long minutes of one-directional conversation and still as friendly and likeable as when he arrived, David leaves with a wave, only to be met with the same front of rudeness. The children look at me like three little dogs.

"What happened to you all?"

"Well, we don't know him," replied Eva.

"So what? He's a person. He's not a chicken or a curtain. He's a very friendly person who wanted to get to know you, and he asked you questions. Where are your basic manners? Don't you say hello to the butcher when—"

"We don't know any butcher," points out Eva.

"Or the fishmonger . . . ?"

"We don't know any fishm—"

"Or the baker or the florist . . . Jeez, do none of these people exist?"

"We know Pastor Paul!" exclaims Bini.

"Yes," corrects Eva, "but we've known him since we were born. He's not a stranger. He doesn't count."

"Anyway," says Aksel, on the way back inside, "all the information that a butcher or fishmonger could provide us, I already know. We buy our products in the supermarket, although less than we used to—meat isn't very sustainable . . . So, Hairy, why do I have to meet a butcher? Or a mail carrier?"

"Well . . . well . . ." Shit, why?

"Because the sound the real car makes is different from the one my toy made."

"Exactly!" I exclaim. "The truth is always better than fiction."

"Okay . . ." Aksel isn't convinced.

"Well, perhaps not always, but how many people have you spoken to this week who have twelve siblings, hmm?"

"We'll be late for Mandarin and tennis," replies Aksel.

We leave the house, and I fasten my seat belt after Aksel reminds me three times.

We're about to turn into the club when I see Samantha, out running with some friends. I get a flashback to the night of Six's party, when I saw her with a guy who could be her son as I was crossing the yard with Rachel before the big event. I slow down, intending to ask if it really was her, but she gestures to say not to stop; we'll talk later.

I go into the club to drop Bini at tennis.

"Do you think Queen Maria Theresa of Spain really had a Black son?" asks Eva from the back seat. "Or was it all a plot to humiliate Louis XIV while he was trying to build Versailles?"

"Well," replies Aksel, punching the back of the seat in front of him, "historical records from the time are very detailed. As was customary, the Spanish queen had a Black dwarf as a servant, and bearing in mind what we know of the king's lovers . . ."

Bini is heading for the tennis court, dragging his racket with all the enthusiasm of someone going to the doctor for an injection.

Mrs. Gee is saying goodbye to the children in her previous class with a bag of candy big enough to keep them busy for a week. Before they even leave the court, they've replenished the calories burned during the lesson. Multiplied by one hundred.

Mrs. Gee has a slightly hunched back, and it looks like her knees are giving her trouble. But when she picks up the racket, that's all forgotten. She transforms. She has the American flag on her cap, on her dress, and on the gold medallion hanging round her neck.

"Today, I'll do racket in the oven with a squirt of cloistered nuns; you see the hole in the rosebush?" Mrs. Gee takes me gently by the arm. She speaks as though her tongue were wound up tight, and each word is a soft rotation as it unwinds. As though she were from a remote village on Mallorca.

"She says," Bini interprets, embarrassed and annoyed, "remember to come slightly before the end of class . . . to . . . to play with me."

"Yes, yes, yes . . ." I take my leave.

I go back to the car and turn on the radio. "Unwritten" is playing; it's everywhere at the moment. Before I get to the exit, I see John pulling up his socks as he goes on the court.

"See you tonight!" he shouts.

I raise my arm and nod. I think I might wear my navy-blue dress, the short one, and my new sandals. And this time I'll shave right to the top of my legs.

I start to sing, checking the kids in the rearview mirror. Eva has her hair gathered in the usual messy ponytail that spills down her back and covers half the letters on her science camp T-shirt. The curls around her forehead are backlit against the window; I imagine her in a few years' time, a surfer chick recently graduated from Harvard. Beautiful. Brilliant. Unstoppable. She is concentrating hard. On her skinny knees, she's holding the velociraptor folder in which she's copied Barça's 2006 attack strategies, trying to decide which of the kids in her class can be Xavi. She's making an effort, so much effort, an effort comparable only to the complete lack of desire to kick a ball. But deep down she knows, with the same clarity with which she told me she would be the class coach, that sooner or later she's going to have to do it.

Meanwhile, on the other side of the back seat and to the complete indifference of his sister, Aksel is rapping. He has one hand over his mouth, closed in a fist, and he's issuing dry and nonsensical noises as he moves the other hand with movements that are far from graceful. I suppose it's too much to ask for his motor skills to be as brilliant as his mind; the only artistic thing about him is the unruly mass of preadolescent curls on his head. But none of that seems to bother him; he writes rhymes in secret on a crumpled piece of paper he keeps in his pocket. Because, whenever his mind isn't occupied by something, Aksel starts to rap.

I don't know whether he's aware that I'm watching him, but I like the idea that he allows himself to rap in my car and not in his parents'. But then he catches me watching and, despite my encouraging smile, he falls silent.

"But . . ." Eva bites the tip of her pencil, looking out at the intersection. "Hairy, I don't think this is . . ."

"Huh? No! No!" Aksel jumps in his seat as though we've driven into the Bronx in the 1980s. "Hairy! You've gone wrong—it isn't this way! Mandarin class is that way!"

"I know. Shut up."

We continue along North Highland Avenue, toward Virginia Highlands. This is where the oldest houses are to be found, with proper stone wells and ivy that looks like it's been clambering over the shutters for more than fifty years.

"Look, Spanish moss!" Eva points at a delicate plant falling in cascades from the tree branches.

I look up. The light cuts through and illuminates it as though it were cotton.

"Yes," says Aksel, who seems unsettled by the new route, "it grows in habitats that only get partial sun and . . ."

"But where are we going, Rita?" The uncertainty is eating away at Eva too.

I turn up the volume on the radio and continue in silence, until I pull up at the edge of Piedmont Park.

"Kids, get ready!"

"Ready for what?"

"We're going to rap and play soccer!"

"What?"

The Atlanta skyline is silhouetted above the perfect grass of Piedmont Park. Half a dozen buildings stand like a colorful miniature city on the other side of a flat expanse with five soccer fields.

The trees lean toward the lake as though they were giant, furry animals, about to take a drink. The green is still there, but it's losing its strength. The cool note in the air and a handful of pale leaves drifting on the water announce a change, the approach of fall.

"But, but, but . . ." Eva has too many questions.

"Don't worry, before you have a heart attack, you should know that Lei Wei—"

"Her name is Lan Wan," Aksel corrects me indignantly.

"The Mandarin teacher is ill and can't hold the class today."

"And how do you know?"

"She called the house and told me."

"And are you sure you understood properly?"

"Of course I understood properly." To tell the truth, I didn't understand a word of what she said; I had to ask Conchi to speak to her. "So, I thought we could come here, to the park, since it's such a beautiful day. Don't you think?"

"Mom and Dad won't like it at all," says Aksel as he unfastens his seat belt.

"But what are we going to play?" asks Eva.

"Well, play, run, can't you see the open ground in front of you?" No answer. "I've brought a ball. If you like, we can practice shooting . . ." Aksel looks at me as though he's calculating a very difficult square root. He says something quickly, and they laugh. "Come on!" Little jerks. "Everyone out!"

The touch of the ball beneath my feet takes me home, to the yard, to Albert. I think about when we were the same age as these kids, when the ball was an extension of our legs and our soccer field stretched up the meadow to the mountains of Alp, and nightfall was the only referee to make us stop. And now I look at Eva, about to kick a ball for the first time at the age of eight! And I also think about all the things she knows that I don't. Like Maria Theresa of Spain having Black children. And I don't know which version is better or worse. In any case . . .

"Shoot!"

On her first attempt, she completely misses the ball.

"No worries. Come on, try again!"

Eva focuses hard on the ball and tries again. This time she makes contact and gives it a good kick. Control and intent. Not because she's done it before, but because she's a natural, like my brother. This girl has a gift!

"Wow! Eva! That's very good!"

"Okay, but I don't want to be a cheerleader."

"Huh?"

"I don't want to be a cheerleader like Tracy. I want to go to Harvard."

"But what are you talking about?"

"Well, instead of being here, I could have been studying strategies or making progress with the C volume of the encyclopedia."

"Look, honey, knowing how to kick a ball decently won't stop you getting into Harvard. It's more than that; it could open more doors than you think. To start, it will help you pass the subject you need."

"What do you think? That I haven't pondered the importance of sports for getting into an Ivy League college?"

She said "pondered."

"And so?"

"So, I would rather make up for it in other fields, like volunteering and—"

"Wonderful. Shoot! Put your weight on your right leg and—"

"Hairy . . ."

What does she want now?

Eva rests her foot emphatically on the ball and puts on a teacherly face.

"Fifty thousand years ago"—not again, please—"women were gatherers. We stayed at base camp to care for the children and the elderly. That's why we're the ones who invented language, because of the long hours we spent forging relationships and identifying the good and bad plants."

"Eva!"

"And! And"—she lifts a finger in the air—"because of that, we have greater cerebral complexity. Not to mention our incredible capacity to distinguish color tones. Men, instead, were cavemen, and that was all. You just have to look at my two brothers. They devoted themselves to hunting—they had to run and protect the tribe. They're much simpler, but let's face it, in general their motor skills are better. They're better at sports."

"Have you corroborated that?" I don't know why I'm asking.

"I don't need to. Everyone knows it. But when we get home, I can log into *Nature* to confirm it. We have a Premium subscription."

I never would have guessed!

"I find that theory not particularly scientific and very sexist."

"But I don't want to kick the ball!"

"But you just did it perfectly, Eva!"

"I know, but I don't care. I want to strategize."

"And that's wonderful, but for this subject, you have to kick the ball as well."

"I'm not going to get famous behind any ball."

"Tell Serena and Venus Williams that! Now be quiet and try again!"

We practice for much longer than I expected. And Eva doesn't want to admit it, but when we finish, she can't help but smile with pride.

During the time we've been on the grass, bickering over our *Homo sapiens* origins and analyzing the perfect velocity and curve of a corner kick, Aksel has been writing verses in the shade of a weeping willow.

"Will you show me what you've written?" I ask.

Away from his younger siblings, he seems embarrassed, no longer required to be the intellectual role model. And now, in front of an adult woman, Aksel bows his head because his rhymes come from his soul and make him vulnerable. Perhaps I would find some lines from Hannah Montana in there. He looks up with a slight smile and says, "No . . . You wouldn't understand."

Bini is sitting on the bench; it's his turn to plunge his hand into the bag of candies.

"Fried eggs with juice, ma'am!" Mrs. Gee hands me a racket.

As soon as he sees me, Bini comes down from his rain cloud of ideas and grabs a racket again with resignation. He hates tennis with all his soul. Mrs. Gee looks at me and starts to explain the game.

"Why don't you just learn English already?" Bini begs me to make an effort from somewhere around the height of my waist. Perhaps I should have considered his pathological embarrassment before roping him in as my official interpreter. But I say nothing, and he translates: "The game involves hitting the ball ten times, you on one side of the net and me on the other."

Even from the remotest lakes of Alaska, it would be clear that the game will be a disaster. Bini only manages to hit one ball, and he sends it into the swimming pool.

Mrs. Gee asks the spectators to applaud from the benches. Half a dozen kids with intermittent teeth clap with generous, American enthusiasm. Mrs. Gee tells Bini to sit down.

"Now you." She gestures at me, and in the middle of one of her unwinding phrases, I catch the word "play."

"The tradition is that she decides whether you get into the club or not," Bini informs me.

To begin with, I hit the ball short, gently, because, well, the woman is about three hundred. But her arm moves like an independent entity, as though possessed by Serena herself, and before I know it, she's two points up, her pupils applauding devotedly.

All right then, old woman, all right. I dig out moves I haven't practiced for years: my wrist, my back, the swift movement of the feet. I make the most of the clay court to reach the ball comfortably. My backhand is much better than my drive; I hadn't remembered. Oh, I do enjoy a good game of tennis.

After several restrained returns, my competitive spirit inevitably takes over. I forget that the point of this might be to demonstrate the honest values of sport and that some members of the audience are probably in diapers. I have to beat the old woman.

I win one point, two. And the third is clear and strong, straight to the left sideline, the opposite side from where sweet Mrs. Gee is standing. I win.

I look at the members of the audience who, despite the sugar overdose and their tender age, know I've gone too far; they're saying things in English, and they aren't good. They get up to take Mrs. Gee by the hand and help her to a seat at the side of the court. One child gives her a banana Laffy Taffy.

I look around me, grateful for the solitude and birdsong, before approaching the coach, hiding my shame. I apologize for the final point, and she says it's no big deal; I played very well, and I should turn up for class next week.

"She says you're in the tennis club," Bini tells me, unable to hide a note of pride, "and that your doubles partner will be John. John Lapton."

The Story of a Frappuccino

I enter Starbucks, full of conviction. Today's the day. Today I'm going to do it. I join the line and go over my pronunciation once again. My commitment is admirable—ice cream, I scream, you scream—jeez, it's almost as if I were born in Atlanta!

Andrew—the other day I learned that Left Ovary's name is actually Andrew—greets me with a long, garbled phrase from behind the counter. I don't understand it, but he rounds it off with a smile that cures all ills. I study the menu and the specials. Shit, there are lots today: Ethiopian cinnamon, heart-shaped pumpkin toppings, an organic milk from Wisconsin, and three options I don't understand.

"Good afternoon, Rita! How are the hamsters?"

"The hams . . . ? Fine . . . fine. Good afternoon, Andrew!"

"What'll it be?"

"A Frappuccino. Mocha. Light. Decaffeinated. Lactose-free." I got this.

"Size?"

"Large."

"Milk?"

"Lactose-free milk." Shit, Andrew, I just said that! And I said it with an Atlanta accent! Don't put me off my game!

"Do you want Wyoming garlands?"

“Weren’t they from Wisconsin?”

“What?”

“It doesn’t matter . . . No, I don’t want garl—no.”

“If you like, I’ll add a caramel sprinkle . . . and a hamst—”

“No, thanks. A normal Frappuccino.” Come on, I got this.

“It’s for here, yeah?”

“What do you mean?”

“Do you want to drink it here, or shall I make it to go?” Andrew is puzzled at my concentration. It’s like I’m calculating something for NASA.

“Here, I’ll stay here, thanks.”

“All right, that’s everything.”

I pay.

I stand at the end of the counter and await the verdict. I remember the first time I went in and ordered a simple coffee and, after replying yes to every question, the Taj Mahal appeared at the end of the counter. But I’m no longer that girl who accepts a Taj Mahal instead of a simple coffee.

The cup arrives quicker than I expected.

“Here you are, Rita. Frappuccino-mocha-light-decaffeinated-lactose-free with a caramel sprinkle . . .” Nooo!

“But . . .”

“I added the caramel sprinkle because I like you.”

Eureka. A resounding victory.

Absurd, isn’t it? The fact that I get a lump of emotion in my throat because of a cup of mutant coffee. Feeling victorious because I’ve finally been served what I ordered. An everyday moment like this becoming a great triumph. That’s living abroad for you: surviving the everyday moments.

It would seem that today, at last, English and I have made our peace.

John's Inheritance

"I thought I heard you mention 'Toulouse' when you were on the phone to your parents the other day."

Hanne's words glide through the study door to the sofa, where I'm sprawled, looking up "illiterate" in my Spanish dictionary.

"Not that I was trying to eavesdrop, but you speak so loudly, it's impossible not to hear everything."

"Ah, don't worry," I reply, without raising my eyes from the dictionary. "Yes, I said 'Toulouse' because a friend of mine has just signed on with the HR Department of Airbus." And Edu's working for the University of Birmingham and Núria's with a bank in Andorra and Maria's with a market research company in Barcelona, but I don't tell her all that. "Why? Do you know someone in Toulouse?"

"Ah . . . That's good, isn't it? Airbus is a good company, very interesting . . ." She leaves a pregnant pause, a parenthesis, then continues, "What about you? Would you like to work for any particular company?"

I turn over a page, two, three. I scratch a foot.

"Hmm . . . Yes, I suppose . . . The question is figuring out which one."

"Which branch of psychology do you like best?"

I realize that Hanne is assuming that if I tolerated four years of college, it wasn't for lack of anything better to do, but because there was some meaning to it, because I was following some kind of plan.

"Rita?"

"Child psychology."

Hanne sticks her head out of the study door; she looks at me, and wrinkles her nose.

"The truth is, I don't know." I close the dictionary. She comes out of the study to hear my next words, leaning against the doorframe, her body arched as though she were clutching a glass of chardonnay. "And I have nothing else to say, Hanne. I'm lost; you know that. I try, I keep an open mind, but I can't seem to identify anything resembling a vocation. It isn't easy."

"The distance will do you good." She's in the kitchen now; I can't see her. "Besides, your vocation isn't really something you decide on . . . It comes on its own; it appears to you."

It seems like everyone has their own version of how to find a vocation. All I know for sure is that it isn't piano or quantum physics or ballet. Or psychology. Especially not child psychology.

"Come on! Put on Serenade No. 13. It can't help but lift your mood."

Eva happens to be passing the sofa, clutching the sketch of her next Van Gogh; she identifies the Mozart vinyl from memory, grabs the needle of the record player with all the delicacy allowed by her eight-year-old fingers with blue-painted nails, and floods the living room with the crackling sound of the old record.

"So, what's happening with John's dinner tonight?" I open the dictionary again. I still haven't found the word.

"It's the Volunteer Fresh Tuna, one of his big charity fundraisers. It's the most anticipated event in the neighborhood . . . especially for single girls."

"Ah, I'm not surprised—John is hot . . ."

Hanne looks at me. Shit, have I gone too far? Let's not forget that women here cover their asses and bellies with a curtain to go to the pool. But she's laughing. She was born in Boston, I suppose.

"Do you know who John is?" Now she is indeed clutching a chardonnay and has an aura of infallibility.

"Shoot."

"Does the name Asa Candler or Robert Woodruff mean anything to you?"

"No."

"What about John Pemberton?" Hanne plays it mysterious, enjoying the lead up to the big reveal.

"Was he the mayor of Atlanta?"

"John Pemberton invented Coca-Cola." Bam.

"Are you saying John is the Coca-Cola heir?" Is Hanne telling me that my doubles partner is the fucking heir to Coca-Cola?

"No. Wait." She's really annoyed at me interrupting her. "After John Pemberton invented Coca-Cola, Asa Candler came along. He bought the formula and founded the company. He popularized it nationwide, beyond Atlanta, started to advertise, and also hired two smart guys to bottle it. The famous one-dollar contract that changed history and—"

"And John?"

"Rita, I'm getting there."

"But you don't need to tell me the whole history of Coca-Cola . . ."

"I wanted to tell you about the Woodruffs, but it doesn't matter: Who out of all the people I've mentioned would you say is related to John?"

"As you can imagine, any of them would be nice."

"Lapton."

"Lapton? You didn't say that name."

"That's because you interrupted me. The Laptons were the smart ones who bought the rights to bottle Coca-Cola. And they closed the contract with the historic figure of one dollar."

"Wow." Wow, wow!

"So, in a way, yes, John has part of the Coca-Cola legacy. And the truth is that John is a very interesting example of how an inheritance should be invested properly . . . But, well, not everything is sunshine and roses."

"I suppose it never is in those families. But I'll never know—that's for sure."

"John doesn't speak to the rest of the family. And no one knows why . . ." She raises a finger to her mouth; she'd probably love to have the chance to throw herself at John. "I don't know . . . There are a thousand versions and some nonsense including murders and kidnappings, but no one has ever gotten to the truth."

"Murders? Kidnappings? *What?*"

"I'm sure they're exaggerations. But it makes it all even more mysterious."

"Hairyyy!" Bini's voice shoots out of the bathroom to demand my skills with the toilet paper. "Please . . ."

"Coming!" I get up and address Hanne. "I'll try to find out more tonight."

"How?"

"I played tennis earlier and I'm a bit sweaty, but I'll take a quick shower and be ready in five minutes sharp."

"But . . ." She laughs, surprised. "You can't come, Rita . . . Who will look after the kids if you're not here? You're the nanny, remember?"

I'm struck dumb. This can't be. But Aksel is ten! And I have friends who lost their virginity at thirteen!

"Sure, sure . . ." I reply.

I deal with Bini and ask him to show me his agenda so that I don't have to return to the kitchen.

Hanne says goodbye to the kids and something I don't catch about a Fête Galante and other nonsense, and they laugh and hug her. She's wearing the same "capsule wardrobe" black dress as the other day. The same orthopedic shoes, the same pearl stud earrings.

Fulbright goes into the study and switches off the light and the computer to be sure that no one except him sees Federico Chitawas's Machu Dicchu. With abrupt euphoria, he comes and stands in the middle of the living room, where I have just sat down, clearly in no mood for bullshit. He unbuttons his sport coat, opens his arms wide, and, tapping his waist, shouts, *"Panem et circenses!"*

Wow, another lunatic. I watch him from the sofa as I flick through *Vogue*, raising it to cover my face.

"Aegroto dum anima est, spes est!"

I turn the page, sick of all this Latin nonsense, but he demands my attention again and, gesturing at the magazine, translates: "While there's life, there's hope."

I don't laugh. They see my reading *Vogue* as frivolous, but there's plenty of culture in fashion, and a lot of politics too. But what would they know?

The garage door closes, and the car pulls off to join the neighborhood exodus heading to John's party. I hear the kids fighting and go calmly down to my room, fill the bathtub, and immerse myself in the last chapter of *The Catcher in the Rye*.

Roberta

When I finished *The Catcher in the Rye*, I spent some time reading up on Salinger's life and underlining a few phrases. It's true, I thought, what he wrote about how your feelings about someone don't end even when that person dies.

Then I finished writing an email describing what William Hernandes told us on the campus tour; I even explained about the fraternity students who had crewed Apollo 11, and, naturally, I didn't forget my Venezuelan classmates who wore rings the size of chickpeas. And of course—how could I not?—I also gave the broad brushstrokes of John's story. I didn't reveal his surname and everything I knew about him, which unsurprisingly created great expectation among my friends. The first few to reply couldn't care less about some rich students on Apollo 11. There was only one question: Who was John?

Hanne and Fulbright returned shortly after midnight. I was sitting on the edge of my bed and heard them laughing and saying shhhh every two seconds.

The pair was very tipsy, which made me like them a little more, but I didn't want to talk or for them to hear me. I didn't want them to see that I liked them because, apart from being unbearable intellectual snobs, they also appeared to know how to have a good time.

I stayed where I was until I heard water running from the faucet in their bathroom. And after a few prudent minutes, I went out to the street.

Outside, the summer was drawing to a close, but the humidity of Atlanta still clung to the skin.

I saw the shadow of a couple dancing, backlit behind a curtain. A teenage girl with acne was saying goodbye to the family in the yellow house, where the parents were giving her a tip, more generous than she had expected.

I left my cul-de-sac and made my way up Oak Paths Drive. It was twelve thirty, and, from the number of cars, rather than a Monday night, it felt like midday on Saturday in summer after a county swimming championship. Given that the average age of the adults in this area is forty-five and over, with most of the children under ten, it was one hell of a social anomaly.

John's party must have been memorable. And I had missed it because I was playing the nanny. Because, damn, let's face it, I am a fucking nanny.

"Reeda Racoons?"

"Here!" They can say "Milwaukee" but not "Racons"? I raise my hand before the expectant class. We all want to know which group we're in.

A teacher with gold-rimmed glasses and white curly hair gives the verdict:

"Racoons: grammar, level three." Three out of five, incredible, a resounding success. I won't tell the Booklands, just to be on the safe side. "Oral communication: level two. And creative writing"—she pauses and peers at me over the top of her glasses—"level four." What?

My phone sounds, and I read the message:

We have to get tickets for Radiohead in Las Vegas! Shall I get you one? I'll get you one! Las Vegas, baby!

(Six's job really does seem to give her all the time in the world. No free gas, though.)

It'll be a fucking blast! I'm a creeeeep! Las Vegas, Rita, Thom Yorke!

After announcing everyone's level, the teacher explains something about the pollinizing of sausages. Then she becomes more serious, picking up three books from the table with a solemnity that would suggest that this is a habitual but significant ritual. She runs her fingers over the titles, stroking the covers and walking between the desks. The first ochres of fall glow through the window.

Tek Soo tosses a folded square of paper onto my desk. I run my finger along the soft fold, the roughly torn edge; I'm right back in middle school.

The teacher is choosing three pupils to give a book to. And she does the same every week.

The first of the three books goes to one of the Venezuelans. The teacher explains something to her, but I can't hear properly from where I'm sitting.

Then she gives the second book to a Colombian guy I didn't notice the other day but who is the spitting image of Gael García Bernal. He's very good-looking. He's so happy the teacher gave him the book that he stands up and shakes her hand.

"Miss Rita."

The teacher must be about sixty, and she's in good shape—tall and robust and, at the same time, strangely muscular. Her skin is dark brown, and her nose is covered in freckles that make her even more likeable. She looks at me, and I feel her calm, the sense of security given by being in the place you've chosen to be, doing exactly what you were born to do. To teach, to be a teacher at this college. To be here now. She pushes her glasses up with her index finger in a familiar but not automatic gesture and smiles at me, as though we already know each other.

"Yes?" I reply.

She holds out the third book, in front of the watchful gaze of the rest of the class.

"My name is Roberta, delighted to meet you, Rita." She smiles at something, or perhaps she finds me funny. "The third book is for you: *The Martian Chronicles*, by Ray Bradbury."

For me? But why? What does it mean to be given a book?

And even more pertinent: Is *The Martian Chronicles* even a book? Isn't it a show on Telecinco where Boris Izaguirre gets his cock out?

I take the book in both hands.

"Do you know Ray Bradbury?" I shake my head. Why can't I speak? She's talking slowly. "You'll like it. Pay attention to the way it combines poetry and practical information. You'll come to that, but first you have to get used to it, to learn from the rhythm, from the chocolate of the words." What is this woman saying? "You have to work on your grammar. You have a base, but it's still very poor. But that's why you're here, to start writing from scratch. The important thing is that, in your text, you showed me you aren't afraid." She laughs, as though recalling a certain phrase. "You made me feel something, you've soothed my carrots, and that's the most important thing." She picks up the book again, unhurriedly searches for a particular passage, and turns to read it out, loud and clear. The whole class listens, the morning sun filtering through the windows making dust motes dance in the air. She reads to us about the nature of time itself—what it might smell like, look like, sound like, taste like.

Roberta hands me the book with both hands. And she smiles, full of joy.

"You have to make me feel that, Rita."

And I feel a strange warmth, because for the first time, a teacher has paid attention to me.

After going to the final class of the day, of which I estimate I understood a third if I'm lucky, I leave with Roberta's book under my arm and a childlike smile that at some point curls its way onto my upper lip. What is *The Martian Chronicles* all about, anyway?

Tek Soo comes up and gently informs me that I have to go get my essay from Roberta's office. It turns out I have a personal assistant.

"Hello, Roberta!"

"Ah! Reeda, come in, come in." Roberta searches for my essay among a mountain of files.

"Thanks."

"Reeda . . . Reeda Ra . . ."

"Rita Racons." With my strongest Alp accent.

As expected, her office is like a movie set: books everywhere—ancient, worn leather-bound tomes—mountains of papers on the desk. The light picks out the relics on the top shelf, and I see a portable record player, a coffee grinder, and two Aztec figures bending over, their asses forming miniature drums. But more than anything, there are photos. Dozens, perhaps a hundred, photographs of Roberta all around the world.

"Racoons! Reeda Racoons!" Milwaukee. "Here we are . . ."

Her white curls bouncing against her dark skin, backlit by the window, paint an idyllic scene.

The pages are covered in notes. No teacher I've ever had in my life, at elementary or high school or even at college, has ever done anything like this. No teacher has paid so much attention to a piece of my work.

"How are you?" she asks cheerfully.

"Good, happy, thanks for . . . the book."

"As I said, Reeda, I saw something between the lines of this text that soothed me with carrots. Your voice has drapes, that's why I gave you the book, but I'll also say that you'll have to make an effort, that you won't win the competition with texts like this."

"Competition? What competition?"

"What do you mean, what competition?" Roberta adjusts her glasses. "The text that *The Georgian* selects every year to publish in its final issue! I've just explained it all to the class!" Ah, the pollinizing of sausages.

"Oh, yes, yes, the competition . . . *The Georgian* . . ." Roberta said "win." My English is worse than a walrus's, but I definitely heard "win."

"To win it, you'll have to write something from your heart. Something inspiring, memorable."

"All right."

"What are you doing now?"

"Now? I'm going to fetch the children I look after."

"Ah, wonderful! Wonderful!" She stands up. "Well then, pay a great deal of attention. Practice with everyday scenes and write something good. What you're experiencing now, today, won't be repeated. Make the most of it. Make the most of the reality of those children; draw inspiration from them. I want to know it all. I want to feel it all."

Today, I showed them how to make my favorite snack, *pa amb tomàquet*. And before drizzling olive oil (the good stuff, of course) over the tomato-smeared toast, I made them try the oil just so they could appreciate the fruity flavor. But first we smelled it. It had apple and a hint of banana. And then, unless I was very much mistaken, they said they noticed the sweetness. Anyway, no one said "yuck," so the afternoon got off to a good start. There aren't many crumbs left on the plates scattered across the long table in the kitchen porch.

"When glutamic acid ionizes, *my dear*, it's glutamate," Aksel corrects his sister.

"But in the example I gave, it isn't ionized, *darling*." Eva sharpens her pencil.

A gentle breeze combs the lavender bushes. There's no one in the street, apart from the four of us, our homework, and the squirrels.

"Would anyone like another slice? Like this, with good olive oil . . ." I ask.

"No, thanks. What's glutamate?" God bless Bini Bookland.

"Glutamic acid," Aksel says to the air, "exists in three optically isomeric forms and is found as L-dextrorotatory, which—"

"Aksel," interrupts Eva, "I don't think you need to specify the hydrolysis of gluten and all that. Glutamate, Bini, is one of the twenty amino acids of which proteins are made."

"Okay," answers Bini.

"What do you mean, okay?" I cry, amazed, from the easy chair at the head of the table, as I crunch on another slice of *pa amb tomàquet*.

The three children turn to me in surprise.

"See?" Aksel bristles. "How do you expect me to explain glutamic acid without mentioning the hydrolysis of gluten?"

Roberta doesn't know what she's asked of me. I open the computer and start to write.

And I Love You, *Mi Arma*

"Yaya?" I hear a "comin'!" that echoes through every corner of the house. "Come on, hurry—Rita's already here!" Albert turns back to the camera. "Mom and Dad will come when they can, but service is dragging on. Yaya's coming now—she's just fixing herself up."

"Fixing herself up?"

Her footsteps clatter down the hallway. I can almost smell the Nivea and hairspray from here. Yaya bursts into the office, and Albert offers her the seat with exaggerated reverence.

"Pah, this guy, what an idiot. Show-off."

She's in the sunflower dress she wears on special occasions, her good earrings and—I can tell—an impeccable manicure. She's been to the hair salon for a color and perm, and she's clutching the little gem-covered purse she uses for Mass.

"Wow, Yaya, what a sight for sore eyes! You're stunning!"

She's a little embarrassed and pretends to be annoyed for an instant.

"Dontcha have any frien's there, Rita? I want to meet them. Introduce me to whoever you like—today I'm prepared. Go on, put on some music, José Perales or Manolo Escobar! No, no, better La Pantoja!"

Albert leaves for a moment to help in the kitchen, and she sits with her back straight, as though ready to testify in a court case she has a good chance of winning.

"Well, to be honest, I'm home alone, Yaya. I'm waiting for the children to finish their homework."

She relaxes a bit and puts the purse down on the table.

"What are you eatin', my love? You look happy, yes you do." For a nanosecond, I glance away from the computer, and my upper lip spasms slightly into a smile as I remember my night with Rachel, but it's fleeting, absolutely imperceptible to the human eye. "Ohh! Somethin's happened"—impossible, there's just no way!—"somethin' good, somethin' good happen' to you, yes it did."

"Yaya, what are you talking about? I haven't done a thing. I'm perfectly normal! For God's sake, you've got cataracts in both eyes!"

"Caratacts . . ." She laughs with a superior air and lifts her hand to her bra. "Rita, please . . . All right, you tell me when you're ready." She takes out a little mirror and wipes pink lipstick off her teeth. "An' that book?"

"My teacher at college gave it to me. Yaya, she gave one to me and two others in my class, that was all."

She snaps the mirror shut, surprised.

"Well, look at you! That's good, isn' it?"

"Yes, yes . . . I suppose so."

"Well, if she gave it to you, it must be for some reason . . . I always knew it . . ." She pauses to lean back in the armchair and shout "Whaaaaaaa'?" over her shoulder, so loudly it makes the connection vibrate. "Your father, my dear, I already told him we're out of liver terrine and to go out and get some, yes I did."

"Oh . . . I'm jealous, Yaya, what I wouldn't give for a slice of liver terrine. Have you sent me a package of cold cuts yet?"

"Yes, Rita, God, what a pain you are with your cold cuts, yes you are! Your mother told you the other day she sent 'em already. All right, tell me, tell me, how are the children?"

"Pff . . . they spend all day reading and talking about science and philosophy and history. They're hard work. Today they were going on about glutami—it doesn't matter. The other day, I asked their parents if I could take them to the movies, and they said it would be better if we went to the museum. We've been three times to see the exhibition on fossils and velocirap—some goddamn dinosaurs. They're kind of boring, and they didn't like half the cured sausages."

"Hard work, no kiddin' . . ."

"But the other day, I took them to play in the park, and we had fun."

"Give it time . . . When they know you properly, they won't be able to tear themselfs away from you, no they won't. What about you, dontcha read when they do?"

"Well, yes, I read, Yaya. I've read, like, fifteen books since I've been here."

"Fifteen books? Whoa!" I hear a noise coming from the kitchen. "Your brother's laughin'. He says no one beliefs that, it's impossible."

"He's an idiot."

"Shut up!" she shouts to him and laughs. "He says he's dryin' his tears of laughter."

"What does he know—he's never dissected the mass of a proton."

"A wha'?"

"Nothing." Did I just say proton? Who am I?

"Well then, what about this teacher of yours, hmm? Hmm?"

"I like her. She gave me this book because she says I have to learn to write from scratch."

"But you already got a job. And so? Any hint of a job you'd like? Are you gonna be a hairdresser or an astronaut? I could see you on Jupiter, yes I could."

"No, Yaya, not yet. Maybe I won't discover it. Maybe I'm meant to live just like this, without a vocation."

"I don' think so." She rummages for something in her bra again.

"Yaya! Can you stop with the bra?"

"Oh, *mi arma* . . ." She laughs—she always finds it funny when we talk about her bra. "You can laugh, but there's no safer place on this earth than a woman's bra. And you know for sure that these breasts have never seen the sun." She pulls out a handkerchief, wipes her eyes, and continues, "We're really missin' you, my love. Your parents are crawlin' on the floor . . ."

"As if! Ha, ha, ha! Don't talk nonsense."

"Well, the other day, I saw your dad open your bedroom door and stand starin' for ages. The years pass quickly, just look at me, I'm eighty-four years old, but this year, with you so far away, is passin' very slowly, yes it is."

"Oh, Yaya, you're going to make me cry . . ."

"Don' be silly! You stay close to those kids when they pick up their books—that's always good." The connection is getting worse. I try to tell her to hang up, but she keeps talking. "And you know that Saint Rita is the patron saint of the impossible! . . . Then you add chickpeas and spinach and pour on a good glug of olive oil, the good stuff . . ." And she goes on, and on, and I listen to her as though I were sitting in the kitchen at home. "I'm sure Trini has a new boyfriend—I don't know how people don't notice; it couldn't be more obvious, no it couldn't . . . And they didn't know if it was a boy or a girl cat . . . No one lives in that apartment! But eventually they caught the cat! Ha, ha, ha. Anyway, you listen to that teacher, my dear—it'll do you good . . . And do whatcha want, hairdresser or astronaut, as long as it makes you happy! And I love you—I love you very much, *mi arma*, yes I do!"

The connection goes dead. I try to call back, but I can't get through.

Aksel is picking at a scab covering half his elbow, down to the raw skin, as he studies an A3 sheet between his legs, which are open in a triangle. Now he says he wants to build a computer from scratch. Just like any other ten-year-old on a Tuesday afternoon, why not?

The other day I found out that Hanne's maternal family comes from Norway, which is why they spell Aksel with a *k* and not an *x*. And hence the unbelievable immunity these kids have to physical ailments: none of your stereotypical nerdy weaklings here. I've seen them headbutt marble bars and bump into table corners hard enough to make even a

Basque woodman faint, but the only effect it seems to have on them is to divert the parabolic trajectory between points A and B.

Aksel never hesitates under pressure; he always has an answer ready on his lips. And he always gets it right. It's exhausting. When he has a book in his hands, he disconnects from reality, and his face vanishes beneath those ash-blond curls for hours. I have to admit that he's handling prepuberty pretty well so far. The fuzz on his chin, the fiercest enemy of any preadolescent—trust me, I know what I'm talking about—is a very subtle blond, which instead of shadowing his face gives it a touch of light that brings out the sky blue of his eyes. He'll never know what a lucky bastard he is. Even now, on the cusp of the age when the clothes he wears will assume utmost importance, the demands of fashion are like water off a duck's back, in line with the family philosophy. He wears T-shirts showing Boy Scout slogans or from his latest math camp; they're old and unoriginal—either that or I don't understand them—the complete opposite to the adjectives I would use to describe his mind, so rare and exceptional.

He doesn't know it, but he'll be irresistible. He's cut out to be a leader and he's a good speaker, but if he hasn't mastered the topic—which is hardly ever the case—he feels lost, laid bare, and he gets angry. And he does everything in his power to prevent it happening again.

Although he does his best to hide it, Aksel is the most sensitive of the three. I'm not saying that because I've read the romantic verses he hides among his copies of *Nature* magazine in the false bottom of his closet, nor because I've seen him snuggle in between his parents, making baby noises . . . I'm saying it because of his gaze: There's no doubting the sweetness in his eyes.

For some time now, he's been pretending to do complicated calculations. He wants to tell me something and doesn't know how.

"Aksel, what are you doing?"

"Nothing . . ." He closes his eyes without lifting his head; he seems very embarrassed.

"You know something? I've been put at level two for oral communication. Level two, out of five!" I laugh.

This prompts more of a reaction than I expected. I've jolted him out of his suffering.

"What? But, Hairy, that's impossible!"

"Nothing's impossible, my boy." I point at my face with a grin. "You have the proof right here."

"If I were you, I wouldn't tell my parents, or . . . or . . ." He laughs; he's cheering up. "Yes, actually, maybe you should tell them." The laughter has relaxed him. Finally, he goes for it. "Hairy . . ."

"Yes?" I still can't believe I'm answering to that name.

"I need your . . ." He swallows, sweating. "Your help . . ."

"Sure, Aksel, tell me."

"Will you help me rehearse a rap for the end-of-semester show?" I stay quiet; I never want this moment to end. "My parents would never let me do it, clearly."

"But why not?"

"Trust me, I've analyzed the possibilities."

"All right."

"And the school won't either. I've thought a lot about it, and I want to do it anyway. I need to do it . . . The end-of-semester presentation will be the only chance I get to show everyone that rap is a true art, that verse and science are compatible, and that together they're unbeatable. But I need your help . . ." Finally, he lifts his head and looks at me. "I need you to help me find the flow."

Wild Souls . . . and Samantha's New Life

I had thought that when the time came to play doubles with John, I would be too distracted, but apparently my pathological competitive streak is strong enough to take my mind off admiring his quads. Or is it possible that my night with Rachel has anesthetized my libido? No, no . . . the urge to look at John's legs is real. Apparently, I'm still teetering on the brink of bisexuality with impressive calm. Anyway, he's just as competitive as I am.

We lost, but it was a good first match. And it gave me the chance to confirm that his sweat smells nothing like the terrible stench of onion or damp groin; quite the reverse: Whenever we passed each other or clasped hands to celebrate a point, I got a fleeting, faint burst of Tom Ford for Men Extreme, mixed with Gatorade.

I played well. Halfway through the match, Hanne and Fulbright appeared to cheer me on. Americans. I'm sure they came to watch John as well, but just as they sat down, I happened to score the best point of the match. The cheers from the half-dozen-strong crowd were momentous, so American, that by extension, the Booklands were effectively being applauded too. The satisfied look on their faces was unmistakable, particularly when they saw John's clear approval. They no longer had Miss Universe as an au pair, but it turns out that the

Pyrenean she-goat is pretty good at sports. And that's cool. For most Americans, such aptitudes are not just admirable but mandatory.

It has grown dark during the match, and I've only just noticed. The bluish floodlights illuminate the tall, thin trunks around the courts; the silence is so clear we can almost hear the squirrels' claws as they shimmy up the trees.

John sits next to me and we high-five as he listens to the voice messages he's received over the last hour. Perhaps it's the president of Coca-Cola, sharing the day's sales figures? "One hundred billion cans. Thanks." Perhaps it's George W. Bush? Or the new Democratic candidate! What's his name again . . . Mojama? I hope it's Mojama. He seems to have quite a few messages, anyway.

I take a slug of cool water and mentally thank Bini for having convinced me to take one of the semifrozen water bottles from the freezer. "I never drink water when I'm working out, Bini, not even when I was skiing in the morning and playing two basketball games in the afternoon, because it gives me gas."

"Hairy, please," he insisted, closing his eyes.

I watch our opponents enjoying the wonderful calm and burst of serotonin that come after two hours of exercise; "You did really well, Rita," says Prrr. I'd like to chat about some of his moves and that brutal clip he sent me just before he fell to the ground, and that backhand, and I'd tell him to work on his serve, but I smile with contained frustration and say, "Thanks." I must improve my tennis vocabulary. They're drinking from their bottles—also semifrozen—and allow the water to trickle down their flesh-colored tops.

John finishes listening to his messages, snapping his phone shut. He says goodbye to everyone—I feel sure he's just invited them to his house—and before getting into his car, turns to me and says, "Follow me."

He's barely gotten the words out of his mouth, and I've started the engine. Now it's my turn to listen to my voice messages. I have fifteen. Six says that last night—whenever "last night" was—she was so horny, she hooked up with a guy (she does that sometimes, sleep with guys; apparently "it's the easiest thing in the world"), and when she got up in the morning, in his house, she found him naked in the living room, praying with open arms in front of a huge altar of flowers and candles. And it wasn't even nine o'clock in the morning. She also says she thought he was Black, but he turned out to be white. And that he was twice as fat as she seemed to remember. Or perhaps it wasn't even the same guy. And that we should get brunch at Murphy's tomorrow. And not to forget that next weekend we're going to Las Vegas, and yes, I can do it. And that I should join Facebook, because then we could chat for free and upload photos. But who's going to see those photos? I don't get it.

I shut my phone by the seventh message—just as Six is explaining the countless advantages of mixing MDMA with Jäger—and put on the new Radiohead CD. It's incredible: I rented *In Rainbows* from my basement room the day before yesterday on this platform called Netflix, and this morning I had the CD in the mailbox in a red envelope. The United States is a wonderful place. Mind you, I'd never be able to find a cassette of Manolo Escobar at any old gas station.

We leave the club in a procession of luxury all-terrain vehicles, but the line soon disperses, and only John's vintage convertible and my bougie BMW are left. Have I missed something? We merge onto a highway I don't think I've ever driven on (although I've almost certainly been here thirty times), and, as "Nude" is playing, we stop at a red light, in front of Atlanta's White House, a replica of the original White House, but a bit smaller and with the shrubs outside pruned into the phrase "God loves you." I call Fulbright to say that I'm eating out and I don't know when I'll be back. I don't tell him I'm going to John's house because, given how happy they were after the last party, I wouldn't put it past them to force me to go home so they can take my place.

Decatur at eight o'clock in the evening is like an August dawn on the upper Diagonal in Barcelona. Not so much as a stray dog.

We make our way along Clairmont Road, passing a couple of cookie-cutter shopping malls, and pull up at a red light. On the left, I see a large industrial building with huge letters on it. It's impossible: YMCA.

"What?" I shout. "Whaaat?"

The YMCA is real!

Shit, the YMCA is a gym!

The light changes to green, and John makes a right-hand turn that I can barely see. I'm singing "YMCA" with the windows down as I follow him onto a narrow road just about wide enough for two cars. All around me are multicolored trees: yellows, oranges, and browns.

Finally, John's bottle-green BMW—vintage and gleaming—slows down and pulls up in front of some wrought-iron gates that open with cinematic slowness.

I stop singing. The gates open into a driveway that meanders generously upward to disappear across the crest of a hill. John pauses at the top, at the precise point where the black outline of the car stands out against the dusky sky, as if savoring the prelude, making it clear that, once this line is crossed, everything changes.

The house appears below us; it's not a steep drop so much as the start of a vast expanse. In front of the house, there's a giant pond, as big as . . . well, as big as a lake.

Down the hill, heading toward the night, I drive slowly, absorbing all I see, the moment, the house, and the entire halo of mystery that always surrounds John. The blurry reflection of my car in the water appears to me like a kind of delirium.

I park. Before I get out of the car, I give myself a quick sniff. All good. I have privileged DNA. I walk over to him as a damp breeze reaches us from the wood surrounding the gardens.

The note of intrigue reminds me of the old villas in the golf district in Cerdanya, constructed by the first bourgeois families in the late nineteenth century. Whenever I cycled that way, on summer nights,

I would stand up on my pedals to peer in. I liked seeing how, little by little, the darkness of night turned the ivy-clad facades into hidden corners full of stories. This house, unlike the ones by the golf course, is made of real stone.

John opens the trunk and takes out the rackets. The crunch of his tennis shoes on the gravel gives way to the squeak of rubber on tile as we enter the porch.

"And the others?" I ask.

"Who?"

"From tennis. Aren't they coming?"

"Ha! A couple of nights a year I make them cod boots."

"Ah . . ." He's smiling; he must think I'm nervous, but I'm not really, only a little bit, the right amount; I'm not sure if he's interested, anyway. "One question . . ." Although I'm not really nervous, if he doesn't say something soon, I'm probably going to start babbling compulsively on random subjects. "The YMCA . . . you know?" I do the movements with my arms. "YMCA, do you know if the gym or the song came first?"

"What?"

"It doesn't matter."

We go inside. Beyond a small landing at the entrance, a thick stone arch demarcates the hall. And beyond the arch, I see two wide Chesterfield sofas, facing one another, upholstered in worn brown leather that changes color depending on the light.

I'm wondering whether or not to take off my shoes, when a man appears. He stands very straight, must be about fifty, and is dressed impeccably. His skin glows up to his hairline, the kind of man who always looks like he's just stepped out of the shower. Is he British? Or gay? He's carrying a tray with a jug of water, ice, and lemon, which is covered carefully and symmetrically with a white cloth; next to it are two crystal glasses like the ones my great-grandmother had, etched with a feather design. They also contain water and ice, with a slice of lemon slotted over the rim of the glass.

"Phillip"—he just had to be called Phillip—"allow me to introduce Rita."

"Oh"—it's a very British sounding "oh"; it must be these surroundings—"nice to meet you, Phillip." Is he a butler? Are butlers allowed to wear jeans? Is John gay? No, please! Maybe that's why Fulbright was so happy to go to his party the other night? Who has a butler in 2007?

"Come on, let's go to the terrace." John grabs one glass and offers me the other.

I take a long drink. It isn't water. It's gin and tonic. I've just fallen in love.

We cross the entrance hall and the living room, or perhaps it's still the entrance hall; shit, it's all very confusing. I follow Phillip with my eyes and watch him repeat his journey in reverse, with the same steps, slipping through the door at the same angle.

"Phillip's a family friend. I've known him all my life. It's like . . . like I'm Batman and he's Alfred. You know who they are, right?"

"Of course, do you think I'm"—an orangutan, a duck-billed platypus, a wild boar—"stupid or something?" He laughs. "And . . . and do you have a Robin?"

He laughs harder, but doesn't seem to feel the need to answer.

We're standing in front of a pair of huge windows overlooking the garden. Before we move on, a photograph on the wall catches my attention. It can't be. Yes, yes, it's them. Or is it Euro Disney?

"That's Euro Disney, right?" I'm a bit scared to hear the answer.

"No . . . it's here." He gestures toward the area with the Chesterfields. "They came to the house, last summer."

"Are you telling me . . ." I'm sweating more than I did in the entire tennis match. "You're telling me you know Luke and Leia?"

"Yes." He takes a long drink.

"Leia and Luke have been here. Here. In this room. There. Here. And now you're going to tell me they're friends of the family too . . ."

"Something like that."

"And . . ."

A murmur of young people and a festive air start to fill the living room/entrance hall with its ten-foot floor-to-ceiling height. I don't see anyone from the tennis team. I'm the only one not wearing shoes. John seems unfazed by the arriving guests. He looks out of the window, smiles at the sight of a row of cars, and says, "Today it would appear that the clothes pegs will eat gazpacho."

"All right," I say.

"All right?" he asks.

"No?"

"It's party time! Clothes pegs."

Phillip appears behind us with another couple of gins. He's worked out the speed at which John drinks his, particularly if a Mediterranean girl with hairy arms is making him uncomfortable. This time Phillip has switched gin; from the sweetness and strawberry note, I would say it's Citadelle. I want a Phillip in my life.

"Citadelle?"

Phillip cranes his neck in surprise, followed by a small bow in my direction that seems to substitute a simple, mundane "yes." His movement releases a light, elegant waft of a woody perfume, pine and orange.

"Come." Jazz is playing. John grabs me by the hand and pulls me behind him.

We continue down the hallway where Luke and Leia are hanging. I'm freaking out at the people in the photos. They all look rich and important, but I don't know most of them. I see Bill Clinton (having a photo taken with Clinton seems to be a requisite to live in this neighborhood). I see Bruce Willis and choke. And then I see a photo of Michael Jordan blocking a teenage John. Michael Jordan. Michael Jordan! The only poster I've ever hung on my wall in my life is of Michael Jordan!

"Come on, Rita, don't get carried away," says he, the one who had them framed. "Come on!" His voice fades as he heads downstairs.

"But . . . but . . . but Michael Jor . . ."

John is waiting for me with a smile that makes my knees go weak. I go down the last step, pick out the strawberry from my glass with my fingers, and eat it in tiny nibbles; I think this pseudosexual scene might compensate for the fact that I'm wearing a church logo T-shirt and my hair is currently being held back not by gel but by sweat.

"Do you know this man?" John is oblivious to both the hair and the pseudosexual nibbles. He carefully picks up a photo from a desk and holds it out to me with both hands and a hopeful look on his face. "Tell me, Rita, do you know him?"

In the photo, a very young John, wearing an open shirt and a tired, tearful smile, has his arm round Juanito from La Boqueria market. It's fair to say that, after Antònia, he's the last person in the world I expected to see.

"It's Juanito, from Pinotxo in La Boqueria . . ."

John takes a step forward and grabs my arms.

"Is he still alive?" His eyes are teary, his voice faltering.

"Yes, of course he's alive! Juanito is immortal!"

He closes his eyes and opens them again to absorb every last bit of my response.

"Do you know him well?"

I met Juanito on the way home from a night out. We were leaving Apolo or La Paloma, and we were starving, so we made our way to La Boqueria. Barcelona still hadn't woken up. At that time, the market was still a dark-blue ghost, and the only glimmer of light was the orangey glow of Bar Pinotxo, with steam belching from its coffee machine. Juanito is responsible for serving breakfast to the first workers of the day: butchers lugging carcasses, fishermen with boxes overflowing with ice, garbage collectors; as well as those on their way to bed: nighttime radio presenters, the dancers from El Molino. I just loved that fine line between night and day: the start and the end, sleep and wakefulness. It was pure magic, and he was the guardian, the official soldier at that ephemeral border post.

And we became friends. I spent a month leading gastronomic tours for Argentinian tourists who came to Barcelona for some kind of conference. So, every morning, I would run the tours, and in the afternoons, I went to college. And the tours always started in La Boqueria, with Juanito's story. I knew all about his life. I had read and asked everything about him. He was my favorite story.

I would tell my group that he was the person who received the Olympic torch in 1992 on Barceloneta Beach and carried it up Las Ramblas, on what, according to him, was the happiest day of his life. Often, when I finished the tour, I came back to La Boqueria and sat at the bar in Pinotxo to watch Juanito grinning at his customers and any fans, even if they just came up to say hello and take a photo.

That bar—those customers, that little corner with the clouds of steam and thin paper napkins hanging from the ceiling—is his life. But it's also the life of many other people. And that October, it was mine.

"Rita, for Christ's sake, how do you know him?"

"From some tours. I know him from gastronomic tours."

"Oh my God!" He looks emotional. "This is incredible . . ." He lights a cigarette and grabs a bottle of Macallan.

He speaks euphorically and opens a refrigerator that doesn't even look like one, taking out an ice cube the size of a fist. He chips at it with some kind of pick before tipping the sharp shards into each glass.

"Do you have some water, please?"

"This man changed my life . . . A free fly, the bottles, pigeons in a pan, the bottles of shit!" He hands me the glass with the whiskey and jagged icebergs. "When are you going?"

"Me? I'm going to Las Vegas tomorrow, but not until the afternoon . . ."

"No, sorry, I meant when are you going back to Barcelona?" Shit. Back to Barcelona.

"Well . . . well, in the spring . . ."

"Ah! You still have a while! When you leave, I'll give you something to take to Juanito."

"But why? What happened? You're pale, and you've got goose bumps!"

"Rita"—he grabs me by both arms—"I'm so glad you're here."

He takes my hand again; apparently, learning that Juanito is still alive has given him a strange peace. When we close the door behind us, John kisses me on the lips. A short, European kiss. Then he says, "And now, Rita, let's go upstairs, the clothes pegs must be fucking by now."

Two young men wearing white tank tops, their legs intertwined on one of the Chesterfields, are fighting over a pill with the tip of their tongues. Wow. They have gelled-back hair and olive skin. More or less like me. Both things. From the ease with which everyone is moving about and looking at each other, they don't give the impression of being in someone else's house. Or perhaps they all live here?

The jazz is swelling, in rhythm and volume. People are scattered all around the hall, the living room, and the staircase, holding glasses or cigarettes with limp wrists. Bohemian artists and off-duty politicians who don't much care what everyone else is doing. Drag queens in wigs, platforms, and epic amounts of makeup. The guests greet John, raising their glasses and nodding at him with familiar but no less sincere gratitude.

Since the day I arrived, it's been clear that I'm a disappointment to the male population of the neighborhood as a replacement for Miss Universe. But even so, whenever I go into the club, every time I go to fetch a child from a house, or fetch Bini from school, there's always someone who, either surreptitiously or openly, checks me out. After all, I'm young, European, and, well, I'm from Barcelona, and that makes me exotic. But here, although I'm barefoot and in tennis gear, wearing very short shorts, with dust-covered legs and sweaty hair sticking up several inches, well, damn it, I'm looking good! And yet no one here has looked at me for a single, paltry second.

A trumpet starts playing in the room next door. And a clarinet. And a sax and a guitar. Four men are improvising around a low wooden table with the silhouette of Atlanta glowing in the distance. How long have we been downstairs? And what do all these people mean? And what day is it?

"This is your first time here, isn't it?" A delicate, transparent hand, perfumed with rose and cotton, extends from a Chanel tweed sleeve and hands me a G&T with raspberries. "It's lovely to see you, Rita."

"Samantha! What a surprise!" I kiss her on both cheeks, automatically, uncomfortably. "Where are the others?"

"Oh, Rita . . ." She laughs. "The tennis crowd only comes for the unicorn tuna fundraisers . . ." She raises her glass to the air and gestures to the guys in the tank tops, who are no longer wearing them. "This is the fucking Deep South!" She said "fucking." No trace of the timid, defenseless Samantha at the door the other day. She downs the rest of her gin. "Anyway . . . I wanted to apologize. The other day . . . in the Jacuzzi . . ."

"In the Jacuzzi?" I ask.

"In the Jacuzzi? No! No . . . Who said anything about a Jacuzzi?"

"Sorry, I didn't understand. The other day where?"

"At the party in that old school in Little Five Points . . ."

"Ah, yes, yes, sure."

"You see, it was the first night I went out alone, and I bumped into you . . . I didn't think I'd see anyone from the neighborhood . . ." She pauses at length. "And the truth is, I didn't know how to react. I'm sorry . . ."

"No problem." I don't understand her apology. People here apologize almost pathologically. A "sorry" before and after everything they say.

"The thing is . . ." She shakes the final drops of G&T into her mouth with as much elegance as is possible with such a vulgar gesture, the ice clinking against her front teeth. She's tense, but she's just decided to let herself go. "I've just . . . I'm recently divorced, you know? Just a month ago. The night at the school was my first as a divorcée." Her chin trembles, and she pauses. "And sometimes it feels like rather than getting divorced, I've committed a crime. There are a lot of people around here who will put up with a marriage for the sake of appearances, or because the women haven't worked for twenty years and wouldn't know where to start. But I've taken that step, you know? I got married when I was twenty. I gave my youth to the kids and my husband's career. Ex . . . ex-husband. That's not so unusual, is it? That isn't so hard to understand? That I want to live? Is it, Rita?"

"No, no, of course not . . ."

"I've been an exemplary mother, and I've only slept with one man in my entire life. Well, it's two now. This isn't the 1950s, damn it! Light bulbs! Cactus! Me wanting to sleep with other men is the most normal thing in the world! Nature! I should have been born in Europe. Shit." She tips up her empty glass. "Anyway, I'd be grateful if you didn't tell anyone . . . I owe you one . . . Sorry."

"Don't worry. You don't owe me anything, I wouldn't hear of it. And I agree with everything you say! Cactus!"

"What did you say? Cactus!"

"Don't worry. I won't tell anyone."

Samantha glides away toward the bar, indignant and unbalanced, and helps herself to another glass. I watch her aura, how it makes everyone around her fade into the background.

I touch my hair and search for a mirror, but the sight of John sitting on a sofa in an unbuttoned white linen shirt stops me short. He's about to play the trumpet.

A girl smoking two cigarettes at once, a pearl necklace hanging down her naked back, is playing the piano. Everyone goes wild, the tank top pair abandon the Chesterfield to go and watch John. The rest of the musicians have been playing for a while, and their faces are gleaming with sweat. The trumpeters climb onto the sofa at an opportune moment, and John grabs a microphone.

The movement of his shoulders, the angle of his neck, the flexing of his knees, have the same elegant, rebellious, and implacable style as when he plays tennis, when he walks, when he simply exists. At the chorus of "*Tu Vuo'fa l'Americano*," the audience dances as though it were ska, jumping, liberated, bumping hips at random. I let myself go in the general euphoria. I dance as though I know everyone or don't know anyone at all, the raspberries leaping out of my glass and G&T sloshing down my legs, tracing transparent paths down the clay stains.

I'm powerfully aware of my body as I lift my glass in the air. I don't think I've ever moved the way I'm moving right now. My arms, my head, like this. I like it. I'm stronger; I'm sexier. I'm caught up in the energy of the room, the pearls bouncing off the naked back, the music making the trumpeters dig their shoes into the sofa, liberated Samantha, the Atlanta skyline glowing against a midnight background. I wink at someone; he doesn't see; I don't care. I wink again; he doesn't see me again; I don't care.

I like who I am now, here. My hair, held back by sweat. I think I have to make the most of Atlanta. I drink. I have to make the most of the intellectual nights at the Booklands'. Six and Roberta. Mrs. Gee's patriotic flags and Andrew's psychedelic coffees. My lone drives in my bougie BMW and straight-punching Conchi. It can't be pure chance that I've ended up here with this family. After all, the universe and I have always gotten on well. This must be good; it has to be. Now that I've gotten this far, I have to get something out of it. I drink. I chew on a raspberry. Everything I'm feeling now is new and potent. This room, Princess Leia, a butler called Phillip. John. John. I let my head tip back and watch my arms in the air. Have I shaved my pits? Of course not. It's been two weeks. I wonder whether it was the fact that I know Juanito from La Boqueria that caught John's attention, or perhaps it's because I'm from Barcelona that he opened the doors to Sodom and Gomorrah for me. Or perhaps it's neither of those things. Perhaps it was me, just me. I feel proud. I feel like I own the scene. I think, in fact, that the only person who brought me here was me.

John and the other musicians are singing the last garbled words of the song, mouths wide, teeth white, chests hairy. With one final shout, John hugs his companions on the sofa; one kisses him on the mouth. The crowd goes wild. Atlanta is glowing on the other side of the window. And I think that this house, this moment, has to be, most definitely, the center of the universe.

Palamós Prawns or a Gun

Once I went clubbing in a ski suit. A competition ski suit, one of those tight ones. The night had started off at the Niu de l'Àliga mountain hut, on the highest peak of the Masella and La Molina ski resorts. And somehow, I ended up in Trànsit in my Spider-Man ski suit singing along to Raphael at the top of my lungs. Life.

Tonight, I'm trying out my tennis kit as party wear. The party has been extraordinary, in the literal sense of the word; I've never seen anything like it. I was totally unprepared, and it's become one of those "I'll just come for one beer" nights where you end up doing the bull run in flip-flops, hair dyed orange, running for your life, holding hands with a man in a braid. It's the music, the house, the oddity of the mix, but mainly it's John's flair for bringing together lost and wild souls, people who come here to be who they are and who don't care if it's a school night. You only get one life, and it happens at night.

It's six o'clock in the morning, and it's still going strong. The girl with the bare back has lost her pearl necklace. She's sitting in a corner doing a version of Amy Winehouse's "Back to Black," with a mournful trumpet. Phillip is sleeping on a sofa between two men with naked torsos. The politician is mixing another cocktail, and two drag queens are playing chess with their makeup still intact.

John and I are lounging in two armchairs at the end of the living room, next to large windows overlooking the gardens, which in turn overlook the wood. I danced so much, I've sweated out all the gin. We're tired but awake. Grubby and uninhibited.

"How are you?" John gazes out of the window contentedly.

"I think I'm getting the hang of it." I'm wolfing down a plate of spaghetti with pesto that I found in the refrigerator. With a Coke from a glass bottle.

John takes a sip of whiskey with the same moderation he showed with the first glass of the night.

"I never knew you were a singer." Or that you had such a hairy chest. How wonderful. "Or that you were so good at Italian."

"Italian's easy, if you know Spanish."

"You know Spanish? And you're just telling me now?"

"Rita, please. I can hold a conversation in Esperanto. Are you really surprised that I know Spanish?"

"You speak Esperanto?"

"I speak Esperanto. It's no big deal."

I finish my Coke in short sips. A weak light is starting to stain the treetops ochre, and a flock of birds is crossing the sky, decisively, as though they were running late.

"I don't suppose I need to tell you, but all this, tonight, these people . . . it has nothing to do with money or who my family is."

"I guess we'll never know."

"I hoped you'd notice that people here can feel free to be themselves."

"That's obvious. But why are you telling me? If you have to say it, it makes it less classy. Now you seem insecure."

"It's important to me that you understand that I'm more than my last name."

Then he grabs my fork and twists a roll of spaghetti. I let him chew. I let him swallow. He makes as if to light a cigarette but changes his mind. He leans back in the armchair, sliding his ass to the edge of the seat as though wanting to hide. He's less contented now, seeming to wrap himself in a heavy, transparent cloak of sadness:

"Rita, that night when I met Juanito, I had decided to kill myself."

Suddenly the trumpet is even more melancholic and shrill. I realize I have too much pesto in my mouth and I'm thirsty. I can't see the garden or the wood anymore. All I can see is John; all my attention is focused on him, not through curiosity, but because suddenly we've become real friends.

"What?"

"I was passing through Barcelona, on business, with my family. I used to travel with them. That morning, we had received a call telling us that someone had some photos of me . . . in a compromising situation . . . Compromising enough to ruin my family's image."

"I see . . ."

"It was a friend. I was eighteen, and all I wanted to do was to discover the world: Atlanta, New York, India—it didn't matter where, but alone, far away. And since I couldn't, I couldn't break the tie with my family and go wherever I wanted, when I wanted, sex was the only thing that sated me . . . that made me feel. Discovering emotions through women's bodies . . . and men's. Atlanta is a big city, but it's not so big when your name is Lapton. I don't know if you can imagine what it means to grow up in a conservative family in the Deep South."

"Well, no."

"I don't suppose any parent would like to receive a photograph of their son in the middle of a . . ." He sinks a bit deeper into his chair. Twenty years have passed, and the panic is still there. "An orgy . . . But if the photo comes with a demand for a million dollars and the threat of damaging the family's century-old reputation . . . Fame travels fast, and photos too."

"Shit, but that must have been the 1970s, no?"

"The 1970s? How old do you think I am? It was the 1980s, almost the 1990s . . . In the middle of the . . . the AIDS crisis."

"Shit." Shit.

"My family couldn't allow such a scandal, and they paid up. My family"—he wipes away a tear without hiding it—"my mother, my father, my siblings, it was never the same again."

My throat feels dry.

"And Juanito? What does he have to do with all this?"

"That night in Barcelona, I was alone, drifting from bar to bar. I'd had a lot to drink, but my mind was clear. And . . . and I was carrying my father's gun in my pocket." The word "gun" makes me shudder. "I waited all night.

"I wanted to go down to the rocks, by the sea, and shoot myself when the sun came up. I wanted my parents to find me dead next to the homeless, the junkies, the destitute . . . That was how they saw me." He pauses for a long time. Another tear rolls down his cheek. "I don't know if I would have actually gone through with it . . . but . . . just when I caught sight of Columbus, pink in the dawn light, at the top of his iron column at the foot of Las Ramblas, the feel of death still there in my pocket, it was the smell of prawns that stopped me."

"What? Did you say 'prawns'?"

"Yes, prawns. I know, it sounds stupid."

"It's the most sensible thing you've said all night."

"So, I followed that smell. It was a quarter past six in the morning. I remember perfectly because I checked my watch, looked up, and saw the wrought-iron arch saying 'Mercat de la Boqueria.' And standing beneath it was a short, brawny man, who seemed to have all the energy I was lacking."

"Juanito."

"Juanito. Two women were just leaving Bar Pinotxo, and then it was just me and him. The prawns were for him, but when he saw me, he decided to share them—it was like he had read my mind. It turns out that Juanito recognized the look on my face. He'd seen it years earlier, when a friend of his went to the bar for breakfast, as he did every day, but on that morning, he had decided to drink cyanide and died right there, in his arms. Juanito told me all this, but without making any comment about my situation. He told me everything, all the big things, the little things, that his friend had loved and decided to give up forever. Love, friends, the sea, his children. The simple beauty of life. Like the beauty of that moment. In Juanito, I saw the sorrow of a true friend. And I thought, okay, I didn't have the family I wanted, but I was able to choose my friends, true friends." Another tear and a smile. "Barcelona was waking up to a damp half-light, and Juanito and his prawns saved my life. I don't think he was fully aware of what had just happened, that he had just saved me. Before he left, he gave me a paper napkin that he made me sign with a blue ballpoint pen and a few tears. He wrote a phrase in Catalan that said, 'Whenever you come back, I'll be waiting for you behind this bar.'"

"Well then, we should go to La Boqueria together." My throat feels unbearably tight.

"Perhaps, but I don't know if I'm strong enough to go just yet. For the moment, when you go back, you can take him the napkin."

Atlanta is waking up in the distance, and two foxes creep across the garden. John and I sit in silence for a while, and I take his hand.

"Were they red?" I ask eventually.

"Red? Were what red?"

"The prawns, were they very red? It was a moment of such emotional intensity, you must remember the prawns."

"Yes, they were very red."

"Knew it. Palamós prawns. Nothing better."

"Jesus Christ, Rita."

When I wake up on the armchair, John has disappeared.

"Oh! My favorite rock star!" Phillip is opening letters at a desk in the entrance hall, looking impossibly fresh. His skin, his combed-back hair, the spotless shirt. Around him, a squad of cleaning staff is erasing all traces of the nocturnal epic.

"Good morning, Phillip."

"You look terrible," he says, "but, my word, you were quite the dancing queen last night! I love seeing someone dance with such a lack of inhibition!"

"What? It's no big deal . . ."

"I've drawn you a bath. On the second floor."

"Don't worry . . . I'll shower at home, I . . ."

"I won't hear of it. Go, and I'll get breakfast ready. In this house, we're professionals when it comes to hangover cures."

Never again will I criticize people who have a butler. He's a fucking wonder. Mind you, what Phillip has just said is exactly what Yaya tells me when I get home from a night out. Those two would hit it off.

The towel was very thick, the water pressure perfect, the shampoo magnolia scented. Red fruit. Green juice. An egg-white omelet. Pancakes.

"I'm going to Las Vegas later," I say. "To see Radiohead."

"Las Vegas? How tawdry, darling . . . But if you must go, eat at Osteria del Circo and ask for Rocco. Tell him I sent you."

The phone rings. I'm halfway through my omelet. I can't help watching with a touch of guilt as the employees sweep the floor and wash the windows. I'm not used to being on this side of the bar. Suddenly, an indignant head of curly hair appears from behind a curtain.

"Chancha!" Conchi looks like she's seen a ghost. "But . . . but . . . but, what the hell are you doing here?"

"Conchi! What are you doing here?"

"Well, working, isn't it obvious? I come as often as I can. No one pays as well as Mr. Lapton. God bless him." She crosses herself. "Don't tell the Booklands you saw me here, okay? Well, you can mention it to Fulbright, he knows, but not Hanne!"

"But why . . . ?"

"You shut up and don't answer back. Did you sleep here? Huh?" She checks that Phillip is still on the phone, coming so close I can smell her herby breath, and adds, "Did you . . . did you sleep with Mr. Lapton?" She crosses herself again.

“Conchi, please!” I laugh. “We were just hanging out until late, a group of us, and John . . . and Phillip, yes, John and Phillip invited me to stay over. I told Fulbright . . .” I take a slug of green liquid. “Have you seen John?”

“Rita, a bit of respect, please, this man is offering you his house. It’s Mr. Lapton. Hey, don’t you have to go pick up Bini? You’ll be late! I really don’t know why they haven’t thrown you out already.”

Chitawas and a Spectacular Gift Invoking God

The excuse worked. I think. I told the teacher, Miss Moore, that I was stopped by the police to take a breath test. But then she, who, to be fair, hadn't asked for any kind of explanation and was just putting green stickers on the Penguin class's paintings, froze and asked why the police stopped me. I said I didn't know, but that clearly the test had been negative, 0.0. She didn't laugh the way she usually laughs when she says goodbye.

"Sorry, Bini, were you waiting long?"

"A bit . . ." He isn't very happy, staring at the horizon from his booster seat.

"I'll make some pancakes when we get home, all right?"

"All right . . ."

Surprising. Shit, I've played my last card.

"Are you okay?"

Silence. Angry lips. Finally, he blurts it out.

"Today I saw a dog just like Goldie." Goldie is the neighbors' dog; Bini is wearing a yellow cap that's too big for him and obscures half his field of vision. "It was just like Goldie, but it wasn't Goldie. But just the same. Identical."

"Mm-hmm . . . and what about it?"

"Well, I went to say hello."

"And?"

"Why has no one ever told me there are ten, fifty identical dogs? It's very strange. Like, it would be strange if there were a thousand Evas or Aksels, wouldn't it? Or a thousand Miss Moores?" He must have gotten embarrassed when he went to pet the dog. "Why don't they tell you on the news?"

I make him pancakes anyway. He's so indignant about Goldie and the massive dog-cloning scam that I feel sorry for him. I have an hour to pack my bag.

Eva's playing in the games room downstairs; she has a playdate with Mary, the daughter of Pastor Paul. In this country, pastors have children, and there's a name for a friend coming to play at your house: a playdate.

"Rita, could you come here a moment?" Aksel's very red face is waiting for me in his room. He wants to talk rap.

"Shoot."

"I'd like you to take me to these bars." He hands me a list with the address of each venue. "I have to see how they perform." He pulls at a hangnail and adopts a serious expression to hide his nerves.

"Bars? MJQ? I know that one. But, Aksel, these bars are only open at night."

"I can jump out the window—it wouldn't be the first time."

"What?" He's just gone up in my estimation, way, way up, but I have to play my part. "Are you crazy? If your parents caught us, they'd send me straight back to Barcelona."

"Rita"—he looks up—"I have to go. It's vital. You said you'd help me find the flow, didn't you? If I don't see live rap, I can't feel it."

"Okay, let me think about it. Right now, I have to go—my plane leaves soon. What's all this?"

"It's a computer, can't you see? I've just finished it. I just need to give it a name. I like 'Chitawas.'"

"Chitawas?"

"It's a canal in Nicaragua. I saw it in a book about the country's indigenous toponymy. It's a remote region that—"

"But why did you pick that name?!"

"The other day I saw it on a note on Dad's desk."

"One moment."

I go to Ful's desk and look at all the notes, but there's nothing that says "Chitawas." Aksel's at the door. "What are you doing, Hairy?" he says with a long, hard look.

Shit, I'll miss my flight.

Backpack ready for two days: concert and party. I'm going to see Radiohead live! Radiohead! Live! Four pairs of panties, three dresses, and the writing notebook Roberta gave me. Condoms? But I'm only going to hook up with a girl!

I add a final PS to the email I'm writing and click send. I peek at Eva and Mary through the games room door. Sitting side by side on the floor, they're labeling creepy-crawlies in Spanish before sticking them to different parts of a giant tree set out in the middle of the room.

I still need my toothbrush and passport. I open the drawer of my nightstand to get my passport, and freeze. Oh, look: two old friends. The memory is so strong, I have to take a moment and sit on the edge of the bed. I still have time.

I remember every detail of the night I received them. The annual dinner with all my friends should have been two weeks after I left, but we brought it forward so that I could join in. It was a great night.

The first part of the gift came with the batteries in, already switched on, inside a shuddering bag. I grabbed it, not really knowing what to expect, and, surprise, it was a vibrator with a dolphin's face, grinning naughtily. I couldn't imagine a better gift.

The second part was a little stuffed-pig keychain. Not just any old keychain, or any old pig. In addition to its luscious blond hair, the pig has an oversized member between its legs. The Incredible Penis, as well as having a glans like a rocket, has an extra function: The penis extends and withdraws. And it does so, shuddering, to the beat of "I Want to Break Free." (I can only imagine the reaction of the parents of the pig's designer, on learning that this is the outcome of the degree they paid for.) It's the best gift in history.

"Ritaaaaa!" Bini's wild cry brings me out of my phallic reminiscence. He's even more hysterical than usual. Something's up. I've left the stove on; I've left the stove on! The house is exploding! "Ritaaaaa!"

I leap up the stairs three at a time, heart in my mouth. I go into the kitchen, but the stove is off. Aksel sneaks out of his parents' study, crying with laughter. Bastards, I'll get them.

"What the fuck is going on, Bini? Shit, you scared me!"

I'm hyperventilating. Bini is sitting at his father's computer, and he doesn't like what he sees on the screen. Shit. He sticks his head out on one side and, with absolute calm, says, "I'm going to tell Mom and Dad that you said 'fuck' and 'shit.'"

"Look, Bini, I've told you a thousand times not to shout like that, you hear me? What the fuck is going on?"

"You said 'fuck' again."

"Bini! I'm leaving."

"No, no, Hairy, please, come here! Aksel says that all Goldies are the same. That they're really clones. That they all know me. That all dogs are like this sheep. Look at this sheep!"

Dolly is on the screen. I hear Aksel cracking up in his bedroom.

"Bini, dogs aren't clones." He's on the verge of tears. Chin wobbling at supersonic speed. "Take it easy, they really aren't clones. Only Goldie knows you. The only thing is that it's hard to tell them apart because they look a lot alike. If you come to Barcelona one day, I'm sure you'll see clones of me too."

"What?"

I don't know if I've convinced him. I just want to open Fulbright's email. "Go and check over your homework, Bini."

"I've already done it—it's all fine."

"Well, draw a house or stick some stickers, or do that thousand-piece puzzle."

"I've done it."

"What?"

"I finished it last night."

"And when did you start it?"

"Last night."

"All right then, read, Bini. Grab a volume of the encyclopedia like a normal Bookland and read!"

"All right, Hairy."

Now for some serious business: HunkPorn.

> You have one new message from Federico Chitawas in your inbox.

Contact has been made! What do I do? If I open it, will I be able to leave it marked as "unread"?

> My dear, dear Fulbright, we're going to meet in person at last. I'll meet you at the Atlanta Marriott Marquis on December 15 at 1 p.m. I can't wait.

Each word of the message makes my body temperature drop another degree. I feel as though I've just stolen something expensive.

Ding-dooooong.

I close all the tabs, Dolly included, and go downstairs.

"Hello, Rita, dear! How are you?" Pastor Paul holds out his hand, large and strong. He's wearing an expensive suit jacket, white linen (but it's almost winter, sir!), and a black tie with a dove at the tip. He looks like Michael Jackson.

"Ah, Paul, hi. Fine, fiiiine . . . The girls are having a great time! Eva has a giant tree, and they've decorated it with the names of animals in Spanish."

"Sorry, what did you say? What have they done?"

"Decorated a tree. And put the names in Spanish."

"Wonderful, wonderful . . . If you could call them, please. We're in a hurry. I'm giving a service in less than an hour."

The girls have heard Paul's deep, celestial voice and are running noisily around the games room, adding the finishing touches to whatever it is they've been doing all afternoon.

"Ladiiiiies . . ." I put on my best devoted and responsible au pair voice.

The door doesn't open. Paul looks at me expectantly, hands crossed in front of his groin, and he clears his throat. Finally, I open the door, and the spectacle unfolds.

The floor is covered in blankets that are the sea, books that are boats, and Ping-Pong balls that are buoys. The most interesting thing, however, is happening on the island.

The two girls, sweaty, unkempt, dirty, and happy, present their work with open arms.

The tree has become a kind of party house where beings of all species and categories come together. The little creatures and fruits with Spanish labels, "*tomates*" and "*plátanos*," have been usurped by an invasion of Barbies, Polly Pockets, Playmobil figures, and soldiers from the American Revolutionary War. Every room is having its own party.

At the bottom, submarine Barbie is drinking tea with the Playmobil chemistry teacher. A Post-it labels the scene as "The periodic table isn't just Mendeleev's."

One floor up, we see Ken with a snake around his waist, showing off his muscles to three Polly Pockets.

On the next floor, American Idol Barbie (how many Barbies has Mary brought with her?) is singing next to a Playmobil figure in a Mexican sombrero, the token Latino of the group. Behind some palm trees, a surfer Ken is recounting anecdotes to a line of Native Americans that the girls have pulled out of the Black Hills War, just when Aksel had them all positioned properly. The scene is spectacular.

I'm sure you could sell this as a multidisciplinary educational exploration of the mixing of ethnicities, religions, and cultural interests. But when I look at Paul, I don't understand what's gone wrong; his mouth is agape, and he's transfixed on one specific spot.

I follow the invisible line of the pastor's glare and reassess the tree to realize that I haven't yet looked at the very top, where gold glitter spells out the word GOD.

A lone figure is enjoying the most privileged views this Friday afternoon. Alone, radiant, spread-eagled. I feel slightly dizzy. I move quickly, with no thought other than to speed up their departure; I babble any old nonsense, random ideas. I even laugh, but it's all useless. It's too late: Pastor Paul, the most important man in the Methodist church in DeKalb County, the deep voice that soothes every resident of Leafmore and elicits reverence wherever he goes, has seen it: the pig, the Incredible Penis.

"One moment!" exclaims Mary.

The pig's extendible penis has gotten stuck on the third floor, between the Latino Playmobil's guitar and a pop-star Ken's microphone, but only until the tiny fingers of sweet Mary, the pastor's daughter (I sure hope he doesn't have a gun hidden in his Michael Jackson jacket), manage to free it. And to the sound of "I Want to Break Free," bouncing between Playmobils and Barbies, the giant foreskin slowly climbs back to the top to find the body of God and the heat of his blond balls sitting imperiously on the celestial throne.

It takes all my strength to turn and look at him. Pastor Paul is grasping some kind of religious ornament hanging round his neck and issuing unintelligible prayers, his gaze lost. Lost I don't know where. Eva is no longer laughing, and Mary is watching her father.

"Dad?" asks Mary, pushing her hair back with the dolphin vibrator that I've only just noticed. Jesus Christ. My toes go numb. "Dad?"

But her father doesn't reply. He's too focused on invoking all the saints and enough testaments to part the waters.

"Mary, let's go." His tone is terrifyingly calm. "Let's go right now."

"Yes, yes, of course . . . I'll see you to the door," I answer.

"No need."

His oceanic blue eyes bore into the back of my brain. Pastor Paul and sweet Mary climb the stairs painfully slowly; he opens the door and lets his daughter go out first. He throws me one last deathly stare (shit, it isn't all that bad, is it?), and before he can say anything, I get in first:

"I'll be at church on Wednesday, Paul."

But Paul doesn't answer and shuts the door, making it clear that this doesn't end here.

I look at my watch and realize that I've got an hour and a half before my flight to Las Vegas.

The Grand Canyon

"Racons, Rita Racons, with just one *o*, Racons."

The airline employee is blond and pretty. She checks the list again and the heart-shaped diamond on her teeth sparkles hypnotically.

"Oh, Racoons!" The diamond is still glittering. "That's you." She looks up; she's not smiling now. "My dear, we called you over the loudspeaker an hour ago!"

"Oh, ah."

"I'm sorry, dear, you've missed your flight."

My only thought is that I want her to keep flipping the pages so I can watch her teeth scatter the light.

"That can't be right! I got here on time!"

"Well, no, you didn't. You missed the tulips. The next available flight to Las Vegas leaves in seven hours and will cost an extra four hundred and thirty-two dollars."

I don't have four hundred and thirty-two dollars.

"Shit. It's very important. I have to catch another one. I have to fly as soon as possible . . . I have a wedding." I'm lying. I want to see Rachel.

"Yes, I understand . . . I wouldn't want to miss a Las Vegas wedding either."

Oh shit, yes, the cliché, brides dressed as Marilyn, grooms as hot dogs.

"Are there any other options?"

"Other options, dear?" I don't reply. "Well, you could fly to Phoenix, pray inside a car, and—"

"Pray inside a car?"

"Pray? Inside a car?" She lets out a little laugh, but tries to cover it up. "Sorry, my dear, I don't understand . . ."

"Nothing, nothing, please continue . . ."

"I was saying that you could pray inside a car and reach Las Vegas in around five hours. Don't worry, if you've managed to go . . . how old are you? Twenty-six, twenty-seven years without going—"

"Twenty-three." I drink too much.

"Twenty-three years without setting foot in Las Vegas, you can manage another day."

"Yes, and the wedding isn't today—it's tomorrow."

"Let me see . . . There's a flight to Phoenix in an hour and a half, and it will cost an extra hundred and seventy dollars, dear."

I'm glad when Six doesn't pick up and I can leave her a voice message. I apologize for the change of plans, tell her not to have a fit because I'm not coming the way she planned. "Hopefully I'll be able to sleep on the way . . . I'll pay for the night at the hotel either way." I hope I have enough money for everything.

I catch a driverless train to Terminal C. There, I take a moment of respite to sit at one of the computers and rent the cheapest car in the entire southern fleet.

"With just one *o*, Racons." I'm in Phoenix already.

"I've got you." The woman at the car rental place doesn't look at me. She has several inches of roots showing. "Dang it . . ."

"What is it?" What the hell has gone wrong now?

"We don't have the model you asked for, but don't worry, I'll give you an upgrade. Wait here."

Outside the windows of the Phoenix airport, I see a brownish mountain with three peaks, superimposed against a blue sky that's starting to turn pink. I've gained three very necessary hours through the time change. All the more necessary given that I haven't the faintest idea where to go now.

"Joe will bring it round for you." The accidental surfer emo returns to her place, still without looking at me. "I'll give it to you for the same price. Now I need a signature here, here, here, and here. And here, here, and here."

I feel like I've just signed for a mortgage.

"Ready, then. I'm going to Las Vegas, you know?"

"Hmm . . ."

"To a Radiohead concert," I continue in Catalan. "And there's a good possibility I might fuck a girl. For the second time."

"Turn around." She raises her head and finally looks me in the eye. "It's here."

A wrinkly man arrives at the wheel of a Mustang convertible, all red and shiny—the car, not the man—and from the pristine state of the wheels, it looks like it's never left this parking lot in the middle of the desert.

"You're the first," she says, now with a winning smile. "I guess today's your lucky day."

That afternoon on the roof terrace with Yaya, when I imagined America for the first time, I thought of all the classic, hugely predictable scenes of what I might do here. Spitting from the top of the Empire State Building, spitting tobacco into the grass at a baseball game.

But I also pictured the image from that Lonely Planet cover I used to see for years on the shelf in the travel section of Puigcerdà library—that dead-straight, endless highway surrounded by desert and sunshine with a single car heading into the unknown. I can't remember who was driving, but the image of the girl in the passenger seat with her hair flapping in the wind, arms raised, was as clear that afternoon on the roof as it was in the library.

Who would have thought, when I sat in the library, chatting with the oldsters who went there to read the newspaper, that one day in the not-too-distant future that windswept girl surrounded by desert would be me. And that I'd be alone, in the driver's seat.

In fact, your hair blows about much less than you'd think when you drive with the top down. I'm going at eighty-nine miles per hour, with the windows open, and I can still hear my music and keep my ponytail in place. "Born in the USA" is on the radio, which seems terribly apt.

I pass through a hamlet of six houses and a gas station, stalled in the 1960s, and from the faces of an old couple making their wooden porch creak with the movement of their rocking chairs, I can tell this isn't the direct route to Las Vegas.

I drive as though I'm the star of a life-affirming art-house epic, and I shout out loud. It's very cold, but I'm well wrapped up, a hoodie cocooning my head. The *Thelma and Louise* of the Pyrenees. I take a certain pleasure in not sharing this moment with anyone, being alone in the middle of nowhere, far away from the children and far away from important decisions about who I am and what I'm supposed to be doing right now. Far away from not finding what I've come to look for. I haven't even brought my camera. I'm going so fast, it feels like I'm running away or I have to get somewhere, but neither of those things is true; the fact is that the car is fucking incredible. I'm not thinking about very much at all. I don't really know where I'm going, and for the last two hours, I've been crossing something called the Tonto National Forest.

I look all around and find a new landscape, rugged and brown. I've never seen anything like it, not even at the Monegros Festival, in the middle of the Aragon desert. Never-ending plains disappearing into the horizon, now an angry orange. Three-armed cactuses as tall as trees. Brown dunes, reddish sky, my convertible, and me. I think I'd like to see a snake. A freight train advances at the same speed as me; car after car cutting through the landscape without disturbing the color palette. I can even hear its creaking chug along the tracks.

I'm in the fucking Wild West.

Night is falling, and I'm still driving without turning the wheel, except when I overtake huge trucks with two trailers covered in lights. Where's the fun in driving like this? Two hours later, at the end of that long, straight road, I reach Flagstaff, the village where backpackers stay when they visit the Grand Canyon. Ladies and gentlemen, I'm at the Grand Canyon, damn it!

The truth is that I really want to see Rachel, Six, and the Las Vegas trash in general, but what kind of degenerate passes the Grand Canyon in a red convertible and doesn't stop?

Cold

"Are you on your own?"

"Damn, did you just use the most clichéd pickup line in history?"

"Yes." He laughs and holds out his hand. "Michael."

"Rita."

"Can I buy you a beer? And yes, that's the second most clichéd line."

Man, what a clean accent, what clear English. Or perhaps . . . am I finally getting the hang of English?

"Where are you from?"

"I'm from Portland, Oregon. Two-quarters Norwegian, one-quarter Irish, and one-quarter German."

And a whole stick of smooth butter.

Michael couldn't be more white or more blond. From his muscular back, I can tell he must do rock climbing or extreme kayaking, and his entire upper body seems to tilt slightly forward, as does his chin. Although he might not sound very promising from my description, Michael is actually pretty good-looking.

Janis Joplin is singing "Me and Bobby McGee" from a loudspeaker in the corner of the stone courtyard full of day-trippers and travelers.

"What are you doing in Flagstaff?" He's friendly and has very pale eyes.

"See that car there? That beauty?" I've parked right at the entrance. Michael and I are leaning on the wooden railings separating the hostel veranda from the parking lot. "It's the one to blame. It brought me here."

"Well then, let's drink to its wise decision." We take a long drink and fall into a comfortable silence. The night has become warmer. "You're reading *The Catcher in the Rye*?" The book is poking out of my backpack. "Didn't you read it in high school?"

"Yes, of course I read it, of course I did!"

I haven't taken it out of my backpack since I finished it. Often, when I embark on a writing piece for Roberta, I copy a chapter with the aim of starting off with rhythm and hope.

"All I can remember is the bit where it says something like 'Why do we have to stop loving someone when they die if they're better than those who are still alive . . .'"

I show him where I underlined those words in the book.

"Wow!" He raises his beer.

"Thanks," I reply.

"And what are you reading now?"

"Capote. Short stories. I love them."

"One of the most exported writers in the history of America. I don't like him. Not because he was popular, of course; that's a good thing. It's his style, I don't . . . Too much character description. Have you read *In Cold Blood*?"

"Not yet, but I'll get to it one day. What about you, Michael? What are you doing in Flagstaff?"

"I live here. I'm a guide. My job is to go down into the Grand Canyon, to the river. Once we're down there, we camp and drink wine and eat cheese bagels and chicken. You could say I'm paid to watch the most spectacular night sky you'll ever see. I have the best job in the world."

"You make me jealous saying that."

"Don't you like your job?"

"Yes, but it's a temporary job, just for now. Truthfully, I'm on the hunt for the job of my life, but it isn't that easy."

"Of course not. Finding what you want to do in life is something that should be approached with calm. Like truly falling in love, and that doesn't happen very much."

"And you can fall in love more than once."

"Sure. Perhaps there's more than one vocation. Maybe one day it will end and another will appear. What I do believe, however, is that if you have the slightest bit of self-love, you should sit down one day and grant yourself the privilege, or pain, of planning it."

"Amen to that." I raise my beer. Michael laughs. "Anyway . . . what you were saying about the sky . . ."

"The most spectacular night sky you'll ever see in your life," he repeats.

"You only say that because you've never seen the sky over the Pyrenees."

"Maybe, but there's only one way to find out. Shall we?" he asks.

"Now?"

Michael grins from ear to ear.

"Right now."

"You're telling me you want us to walk down there right now? The bottom of the goddamn Grand Canyon at eleven o'clock at night?"

"Life is short!" He drinks.

"Michael, that's your name, right? Michael?" He laughs. "I've known you for three minutes, and you're asking me to go on probably the most memorable excursion of my life with you."

Shit, now I don't know what to do. At reception, they said that there's no phone coverage at the bottom of the canyon, and no doubt when we reach the river, this quarter-Norwegian, four-ninths German, eight-sevenths whatever, and Yankee from top to toe will murder me, cut me into a thousand pieces, and chuck me into the river. Coyote food, et cetera.

"Come on, then, let's go!"

"What? Really?" He's obviously amazed.

"Really. Yes, let's go."

Michael sways back and forth weirdly and starts laughing.

"Shit, woman, you're crazy. I was joking. It's eleven o'clock at night, and I've had four beers."

"Oooooh . . . That's disappointing."

"You don't know what you're saying."

"I'm in very good shape."

He keeps laughing, shakes his head, laughs some more.

"Look," he says, "why not wait six hours. We'll get up before sunrise. We'll start along Bright Angel and reach the river in time for breakfast."

"It's a tempting offer, but I'm going to Las Vegas tomorrow. I have a date with Thom Yorke."

"Shit! You're going to the concert? Nice . . . All right then, I know I don't stand a chance against Radiohead. But if you change your mind, I'll be in the hotel parking lot at six tomorrow morning."

It's been a long time since I opened my eyes at six o'clock in the morning. Of course, it's not every day you get up knowing you're going to see Thom Yorke. When I wake, it's still dark, but the first glint of sunlight is starting to erase the stars from the sky. I think about Michael's sad puppy eyes, so cute; him in the parking lot, the Grand Canyon waiting for us . . . But the idea of hearing "Creep" live makes me snap them shut again.

I share a shower with a couple of Norwegian girls. I don't pay any attention. Not even anthropologically speaking. I wash my hair—who knows what will happen when I reach Vegas or when I'll next have time to shower—and I go to see how my love spent the night. I head for the parking lot and find her there, as red, shiny, and spotless as when I met her yesterday.

Now I'm sitting in the hostel kitchen, surrounded by adventurers like me, who are preparing a hearty breakfast.

Well, "breakfast" . . . It must be harder to cook that round of yellow plastic they call an "omelet" than it is to break an egg in a pan and let it cook itself. For the love of God, what a strange omelet; if Yaya saw this, she'd use it to wipe down the counters. Admittedly, the sausages aren't bad. I've wrapped six in a napkin and stuck them in my pocket. And one of those omelets too; it's protein after all. Anyway, it's quite the scene: a Styrofoam plate, a round, beige omelet, and bacon so greasy, it dribbles down my chin. Climate change for breakfast. And to think that just twenty-four hours ago, Phillip served me an egg-white omelet worthy of El Bulli. Life, eh.

I toss my backpack onto the back seat, pat the sausages in my pocket, and look up. The sky is vast. The clouds move slowly, in elongated shapes, and a piece of paper flutters against the windshield of the Mustang: *Look me up on Facebook: Michael McAfee. Yes, like the antivirus.*

All right then, I'll have to join Facebook. I wouldn't tell her as much, but Six is usually right about everything. I'm sure I'll get hooked.

I drive for just over fifteen minutes and leave the car in one of the parking lots. The few cars there are all American, license plates from all the states, and I'm rather pleased to recognize the Georgia peach on a huge Jeep. It's sunny and it's cold and it's fucking amazing.

I'm nervously excited. I'm about to see one of the wonders of the world.

I grab my backpack, walk over to a secondary viewpoint, aware of the significance of the moment, and before I even raise my eyes, I'm grinning impulsively: The Grand Canyon, quite literally, is at my feet.

The word "enormous" doesn't do it justice. From here, it seems infinite, much bigger than I ever imagined. I can't help myself: I look to either side, confirm that I'm alone, that none of the overweight security guards are watching, and I jump the fence.

I make my way down a narrow dirt path, barely wide enough for both feet side by side, and continue to the end, where a sheltered stone in the shape of a seat seems to be waiting for me.

It's incredible.

The noises are becoming fainter. The cries of children, car doors slamming—it all fades away. The light creeping between the mountains picks out the varying shades of brown in the canyon. I settle my back into a comfy nook, not caring if my white sweater gets stained by the red earth.

Although it's barely an hour since I had breakfast, I eat a sausage. It's not hunger. It's to control my sense of overwhelm, what Astrid once tipsily diagnosed as Stendhal syndrome. Whenever I find myself gazing at a landscape as stunning as this, I feel like I'm not equipped to absorb it. That it isn't enough for me to look, listen, and touch it—that I need something else—and activating my taste buds always helps. I need to occupy all my senses to assimilate the moment fully. Even if it's an overcooked sausage.

The sun rises and shortens the horizontal shadows of the craggy precipices. I think I'd like to listen to the Bob Dylan song "Blowin' in the Wind." Yes, I'm a romantic. But when all is said and done, you can always find the answers in the wind.

My phone rings.

"Albert?"

"Rita?"

"Broooo! Fantastic! Albeeeert! How are you calling me here? How did you do it? It'll cost you a fortune! Man, you won't believe where I am! Right now, right at this moment, I'm . . . can you hear me?"

"Yes."

"I'm at the Grand Canyon! Albert, the Grand Canyon! It's right in front of me, below me, well, inside me! I mean I'm inside it—I'm in the Grand Canyon! It sounds impossible, right?"

"Jeez, Rita . . . That's exciting, how cool . . . I'd love to be there with you! But where are you exactly?"

"Here, on a rock, hidden away where no one can see me. It's so, so impressive!"

"But could you fall?"

"Fall? What do you mean? Are you crazy?" I laugh.

"Rita . . ."

"What's up?"

"We tried to call you at home, but there was no one there. We didn't know you'd gone to the Grand Canyon. Wow . . . that's awesome."

"Albert . . ."

"Are you alone?"

"Yes, what's happened?" He won't say it; I don't understand. "Hey, man, you're scaring me. What's happened?"

"It's Yaya." An electric shock goes through my brain.

"What? What's happened?" He doesn't reply. "Albert!"

"Yaya developed pneumonia last week . . ."

"Shit, okay, and how is she?"

"Rita . . ." Albert's voice breaks. "Yaya is dead."

A dense fog invades every corner of my body, crushing down on my shoulders and my eyelids. I can't see clearly, I have goose bumps on my forearms. My throat closes over. I can't breathe properly, and I lose my orientation for a moment.

I hear my brother's voice at the other end of the line, but I can't make out what he's saying. I can't get any words out. I try to remember how to breathe. Albert raises his voice, but I don't react. He shouts, "Rita!"

"I'm . . . I'm here."

"Can you hear me?"

"And . . . and Mom? And Dad?"

"They're fine, everyone's fine . . . but I wanted to be the one to tell you. Rita, Rita, I love you, and you have to be brave. You hear me?"

I can't speak.

"Is there a café nearby? Do you have water? Is your friend there?"

"I'll . . . I'll go to the airport right now. I have a backpack . . . and an omelet. I'll get the next plane. I still have sausages. I'm on my way. I have my passport. I'll go to the airport."

"Listen to me . . ." He speaks slowly; I can tell he's struggling. He takes a deep breath. "Listen . . . Yaya made me promise not to tell you until today."

"What? Why today? I reckon it'll take me twelve, fourteen hours to get to Alp . . . Perhaps a bit longer. Hopefully I can find a direct flight. I have . . . I have to see her."

"Rita, listen to me. Yaya made me promise . . ." He's crying; my brother is crying. "She made me promise not to tell you until today . . . Until . . . until we'd buried her."

An invisible hand crushes my heart, making my body shrink in on itself.

"What? No. That can't be . . ."

"She knew she was dying, Rita." Albert tries to sound strong, but his voice is wavering. "I saw it in her eyes . . . and she told me. She made me promise because she knew that the moment I told you, you would want to come. She wants . . . She wanted you to stay there, in Atlanta, in the States. She said you shouldn't come back yet. She said that if you stayed for longer, you'd find what you're looking for."

"No. I can't believe it."

"Rita—"

"I don't care. I'm going."

"Okay, whatever you want . . . Rita?"

My body is levitating; the fog is now a cloud, a very heavy cloud. I press into my eyes with my fist.

"Albert." I can no longer take in what he's saying. "I have to go, I need to be alone, I'll be fine, don't worry about me."

He says something, and, from the tone, I gather that he more or less agrees.

After an hour, or three, I don't know, my body uncurls. As though, after fighting my way through the chaotic spiderweb of an absurd unconsciousness, suddenly the light has come on. I start walking downhill.

A dirt track cuts the steep slope in a sharp zigzag. The hillside is so sheer that the lines are almost horizontal, turning at very sharp angles. I move away from my hidden rock as if there's a way to escape what just happened. What I've just felt. I'm at the Grand Canyon, and I feel claustrophobic.

I was driving a red convertible, and Yaya is dead.

I look at the sky, trying to sharpen my gaze, as though seeing for the first time. Or is it the last time? My brain and my heart are devastated, white, hard, sterile surfaces. All I feel is cold.

I look at the recent calls on my phone to make sure that Albert's call actually happened. Because it's impossible. It has to be impossible. But I see it on the screen; I'm not dreaming.

What was I doing two days ago? How come I didn't feel that she was no longer there, that Yaya had gone? I didn't notice a thing. And why didn't she call me? Why didn't she call me to tell me she was dying?

I want to call her to tell her that she died.

Dust

I've been walking for three hours, and I still haven't seen the river. My eyes are red and swollen, my mouth full of tears, and try as I might, I can't seem to remember her face. My only memory is of the time when I wanted her to pass me the Marcilla coffee, but it came out as "morcilla" coffee, and then she started laughing so much, she had to go out to the vegetable patch, because morcilla is blood sausage and not the kind of thing you'd want anywhere near your coffee. All I can see is that image, her faded tunic, the curlers in her hair held down by my brother's red bathing suit, her back to me, her smell of bleach and orchard. That's all I remember. Over and over. Over and over.

The paths are covered with mule shit, round and black. I have no reception.

For hours I've been walking, puffing with rage, sadness, and panic, hours witnessing the history of planet Earth traced in the lines of stone, cream-colored stripes on orange. Centuries that don't even come to an inch in depth. Yaya's life isn't even an inch. She's no more than a miserable speck of dust in this six-million-year-old ravine.

So, what does all of this mean? Is that it? All those years, when she was young, picking olives, cleaning rich people's houses, when she had to hide from her mother's beatings? Where does all that go now? Her voice, her infinite joy, her spotlight on the stage . . . it's all turned to dust.

I stop to catch my breath at a bend overlooking a cliff. I sit with my legs dangling. In every direction, a horizon of dusty ochres with a scrap of green from the pines. I look up and see that the wooden railing and the first zigzag in the path are out of sight. I'm inside the canyon and not entirely sure how I got here. I haven't met a soul. I'm still descending, along little paths down such steep slopes that in some places I have to skid on all fours. I don't know if I should be going down here. I'm tired and thirsty.

Right now, I should be with my family. I should have been in Alp two weeks ago, to wrap her up warm, to tell her not to go out to the vegetable patch without her jacket, that it's cold. To scold her. To take care of her, to laugh with her, to tell her I love her, to tell her I hate her for doing this to me.

I curse every day I've spent here, every day I wasn't with her. I curse the Booklands and Atlanta and Six and Roberta and John. I give it some thought, but I can't think of any moment in my life that fulfilled me more than when I was at home, with my family, when I was with her, when I knew that Yaya was alive. Everything else now strikes me as absurd.

I've been walking for more than five hours. I'm pretty tired. Not so much because of the time I've spent walking but because of the continual, eroded slope of the mountainside. Because of the pain. I must have come down several thousand feet. I'm right inside it. It's getting colder, and I'm seriously thirsty. My tongue is covered in dust, and my face has a coating of fine red dirt with transparent lines of tears and snot; I think of Wilson, the volleyball Tom Hanks adopted in *Castaway*.

From up here, I can see where the path continues, stretching on and crossing a vast, green plateau until it finally disappears, dropping down the precipice. The path is like a fine crack, a white scar. And I'd swear, if I'm not starting to hallucinate, I can see the river. Yes, I can see it. I'm closer to the river than the sky.

She said that if you stayed for longer, you'd find what you're looking for. Albert's words echo over and over in my head.

Water

I followed the white path cutting through the green like a crack, and when I reached the end, I found that I hadn't been hallucinating: The river wasn't close, but it was within reach.

My last few steps took me over a suspension bridge spanning the Colorado River. I grabbed firmly onto the steel cables and walked until I could feel the earth beneath my feet again. I passed a small stone arch and came out on the other side of the mountain, where I found a small group of people washing plates in the river.

Michael was sitting on a rock, holding a piece of rope between his teeth and tying a knot with the remaining length. Each dry tug to tighten the knot accentuated his glowing white triceps, and I wondered how the hell I could be thinking about Michael's triceps at a moment like this. When he finally saw me, his mouth dropped open so far that the rope fell to the ground, and he got up slowly, as though he couldn't believe what he was seeing.

"What the . . . fucking hell," he said out loud, as though seeing a ghost (a ghost with a face like a red volleyball).

When I utter the words "My grandmother is dead" for the first time, I burst into tears. Michael just hugs me. And, when I stop crying, he feeds me like a puppy. Then he heats some water, wets a towel, and gently wipes my face, hands, and arms. And he insists—a bit—on giving me the clean clothes he brought for tomorrow, which consist of a Sleater-Kinney T-shirt and some dry white socks.

Michael's clients today are two very nice, very American couples, who are very keen to console me. One pair is redheaded, the other white-blond, both of them.

I thank the multicolored group for sharing their breaded chicken, nachos, and vanilla Coca-Cola with me, and I take my leave.

I grab the sleeping bag, courtesy of Michael who brought a spare, and walk along the river. The last light of the day is saying farewell to the stones of this deep ravine of muted ochres, and suddenly a wave of purplish light brings the cold. The light fades as though it has simply run out of strength, and I feel the cold weight of this black day.

I take a very narrow path flanked by two very high walls that I stroke with my open arms, and end up somewhere surprising: a small semicircle of sandy beach, where dinosaurs must have napped millions of years ago. A small bay in the middle of the mountains.

It's just the night and me. There's no more light, or thirst, or cold. Now all I have is fear.

It's an incipient nostalgia for the future—the fear that I won't be able to tell her everything that happens to me from now on. I'd like to tell her that I still haven't found my vocation, and that I might never find it, but that I'm glad I listened to her that day on the roof with the clothes on the line fluttering against the light. That I'm happy to have discovered Atlanta, to have met the Booklands, Six, John, and Roberta . . . to have faced up to myself. I'd like to tell her I loved her and that she would be proud of me.

I close my eyes with a sigh of utter exhaustion. And I fall asleep with a sudden and absurd question: Did I lock the car?

I dream that I'm in the shaft of a dark well, that I'm shouting, but no one can hear me. Then an urgent gulp wakes me suddenly. I can feel my heartbeat in my mouth; my teeth are tingling; I'm struggling to breathe. I press down on my chest with both hands, as though I could curb my heart. Intense.

I look around me, trying to figure out where I am.

How long have I been asleep?

Little by little, my breathing calms and synchronizes with my heartbeat . . . I lie down again.

I close my eyes, inhaling deeply, taking in the scent of dust and water. And when I reopen them, I'm met with an epic scene: The most amazing starry sky in history is blanketing me like a *National Geographic* poster.

The universe is spread out before me in a shimmer of colors. It's incredible, absolutely incredible! This must be what it's like to travel back to prehistory, or into space, the Milky Way like an open wound in the sky, gushing with millions of stars.

Suddenly, the memories start to flood through me, as though they were raising their hands one over the other and begging me not to forget them, for me to describe them, to write it all down.

And each and every one, no matter how old, now appears so clearly, it seems impossible that one day they might fade. But I can't bet on that.

I take out my notebook and pen, and I start to write.

Each word, each image I remember of her, seems to give me a little more peace. The agony and fog that overpowered me this morning, on that blighted rock, have started to dissipate.

Some of the memories come from long ago, in shapes and colors and textures that I was too young to understand at the time.

I write about her hands, the strange iridescent, beetle-like shades that she used to paint her nails; the elongated holes in her ears from her dangly earrings; her white breasts "that have never seen the sun."

I think I'll need a thousand years to describe every corner of her room. The supermarket bags stashed everywhere. I remember the snow. Snow is one of the clearest images. When the first snow of winter started to fall, wherever she was, whatever she was doing, Yaya would stop and drop everything to run outside and watch the silent, opaque sky that only comes with proper snowfall. By the end of winter, she would be cursing it, but that first fall was magical. I found it amazing that, after so many years and so many winters, she could still be so surprised, but her little-girl's grin at the sight of the flakes, with their impossible geometry, melting into the palms of her hands, was almost restorative. "But how is it even possible? Water in the shape of a star?" she would repeat every year. "It's the most beautiful thing I've seen in my life!" Snow was Yaya.

My hand is aching; I haven't got it in me to write it all down. I describe how beautiful she was in that black-and-white photo from when she was sixteen. I run through all her relics, the tapestries she left unfinished, the speeches she recited to the plants. The time she called the radio station to ask them to wish me a happy saint's day. It would be impossible to write all the jokes, all the idioms and verses her father taught her. I hope she listened to me and wrote it all down in her notebook.

I get to the poverty: the rituals inherited from her impoverished childhood, like the cookies and little soaps she pinched from hotel rooms when she traveled round Spain on Social Services outings. I think about the last postcard I sent her, showing a man with a hairy ass and the Eiffel Tower behind him. If I'd known it would be the last, I probably would have chosen something else. Or perhaps it's funny that it was that one.

The pain is unbearable; my longing tortures me, chokes me, and I wonder if I'll ever be able to climb to the top again.

Sometimes, when she was waiting for her friends to come and sit with her, on the same old bench as ever, I would spy on her, because she often talked to herself and I found it funny, but also because sometimes I caught her looking at our house, as though, after all these years, she still couldn't believe she had managed to build it. To build that life.

Right now, the Milky Way is so brazen, so clear, that it seems unreal. I could do with a sausage to chew on. The Grand Canyon drawn with thousands of stars and waves of light, blues and lilacs and yellows and blacks. The sky reflected in the river. The canyon reflected in the sky.

How is it possible to see yourself like that, from Earth? How strange. How ironic, too, that on the darkest night of all, I'm gazing at such an extraordinary starry sky.

"You should get some sleep."

Michael has left the main tent to check that I'm not slitting my wrists. He hasn't said a word until now, but I saw him arrive. I give him a nod of welcome to my small camp, and he sits next to me.

"You should know that the ascent is much harder than the descent. And you're weak. You have to sleep."

I don't know how to reply other than with a smile of gratitude and defeat. Michael, that stranger whose identity is split into percentages, grabs his sleeping bag and lies next to me, extending his brawny white arm beneath my neck, and I let myself go as though I were in the bed I'd slept in since I was a child.

I close my eyes, still clutching my notebook, the pages wrinkled by the earth and my tears, my fingers stained with ink. And when we're both asleep, in the cradle of the Colorado River and with the Milky Way as a nightstand, a shooting star, glowing and determined, crosses the sky.

In my dreams I feel that star drawing a trail of bleach and tomato, laughing out loud and telling me not to worry . . . that it will all be fine.

Snow

Going down is optional; going up is mandatory.

This is the message carved behind the bathroom door in the shelter next to the Colorado River. Words we all read when we use the toilet, making us curse all those times we skipped the gym in favor of a beer (which, in all honesty, I wouldn't change for anything).

As expected, the café is pretty Spartan, not much more than four wooden tables and three types of doughnuts in a plastic display case, but the selection of postcards is decent—and that's why I came. I waver between the classic aerial shot and the one with the turquoise river, but in the end, I go for an old mule tottering down the Bright Angel Trail. I write my home address with pride and pain.

This is the first postcard of the rest of our lives. Everything will be fine . . . She told me that.

The girl in the café has a black wavy ponytail that reaches to her waist (and looks a lot like the mule's tail in the postcard). She picks up a worn wooden stamp and makes an inky imprint on the postcard that reads, *This postcard was sent from the bottom of the Grand Canyon, Colorado, November 2007.*

"What does it say?" she asks with the tranquility of someone who has all the time in the world.

"It says that today has changed my life." My chin trembles. "And that I think it will all be fine."

She turns serious and looks at me as though she knows what I'm talking about.

"You should know that not everyone is brave enough to come down here . . . much less alone."

"How do you know I came down alone?"

She leans her arms on the counter, lifts her feet, and tilts forward to within a couple of inches of my nose.

"Going down is optional; going up is mandatory."

Michael's feet aren't straight when he walks; the toes point together, as though his feet are twisted or he has bandy legs. It looks like every step is an effort.

After the much-anticipated toasted bagels with a smear of Philadelphia and a disconcertingly good coffee that Michael made with the portable stove, our little group of multicolored heads started the ascent via Bright Angel—what an opportune name.

The sun still hadn't poked out its head, but a breath of clarity announced the end of the dark night. The light started to pick out the relief of the orangey stones and caress the low water of the turquoise river.

I insisted on carrying the cooking utensils in an extra backpack, for which the group was eternally grateful, given my "situation," but I felt a strong urge to do something.

I carefully arranged the stainless-steel plates, small pans, wooden spoons, salt, and forks and put the backpack on, feeling like I was carrying a little more of Yaya with me.

We've been walking for nearly an hour. The first ray of sun shoots out, demanding that we stop and take in the harshness of our surroundings. It's cold, but it seems like today, so beautiful and sunny, is endeavoring to help me all the way back up.

"I've had bad knees since I was born," Michael tells me, without bitterness as he carefully removes the forty-five pounds he must be carrying on his back. "But don't tell me that the extra effort doesn't make up for experiencing this whenever I want."

The sun is flooding every crevice now, covering every mile between us and the horizon, and it warms our path. Michael offers me a dented metal canteen, takes a deep breath, and closes his eyes, as though he can see more clearly that way.

"Look for a job like this, Rita. Get a job that makes you forget the effort, that makes you forget that your knees or back hurt, where it doesn't matter whether it's Monday or Friday, something that makes up for everything else."

And I look at him and think that perhaps Yaya visited him in his dreams to remind me of her last words during our eventful video call: *Do whatcha want, as long as it makes you happy.*

We've taken less time than I expected to reach the same white path across greenish stone that first led me to the river. I imagine an aerial view of our little group advancing, treading the same gash in the earth where I cried yesterday, but now that I'm traveling in the opposite direction, I feel a certain closure, a first peninsula of relief. Like sewing up a wound or pulling up a zipper. It's as though with each step I take, the path is explaining that it will never leave, that it will always be here, like a scar, but that when spring comes, the grass will grow around it and cover it with flowers and life.

Michael announces that this will be our longest stop, on a terrace of flat, squarish stones. I take off my backpack, to the metallic clink of the pans. The blonds and the redheads sit down alternately, and I think that if only we had two more heads, we could draw the Catalan flag, but for now, all together, we only amount to a box of Playmobil figures.

An oldish man appears, looking like he hasn't seen a shower since 1998. He could be anywhere between fifty and a hundred, wearing a cowboy hat over sun-bleached hair and dressed like a Native American. A strange mix to say the least. Most disconcerting, however, is the fact that he's clutching a very long bamboo cane with a human skull at the tip to help him walk. I can't take my eyes off the cranium.

"Today!" The man adopts a ceremonial stance, as though we've all come here to listen to him. "Today . . ." He's a shaman; he might say something important. The intrigue is killing me. "Today will be sunny!"

And he shakes the skull. He sees that his announcement hasn't aroused as much enthusiasm as he would have liked, so he shakes it harder. Until the skull loses a tooth. And the audience is struck dumb.

But, instead of vomiting or being horrified, for some absurd reason I get a fit of the giggles. And I can't stop. I can't help thinking that right now, Yaya would be joking about turning herself into a toothless skull pronged at the top of a bamboo cane guiding the path of a dubious shaman.

The shaman isn't remotely amused at my laughter, and as he picks up the tooth in both hands, like a piece of treasure, he glares at me. Michael goes over to explain my "situation," that "she isn't well." And as I wipe away my tears of laughter, I think that perhaps he's right, I have gone crazy. As crazy as Yaya.

Five hours later, after skirting clifftops, walls, and mountains with more than one outburst of tears, we meet the first zigzagging path I came down. And at the top of it all, the corner where I spoke to Albert.

I look at it from below, as though the color of the earth is different, as though the corner has become larger, as though a million years have passed.

I launch myself into the final stretch with determination, my feet steady with each step. I feel the void inside, the compass running wild, but I grip firmly onto the straps of the backpack.

We reach the top.

The sign announces the end of the countdown: "BRIGHT ANGEL, 0 MILES."

The end and the start at the same place.

The strange feeling of asphalt beneath my feet. Day-trippers, wearing jeans and scarves, look at us as though we were heroes. Parents crouch to grab their children around the waist and point us out. Michael speaks to the park ranger, who smiles proudly and gives us a half bow. Someone breaks into spontaneous applause.

I meet the audience with a tremulous smile, wavering between pride and uncertainty. I wasn't expecting my return to civilization to be so momentous. I feel more lost than ever, but also that I have a clearer way to find a direction: myself.

And do whatcha want, as long as it makes you happy.

Suddenly, as if by magic, a drop of water in the shape of a star falls into the palm of my hand. It's starting to snow.

PART THREE

There's a Whore in the Dining Room

Thirty-six missed calls.

Twenty-seven voice messages.

Let the show begin.

The messages from Six complete the cycle of emotions: Anger. A whole lot of anger (plus various insults). Doubt. Concern. Ecstatic joy (Thom Yorke singing "Creep" in the background, Rachel asking why I'm not there). Incomprehension. "If you're dead, I hope at least you left me a handwritten letter and your vintage Converse."

But of the twenty-seven messages, Fulbright's is the one that worries me enough to pause midway as I lower the convertible's soft top: "Rita, we don't know where you've gone, we don't know what's going on, we hope you're okay, but you need to call us urgently. Your friend doesn't know where you are either. This morning, Pastor Paul called to tell us about the incident the other day. With the pig . . . ? My God." He breathes out; I could swear he laughs for a split second, but then he turns serious again. "Meanwhile, we've also received a communication from Bini's school. Miss Moore says that the other day you were late to pick him up because you were stopped by the police for alcohol abuse. At eleven o'clock in the morning? Rita, this is serious. Call us as soon as you can. We're worried."

Adults are a real drag. I lower the top of the Mustang all the way.

I know I've been here a few months, but I guess I can still blame it on language. The breath-test excuse is a classic that always worked for me when I was late arriving in Barcelona; I don't know what Miss Moore understood—I made it perfectly clear I hadn't had anything to drink. And as for Paul . . . Two little girls using a pig with an extendible penis to play God is rather more complicated; although, if it means that we're all his children, it seems quite reasonable to me. I think it must be a cultural thing.

Atlanta is blanketed in cold. Finally, the sweltering heat has lifted, and the highways are grayer and more spacious. Some yellow and red leaves are still clinging on, but the first naked trees are visible. I imagine the trees in Piedmont Park, like waiting skeletons, their coat of leaves waiting, too, hibernating.

When Hanne discovered that I'm alive, she decided to postpone the avalanche of questions about my disappearance for a face-to-face interview. Let's not forget that they thought I was going to Las Vegas to see Radiohead, and Six called them to ask where I was.

Hanne insisted on coming to get me at the airport, but I told her Six would drive me. A shameless lie. I just couldn't face a whole journey of questions and compassion. I planned to take a taxi, but a girl offered to take me in her car because we were going the same way, and she charged me less than half what the taxi would have cost. The car was amazing. I told her she could offer this service professionally, and she said she'd think about it; I also suggested she could offer a bottle of water to every passenger. What I didn't say was that this is the kind of brilliant project a certain five-year-old dreams up every four hours, although without any *s*'s because his front teeth have fallen out.

That five-year-old is waiting for me now on the other side of the little windows on each side of the front door, drawing transparent planets on the glass, and running out to greet me with open arms before I've even set foot outside the car.

"Hairyyy!"

"Bini!" The best hug in the world. I needed that.

"Hairy, there's a whore in the dining room. She's waiting for you."

"Huh? A . . . what?"

"There's a whore, a whore even taller than Daddy!"

"Ah, a whore."

One of these days I'll have to explain to Bini that a whore isn't a very tall woman. The day Eva asked me from the back seat whether "whore" meant a very tall woman, I found it so funny that I said yes. I assumed they wouldn't use the concept all that much, and to be fair, I've never heard them say it again. Until today.

I take off my backpack in the entrance hall and climb the four stairs to the living room, announcing my arrival with the loud creaking of each step. Who could the whore be?

When I find out, I can't believe my eyes.

The boss of the au pair sect from New York, the raspy-voiced woman with the shaved head and jowls, is sitting on the sofa with her legs wide open like a Wyoming lumberjack. Fulbright offers her a cup of tea. I quickly calculate the days until his "meeting" with Chitawas. Seventeen.

"I always had the feeling we'd meet again." She stands and holds out her hand to me. What on earth is that woman doing here?

"Oh yeah?" Be quick, intelligent, this is your house. "Well, I didn't. Welcome to Atlanta"—I can't remember her name—"ma'am."

"Do you have a moment, Rita?" Hanne asks me.

"Sure," I reply.

Raspy puts her cup on the table as though it were a log she's just ripped up with her bare hands and launches into her speech automatically.

"The truth is that I came to Atlanta with the intention of meeting leaders from Druid Hills and Alpharetta, and returning to New York tonight. But when I come to Atlanta, I always drop in to see my friend Karen Tucker—I suppose you know who she is, right?"

"Hmm . . . Not off the top of my head." I smile, feeling generous.

"Karen Tucker is the director of the language school at Georgia Tech, an excellent professional who's made the institution into a national point of reference, both for the integration of foreign students and for its promotion of American history and literature beyond our borders. And, well, we were chatting about future collaborations, about how Au Pair in the States could offer a link to the Smart Girls Program and that we should be on the lookout for smart cooties"—did she say "cooties"?—"and of course we immediately thought of you. What a surprise!" Her tone is dripping with honey; it's terrifying. "As you can imagine, I never forget the face or name of any girl who passes through my class." She pauses and raises a finger: "Curtains of training for excellence in the care of American children. So, when Karen mentioned the au pair Rita Racons, I thought . . . let's drop in and see how *our* Rita is getting on." She picks up her cup in the palm of her hand, as though it were bourbon, and takes a long, calm drink, the silence implacable. "So, I came here to Oak Paths Drive. Your family welcomed me into this excellent, most excellent home you've been lucky enough to be allocated, my dear. And who would have thought it would be my lucky day!" With teary eyes, she looks up to the sky. Where is this going to end? "No sooner had Hanne eaten the first bus candy I brought for the occasion, than our Lord blessed us with an unexpected visitor. Oh, what joy, what a delight! Who should ring the bell, but Pastor Paul, one of the most esteemed pastors in all of DeKalb County, and I would go so far as to say the entire state of Georgia." Her voice has become deeper, a touch colder. Hanne and Fulbright look at me with resignation, as though it's out of their hands; they're powerless to stop the beast. "But he didn't come with the halo of benevolence and parakeets that always surrounds him when he shares the Word of God with us, oh no. It would seem that our Lord God abandoned us on that particular day . . ." She glares at me. "And you know why, don't you, Rita? You know perfectly well."

"It . . . it was an accident, I'm sorry," I respond dramatically. Shit, Yaya is dead, and I have to apologize for a fucking toy wiener.

"And we understand," adds Hanne, lowering her voice, touching my knee. "We get it . . ."

"But it was unacceptable!" thunders Raspy. And it comes again: Her ears start to sweat. "As it states in paragraph three of page three hundred and eighty-nine of the protocol guide for au pairs, 'You will never make reference to or show to the children any'"—she sighs, closes her eyes, and crosses herself—"'any kind of sexual object.' And for them to use it like that, oh my Lord."

"We're fully aware," adds Fulbright, trying to calm her.

"The protocol is very clear, Dr. and Dr. Bookland. The code of ethics indicates that the au pair should be removed from the country."

What?

"We're fully aware of the situation," repeats Fulbright, rising from the sofa and initiating the goodbye process. "Leave us to reflect on it today, and we'll give you an answer tomorrow."

What do you mean, reflect on it?

The whore stands up. She stuffs herself into her XXL fleece from 1993 with the embroidered logo of Au Pair in the States, shakes hands with Fulbright and Hanne, and then squeezes my hand with contempt and a glimmer of hatred. I suppose the fact that an au pair who attended her most excellent class is capable of introducing an extendible penis into a family home is a black mark that will besmirch her divine résumé forever.

Today's dinner-table topic was "When Hannibal Crossed the Alps." Aksel spoke about the financial cost of hiring Balearic slingers and the military weaponry used to attack Rome. And it's only Wednesday. He even mentioned "rounding off the bends in the river to achieve a perfect parabola for launching projectiles." Eva provided all kinds of details on the supply system and the transportation of food on the elephants' backs. And, to round it off, Bini made a comparative analysis of the current vegetation of the Alps and how he thinks it must have changed since the year 218 BCE. "I think climate change has made more ice melt, and so it will be greener now."

I didn't utter a word. I was happy to let them think I was upset about today's surprise visit, but, truthfully, I couldn't have contributed anything to the conversation. I didn't even know that Hannibal crossed the Alps. Or that he did it with elephants. And, let's be honest . . . I didn't know who Hannibal was either. Then I decided that I'm fine not knowing.

And after Hannibal and his parabolas in the bends of rivers, I don't know how, but we've ended up talking about nihilism.

When I hear the word "nihilism," I'm about to go look it up on Google, but luckily Eva and Bini don't know exactly what it means either, so I listen to Hanne's explanation to refresh the little I remember of what I learned at college. And to confirm that, actually, what I remember has nothing to do with nihilism.

I've been fairly downcast during the whole of dinner. I still am. Obviously it has nothing to do with Raspy; I couldn't care less what that freak thinks. And I suppose I could say the same about Ful and Hanne. Given that they have the Democratic Party flag hanging in the garage, I can only hope they're not so appalled they send me home, just because their daughter played with an extendible penis. But then . . . is it their decision to make? Or is there really an ethical code for au pairs, and they're really going to deport me? Fanatics.

I can't leave now! I don't want to leave! After my ascent at the Grand Canyon, as I was driving back in my convertible, this house kept appearing in my mind's eye. The certainty that this cul-de-sac I've ended up in is actually a lottery win. It's a miracle that these cum laudes still haven't thrown me out. The fact that I'm still here must mean something. And now they know who I am. They know I look everything up on Google and that I eat their Argentinian sandwich cookies, the only food they asked me not to eat because they're really hard to find. When they told me that, I searched Google to find out what a sandwich cookie was, and that's when I started eating them. They also know

I've never known the difference between the theories of Hobbes and Rousseau. Or who Hobbes and Rousseau are, for that matter. I don't know most of the subjects they discuss at their weekly themed dinners, and I can't follow the most basic medical jargon. ("Acetylsalicylic acid" isn't medical jargon, so I'm told.) But they know I listen to them. That I'm interested in them. Against all odds, I'm interested in them. Perhaps that's why I'm still with them. Simply because I listen. Just like they listen to me. Each of us from our respective sides of the intellectual barometer. I can't leave this house.

So Raspy and her XXL fleece slammed the door and sent my future flying into the air. Whether I stay in my house on the cul-de-sac or I'm deported for a toy penis is as yet a great unknown. The only thing that's clear is that Hanne, Fulbright, and I have to talk. So, when we've put the kids to bed, I don't say my habitual breezy good night before going down to my room and sending the usual emails across the Atlantic.

Today I come back to the kitchen. Because we have to talk.

"So," Fulbright begins, clearly pondering as he collects the NASA spoons from the kids' table, "according to Nietzsche's theory, it's impossible to distinguish existence from nonexistence. And let's not forget the negative sense, because nihilism relates to the long process of decadence of Western culture that started with Socratism and extended through Platonism and Judeo-Christian religion . . ."

"Of course!" adds Hanne, pouring another glass of shiraz.

"She's not listening," he says, "this woman isn't listening to me . . . Rita, let's go back to the start: According to nihilism, the concept of existence in itself has no meaning, only nothing exists . . . What do you think?"

"I don't think any human being should say the word 'nihilism' before the age of twelve."

They both freeze for a second. I don't know if I should be taking such liberties, given my precarious status in this country. But they laugh.

"Come on, didn't you study this at university? Surely Nietzsche is mandatory reading for any degree," he continues.

"Yes . . . let's see . . ." I sit down at the kids' table.

"Come on, psychologist." Hanne smiles, her teeth stained purple by the wine.

"The symbol of active nihilism is the lion." I found this on Google in the bathroom. "It symbolizes the destruction of established values. It's the human being who fights against idealist morality with their divine will." I've always been a machine at memorizing texts. "And it's this fight against the established values that creates freedom." I smile.

"You Googled 'nihilism' when you went to the bathroom, right?" Son of a bitch.

"Possibly! Is that what you think of me?"

"Oh, freedom . . ." Fulbright is getting a second wind. Hanne pours herself another glass. "Freedom—"

"Freedom is the ability to choose," I cut in.

"Oh!" He stops short again, now in the process of opening a second bottle of wine. "*Fahrenheit 451*?"

"What do you think I do while I'm waiting for Bini to finish tennis?"

"But you're always late!"

"Precisely."

"Aha . . . Interesting, very interesting."

"I really liked *The Martian Chronicles*, and I wanted to continue with Bradbury. *Fahrenheit 451* is much darker, but I love the way this man writes . . ." He looks at me as though expecting me to say something else, and I quote him a line about filling your perception with wonder. He's delighted; if I were a man, he'd have fallen in love right then and there. "Of course, I'm not sure whether 'wonder' relates to the Spanish *maravilla* or *pregunta*?"

"Aren't they the same thing, dear Rita . . . ? Aren't they the same . . . ? To wonder! To wander! Bradbury talks about book burning due to agoraphobia caused by having too many ideas, the vulnerability of realizing we don't know anything. It isn't easy to have every choice available to you, but you have to be brave enough to face it. Do you think you've started to face it now, Rita, with all your questions?"

I don't feel like telling him I spend much of my spare time now reading and writing. And in fact, I'm not sure if that means anything, if I'm honest. But I really want to go to bed. I'm very tired.

"I think so, Fulbright, I think so." I look at him with all the sincerity I can muster. "So, you want to talk about the pig, right?"

Hanne decides to make the difficult conversation more pleasant by filling the room with Bach's Goldberg Variations. When she presses Play, the slight pressure on the button makes her spill a little wine on her turquoise turtleneck. Is it new? Hanne's wearing a new sweater!

"Exactly, we need to talk about 'the pig.'" She does air quotes with her fingers.

I sit on the armchair; the two of them are on the sofa. Hanne starts.

"Explain to us what happened with the pig, in the games room, exactly."

"We already know what happened, exactly, honey. There's no need to go through it all again . . . for God's sake," says Fulbright.

"Exactly, for God's sake . . ." She laughs as though she were eight and just heard the word "penis" for the first time.

"The truth is, I don't think it's such a big deal. It's a silly gift my friends gave me and I had it stashed away in my room and . . ."

"Sure, sure . . ." They aren't laughing anymore. I've never seen Fulbright so serious. He continues, "The real issue is that you were drunk when you went to pick up Bini the other day at school. And that's very, very serious."

"What?" *What?*

"You were drunk when you went to pick up—"

"No! I wasn't drunk . . ."

"Well, we were notified by the school, and that kind of information must have some kind of basis. Rita, it's possible that the school reported you. And if they reported you, according to the contract, you'll have to go back to Barcelona."

"But, well . . . honey . . . we can't let you go now . . ." says Hanne. "Now that Eva finally seems to be passing phys. ed."

"How did you know she was failing?"

"Please, Rita, they're our children . . ." he replies.

"So you know about Aksel's rap too?"

"Aksel's what?"

They look at me, puzzled. I'm an idiot!

"His . . . rap . . . his computer, he's built it from scratch . . ."

"Well, sure," replies Hanne. "As I was saying, we can't get another au pair now. And Aksel wants you to stay, Rita." I feel a lump in my throat. "And Bini . . . Bini too."

I'm surprised to find myself thinking that the worst thing that could possibly happen now would be to be separated from the kids.

"But you were late because the police stopped you. That's what you said. Had you been drinking . . . ?" Silence. I can't tell them I was late because I stayed over at John's house. If I do, they'll be jealous because they weren't invited to the place that makes them feel cool and young and alternative, and they'll hold a grudge and make me sweep up all the branches and organic waste in the yard. "I know your private life is none of our concern, but at that time you were working, and we need to know why you were late. We need to know if you were drunk, Rita."

"I was at John's house, after a party . . ."

"What?" The reaction is stronger than I expected.

"It was after tennis . . . It was . . . it was spontaneous. I . . . the thing is I didn't want . . ."

"A party at John's house?"

They exchange a look. Their indignation grows. Hanne puts down her glass. Adult life is a fallacy. We'll always be eight-year-old kids in the bodies of older people who want to be invited to their friends' parties.

"And how was it? Who was there?" Hanne quizzes me.

"It was kind of boring." I picture John with his shirt unbuttoned. Phillip sleeping between two men in tank tops. The tongues. The pill.

"Boring? I don't believe that," says Fulbright.

"There was no one from around here." Samantha, when she finally let herself go, arms around that woman. "I didn't know anyone, but it was getting late . . ." Eight in the morning. "And I thought I'd better stay over rather than drive because I'd had a couple of beers."

"A couple of beers!" Hanne bristles. "Just because we're Harvard graduates doesn't mean we're idiots."

"Okay, so I woke up late and arrived just in time to get Bini. I gave the excuse of the breath test because it always works in Barcelona."

"Sure . . ." They're clearly hurt. They wanted to go to John's party, and they weren't invited.

"Fine." Ful won't look me in the eye. Hanne is staring into the void, weighing the situation, imagining the party, John. "Matter closed, then. We'd like to ask you not to arrive late again, because it's a bad habit, and we don't want our children to pick it up. And, Rita, when you have a moment, we'd appreciate it if you could sweep up the branches in the yard . . ."

They're very, very angry. Their cool level has dropped to zero. I need a good counterattack.

"Fulbright, Hanne . . . my grandmother died."

The Hardest Job in the World

Today I was really keen to get back to class. To normality.

I arrived early, before anyone else, almost. I saw Tek Soo waiting outside, his body draped over six steps as though he were on the cover of a K-pop album.

I sat with him on the stairs and told him all about my weekend. Except the bit about Yaya. I don't know if he entirely understood, because he didn't show much enthusiasm when I told him I trekked ten miles down to the bottom of the Grand Canyon. I suppose I forget all too frequently that his grandfather was from Japan and was an actual ninja—it would take a lot to impress you after that.

He gave me a little cookie he said is typical of Seoul and, in the handover, brushed my finger with his and blushed.

More than anything I wanted to come because Roberta is giving us back our last writing assignment with corrections. I worked hard on this one. Who would have thought it, a well-written and creative text, in the English language. All those sentences together. It's nothing short of a miracle.

"Good morning, my dears!" Roberta bursts into class with her usual energy and gets straight to the point: She holds up the corrected essays in the air. "These are you. I have you in my hands. You're mine, but only for a moment. I'm nothing more than a string bean, the guardian of one of the many barriers you'll find on the path of art and literature, the path that will open doors for you. Nirvana!"

She's a prophet. She'd get on well with Fulbright. I'm nervous, my palms sweaty. I think I did a good job. I titled the essay "American Ink," and it was about John (Jack, in the essay) and Coca-Cola, but it also compared the two cultures, everyday life in Atlanta and Barcelona. The waiters, Southern hospitality, okra versus *escalivada*. It's a predictable topic, especially when you go to live in another country, but it's from a Cerdanya perspective, which always adds points.

"Rita."

"Yes?" I laugh with trembling lips, blushing.

"What did Hemingway say about good writing?"

"That no one knows the secret." I've learned this; I'm a book nerd now; no one would recognize me. "But he said that he knew it, that the secret of a good text is that it's poetry written in prose . . . and that's the hardest job in the world."

"And how right Mr. Hemingway was. In fact, he said a lot of things, especially after a few daiquiris." The class laughs; I'm lapping up her words. "He also said the most essential gift for a good writer is a good bullshit detector."

There's every chance I'm drooling. I gaze at Roberta with admiration and love. I watch how her white curls tangle around her gold glasses, I look at the brown skin on her beautiful fingers when she hands me my grade for the best thing I've ever written.

"Rita, this is shit."

"What?"

I'm three years old, and I've pissed myself in front of the whole class.

"This assignment, absolute shit."

"Ah . . . okay."

Someone laughs.

"Don't take it badly."

I'm twenty-three years old, and I've pissed myself in front of the whole class.

"Ah, no, no . . ."

"I think you have a good bullshit detector, Rita, but in these lines, you're as subtle as a walrus in heat. What you gave me is no more than a list. An anthropological analysis of American life and culture. An analysis with no soul."

"But I did that deliberately. There's a crescendo of meaning . . ."

"I wasn't drawn in. I have to admit that you've made me plant geraniums on the fact that we Americans are saying 'sorry' all the time, and the girls who speak with a nasal drawl need a good slap. But it lacks depth, analysis, poetry, and prose. And this Jack, what's he got to do with it?"

"I wanted to create mystery . . ."

"But here Jack is making necklaces with macaroni! It's too obvious! Some parts are interesting, but they're poorly ordered and too superficial. Try again."

Boom.

I walk past the director's office, where the door is always open, and I read the name: Karen Tucker. I can't help but smile as I think of Raspy.

On my way out of the door, I bump into Roberta again, who has a disgustingly jovial smile on her face. She grabs me by the shoulders.

"Rita, try again."

I go to the parking lot, get into the car, and check my cell phone. A message is waiting for me:

> I've just gotten you a date with the best rapper in the South. Bring the kids to the house this afternoon. John.

Sinatra Died on a Plane

"Hairy, why do you always give us breakfast food? It's four in the afternoon . . ." Bini opens his mouth wide as he munches on toast with peanut butter and jelly, perched at the kitchen counter.

"Don't you think it's the best food of the day?"

"If I could eat chocolate ice cream for breakfast, then yes. Hairy . . ." He can't open his mouth any wider. "Where are we going today?"

"Today? Why do you ask?"

"Because you're wearing a lot of perfume."

"We're going to see a friend of mine who's going to introduce us to a girl who will help Aksel with his end-of-semester project."

"A rapper?"

"Yes, a rapper. But remember that we can't tell Mom and Dad until the end of the year, okay? It's a surprise!"

"Hmm . . ." He isn't convinced.

"Do you want some chocolate ice cream?"

I enter the code at John's gate like I'm a marchioness. Such security, such a sense of belonging, such a continual need to win these kids over. I check the rearview mirror and notice how I'm accruing "cool au pair" points as we head up the little hill, with a golden bonus as we cross the brow.

"This must have a bigger square-footage than the White House!" says Aksel.

"Are we at Camp David?" asks Bini.

"Who is this John?" adds Eva.

I guess that, however intellectual they are, for all the Hannibal and nihilism, a rich person's house will always be a rich person's house.

By day, John's house has a more romantic air. The drama of the initial descent, the truth of the bare stone . . . It all looks like something out of Jane Austen. But here, instead of a contained and repressed Mr. Darcy, we have another more obvious lead character, with more drug-orgy tendencies.

A lead character who comes out to meet us wearing his at-home uniform: million-dollar jeans, white shirt, and a camel-colored coat that swishes a perfectly calculated inch above the floor and that any sane person would only remove from their closet for the summer wedding of a close relative.

"You must be Bini." John shakes Aksel's hand. "You must be Aksel," he says to Eva. "And you, without a shadow of a doubt," he says to Bini, "must be Eva."

Yes, it's an old joke, easy perhaps, but he says it so funnily, with a smile of feigned confusion, that he makes us all genuinely laugh.

"And you, madam"—he takes me carefully by the hand and gives me a velvety kiss—"you must be the famous tennis coach, Mrs. Gee."

That makes us laugh even harder. And I would happily rip his jeans off with my teeth.

Phillip is waiting for us in the kitchen with a snack worthy of an American funeral. A couple of silver dishes, not huge but laden with food, one with chicken curry and another with vichyssoise, and next to them, arranged in a perfect diagonal, an array of sandwiches wrapped in little papers like you get at expensive cake shops.

He gives us the choice of hot chocolate, coffee, or green tea. Eva thinks I'm not looking and points at the coffeepot. She knows she shouldn't. Phillip serves her the forbidden liquid with no questions about the effects of caffeine on an eight-year-old body. Eva accepts the cup as though this is common procedure and unknowingly, taking pleasure in the novelty and mystery of it all, joins the long list of people hooked on this palace of hedonism.

"Thanks for all this, John." I wipe my chocolatey lips and scan the back of the Aretha Franklin vinyl he's just put on. "Have you taken the day off?"

"You can't bear the curiosity, can you? Not knowing my job? Where I come from?" He laughs.

"Ah, but do you have a job?"

"Soul should be arriving any minute."

"Kiom de iaroj vi havas?" Eva is talking to Phillip.

"Kids . . ." I interrupt. "How many times have I told you not to talk Latin!"

"Hairy," Aksel stops me, and they all laugh. "That's not Latin—it's Esperanto!"

"Whatever it is, don't speak dead languages that no one knows!"

"Mi bedaüras," Phillip replies.

"Finu vian mangôn ĉar ni baldaŭ forlasos!" adds John urgently.

"Just what I needed."

"Mia amo, vi aspektas bela hodiaŭ, hara," he tells me.

"What did you say?" Who would have thought I'd ever feel left out for not speaking Esperanto.

"Is . . . is that a plane?" Eva points out of the large dining room window, beating her feet against the tall stool with the heels of her shoes. The caffeine is starting to kick in.

"It's not just a plane, my dear Eva," replies John. "Her name is Lola, and she's waiting for us."

In the middle of the lawn, on a small circular cement helipad, there's a light aircraft—and I'm not in the slightest bit surprised. Eva and Bini jump from their stools and run to the window, shouting and smearing their hands and noses against the glass. But Aksel stays in the kitchen, petrified, transfixed on an apparition with long, pink hair that he's just seen in the doorway.

Soul must be about my age and is Black. Her straight hair is dyed light pink, almost gray, and reaches down to her navel. She stands there quietly, her gaze obscured by a black hood, with only her embarrassed smile visible, and yet despite her pose of absolute defenselessness, the calm and confidence she conveys from a distance are hypnotic.

"Soul!" shouts John, striding over to greet her with open arms, as if we all know what's going on, as if he had to rescue her. "Welcome!"

(Is this the famous rapper who's going to save our asses so that Aksel doesn't make a complete fool of himself in front of the entire school?)

Aksel has finally jumped off his stool, paler than usual. On any other occasion, in front of a girl like this—a lady, he would say—his legs would go weak and he'd use what little balance he had to run off. But he can't. He can't appear to be cowed by the presence of the face he has admired for hours on his computer screen, imitating her gestures and voice, noting down her best verses. Aksel doesn't see a pretty or exotic girl; he sees Soul, and fills with hope, ready to cling to her with every fiber of his being, to listen to the answers to all his questions, because he knows that today, at last, his flow is closer than ever. He walks over and stutters for a few seconds before saying his own name and holding out his hand.

I could never have predicted we'd end up drinking hot chocolate and flying over Atlanta in a tiny plane with a multimillionaire and a rap star. But that's what happened.

"Do you think I should call Hanne and Fulbright and tell them I've taken their kids up in a tiny plane that took off from a garden?" I ask John as he puts on his pilot's earphones. But the look he gives me suggests I've just asked the most boring question in the world, and I care much more about looking good in front of him than the inevitable crisis that will break out tonight if any of the three kids lets slip that, instead of going to their Mandarin lesson, we went flying.

"This is your captain speaking," says John, six feet in front of us, laughing in the mirror. "How are you, kids?" The children reply with smiles of extreme excitement and give John a thumbs-up. "Attention, please: This plane isn't just any plane. Lola, this jewel of the 1970s, belonged for years to one of the most extraordinary voices the world has ever known. In fact, he was . . . 'the Voice'!"

I glance at Soul to share my surprise, and she eventually responds to my arched eyebrows with a smile.

"Yes! Frank Sinatra had this plane for his own personal use and took his countless lovers up and down in it."

The children listen to the list of Sinatra's lovers as if it were a speech about the Late Cretaceous. "He fell hopelessly in love with Carmen Sevilla, a Spanish woman every bit as lovely as our Rita here, and he sent her a bunch of red roses every day; but the lover he desired the most was Mia Farrow, twenty-nine years younger than him."

The noise of Lola's engine isolates us all for a while as we continue our ascent. The residential streets of Atlanta reappear just as I saw them the first time from the air, like scars, sewn up with stitches, like thousands of centipedes, now in the midst of trees changing from yellow to gray and stretching out toward a new horizon.

Eva and Bini come to sit next to me and hold me tightly, one on each arm; and I don't say anything, but I think we should travel by private plane more often.

Aksel, in turn, is grinning and bearing it as best he can from the back seat, trying not to betray his fear of heights, trying not to look like a child in front of Soul, keeping his chin lifted. She, meanwhile, is gazing out of the window as though she knows where we're going.

It doesn't take us long to get used to the roar of the engine, to seeing clouds pass beneath us. Georgia dressed for winter.

"Won't you tell us where we're going?" I shout.

"What?" replies John, laughing. "Do you all have your seat belts fastened?" He glances in the mirror to check as Bini and Eva scamper to their seats and fasten up. "You want to know where we're going?"

"Yesss!" shout the little ones.

"You know that wise saying about how it's not the destination, but the journey?"

"Yesss!" They have no idea.

"And not just that, the journey has to be done right; we have to make the most of it; you have to learn from the people you meet and be able to deal with every unexpected turn. The journey is always the answer!"

"Are you a fucking preacher now, or what?" Soul has a voice, and she isn't taking any shit. "Can you tell us where we're going?"

Aksel starts to drool.

"All I'm saying"—John laughs—"is that when sudden changes come along, it's important to know the people you have around you."

Suddenly, he lets the plane drop.

My stomach rises to my throat. It's such a shock that I can't even reproach him; all I can do is close my eyes, scream, and scratch at my seat. Against all odds, Eva and Bini are laughing, with tears in their eyes; they can't stop; they abandon their bodies to gravity, levitating as far as their seat belts will allow, and beg John not to stop. I try to look at Aksel, who's sitting behind me, but I can't turn my head that far. All I can see is Soul's pink hair shooting out vertically, getting hooked on the vents on the ceiling compartments, and her smile becomes a grimace of panic. I don't know who's screaming more, me or her. I worry the cocoa I drank might come out of my nose any moment.

John does it again . . . and I'm thinking today's the day, today's the day it all ends. He's shouting like a lunatic, as though he wants to free himself of all his demons. But what demons can this man have left? He holds three orgies a week!

Shit, fuck! I realize that, apart from the orgy he went to in the 1980s that estranged him from his family, I know nothing about John. I don't even know what he does all day! If he does anything at all!

Finally, I manage to turn to Aksel, at the very moment when he can't hide it anymore: His Viking paleness has become an angry red, his mouth unleashing drooly shouts, and, in rage or sheer desperation, he grabs Soul's hand. She looks at him, hesitates for a moment, and then squeezes his hand tightly, sharing the horror. Creating a bond. The bond that John wanted.

That asshole John is still laughing, until eventually, after an eternity, I feel gravity return to my legs. I'm hoarse, and I have to press down on my chest to contain my pounding heart.

"And now that we all know each other a little better," announces John, with absolute calm, "we're going to land in this lovely field in Birmingham, Alabama."

The sandwiches wrapped in fancy-cake-shop paper have survived somewhat better than our faces. As we sit in a circle on grass scorched by the cold, John unwraps beige linen napkins and drapes blankets round our shoulders. Just like that, normally, as if we haven't just danced with death.

No one wants to say it out loud, but now, after the storm, I think we can all admit that the craziness was worth it, that the postorgasmic adrenaline is awesome.

We swallow down brioche triangles without saying much, enjoying the breeze and the exhaustion. Eva looks at me and remembers my face of terror, and gives one of those highly contagious little-girl giggles that makes you forget everything. Eva's laughter is the most wonderful sound on the planet, and when she gives a belly laugh, the world is a better place. I'm holding out, though. Bini, then John and the rest of the suicide squad follow suit. The weak sun brightens this little mound in the middle of the Forrest Gump state.

"Soul, are you a rap star?" asks Bini, his lips stuck with crumbs.

Aksel swallows, terrified at his brother's daring. *"Bini!"* He blushes red as a tomato.

"Yes, she is," replies John, "and she's very good."

"Yes, but don't think for a second that I'm about to start rapping now, after that fucking aerial pirouette."

"Come on, don't be a drama queen. You can't deny I've just given you inspiration for a verse or two," he continues.

"You're a son of a bitch." This girl swears a lot.

John has brought a guitar, two violins, and a ball, but we seem to be incapable of agreeing, so I take Eva to shoot some goals and leave the rest of them to work it out.

"Eva, later on, can you ask John what he does all day?"

"All right. Is he your boyfriend?"

"John? Eva, he's a mature gentleman!"

"Well, Frank Sinatra was a mature gentleman, too, and he married Mia Farrow. And they had the same plane."

From a distance, the sight of Lola parked on the flat and the figures flitting about against the light at the top of the hill looks like a Louis Vuitton commercial.

And to round off the scene, perhaps fed up with my insisting that she try to kick with the inside of her foot instead of her toes, Eva picks up the violin.

"All right, what would you prefer? *Eine Kleine Nachtmusik*, *Polovtsian Dances*, or *Humoresques*?" Incredible, we're all thinking. "Or do you want Mozart? Adagio in E?"

"*The Pink Panther*! *The Pink Panther*!" cries Bini.

"No, no!" cuts in Soul, as though Bini weren't a five-year-old and the cutest thing in the world. "Mozart, damn it! Always Mozart!"

"All right then." Eva is talking quickly, moving quickly, the forbidden caffeine coursing through her veins. "Let's begin with our friend Wolfgang . . . and then *The Pink Panther*, just for you, Bini." She winks at him.

Eva rests the violin on her tiny, bony shoulder, slots the wooden curve under her neck, and closes her eyes. In a matter of seconds, her expression transforms, her concentration is absolute, and the last of the sun's rays shower her hair with light.

Eva gives Mozart an abrupt awakening. The first notes sound loudly, with gusto and youth, and it's such a surprise that my body spasms. The music is quick and cheerful, and then it changes; now it's lower and slower, climbing again in a burst of color and adventure. Eva is playing in fast forward mode, her head nodding wildly, and despite my profound ignorance, I understand that this is genius. I feel hugely proud. Proud to know her, honored to be the one who looks after her and occasionally advises her. Eva is a prodigy! She must never stop playing!

To hell with soccer! Why on earth does she have to learn to play soccer?

The sun went down while Eva played Mozart and two rounds of *The Pink Panther.* Now the sky and our faces are painted a warm purple, and it seems like the circle has no intention of breaking; we're all lying in silence, gazing at the clouds.

"Do you write, Aksel?" asks Soul.

Finally, the moment he's been waiting for. Aksel freezes for a beat, but the need to find his flow is so powerful, it forces him to his feet. He pushes back his dry, unruly hair from his forehead, and replies from the heart, "Whenever I can, Soul. I have scraps of paper covered in verses and rhymes, and I even have some whole songs."

"Brilliant. What's the latest thing you wrote?"

"Some rhymes about when Tesla proposed that Edison change the constant current system to alternating current."

Soul digs her elbows into the ground and props herself up to look at Aksel.

"Fucking Tesla, huh? Go on."

"I've also written about the Boston Massacre, and the inventions of Thomas Jefferson, like the revolving chair and the macaroni machine."

"More. Go on."

"To practice the rhythm, I sing poetry. I really like Walt Whitman and the whole wave of writers he influenced . . . like Lorca, Neruda, and all the Generation of '27."

"Shit, how old are you? Eighty? Shouldn't you have a Rihanna poster?" Aksel doesn't really understand what she means by this, so he doesn't answer. "And have you written about your feelings?"

Aksel's energy wanes, and his shoulders hunch; he knew he would be asked this question, and he doesn't have a good answer.

"I don't think so . . ."

"What do you mean, you don't think so? Rap is all about emotion! When you write about what you feel, you know it! There's no margin for error; it's like love: Either it electrocutes your soul, or it's just smoke, nothing." Aksel doesn't know what to say. Soul sits up and looks directly into his eyes with the complicity of two people who shared a near-death experience just over an hour ago. "Do you want to rap, Aksel?"

"Yes."

"Do you feel it inside, in your heart?"

"Yes. I feel it loud and clear. In my heart."

"Are you aware of what that means? Of the responsibility, the curse, and the privilege of feeling art in your veins?"

"Yes." He's floating.

"Well, if you truly feel it, you and rap have to be one and the same. You have to have a rhyme ready for everything that comes up in life."

Aksel grabs his notebook and starts taking notes.

"What are you doing? I'm talking about life! Don't take notes: Listen to me!" Aksel slams the book shut and widens his eyes and, without realizing, opens his mouth too. "Read the dictionary, read a fucking encyclopedia if you get the chance . . ."

"I'm doing that already. I'm at *F*."

"What?"

"Yes."

"Amazing. Fucking brilliant. You need to always have words ready on the tip of your tongue. As many as possible. You have to master them. You have to be profane and poetic at the same time. You have to sing with the energy of a boxer and the elegance of a ballerina. Talk about what you know, what moves you, what you know better than anyone, whether it's that asshole Edison or that asshole Whitman. You're a frickin' white kid, a nerd, and from Atlanta, Aksel. Speak about that, speak about who you are, and you'll find a new and brilliant voice that will light up everything. You'll find your voice."

"And will I find my flow?"

"Yeah, follow what moves you, and the flow will appear on its own." Aksel is crying inside with joy. "By the way, have you ever seen a rap battle?"

"Yes, all of yours, Eminem's, all—"

"No, no, no, no . . . I mean live."

"No."

"Come tomorrow. John knows where it is."

"But, Soul," John cuts in, "don't you think he's too—"

"He has to see it," Soul says to John. "If he doesn't see it live, he won't be able to feel it. And if you want to do something for real, you have to feel it."

John nods, not entirely convinced.

Then Soul closes her eyes for a few long seconds, stretches her neck to one side, then the other, and starts to move her body in small, rapid waves. And she starts rapping.

Oh me! Oh life!
Oh, Whitman, fuckin' fuckin' Walt Whitman,
You tell us to live
To grab life by the horns.
Oh fuckin' Walt Whitman
The same goddamn question, every time:
What's good in this world, amid all this shit?
Oh me, oh life?
Oh, Walt Whitman, Lola and I will answer the question:
That you are here—that life exists and identity
That the powerful play goes on,
and you, you, you, Aksel, you may contribute a verse.

The Flow

"Does root beer make you hurl?" Aksel's hypochondriac face is wedged between the back of my seat and the car window.

"I told you to have an herbal tea, not root beer."

"But root beer is all there was, and the other day on *Jerry Springer* there was a guy who threw up because he drank too many beers."

"*Jerry Spring* . . . ? And how many have you had?"

"Three."

"Three root beers?"

"I'm nervous, Rita, really nervous!"

I won't admit it out loud, but I'm just as nervous as Aksel. Look calm. Breathe.

"So, are you going to hurl or not?" asks Bini, who ten minutes ago got on his knees in front of the car, begging me to let him come.

"No! He isn't going to hurl because we're here now, and as soon as he steps outside, it will all be fine."

"Shit, shit! This is much closer to home than I thought. I brought hummus for the journey and everything!" shouts Eva hysterically, because obviously I had to bring her along too.

"Eva, please, no more swearing."

"Rita, you're practically . . . we're committing a crime, so I don't think my swearing really matters all that much."

"You might be right . . . Now, be quiet." Don't say you're nervous. "When we get out, we have to convey confidence." Don't say you're nervous. "We have to act as if we have the situation under control."

"But what if . . ." starts Bini.

"And also, Rita . . ." continues Aksel.

"I said not a word! Not a word, *I'm really nervous*! . . . *Shit!*"

"Rita Racons." The bouncer doesn't even check the VIP list to verify my name. "Soul told me you'd be coming." He isn't laughing. "I guess you know this is no place for kids."

I look at Aksel, no longer trying to hide my nerves, and speak to him telepathically: "Aksel, are you still sure you want to go in? You know that once we go through that door, there's no going back. This man isn't friendly, and if your parents catch us, they'll send me to Guantanamo."

"Rita," he replies, through the same telepathic channel, "I'm cold, and I have a knot in my stomach; right now, I can only dream of the glass of milk Mom gets me every night when you finally go downstairs to your room and I can drink it in peace, without worrying you'll think I'm a little kid. I'm also thinking about the complexity of trigonometry and about how the lichens of the lower Amazon can photosynthesize in an atmosphere like Mars, but, despite all that, after everything, I want to go in."

We venture along a corridor covered in graffiti under the light of fluorescent bulbs that issue a metallic hum and with each flicker reveal dozens of insect corpses. The stench of marijuana mixes with a fug of humidity, sweat, and latex. The boys cling close to me, but Eva goes in front, opening a path with her hummus in one hand and carrot sticks in the other. The hum mingles with a murmur of animated voices that grows until Eva stops in a doorway and silence falls.

We're inside a huge garage. In front of us, about a hundred faces have turned to scrutinize us.

We're the only whites in the room. I look at the kids, and they've never looked so white; it's as though they're emitting light; we're fluorescent.

Aksel squeezes my arm with all his strength, and I raise my hand to greet everyone and announce that we aren't Russians or Communists, that we've come because we're friends of Soul . . . but luckily no one hears what I say: My timid "We aren't Russians or Comm . . ." comes out at the very moment the lights go down, and two giant spotlights focus on the stage in the center.

Soul appears on one side of the ring in a silk robe, like Rocky's, but pink—I feel hugely proud—and on the other, a fat guy with a couple of inches of body hair on his shoulders introduces himself by removing his T-shirt and throwing it into the crowd. The presenter tosses a coin in the air, and Soul wins. The show is about to begin.

Soul launches into her repertoire in a low, broken voice, from under her hood. The first few phrases are slow and poetic, nostalgic even; then suddenly she falls silent, yanks off the robe, and kicks ass.

She starts spewing out insults, effing and blinding and everything in between in defense of Black joy, justice, and peace.

Bini looks at me, obviously astounded at this verbal apocalypse, and tries to assimilate this novelty, this creativity. Eva dips a carrot in hummus, but since the show began, she hasn't been able to take a bite. Aksel stopped cutting off the circulation in my arm some time ago, and now I can't see him anywhere. I scan the room and can't find him, until the spotlight shines on the crowd for an instant and his golden hair appears up on a step at the side, far from the world and from everything, unashamed and unaware. Captivated by what he sees on the stage, he's imitating Soul's movements with a serenity that jars with the surroundings; he observes her as though she's an angel—an angel who keeps saying "fuck"—but, in reality, it isn't her or her pastel pink hair that he's watching; it's her art. He's clearly fascinated by her technique and her voice . . . Everything that Aksel hopes to achieve, everything he could possibly want is on the stage: the flow.

And I'm thinking that, if we're caught, this madness that I somehow decided to agree to will have been worth it just for this moment. To see Aksel like this. But more than anything, I think that one day I'd like to feel, even if just for a few moments, even if just once in a lifetime, all that Aksel is feeling right now as he gazes at the stage.

Fulbright and Chitawas Go Up in an Elevator

"And remember at the end when Soul jumped off the stage and everyone caught her?" Bini is overexcited. "And she spread out her arms like this!"

The three of them are eating breakfast with their hoods up. It's sunny, and today's squirrel is climbing the tree in the yard.

"And when . . ." Eva lowers the tone. "And when she kept on saying the f-word?"

Today more than ever they are a team of three; they very obviously feel cool and daring and united. Aksel listens to his siblings with a peace that I've never seen in him before. He looks at me and smiles.

"And when I farted in the car and Hairy laughed?" says Bini.

"Can I ask what's so funny?" Fulbright arrives home from tennis, sweating in his Harvard T-shirt, and climbs the stairs like a slender hippopotamus.

"Good morning, Fulbright!" I adopt an enthusiastic but casual tone, trying to draw a line under the children's conversation. "How was the match?"

"Very good, very good, I played rather well today."

I doubt it.

"And Hanne?"

"Hanne stayed back to play a little more. I left early—I have an important meeting today . . ."

Oh yes, he does. Today is the day: Fulbright is meeting Federico Chitawas.

Aksel launches into a dialogue we've rehearsed to the letter, and Eva picks it up. "And yesterday I farted in the car and Rita laughed!" Bini concludes, skipping all the rules but with a spontaneity that makes him sound more natural than his siblings.

"Now then, Rita . . ." Fulbright becomes serious and clears his throat. "You must realize that I know these three children well enough not to believe a word of what they've just said." Silence all around. "Apart from Bini's fart, of course."

"What?" Guantanamo here I come. "What do you mean?"

"I mean that there's no chance that you saw Ganymede and Callisto, as Aksel says, given the coordinates of Jupiter yesterday . . . That astronomy class you went to last night . . . What I'm trying to say is that you're busted." Shit. "I assume you've started preparing a Christmas surprise or some secret about the end-of-semester show . . . by which I mean I hope you're rehearsing already."

"Yeah!" I manage to articulate at last. "We need to talk about it in private . . ."

"Well, don't take too long—it's less than two weeks until you go onstage."

Fulbright goes into the bathroom, satisfied. Any other day, he might have caught us for real, but not today.

Protected by the unique privacy of his bathroom, perhaps he puts on a Bryan Adams song and, before stepping into the shower, looks at his naked self in the mirror. He'll think about what he's going to do. The doubt. The kids, Hanne, his job, the neighbors, his parents. But he'll also admit that it's too late. The urge, the leap into the void, the truth. The decision is already made. This has nothing to do with anyone else. This is just about him. Today, finally, perhaps for the first time, he'll be who he's always wanted to be.

To be honest, being an au pair is easy: You invite your kids' friends over to play; you wait for them to ask you outright not to disturb them; you pretend to be slightly offended and make them promise not to do anything outrageous, such as emulating God by using a pig with an extendible penis. Then you go to your room and lie on the bed to call Six and chat about the latest Swarovski faucets she's sold and her latest hookup, and to send the latest email.

A few days later, the friends you invited over to distract your children return the invitation; then you wait for them to ask you outright to come and fetch them as late as possible, as a favor, and you make the most of it and go to Starbucks to see Andrew, and to write the next American anecdote, riddled with exaggerations, and you send it off to your list of a hundred and fifty friends. And you feel a little happier.

And that's how it usually goes. But today, instead of writing for five hours with my Frappuccino, I drive to the city center to witness the meeting of the century: Bookland-Chitawas.

I leave the car in the parking lot at Georgia Tech and have to walk three times farther than I calculated until I find the hotel of sin, the Atlanta Marriott Marquis.

I'm dressed in a style completely different from my own so that Fulbright won't recognize me if he sees me from a distance, but I've clearly gone overboard because, once I'm in the hotel and hiding in an armchair in the lobby, a man comes up to ask whether I'm Cynthia. I'm so taken aback, I don't say anything, but the man adds that he's carrying three hundred dollars in cash. I can't believe it. What a cliché. I feign moderate offense and tell him I'm at the hotel because I've just graduated in anthropology and am on my way to get my PhD. And a medal.

I should have known the shoes with the transparent heels were too much. In fact, wearing the clothes that Daniela left to donate to charity is too much. On her, they looked incredible, but I, let's face it, I look like a prostitute.

I ask the waiter for the *Atlanta Journal-Constitution*, grabbing it and angrily putting away the book I'm reading, because the cover is too eye-catching.

I started *Love Story* yesterday, and I think I'll finish it today; I don't know if it will end well . . . I'm engrossed, anyway, and can't stop imagining erotic scenes with Oliver Barrett IV. I want to study at Harvard.

Truthfully, I should have been more careful, because if Fulbright catches me, I have no excuse for being here. I can't tell him I've just been given a medal for my PhD in anthropology. And how would I justify being dressed like this? I suppose I could say that he pays me so little that I have to sell my body. Better if he doesn't catch me.

Fifteen minutes until the meeting.

I lower the newspaper to eye level and scan the hotel foyer. It's impressive. It's like being inside the stomach of a giant whale stretched vertically, opening its mouth toward the ceiling. The long, marble-colored ribs of the balconies run along the insides of the building like a skeleton. In the center, rising up the spine, three transparent elevators distribute tiny people to every rib, until they reach the top, the fifty-second floor, and the light.

Suddenly, I have a crazy urge to go up in one of the elevators. Do I have time? I have time.

I leave my sweater and coffee at the table to keep my place; I take the newspaper to look less like a prostitute (because, as everyone knows, prostitutes don't read newspapers); I smooth down my plasticky skirt and set my transparent heels in motion. The elevator is supposed to be for guests only.

I share my journey with the members of a Lithuanian family who glance anxiously at me, and I give them a warm smile. Mother Teresa in stilettos, I turn and press both hands against the glass, prepared to feel the thrust, to see my armchair shrinking by the second. The elevator shoots up, moving quickly, but not so quickly that I don't see him—Fulbright has just arrived. Americans and their goddamn punctuality.

I witness the meeting of the century from above: Fulbright extends a cordial hand, but the Latino porn star skips formalities and hugs him. And it isn't an American hug; it's a real hug. This is serious. As far as I know, this is the first time they've met, but from the way they're interacting, the way they're looking at each other, it's clear there's a deeper relationship there. As deep as all the times Dr. Bookland pressed Play on the videos. Or perhaps . . . could we be talking about love?

I shoot off. In seconds, I've whizzed past about fifteen marble balconies, and Fulbright and Chitawas have become two tiny specks walking toward the reception desk.

They're getting a room! Will this be the first fuck? (Twenty-fifth floor). Will it be Fulbright's first time holding someone else's penis? Perhaps he's paying for it? Or is it Chitawas who's paying, fed up with porn stars? Does he have a thing for inexperienced professors?

This can't come to light . . . If they're caught, in the superconservative state of Georgia, it's bye-bye, Fulbright. Fiftieth floor, we're above everything! From here, the hotel lobby has become a cave of aliens, a kind of Martian city with a Christmas tree in the background. If Hanne finds out, I doubt she'll be very understanding; I suspect she'll raise hell, and perhaps I'll have to go home . . . And I don't want to—I don't want to go back yet; I still haven't fulfilled my mission. And what about the children?

Fulbright and Chitawas go up in the elevator.

The Lithuanian couple has decided to go back down, after numerous pleas in Lithuanian by their children.

We start our descent. A pointless stop at the twenty-fifth floor thanks to one of the Lithuanian kids. We carry on going down, and I realize I haven't seen them for a while. We're stopping at the seventeenth floor, because of the other kid! I hate kids.

Now it's the mother who's blocking the door sensor—it won't close—and I watch in terror as an ascending elevator slows before stopping at the same level.

I don't have time to react. They're right beside me, two glass walls over, just a few feet away. I don't move. I notice my heart rate soaring and my face burning. Think FBI. If I crouch to pick up the newspaper and cover my face, I'll only draw attention to myself—there's also a good chance my skirt will rip—and I'll be discovered. Bloody Lithuanians. Come on, doors, close! At last, they close, and we continue on our way down. Hallelujah.

But curiosity gets the better of me, and I take one final look. My trust in gravity betrays me, and I see Fulbright's body turning as though obeying a subconscious instinct . . . Our eyes meet. I stand petrified, and he watches me in absolute terror before disappearing into the deepest cavities of this strange skeleton city.

What have I done? Have I fucked up?

Have I gone too far, or have I done what needed to be done? What am I saying? I didn't need to do anything; the fact is that I'm a busybody, and secrecy raises my adrenaline.

I drive home with a sheen of cold sweat, eyes fixed on my phone, waiting for catastrophe's call. But it doesn't come. I continue down the main road through Leafmore, past the club, and still the call doesn't come. Maybe I'm freaking out over nothing and he didn't see me? I'm freaking out. He saw me.

Come on: Keep calm. FBI. I just have to come up with a convincing excuse. Something simple, a classic: I have a boyfriend. We met in the hotel because we don't have anywhere private to meet, and his uncle gives us a discount. And whichever way you look at it, I just happened to see Fulbright—whatever he had gone there to do—we just bumped into each other, period.

No . . . Empathy, Rita, show some empathy: You have a girlfriend, a girlfriend!

I'm sitting in the kitchen with a glass of terrible cabernet, finishing a voluntary assignment for Roberta—I'm unbearable—inspired by an article that caught my eye when I was hiding behind the newspaper in the hotel foyer. It's about the Democratic candidate Barack Obama—not Mojama after all—who said that at my age he traveled around the world to discover exactly who he was. And whether, I quote, "he felt more white or Black." Our twenties are a difficult decade for all of us.

According to the chalkboard in the kitchen, Hanne has gone to pick up the kids from a playdate and taken them to the Centers for Disease Control for a talk about the distribution of vaccines in Kenya. (Where else would you go on a Saturday afternoon?)

The garage door opens. I get goose bumps again. Fulbright comes up, slower and clumsier than this morning—is he tired from all the sex?—as though he can sense exactly where I am, here, waiting for him.

He enters with a smile, half theatrical, half sincere.

"I see you've changed . . ." he starts, defeated.

And so begins the speech: the date; the hotel; the discount from the uncle. I have a girlfriend.

Fulbright's face does the opposite of what it did in the elevator, this time shifting from terror to hope. He's clearly relieved, relieved enough not to confess what he was about to confess, enough to change the plan.

"I was there . . ." he lies, stretching his neck. "I was at the hotel because I was meeting a recent graduate of anthropology. I had to give her a prize . . . a medal."

You too, huh?

Catalan Soup with Curry

Today, after an enlightening class about how to introduce characters and make a story convincing, we celebrated with an international Christmas dinner.

Tek Soo has been telling me how, in Seoul at this time of year, the streets are decorated with a mix of Christmas and Saint Valentine's Day, and that in his house, instead of spending hours cooking broth, they reserve a table at an all-you-can-eat buffet and stuff themselves to the bursting point (which, given his weight, I expect must be equivalent to the appetizer of the appetizer of the appetizer in my house).

Tek Soo, who no longer blushes when he sees me, tells me all about his life whenever he gets the opportunity—and let's not forget that his grandfather was a ninja—describing it in such a poetic way that I'm hooked from start to finish. As poetic as his texts. Tek Soo is an incredible writer. He tells me I am, too, but I know that's just his way of dealing with praise; it's one thing to maintain a friendship with a girl and another thing to accept flirtatious compliments about his writing.

But I'm struggling to concentrate on what he's saying today, because when the other young men in the class try my dish—*escudella i pilota*—they go crazy and start wolfing it down. I'm glad I didn't spend five hours in the kitchen and instead bought five cartons of "Mediterranean Soup with a Hint of Curry," which was the closest I could find to our traditional meaty broth.

Roberta, who thankfully tried the soup before the rest of them got their hands on it, comes over to thank me in person. She's wearing a charming glittery red-and-white vest and, biting the head off a Christmas cookie, says, "About your last assignment . . . I liked the hypothetical situation where you met Obama playing basketball."

"Wow, that is a good Christmas gift. An 'I liked it' from Roberta."

"Don't get too excited."

"The truth is I enjoyed writing it."

"I could tell. Anway, I recommend you read up on his wife, Michelle Robinson. You might not meet her on a basketball court, but you wouldn't be disappointed wherever it happened. Even if it's only hypothetical. I look forward to reading a good Robinson-Racons scene. Bear in mind that she has a great sense of humor."

"I'd probably come up to her knees."

"You see? That's a good start."

"Me holding a conversation with the knees of a potential First Lady. I like it."

After the chat about Mrs. Obama's knees, she tells me she can't recall ever having such good soup in her life. I say she's exaggerating. She says, "Maybe, yes," but that the soup is really good anyway.

I say goodbye to the class, tossing a nice Catalan *Bon Nadal* in the air, which they repeat as best they can, and suggest we meet later for a casual drink in Little Five Points. Perhaps Six will come too; I haven't seen her for days. I know that if I tell her there will be Venezuelan women coming, she'll be there like a shot.

When I started these classes and told her I had met some Venezuelans, she begged me to describe them in great detail—she clearly has a fetish about Venezuelans and Ecuadorians—and she went on about it so much that I gave her an almost obsessive description of each one and, not anticipating they would ever meet, embellished them. Poor Six pictures them as the love children of Jennifer Lopez and Beyoncé.

Message. Six says she's coming. With Rachel. Rachel!

Something's happening in my stomach, but it isn't butterflies. I'm just horny. I haven't seen her since D-Day. She texted me when she heard about Yaya, but she didn't want to push it. She just said she was really sorry and that she was there if I needed her . . . and that she wanted to see me . . .

Maybe I'm a good lesbian?

No, no, no . . . I can't think about parties and sex today; I can't screw it up. Aksel is performing tomorrow, and he needs me; I have to make up for his parents' deficit of understanding.

On the way home, the aromas of international Christmas gastronomy clinging to my hair, I bump into Samantha. She says she hopes to see me by the stage tomorrow, and I say yes and cut short the conversation because an unknown number is calling me for the second time.

"Hello?"

"Good afternoon, Miss Rita. I'm Margaret Teacher from Aksel's impossible-to-pronounce-name school. Could I ask whether you'll be long? We're waiting for you."

"Oh! Good morning, good afternoon! No, no! Of course not! I'll be ten minutes—I'm sorry for the delay. Thanks for your understanding."

Shit! Last week, the director of Aksel's school called to ask whether they could count on my "invaluable support" and if I would "attend their annual celebration of foreign Christmas traditions."

It's clear they've never had anyone from Barcelona. I'm exotic here. Well . . . I'm not surprised . . . Who with half a brain would decide to come to Atlanta as an au pair? New York, Boston, Chicago, San Francisco, Portland, New Orleans—gastronomic capital—or even Texas! But . . . Atlanta! Elena! Not Elena, Astrid!

"Of course I will!" I answered, instantly imagining Aksel's look of horror when he sees me in his classroom. "It will be an honor."

I make my way down the corridor. The Christmas decorations are rather austere, and the only glitter to be seen surrounds a mathematical formula three lines long. Sometimes I forget that these kids go to schools where what looks like Nobel-level physics to me is no more than the morning warm-up to them.

I knock on the classroom door and go in without hesitating, only to realize that, contrary to what I thought, I'm the only speaker this afternoon. From the teacher's stiff smile, I can tell they've been waiting awhile.

"You must be Rita, yes?" Margaret Teacher welcomes me with this resounding question.

"Rita, that's me," I reply, "all the way from Barcelona." Aksel stares at me in horror, lowers his head, and bites his lower lip to control his nerves. "Thanks very much for inviting me. It's an honor to be here."

"Children, how do we welcome our guests?" Hierarchy and obedience permeate every corner of the room.

"Good afternoon, Miss Ritaaaaa!" the class greets me out loud and in unison, with incredible sincerity given that it's the last hour of the school day.

"Tell us, Rita, which tradition are you going to share with us today?" The teacher is so intensely didactic, it makes me nervous. "Perhaps you could sing us a folk song or show us a traditional dance? Flamenco? Or the sardine, isn't that what it's called?"

"*La sardana*, it's called *la sardana*."

"Perhaps you could tell us about your childhood memories of Christmas? Or recite a verse or two?"

Perhaps you could shut up, ma'am?

"We have this log that . . . that poops"—they're ten years old—"a log that poops out presents."

Absolute terror. Aksel begs me with his eyes almost popping out of their sockets, imploring me not to go on, to back through the door I entered and retrace my steps. But I pretend not to notice, and, with each of my descriptions of the *tió de Nadal*, Aksel obviously feels his dignity turning inexorably to shit.

The way Americans decorate their houses and yards at Christmas is amazing, even more outrageous than I've seen in the movies. Next to this, the *Home Alone* house looks like a mountain hut.

"Can you imagine the fortune it must cost people to run all this?" I glance at Aksel in the rearview mirror, but he won't shift his eyes from the window. "Aksel?"

"Do you really not have any other traditions in Catalonia? Didn't you say you have the Three Kings who brought I don't know what herbs to Jesus? The Three Kings are just about the most boring thing I've ever heard, but at least it has credible history, with tangible gifts . . ."

"The *tió* is tangible too . . ."

"Did you really have to come to my class to talk about a pooping log?"

"Well, as you say, the Three Kings are pretty boring, and people have already heard of them. You don't get the *tió* anywhere but Catalonia."

"And have you never wondered why? You Catalans are out of your minds. Who believes a log can poop? And you even put a cap on its head!"

"Well, they asked me to talk about unique traditions . . ." I look in the rearview mirror again and laugh. "And you can't deny that your friends were intrigued . . ."

"No, they weren't, Hairy . . ." He knows they were. "Couldn't you see they were laughing at you? And did you really need to say 'poop' so many times? Poop, poop, poop!"

"But it's your favorite wor—"

"When we say it at home, by ourselves!" He's struggling to contain his laughter.

"Well, I didn't make up the song . . . and it says 'poop.'"

"We could have done without the song, really!"

"All your friends were joining in and crying with laughter . . ."

"But it's unhinged! It makes no sense! Warming up a stick, why? And feeding it tangerines? It's a piece of wood! A *log*!" The absolute incongruence of the *tió* is driving him crazy. "It's moronic! It's obvious that when the kids go to sing or pray in the next room, it's the parents who put the gifts there!"

"You don't know that."

"Man." Aksel doubts himself for a second. "Please!"

Aksel's overcrowded head of hair reflects the neon reds and greens from the houses, augmented by the hazy air of this winter's night. The boy leans his forehead against the glass, and the warmth of his indignant body draws an imperfect circle on it; his gaze is lost, and despite the fact that his entire reputation as a "cool guy" has been put on the line by a shitting log, he isn't thinking about the log, or the stick, or the cap anymore . . . Tomorrow is too important.

"You're well prepared, Aksel. It'll be fine."

"Yes . . ." He doesn't move, doesn't laugh. "I suppose . . ."

"What do you mean, 'I suppose'?"

"Hairy . . ." Now he moves his head away from the glass and stares at me in the mirror; he's terrified. "'I suppose' means that music, rap, well, it isn't an exact science. I can't plan it or calculate it like the velocity of a particle in simple harmonic motion! I don't know what's going to happen tomorrow. I don't know how it will go . . . I don't know if all this has been a mistake."

"Putting yourself out there is never a mistake. And I'll be with you, Aksel."

He falls silent for a moment before asking, "Promise?" His pride won't let him show his desperation, but the need, the risk, is too great for him not to ask.

"Promise, Aksel. Tomorrow I'll be there all the way through, from before you go onstage until you're done. Tomorrow will be a day we'll always remember, you'll see."

I'm in a Sardine Boat and the Captain Looks Mad at Me

"Do you think they'd fix me an egg-white omelet here?" Six's hair is wet, and she sniffs it; she's just come from acroyoga.

"Six, look at the waiter's ass crack."

"What?"

"Nachos with ground beef is considered gourmet here. I don't think they'll do egg-white omelet."

"Something's up with you," she says as she lights a cigarette.

"I'm nervous, woman."

"Because of Rachel?"

"Shit, because of Rachel too. But mainly because of Aksel—it's tomorrow!"

"It might all go well, but if they find out you've been taking them to nightclubs instead of Mandarin class, they'll prosecute you anyway."

"Yeah, shut up, shut up . . ."

Six squeezes her muffin top with both hands, as if she's just discovered it, and returns to her world.

"Hey, so when are the Venezuelans getting here? I haven't fucked for two weeks—it's been months since I've had such a terrible drought."

The waiter comes over with a smile that shows commercial-worthy teeth, but, instead of the usual "Hi, my name is Blah Blah, and I'll be your server today," he stops at the end of the table, amused, as if he understands everything we're saying.

"Just forget about the Venezuelans—you won't get anywhere with them. They're standoffish and religious and wear diamonds to English class . . ."

"Religious, you say . . . They're the best kind. Nothing gets them hornier than repression and sin. And as for the diamonds . . . Honey, you're classist. None of your prejudice here, please!"

"Prejudiced, me? You're the one who thinks that people from Cerdanya are so provincial, we've never been up an escalator and don't have Canal+." I laugh.

"Ha! Look at her! The one who says that folks from Hospitalet have gold teeth and wear our thongs outside our pants."

"I admit I have a friend who went to Barcelona when she was five and asked her mom if the traffic lights were trees." I'm laughing hard.

"That's brilliant . . . And I admit I once had a friendship bracelet with my name on it. And it wasn't a gift—I bought it myself."

"I think we can agree that the snobs of Barcelona think we're good for nothing. Even though they run away when they see a goose. Or a thong, in your case."

"Idiot. But yes, we can agree. And getting back to the point, it's been days since I told you we could include Barbie Samantha in the orgy. She's a lesbian, after all."

"I'm not saying snobs can't be lesbians. I'm just saying you should get those Venezuelans out of your head . . . Anyway, Samantha? You've never even seen her."

"I don't need to, honey, I don't need to. Just like I don't need to meet John to know that he'd take you up against the first Coke-dispensing machine you came across."

"If only . . ." I think about John, whom I'll see tomorrow night at the get-together with the tennis crowd. "You really think so?"

"Rita, sometimes you're so dumb. It's so obvious that all the mothers in the neighborhood hate you because you're hot and a good twenty years younger than them. It's mathematical and anthropological logic."

"You should make a career out of that. Hey, when is Rachel getting here? What do I say to her?"

"She'll be here any minute. She's dying to see you."

My stomach again, I'm nervous.

"By the way, we need to talk about Christmas. What are you doing?" I ask.

"I'm going to drink all the Jägermeister in Atlanta. I fucking hate Christmas." Six's mood changes.

"No, I'm serious. What do you do for Christmas in Atlanta?"

"Nothing, seriously."

Six and I fall silent. She looks away with a profoundly sad expression, which is unusual for her. But then she shakes it off, and we put on the same fake smile to look at the waiter, who's been standing there, immobile at the end of our table, since he arrived.

"Oh! Is that it?" The waiter laughs. "Don't mind me, keep talking! I love Portuguese!"

"What's the strongest beer you have?" I ask him. I can't meet Rachel completely sober.

"If you need to wake up, then Jack Daniel's would be better."

"A Jack Daniel's it is then, please," I say.

"Same for me, plus some nachos with extra cheese."

"What about the acroyoga?"

"To hell with yoga and protein, I'm dying of hunger," says Six.

"But, Six . . . Come on, wait, don't give up." I look at the waiter. "Do you do egg-white omelet?"

"Did you say 'egg-white omelet'?" The waiter bursts out laughing.

"Where do you think you are, Rita?" Six laughs. "In a high-end restaurant in Portugal?"

The Venezuelans arrive as the solid glass tumbler of whiskey draws a damp circle on the wooden tabletop. Six gets up in slow motion, throws her shoulders back, sticks out her chest like a peacock, and, with her innate sales skills, captivates the new arrivals in seconds, making them laugh loud and hard. I tell her she's a predator.

Before we can sit down, she arrives. A romantic French song is playing. Rachel heads toward our table, lips painted purple again, and I, unlike the others, remain standing and break out my welcome smile far too early. Because Rachel stops halfway to greet some friends, and I don't know whether to sit down—she isn't too far away—or stay standing with my smile—she isn't that close either—I down my whiskey in one, and the harshness of the raw alcohol forces my eyes to close—I never drink whiskey—and the empty glass slamming down on the table causes Six to pause in her Venezuelan-cajolement speech for a nanosecond that only she and I can identify, as if to say, *Why are you drinking so fast? Relax, for Christ's sake.*

The Venezuelans are laughing, touching their lips with their perfect manicures, and I laugh along at nothing in particular—I don't know what they're talking about—as I glance at Rachel out of the corner of my eye. I remember that night as I have so many times beneath my sheets, and my mouth fills with saliva. But, now that I look at her again, I realize I don't know her at all, that the only prior relationship I have with her is with her body, so similar to mine, with her bony shoulders and nimble hands.

"Hey, Rita!"

I'm excited, nervous, but the fact that she's a woman makes me feel an automatic closeness, as though we share a code that makes it all much easier, more intimate.

"Hi, Rachel!" The scent of watermelon. "How are you?"

We take the second round of whiskeys in red plastic cups to Six's house, just after Tek Soo arrives with our other classmates (a group she deems "entirely unnecessary"). And as Six shouts, "Christmas is shit! Death to enforced capitalism and the idolatry of real and invented machos!" we enter the code and go into the former school.

But today, instead of going straight to her apartment, Six wants to show off the building to the Venezuelans.

The damp cold stiffens my neck, so I take a long gulp of whiskey to loosen the muscle, and as it trickles down my throat, I notice that the rust around the lock on the main door is much worse than I remember. The alcohol runs sharply down my gullet; I feel it descending from my neck to my stomach, and the bad whiskey warms my skin. I stand aside for a moment, feeling suddenly dizzy.

"Come on! I'm closing the door!" shouts Six, jerking her head toward the Venezuelans' asses.

"You're crazy, Six . . ." I say into her ear. "Can't you see you won't score with them? That it would only make it awkward?"

"Death to fucking shitty Christmaaaas! Death to family dinners!" Six yells in the middle of the hallway, even more out of it than usual. "Death to Santa Claus and the motherfucker that birthed him!"

"Could you please shut up? There are children living here!"

"Even better! The sooner they find out about the deceit, the better! Drink!"

"You know, Santa Claus and the Three Wise Men." I'm dizzy; I've got the hiccups. "And the pages and the shepherds, and the *tió*, they don't make Christmas shit! Come on! Shut up!"

"You see? Jeez, even the fucking shitting log has to be a man! Viva Frida Kahlo, damn it!"

"Who is the *tió*?" asks Tek Soo.

"It's a log from Catalonia that shitssss . . ." I try to say.

"A log that shits?" he asks.

"I can't explain right now, Tek Ssshoo. Not right now."

We're taking the same route I took with Rachel. The display cases, the lacrosse prizes, the basketball court markers from the past that now cut across apartments and passageways. Rachel's watermelon scent. The menthol cigarettes she sucks through her purple lips. The velvet curtain.

"But fucking Christmas . . ."

I've had enough. I take Six into a corner; the others continue.

"Six, stop. Can you please tell me what's up with you?"

"It's . . ."

The pause has caught her by surprise and lessened the euphoria of her hatred. The alcohol allows us to do away with all usual digressions and get straight to the point. Her eyes fill with tears and a fresh rage. She's very drunk.

"It's . . ." She hesitates for a moment, but the surrender comes inexorably. "It's . . . can't you see, Rita? Haven't you noticed all this time?"

"Wh-what? What's up?"

"Can't you see that I'm alone? That I have no family?" A shudder runs through me. "Haven't you realized that no one ever calls me? That I can't grieve for my grandmother's death because I've never known what it means to have one? That I don't know what it's like to have a dad or a mom or a brother? That I don't know what it means to have a home to celebrate a fucking Christmas meal in?"

Another sudden wave of dizziness makes me wonder for a moment if I've just heard what I think I heard. But the tears and anguish of this new Six confirm the catastrophe. I remove my hands from her shoulders with theatrical slowness. Mouth half-open. And now I realize that, on some level, I've known all this since the day I met her.

"I . . . I'm sorry."

"It's okay." She smiles, wiping away her tears. "I've been alone for twenty-five years, and, as you can see, I haven't turned out too badly. But can you just allow me to hate these days of family and patriarchy in peace. For now, it's all I have. And now let's go. The Venezuelans are waiting for me."

Six rejoins the group with admirable ease. I suppose she's learned how to keep self-pity at bay.

I don't want to drink any more. Tomorrow I have to be in a fit state for Aksel, but Six begs me with arms outstretched. And how the hell can I say no to her now? I'm still in shock.

We drink the third whiskey in the laundry room, where Rachel drops all pretense of subtlety, glancing furtively and biting her lower lip in my direction. Her intention to repeat our night together is becoming abundantly clear.

Rachel sniffs my neck, strokes the palm of my hand—it reminds me of when I was little and my mom used to trace circles on my palm, singing "*Ralet, ralet*"—and she drags me over to lean me up against the leather vaulting horse. The Venezuelans are still laughing like crazy, and Tek Soo and the guys have managed to turn on an old radio that was hiding in a corner, under the rhythmic gymnastics ribbons. A punk version of a Christmas carol is playing.

Rachel grabs my face in both hands and kisses me. Everything stops.

Tek Soo's face is so red, it seems about to boil over. The guys let out a whoop—they've clearly seen this in porn—and the Venezuelans look at us as if Satan had appeared amid fountains of lava.

For her part, Six takes advantage of the moment and, in a surprisingly elegant turn, kisses the Venezuelan with the thinning hair, who seems to enjoy it. She enjoys it for as long as she lets herself go—the novelty, the adventure, the gentle touch—but the legacy of five hundred years of applied Catholicism and, even worse, living with South American telenovelas—"Sofia Francisca, get away from Federico Matías José, you depraved harpy!"—make her pull away with a jerk, and the Venezuelans leave en masse. Such drama.

After their departure, in an entirely unexpected outcome, I'm sure—it can't be; it can't be!—I'm sure I see Six getting it on with Tek Soo.

But Rachel's lips clamp against mine again in a steamy aura of whiskey and mint; she takes me by the hand, and we disappear from the room full of baskets of dirty clothes and hula hoops.

Mooooooccc! Mooooooccc!

I'm on a sardine boat, and the captain looks mad as he tugs hard on a rope. It's making a terrible noise. If it doesn't stop, my eyes will fall out; they'll be hanging out of their sockets; they'll bounce on my cheeks, and I'll only see the world intermittently.

Mooooooccc!

My eyes! My head! Make it stop, please! Stop!

Suddenly the light changes, and the captain disappears. I don't know where I am, but I'm not on a sardine boat, and it isn't a siren; it's my phone.

"Hello?" My tongue scrapes my palate with the double *l*.

"Rita?" I hear a familiar voice at the other end of the line.

"Yes, hello . . ." My head. "Who is it?" I see some big windows with bare trees on the other side. I'm on a top floor. Rachel is asleep next to me. I'm so thirsty.

"Rita, it's Samantha . . ."

"Sa-man-tha? How did you . . . ? Has something happened?"

"It's just that, the show is about to start and I spoke to Aksel and he was asking where you were and . . ."

I can't breathe. I look at my watch and realize I have five minutes. My heart pounds so hard, it's drilling into my head. Cold, hot, cold. I cry. I jump out of bed and fly down three flights of stairs.

Apart from a slim, friendly woman at the entrance, Aksel's school corridors are empty, everyone is in the theater. I pass through the security gate and, if it weren't for that woman—who knows I'm the Booklands' au pair and who's seen the state I'm in—I probably wouldn't have been allowed in.

"Top floor."

"Pardon?"

"You have to go to the top floor or you won't be able to get in."

I run desperately and find the theater door.

Although I open it as slowly as possible, the squeaking of the door makes about five hundred indignant heads swivel round to glare at me. It's quite an impression; the theater is huge, and there's a full house. There are parents and grandparents in their Sunday best; some are standing on the stairs and craning their necks to see the stage better.

I must have racked up at least three speeding fines on the way here.

Among the heads that turn with the noise of the door, I see Fulbright, looking at me enthusiastically and pointing at the stage, mouthing, "Aksel! Aksel!"

I'm tense, even tenser than when I used to perform myself. There's no space between my chin and my shoulders; my nerves seem to have eaten my neck.

He'll do fine.

He has to do fine.

Aksel does everything fine.

Always.

Anyway . . . It's not that hard . . .

All he has to do is break the rules of a hundred-year-old school with a nationwide reputation in front of five hundred people. He just has to betray the confidence his class placed in him as the sole representative to exhibit their science projects, in which they analyzed Bohr's theory in five languages—English, Spanish, Mandarin, French, and German—which will be translated simultaneously on a giant screen. That's all.

He'll only have to carry the guilt for abandoning all that. For taking this unique opportunity to demonstrate that science can also be rapped, Bohr's theory included. And he has to do it so well that, when his parents become aware of the fraud, they forgive him because their pride will be greater than their disappointment. And so that they'll accept that these months of lies have been worthwhile because Aksel has finally followed his instinct and found his flow.

It has to go well because there's no alternative. The lights go down. After a round of applause that fills my lungs, Aksel comes onto the stage.

All the spotlights fall on his golden hair.

The applause fades with a few final overenthusiastic claps—mine. Aksel doesn't start right away. For a moment, he looks at the audience and seems to be searching for something he doesn't find. He lowers his head, grabs the microphone firmly and looks at the floor. A giant image of

Copernicus in the year 1493 appears on the screen, behind his back, but Aksel pays no attention. He looks at the audience again, more brazenly now; he brings his hand to his forehead to reduce the glare of the spotlights, but he doesn't seem to find what he's looking for. I'm an idiot! He'll be looking for me!

I get up in the shadow of the top step and wave my arms as visibly as I can, but his parents are doing the same and blocking me out. Fulbright and Hanne look at each other and whisper, not understanding what's going on. Aksel lowers his head in defeat again, and the silence continues.

Seeing the boy's evident petrification, the audience gets up and cheers him on, American style—"God bless you!" "You can do it!" "Come on!"—and I shout as loudly as I can, but Aksel doesn't appear to hear any of what's going on around him, until Margaret Teacher is about to intervene and rescue him.

Catastrophe. Childhood trauma for life. Agoraphobia. Hatred of women. Stage fright.

Or perhaps not. Perhaps now is that pivotal moment that happens in the movies, when Aksel will start to rap like a pro and stun everyone into silence.

Silence. A glimmer of hope. But it doesn't happen.

Aksel turns, looks at Copernicus and the planetary model that inspired Bohr's theory, and starts to talk in Mandarin.

Listening to "All I Want for Christmas Is You" is usually one of my favorite parts of Christmas, but right now, under the shadow of the pine farthest away from the school parking lot, it feels like the saddest song in the world. A nightmare. Mariah Carey's voice blares out of every loudspeaker in the school to remind me over and over again that I've messed up. That all Aksel wanted for Christmas was me, and I wasn't there.

The treetops sway in a cold breeze, and the atmosphere outside the school couldn't be more festive. The parents are waiting for their little geniuses to arrive while discussing who will be the next to host the volunteer dinner to raise funds for research into AIDS or hippotherapy; they're all smiling, and, although I'll never be sure whether they're genuine smiles, today I believe them.

I see Hanne and Fulbright chatting to Pastor Paul; I see Samantha and Prrr and Brrr and Mrs. Gee, and all the other parents who greet me from a distance. All I want to do is leave. But I can't. I have to tell Aksel that I did come, that I'm here; I have to say sorry.

"Hangover?"

Wood and earth. The notes of Tom Ford waft unmistakably over me. John has the double gift of finding me when I think I'm hidden and surprising me as he does it. He's wearing a very elegant, long woolen coat and a white scarf. I give him a kiss on the cheek.

"Merry Christmas, John."

"I'm sorry that Aksel . . . I don't understand what went wrong . . ."

"Best to talk about it some other time."

John stays silent. He greets someone in the distance with a slight nod, confidently, even though he knows that the sight of the two of us could easily start a rumor. A rumor I wouldn't object to.

"What a night, eh?" He's wearing a gold Santa pin on his lapel. "You woke my whole team . . . They send their greetings."

"What?" Now I remember: I called him because I wanted him to come to the party.

"Thirteen calls in total that rang from San Francisco to Atlanta." He laughs mockingly. "I have a new phone, and I don't know how to put it on silent because it has no keypad, and when I answered, all I heard was some guy singing in Korean."

"What were you doing in San Francisco?"

"Things, Rita. I arrived just in time for the performance."

"For the performance. But why?"

"Didn't you see me? I gave the opening speech!"

"You? I don't get it."

"The school was founded by my family. It's one of the projects I feel most proud of."

"What? And you're only telling me now? And . . ." I'm so tired. "And what do you mean you've got a phone with no keypad?"

"Yes, it's incredible! It's the future!" He plunges his hand into his pocket and brings out a kind of black screen. "It's called an iPhone!"

"The phone has a name?"

"Yes . . . Look, it just has one button here and . . ."

Aksel emerges at last. Although he's only ten, he's already proficient in the art of the American courtesy smile. He's always been very good at it, but when he comes out of the school door and sees me, just as Mariah Carey is launching into "youuuuuuu," his smile drops from his face. The worst thing of all is that he doesn't look angry, just terribly sad.

I go to fetch Eva and Bini, who are playing in the playground—I need moral support—and we walk toward him.

"Why do you think Aksel didn't sing?" asks Eva in a confidential tone, her hair matted with dirt and playground grime.

"I don't know, Eva," I reply, broken.

"Maybe he had a tummy ache," says Bini. "Or maybe he needed the spotlight to show him where you were, Hairy."

Parmenides, Empedocles, and the Explosion

"I'm fine," he told me. "Honestly," he said.

I would have preferred a more conventional hatred, a less elegant and mature response, a tantrum to end all tantrums. The worst thing is that he seems to be telling the truth; this isn't just a strategy that will eventually explode in shouts and tears and reproach at my abandonment. He's so disappointed in me that he appears to have turned the page. My page.

"But I was there," I implored him.

"I'm really fine," he replied, not meeting my eye. And he closed his bedroom door carefully and with a smile.

Shit, Bini forgave me when I left his favorite toy figure outside in the yard for four days and the rain washed its face off (I drew it on again with permanent marker, but he had nightmares for a week). Even Eva forgave me when I left her locked in the car for two hours; of course, I paid for that by allowing her to forgo her daily soccer practice and letting her eat pancakes for a month, but it worked, because she didn't tell her parents (leaving a child locked in a car is one of the red flags in the au pairs' bible and means immediate extradition).

The au pairs' bible doesn't say anything about not being present at one of the most important moments in your charge's childhood, but it's worse than the rain washing the face off their favorite toy. Aksel doesn't seem to have much interest in forgiving me.

It's December 24, and I'm wandering around someone else's house, dragging my feet. I don't know what I'm supposed to do. I'm so sad, I focus on some details of the house I haven't noticed for a while, some of the smells I've gotten used to (the fabric softener in the laundry room, the warm wood polish scented with vanilla). The distance between Aksel and me is so tangible, I feel like we're starting over from the beginning, when we were all strangers.

I'm wearing multicolored glittery ankle boots and a black velvet dress with white cuffs. I bought it for the occasion in a supertrendy store called Urban Outfitters that I discovered one day with Six, after brunch at Murphy's. I wanted the ensemble to convey the perfect balance between intellect, fantasy, and the European touch, which would satisfy me and the Bookland family in general. But now the boots are weighing me down. I'm in no mood for glitter.

I drift between the living room, the study, and the kitchen, killing time in case Aksel emerges from his room. Since he doesn't seem to be in any hurry, I go to pee in Fulbright and Hanne's bathroom. I do that sometimes—"We have nothing to hide," she told me one day, and winked—and in there I see that the latest issue of *The New Yorker* has arrived.

I sit on the toilet, in a haze of mint and white lily, and flick through the magazine rack—the pre-Socratic texts of Parmenides and Empedocles, Heraclitus's *Fragments*, an essay about the programmable design of orthogonal protein heterodimers—and I stop peeing mid-flow when I spot an intruder. Perhaps you do have something to hide after all, my dear Hanne.

It's extraordinary, phenomenal: the "trivial and inconsequential" pages of *Vogue*, open at a page with the headline "The Perfect Looks to Welcome in 2008." I can't tell you how satisfying this is. Oh, Hanne, this is wonderful. How many of your core principles did you have to ditch to invest four dollars on this?

Even so, I pick up *The New Yorker* (I read that *Vogue* days ago; there was a chilling interview about Oprah's early life and a wonderful text by Truman Capote). Now I'm reading an incredible story about a girl who wrote her first novel using a cell phone like mine, one so basic you can't even play Snake. I sit there for so long, my legs go to sleep.

I wash my hands with a new soap and see that Hanne has replaced the usual no-brand moisturizing cream with Eau de Rochas, which I decide not to sniff because I'd die of homesickness for my mother's arms. This morning, I put on a bracelet she gave me before I left, but I had to take it off because it got caught in my arm hair and left my wrist bald. So painful. Nostalgia literally burns.

Walking on my heels, I leave the bathroom, trying to wake up my numb legs, and return to the living room to stand in front of the Christmas tree. Aksel is still shut away in his room. There's finally been a truce in the relentless Christmas music, and James Taylor's "Carolina in My Mind" is playing, adding a touch of poignancy to the scene.

The unsightly, unbalanced decoration of the tree would make Monica Geller and the Ferrero Rocher butler want to kill themselves, but on closer inspection, under the reflections of an illuminated wreath in the colors of the American flag, the branches are ordered by theme, and each bauble is full of content.

On some branches, the baubles are handmade, school craft projects from when the kids still colored outside the lines. Farther up, following their chronological evolution, we find mathematic formulae encapsulated in snowballs, Bini's favorite extinct animals, and a collection of miniature impressionist paintings by Eva. On the next branch, in the "national pride" section, hang Mount Rushmore, NASA, and MoMA, and slightly farther up, above a history branch—Lincoln, Luther King, Darwin—the shields of Harvard and MIT dangle alongside the one I bought, from Georgia Tech. All three at the same level, as though cum laude degrees from two of the most prestigious colleges on the planet could compare with a year-long English course. I'm not even enrolled at the university itself, I'm at the language school . . . God, I'm pathetic.

The branch with the greatest weight to bear, however, is the lowest of all: the literary branch. In addition to a collection of classics—on the redesigned cover of *Frankenstein*, Mary Shelley goes by her mother's name, Wollstonecraft—family tradition decrees that every year each member of the family must choose the book they've enjoyed most and recreate the cover in miniature to hang on the tree. A bibliography for future generations. But none of the Booklands is capable of choosing just one book, so every year they make two or three, and the branch is now touching the floor. The truth is that I couldn't choose just one either, and so my additions to the sagging branch are *The Martian Chronicles*, *The Shadow of the Wind*, *Love Story*, and *Cold Skin*, a mix of American and Catalan texts that have taken up residence in my head.

I don't know if it's purely the effect of living with the Booklands that has gotten me reading and writing. Would I have done the same if I'd been with a family of extreme Mormons who were against abortion and coffee? If I was looking after the kids of someone famous, like that au pair from Igualada? Or if I was living in an Amish community and a young man with curly hair and a beard convinced me of the joys of life without electricity?

Aksel is still in his room.

I don't think I'll bring out the *tió* tonight after all. To hell with it. It was meant to be a surprise, but I don't have the energy to create anticipation and put up with everyone poking fun at my log. I don't have the tiniest spark of magic left to bring it out tonight. Or to make it shit out the budget-range chocolates I bought for the occasion.

I fold the last napkins on the plates for tonight's dinner and ask Hanne and Fulbright if I can help them with anything else. But they're distracted, talking about the debate that's been going on for weeks.

"Obama has no experience, he's perfect as a candidate, but as a president . . ." he's saying. "Besides, it was time to have a woman. It was now or never!"

"Look," replies Hanne, "far be it from me to say there shouldn't be a woman president, having had men under me at work for fifteen years. But that's not the point, and anyway, a Black man won! So, for starters, progress and equality have won. And while he's an inexperienced socialist from Chicago, Hillary's establishment through and through! More of the same!" She's drinking white wine. "And, for the love of God, her husband cheated on her in front of the whole world and she forgave him!" It's just an instant, but Fulbright locks eyes with me; the ghost of Chitawas between us, the shame, the passion. "That's inadmissible, just plain dumb!"

"Do you have the soup under control?" he asks, trying to change the subject.

"And let's not forget," she continues, "that the Democrats have competed against a Vietnam vet, a prisoner of war for six years, who was tortured and repatriated. And we've done it with a Black hippie from Chicago and an establishment panderer." She drinks. "So, let's toast! It's Christmas, and in 2008, the country will be Democrat- and Harvard-run once again!"

"Can I help you with anything else?" I cut in.

"Ah! Rita, don't worry," Hanne continues, "we still have at least an hour and a half, so do what you like. You could drop in on your friend John, if you want . . ." She laughs jealously.

Fulbright stirs the spinach soup and says nothing. Since I caught him with Chitawas, our relationship has cooled. It's been ages since he asked what I'm reading, and I'm dying to tell him that the ending of *Love Story* blew my mind. I'd also like to tell him that I'm halfway through Capote's *In Cold Blood*, and that the house in Palamós where he wrote part of the book and spent three summers has been demolished. I'd like to tell him he should let himself go, that it's no big deal, that it's okay to be gay, even in Atlanta.

I go downstairs, breathing in aromas of fennel and cinnamon—neither of which particularly interests me—and look for Eva and Bini.

The door is ajar and I spy on them; on the floor they have the diagram for the electric closed circuit that Eva's building. Next to her, Bini has finished a Lego *Jurassic Park* kit for age twelve and over, with the relevant corrections for anachronisms.

They're about to land on the moon.

"Why do I always have to be Collins?" Bini complains, without relinquishing control of Apollo 11's navigation system. "No one even remembers who Collins is!"

"Because Aksel is Armstrong, and I'm Aldrin," replies Eva, simulating the lack of gravity by hunching her shoulders. "And we've talked about this so many times, Bini, childhood hierarchy goes according to age. It's the tradition, and it works."

"But . . . but Aksel's not even here! He's in his room!" His chin trembles; he's about to cry. "And I still haven't set foot on the moon!"

"All right," replies Eva, and her brother's chin stops. "I'll be Armstrong, and you're Aldrin."

"Yesss!" Bini pretends to push buttons. "Bip-bip-biiiip! Tssshhh . . . Boop-boop-boop! Finally, I can tread on the surface of the moon! I'm entering the *Eagle*, I'm entering the *Eagle*! I'll plant the flag on the moon . . . *One small step for man, one giant leap for mankind!*"

"Huh? I'm supposed to say that!"

"What are you doing, kids?" I interrupt with a hopeful smile.

"Hairy! Nooo!" they cry in unison. "Get out! Don't look! Go away!"

"But I'm not looking at anything . . ."

"No! Go away!"

Although I know they're only shouting at me because there's a half-wrapped gift for me on the floor, the hostility makes a lump form in my throat.

I need to get out of the house. I go to my room and grab my computer.

It's raining. The overilluminated neighborhood of Leafmore hides beneath a steamy fog, shrinking in my rearview mirror until it becomes an intermittent splotch of green and red lights. I drive fast. On the radio, Delilah is trying to cheer up a teenager with a broken heart. I change stations. "Highway to Hell" is playing. I turn up the volume.

My first idea is to go to San Francisco Coffee in Virginia Highlands and drown my sorrows in a double mocha, but I don't have much time. I call Six, and she doesn't answer. She must be enjoying herself at her Christmas-haters dinner. At least she's in the right country; there's a group for everything here. A dinner for hating Christmas. This Christmas. Perhaps I should have gone too.

There's only an hour until my own dinner. I stop off at my usual Starbucks as the water lashes against the glass. I check my reflection hopefully in the rearview mirror, but my tears are too obvious in my red, glistening eyes. If Andrew is on shift, I know he'll ask what's wrong. And I don't feel like talking. So I sit there, listening to gallons of water crashing against my bougie car. I tune back into Delilah, deciding that when they read out the phone number, I'll call in. In the meantime, I take out my computer and start to write.

I write about all the Christmas Eves when I've gone out in Puigcerdà.

I write that, this year, I won't walk through the snow in high heels and thick tights, or get home at seven in the morning, in the scant warmth of the last few dawns of the year to the sound of Antònia's cowbells. I won't get only three hours of sleep or set the table with a hangover offset only by the anticipation of the most delicious meal of the year.

I write about everything that's happening right now, at this precise moment, five thousand miles from here, as I cry in the parking lot of a fucking Starbucks in a city without sidewalks or *galets* soup, the stuffed pasta delicacy that fills my home with the smell of Christmas.

Andrew has spotted me and waves from the counter. He lifts up a cup with an inch of whipped cream. He wants me to go in, but luckily there's a very long line—don't people have a life? It's Christmas!—that means he can't come out here.

I feel terrible. What I really want to do right now is to call my mom, to lie on the sofa with my head on her lap, smelling her clothes and feeling like I'm home; for my dad's face to light up when he sees me, for him to tell me three new jokes and rave about how amazingly clear the picture is on TV today. I want to laugh with my brother, to make jokes that no one else understands. I miss it all. The spontaneous drinking sessions, the sea, and the mountains. The coffee in Aroma. I want to pick up the phone and be able to call whomever I want, whenever I want.

I shouldn't be here now. I should be in Alp, at home, where I can be a fucking disaster, but at least a free disaster who isn't destroying anyone's childhood.

The line in the café is shrinking, but Andrew still can't get away. "All I Want for Christmas Is You" is playing on the radio now. I switch it off. I put away the computer and close my eyes.

To be honest, I can't tell how much of what I'm feeling is homesickness and how much is my terrible guilt at having abandoned Aksel onstage.

I'm plagued by the memory of his little face searching for me in the audience. His bravery, all the effort he invested in that moment that was hanging on me, my presence there. Perhaps that's the problem, that I don't know what it means to truly strive to achieve something. That I've always decided not to think, to take shortcuts instead of risks. That I'm incapable of understanding what it means to feel vulnerable like Aksel did that night. To feel weak and defenseless and, despite all that, get up on the stage in front of five hundred people to defend who you are. I was the only missing piece. He wasn't asking much of me, just for me to be there. And I wasn't.

Aksel has finally come out of his room and seems even more pissed than before.

Hanne is wearing a new dress. She's parked the black polka-dot number from 1998 and has shrouded herself in something shorter, in bottle-green velvet with tiny beige dots, and, despite the usual orthopedic shoes, today she almost looks the age she is.

"Can you taste the soup, please?" she asks.

"You look lovely," I tell her.

She gives me a swift "thanks," looks away, and blushes.

"I think it needs a bit more salt," she continues, "but in this house, we rely entirely on you to be our taster now." She smiles at me sweetly.

I look at Aksel; he always jokes about the precision of my palate, but he's avoiding my gaze.

As soon as we sit down at the table, the Viking Christmas spirit takes hold of the Booklands. I'd like to smile, to let myself go, to climb up on my chair and recite a verse or two, bring out the *tió*, sing "Fum, Fum, Fum!" and eat as though I might be shipwrecked tomorrow. But I can't.

Conchi is watching me wistfully across the table, with a hint of compassion. Today of all days, we're both feeling the distance, and perhaps that brings us closer than ever. It's only my first Christmas away from home, but she's been doing this for fifteen years, one asylum appeal after another. Earlier, I watched her through the crack of the bathroom door and saw her crying and kissing a photo of her son.

Inevitably, there are no corny, preformulated verses here. Everyone has written a verse for someone in the family and hung it from a branch on the tree. Even though we all know who wrote what, it isn't until the end of the meal that we officially discover the authors.

I go first: I had it easy because I had to write about the neighbor's parakeet—Eva insisted on including it in the family—and my verse goes down pretty well. In fact, from Hanne's surprised expression at the last lines, I think I may have won some points.

"Hairy!" shouts Bini when he reads my name on the envelope. "This poem is for yóu!"

The poem starts by calling me Athena, goddess of war, wisdom, and handicrafts. But the author makes it clear that he didn't choose that name for wisdom—thanks, Booklands, that much has been obvious since day one—but because she's a warrior goddess.

One of Athena's main aims, says the second verse, is to protect the city of Athens, but in my case, the city isn't "the powerful polis of Ancient Greece," but the blue house at the end of Oak Paths Drive. The rhymes are impressive. It says that my Athens is more important to me than I think. "And inside that city-state, or polis, whether you know it or not, every last one cares about you a lot." Because within the four walls of this beautiful polis, it continues in verse three, live the muses that inspire me and drive me crazy but whom I always help. "The four divine sisters—oratory, theater, dance, and music—are not muses here; instead, there are three of them; fun-filled, inspiring, and brimming with cheer." "Haven't you guessed yet?" it asks. "Don't ponder unduly: Bini, Eva . . . and this humble apprentice of rhyme, yours truly."

The Bookland family breaks into the loudest applause of the night.

"You surpass yourself every year, Aksel! These are the best Christmas verses you've ever written!" cries Hanne.

"I didn't know you were such a master of rhyme!" shouts Fulbright, getting up. "I'm impressed!"

I'm so moved that I don't notice Aksel's tense expression. He's flushed, his hands pressed beneath his thighs as he kicks the table leg. I get up with teary eyes and go over to give him a hug. But, to everyone's surprise, he springs up and runs to his room, and, before shutting himself away for the rest of the night, he shouts, "I take it back! I take it all back! I wish you'd never come here!" This is awful, I want to disappear. "I mean it! I wish Daniela hadn't gone back to Colombia and you'd stayed in your shitty mountains! Which no one has ever heard of!"

The whole Bookland family is staring at me, utterly bewildered. In shock. Christmas down the drain. They're waiting for me to explain, because, from their faces, I can tell they've never seen Aksel like this. Silence.

"Has something happened between you?" asks Hanne.

"Well, I think that's pretty clear . . ." says Conchi, lifting her cup to her mouth, pinky raised.

"No, not as far as I know . . ." I lie.

"Aksel, Aksel wanted . . ." Bini speaks with the sense of duty of a five-year-old child. "Aksel wanted Rita to see him this morning . . . at the Christmas festival."

"But she was there," replies Fulbright, not understanding.

"Yes, but she arrived late. It must be because of that . . ." continues Eva, taking my side of the conversation.

"Ah . . ." says Hanne, who has her suspicions. "But there must be something else behind it."

"Best to let him be," I add. I want to go to my room; I want to go home. "I'll talk to him tomorrow and apologize."

"Well, only apologize if there's a need to, eh?" Fulbright says. "These kids can be rather rude when they want to be."

My God, I'm shameless. I abandoned Aksel at the most pivotal moment in his life, and now I treat him as though he's crazy. I'm the devil.

Traditional Norwegian desserts are any child's dream. Flans, chocolate brioches, crepes with cream, sugared doughnuts. Any other day I would have tried a bit of each, or even the whole lot. I put on one last fake Christmas smile, my cheeks almost cramping up, and thank the Bookland family for having shared their Christmas with me. I go downstairs and finally shut myself away in my room, counting the hours until Christmas is over and until I can go home.

Barbie's House Isn't Pink

"Re-remember not to tell Rita where we're going!" calls Bini, fastening his belt across the booster seat.

"I think you're creating more hype than the situation deserves," replies Eva, squeezing a stuffed elephant.

I don't know why we couldn't go in my car to wherever it is we're going. I got changed so quickly, I forgot to put on a bra, and I was counting on the emergency one I keep in my glovebox. I open the window, feeling a bit nauseous. I don't know why (and, obviously, I have no need for a pregnancy test).

From my European point of view, Americans—or Americans in Atlanta—have many unfortunate traits. Bikinis with a wraparound curtain are a disaster, the paranoid rules of the Boy Scouts, good wine in red plastic cups, life without sidewalks, people asking me when I'm going to get married, driving instead of walking, the sweetened bread, and "I'm sorry" wherever you go.

I also think they're pretty hopeless in the art of seduction—John being an exception—and the fact that they're always dressed as though heading for the gym doesn't help. But I'm aware of how biased my opinion is, having grown up within spitting distance of the French border, where sex for fun is a national trademark, and in Catalonia, where the wine is always served in proper glasses. Yes, I know,

Bourg-Madame, the French town just across the border that's visible from Puigcerdà, isn't exactly Paris, but it's still in France.

But if there's one thing about these people that warms my heart—apart from the creativity of their postcards and their general zest for life—it's the volunteering. Here, everyone volunteers.

There are companies that allow you to stop working for six months, on full salary, to devote yourself to a noble cause. I've seen Mrs. Gee, in her Ralph Lauren American flags from head to toe, giving free tennis lessons in schools in parts of the city where the balls disappear through holes in the fences. There have been nights when Fulbright and Hanne have come home exhausted from work but have dressed up and gone to a charity dinner they organized, where they've raised $500,000 for one of Hanne's team trips, and then I've seen them leave for Kenya, loaded with vaccines. Although, I have to admit, I thought they were laundering money at first (let's not forget, I also grew up near the border with Andorra).

But after a few months, I realized that no, they're doing it genuinely, with no financial benefit for themselves. They're simply doing it to help other people.

Today, two days after the saddest Christmas dinner of my life, the Bookland family, complete with au pair, is heading to one of those volunteer events. Today we're going to donate toys that the most privileged children have selected for other kids, to make better use of them.

"I calculated the remaining life of the Lego prehistoric creatures set, and it's really long." Aksel speaks loud and clear, albeit with an obvious disdain toward me. "Bearing in mind the wear and tear on the pieces, which is all of 1.456 percent in the last four years, that is, around 0.4853 percent per year, and also adding the probability of a 2 percent loss of pieces (a calculation that varies depending on the child), this toy has a very long life expectancy. At the very least, it could last another three generations; that is, obviating the influence of climate change on the humidity and temperature, and depending on the progressive policies of the Democrats, but I trust in Obama and the speedy development of the G8 roundtable on climate change in Davos, so the environmental factor seems unlikely to affect it."

"Hmm . . ." Eva replies in an equally serious tone. "I don't think you need to go into so much detail, Aksel. I don't know if the children will care about the life expectancy of some plastic dinosaurs. I think you should sell it better. Appall to the emotions . . ."

"Appeal," corrects Aksel.

"Appeeeal to the emotions; that's what Mom does when she wants people to give her money to go to Kenya: Explain how you've enjoyed the game, what you've learned from it, the historical incongruities you've found, how you think it could be improved."

"Brilliant!" exclaims Fulbright. "Well explained, Aksel, and well countered, Eva. As an irrelevant but constructive detail, I think your calculation of wear and tear isn't entirely precise."

"Yes, it is, Dad. I tested it. You're overlooking the fact that 2004 was a leap year."

"V-very good, Aksel. I'm proud of you," Bini cuts in, still gazing out of the window, while the rest of us contain our laughter, surprised at the authoritative tone of his congratulations.

We leave Lavista Road, turn onto North Druid Hills Road, and in a few minutes, we enter a U-shaped neighborhood. The distance between the houses is just a few yards, which, considering the sheer size of the dwellings—I'm not exaggerating when I say that, if they stood alone on top of a hill, they would pass for castles—makes them look like a joke, a decoration.

Emerging from the door of one of the castles, standing straight like Forrest Gump and with so much hair gel, it could take someone's eye out if they're not careful, is Eric, the collector of presidents. The boy born knowing what he wanted to do with his life.

"Don't take this the wrong way, Dr. and Dr. Bookland, but it's been years since I agreed with my parents that we'd only ask Santa for the crucial accessories for my presidential collection. I'm afraid I couldn't bring any unused gifts because I don't have any." This child is eighty years old, he's won three Nobels, and he's wearing a white tank top.

"And which president did Santa Claus bring you this year?" I ask.

Hanne looks at me in the rearview mirror.

"No president this year, Rita. But, bearing in mind that the honorable George W. Bush's days are numbered, Santa brought me an exact replica of the telephone he used just two weeks ago to call the armed forces in Afghanistan."

"Impressive!" says Fulbright sincerely. "This collection is unique. I admire the originality and precision of your work. It's very good that you have such a well-defined goal."

"Thank you, Dr. Bookland. My aim is to amass the most complete collection in the country. My vocation is very clear."

Recently, whenever anyone says the word "vocation," my heart starts to race. I lower the window again.

"Is there far to go?" I interrupt the conversation.

As we get closer to our destination, the traffic increases. We join a line of cars heading toward a gateway on a bend, where two local teenagers, so perfect they might have been drawn with Photoshop, are volunteering to park cars.

The house is tremendous. Tremendous in a good way. Symmetrical and painted such a tasteful grayish blue, it almost makes me emotional. I guess it must be twice the size of ours.

I get out of the car and hold the gaze of one of the hunky teenagers. Cougar. But he holds my gaze for longer, incredibly sure of himself in his perfect body. I'm weaker, and I lose.

Samantha greets me enthusiastically from the top step. She's waving so vigorously that her emerald earrings seem to be dancing a Polish polka. From the bottom of the steps, her legs look more streamlined and stylish than ever, the soles of her Louboutin heels a perfect red. By her side, I feel like a hairy hobbit.

"Oh my Gooood! *Amore!* How wonderful to see you! I didn't know if you'd come. I left you a message, but since you didn't reply, I thought you must be at an orgy or something." She's not laughing; she's deadly serious.

"Sorry, you know I'm hopeless with the phone." Samantha is wearing a white cashmere sweater with a long plume, like a real swan. "What an amazing mansion! I feel like I'm hallucinating, I'm dying to see inside. I hope it doesn't have gold faucets . . ."

"No, don't worry."

"You've been in already?"

"Well, I chose them."

"What?"

"Welcome to my home, Rita."

"What?" She's only fifteen years older than me, and she already lives in a palace.

"My ex-husband is a famous surgeon. And he's free to be a famous surgeon because I've been at home raising his children and taking them to piano and ballet and basketball while he built a career and I didn't." She looks at me, waiting for me to say something.

"You're a great mother." The conversation is interrupted by a disingenuous embrace from one of her ex-husband's star clients.

"Never do that, Rita."

"What, get my lips filled?"

"Shut up, I'm serious."

"Cheekbones? Hag mouth? My tits?"

"You have to build yourself a career, Rita." And we're back on the subject of careers and the future and all that shit. My heart is racing again; it's even worse than in the car. I raise my hand to my chest. What the hell is wrong with me? I haven't even had any coffee today! "Live your life, Rita. These years are so important for your future." Oh yeah? You don't say. "I'm sure you'll do great things, Rita, great things."

"Yes, yes, of course."

At the age of twenty-three, I finally enter the Barbie mansion.

Welcoming me with his toothless smile and so much love it would make you melt, Mike decides to break the welcome protocol and, instead of shaking my hand, buries his face in my stomach and wraps his arms around me. Aksel watches from the corner of his eye and walks away.

"I'm so glad you came! I have a surprise for you!"

"Wow, really?"

"When you go into the kitchen, look next to the salami and prosciutto, and you'll see there's a plate with *pa amb tomàquet*, just like you taught us to make. Mom bought the olive oil you said. The Arbequina one."

"I don't believe it."

"Go and try. I can't, I have to stay here, I'm in charge of saying hello. I'm very important."

"You really are—you're the most important of all. Thanks very much, Mike."

The house is full to bursting. Most of the guests are still crowding into the entrance hall and forming a line of parents and children leaving gifts at the foot of a tree that puts the Rockefeller one to shame. The guests smile, holding proper glasses—this is the first party I've been to where people haven't been drinking from plastic cups—I walk past small groups and catch fragments of conversations: Some enjoyed *The Nutcracker* on Broadway; others are complaining about the quality of snow in Aspen.

On my way to the kitchen, I greet Prrr and Brrr, and the soccer coach and the baseball coach and Sheryl, the short, histrionic woman I played tennis with the other day, who congratulated me afterward because I won with a ruthless backhand. And because "until now, no one from around here has been able to beat me . . ." Well, I'm sorry, Sheryl, I'm just that good.

I keep moving, enjoying the usual sideways glances from people, pretending I don't notice with great professionalism and a contained smile. Deep down, I'm happy because even after all these months they still see me as exotic and mysterious.

On the other side of the dining room, leaning against the mantelpiece above which I could swear there's an original Miró hanging, Pastor Paul greets me, raising his glass in the air, but only out of obligation; he doesn't come over. It's clear that neither he nor God has forgiven me yet for the celestial wiener.

Eva is playing with Mary. Bini is waiting patiently for Mike to finish his welcoming duties, and Aksel has decided to pay heed to his sister and write a motivational annex to the introductory note to the Lego set.

I grab a slice of *pa amb tomàquet* and a strawberry caipirinha made for me by a professional waiter, and take a tour of the house.

I imagine Samantha in this gilded cage; the echo of her stilettos with each solitary step, as she waits for her kids to come home from school and for her husband to finish fucking his secretary. As she feels that life is slipping away from her, just like the sand slips through her fingers on her private island off Hawaii. I imagine her playing a sad song on the grand piano, lamenting the fact that she didn't grow up in an artistic quarter in Europe, where she could walk in flat shoes and feel the air of the old continent on her unshaven armpits. Wishing she hadn't been born in Atlanta, hadn't grown up with a uniform and knowing the protocol for afternoon tea; wishing her father and grandmother hadn't planned her wedding to the very last detail, on the day Samantha turned twenty.

"Hello, Rita, how are you?" Mrs. Gee is even dressed as a tennis coach here.

"Hi, Mrs. Gee! Fine, just fine. And you, how are you?"

"Fine, fine . . . I've been wanting to speak with you for days."

"Oh yeah? Is everything okay with Bini?"

"Yes, yes. Bini's such a polite boy . . . Tennis isn't his strong point, but . . . Anyway, I wanted to speak to you because my son is a psychologist and, since you told me you studied psychology . . ." I cough from lack of air. "I thought you might be interested in talking to him." I smile; I don't say anything. "Well, I guess that this au pair thing is only temporary, that at some point you'll want to start working in the field you studied."

"Yes, yes, of course . . ." My God, has everyone decided to gang up on me today? "Thanks very much for the offer. I'll check my diary and suggest a day."

I trudge downstairs. The murmur of the crowd diminishes behind me until I feel the pleasant connection between my shoes and the fluffy white carpet of the lower floor.

I pass the heated pool and the games room. I pass three matching guest rooms with en suite bathrooms. I pass the vaulted, temperature-controlled wine cellar and the home gym. Finally, I enter a small room with a padded leather bar and six high stools upholstered in navy-blue velvet. It seems like an antechamber to something else.

On the other side of the room, a sofa upholstered in the same fabric and color contrasts with the tropical-leaf wallpaper, over which a series of watercolors is hung. There's also a golden record player and, next to it, a door with an unlighted sign saying "On Air."

A radio studio? A recording studio?

And suddenly, as though it has sensed my presence, the sign lights up.

The moment of hesitation is so negligible, it barely counts. I venture down a corridor with walls covered in the same tropical paper and open the door right at the end.

Bingo.

Around twenty armchairs in bottle-green velvet are arranged in four rows facing a movie screen. The light is dim, it reminds me of the home movie theater in *The Aviator*, the luxury and adventure. Leonardo di Caprio.

"Shouldn't you be watching the children?"

I hadn't noticed the man sitting in the second row. The soundproofing of the room makes the sound of a match striking sound very close. The tiny flame lights up his face.

"And do you always have to appear as though we were in the final scene of *Casablanca*?"

John is wearing a black polo shirt that emphasizes his pecs. His feet are resting on one of the little leather pouffes that sit behind each chair.

"You're funny."

"The kids are big enough, and that's what their parents are for . . ." He releases the smoke jerkily. "How did you know I'd come in when I saw the light was on?"

"Because you're the only person here who would dare to snoop around this much."

"Oh yeah? Well, people are boring. What are you watching?"

"They aren't boring. It's *The Shining*."

"Boring. *The Shining*, the perfect Christmas movie."

"They're conservative, Rita." Something is up with him. "They're scared, like you and me, but I wouldn't say they're boring, and what they're doing is very worthy; don't look down your nose at what's going on upstairs. That money will help a lot of people . . . a lot of children." I say nothing. Now I feel guilty. He takes a long drag. "But you don't give a shit about any of that . . . You're just here in passing. You'll leave before too long, and all this will remain behind. Everything that happens today, here, it's all a game to you." I don't know if he's intense or pissed off.

"For my entire existence, I've always thought that life was like a game. I've never taken anything that seriously, so, for the moment, you aren't telling me anything new." I take a gulp of caipirinha and go down the three steps to John's row. On the screen, Jack Nicholson is talking to the secretary, ready for his job interview. "Anyway, what's the most popular man in the city doing in the fringes of the underworld?"

"I'm not in the mood for it. I don't like Christmas festivities." He offers me the joint. "Good thing you aren't boring."

I feel a tickling in my gut.

"Oh no? You're stoned."

"No, you aren't boring, Rita. Perhaps just for the fact that you've ended up in this corner of the world without meaning to. Anyway, you're the least likely au pair I've seen in my life, and I've known a lot of au pairs, believe me. It's obvious you have no knack with children." He shuffles his ass down to the edge of his seat like a teenager.

"Thanks very much . . . Even if that's true, it kind of makes me mad to hear it."

"Don't be offended. The fact that you don't like children doesn't mean you haven't gotten them to love you. Don't you see it?"

I stay silent.

"But . . . it doesn't matter!" he continues. "You'll leave . . . You'll leave here with what you came to find, and you'll head back to your beautiful Barcelona, and you'll go to La Boqueria and have breakfast with Juanito, and you'll live with your friends and your family and do what you want to do in life. And I'll still be here, raising money for those in need, in a never-ending loop. A loop with no family."

"Come on, don't exaggerate. After I leave, any day you like you can get into Lola, fly across the Atlantic, and land in Alp. We have an airfield, and you'd love my village."

"And Antònia's cows, the Sanavastre trail, skiing under a full moon from Niu de l'Àliga, and blah, blah, blah . . . It's like I've lived in Cerdanya all my life. As though I lost my virginity in Trànsit. See? I listen!"

"Impressive."

"Yeah . . ."

"But have you seen yourself? You couldn't be more perfect, damn it. Stop complaining."

"I'm just having a bad day. Like I said, I don't like Christmas."

"I . . . I haven't liked this one much either. But . . . we'll get through it."

"I suppose. I've hated it for about twenty years now—I'm a pro."

"Well, at least you don't have to worry about January price hikes like the rest of us." I laugh.

"Ha, ha . . ." Before his next drag, he holds my gaze a bit longer and smiles. "I'm sure you'll do great things, Rita. You'll shine bright."

"Shit, here we go again."

He looks at me uncomprehendingly.

"What?"

"I'm fed up with everyone saying that. I can't take anyone else telling me that with such impunity. Why do you all do that? How can you all say it with such certainty, when you have no idea?"

"Say what?"

"Great things! What is 'great things' supposed to mean?" I'm raising my voice. "What are 'great things'?" My heart is pounding; I'm struggling to breathe. "Enough! I just want to find a job I like! And that's it! To have a routine, or maybe not, but to work. For my parents to be proud of what I've achieved. I want to get up in the morning with a clear direction, knowing that the day will have some meaning and I'll have been productive, that I'll have contributed something tangible and interesting to this world, whatever it might be, but something that's meaningful, that gives me enough money to live. I don't want to do 'great things'—jeez, I just want to do something!"

"Sweetie, I get it. Isn't that what we all want, Rita? To discover what we've come here to do?" I don't know if he quite grasps the gravity of the moment. "You'll manage, I'm sure of it."

"But I don't know what else to do! I don't know where or how to look for more! H-h-how . . . I'm supposed to . . ." My heart is racing. Something bad is happening to me.

"Are you okay?"

I jump up. I start pacing rapidly to try to understand and justify my accelerated heart rate. But it doesn't work. I shake out my arms and hands. I jump. I run up and down.

John follows me with his arms open, as though expecting me to fall at any moment. I take off my sweater, unbutton my shirt, and the effort makes me see colored lights.

Jack Nicholson bashing at his typewriter starts to fade. I rub my eyes as hard as I can, but my heart pounds faster still, and the little lights won't disappear. I think about finding a bathroom. (Why? I don't know!) What's happening to me? I need a strong stimulus, so I slap myself in the face.

"Rita! Stop!" I grab my glass and pour the rest of the caipirinha over my face. But it doesn't work. I can't feel my hands, or my feet, or my left arm. Shit, shit, it's a heart attack! I'm having a heart attack!

"Breathe."

But why am I having a heart attack at the age of twenty-three? Isn't my whole life supposed to be flashing before my eyes? I can't see it! Where's Rin Tin Tin? That dog was important to me in my youth! And I can't see him!

"Breathe." John is frightened but manages to speak calmly; he seems to know what's happening to me. He grabs me by the arms. "Rita. Look at me. Breathe!"

"I . . . I can't . . ."

"You're having a panic attack. It's okay." What's a panic attack? "Look at me and concentrate: Put your hands over your mouth and nose, like this, like a tent, and breathe inside the tent." John's stoned eyes are very funny and I'd like to laugh, but I can't right now because I'm dying. "Close your eyes and breathe. Rita, believe me, it's all going to be fine . . ."

I breathe in, breathe out. My eyes fill with tears. Breathe in; breathe out. I can't stop crying. Breathe in; breathe out. I notice the expensive, thick, soft carpet, first in the palms of my hands, then my arms, finally my face. The floor.

It's working. After a long and utterly terrifying time, the tent manages to reduce my hyperventilation and, when my heart recovers its usual rhythm, I stay lying on the carpet, as though I've fainted but am still conscious.

I feel like I've just run a marathon. Like I've just had twenty-six orgasms in one day. Spent. A prickling sensation ripples across my teeth and I can barely talk; I can feel it in my hands and feet too. John says it's normal.

"The animal instinct responded to what your body interpreted as a danger, and your heart pumped all your blood to confront it: to your mouth, to bite; to your hands, to fight; and to your feet, to run."

Very interesting. Please let it never happen again.

The final prognosis of the "great things" expected from me cost me dear. It was the straw that broke the camel's back. Now I understand why the day before yesterday I woke with a cry that left me sitting up in bed, and I also understand the random tachycardia I've been experiencing while calmly watching Obama's speeches. I would have preferred any of the other symptoms of anxiety that John mentioned—except for the suicidal feelings—like backache, for example. And what can I do to stop it from happening again?

"Stop putting pressure on yourself," says John. "You don't realize it, but you do it continually."

A long time has passed, and the two of us are still lying there completely still.

I'll try. I'll try to stop comparing myself to my friends and their professional careers on the other side of the Atlantic; I'll try to stop thinking that I'm too late for everything, that the Coen brothers started to make movies at the age of eight, that Whitney Houston was singing professionally at fourteen. And I won't even look at Lisa Simpson. I'll try to stop thinking that the kids have a much clearer purpose in life than I do. Even Bini. Perhaps it's true, but self-flagellation won't lead me to anything productive.

The background buzz of children's toys on the floor above fades entirely as the end credits of *The Shining* are cast across my face and John's.

If someone comes in and sees us, they'll think we've just had the fuck of the century; I've felt my phone vibrating in my pocket about twenty times, but I can't move. I want to stay here for a million years, or forever, in this home movie theater, with John, watching all the movies ever made. I'd start with *Blue Velvet* or *My Blueberry Nights*.

Breathe in; breathe out. The usual promising scent of wood and earth seeps through John's shirt. My eyes are closed, my face has moved from the warmth of the carpet to rest on his chest, against the pleasant graze of body hair beneath his collar. The damp smack of his lips detaching from the cigarette above my hair. I'd like someone to take a black-and-white photo of us.

I touch my lips and realize that the prickling in my teeth has almost disappeared; I can feel my extremities again. I move my fingers as though waking from a long dream. I stroke my fingertips, my movements so slow and delicate, I don't recognize them. Reality returns; my breathing calms; the movie theater comes back into color.

On the screen, Dustin Hoffman is standing stiffly on a moving walkway. "The Sound of Silence" fills the room and reaches our ears from the velvety reverberation of the armchairs. A thousand dust particles shine inside a perfectly defined tube of light.

My exhausted body slots against John, who is holding me gently. I close my eyes again to visualize the air entering my nose and leaving through my mouth, like he told me to do. As though I was learning to do it for the first time. That's all I think about. Being here, breathing. Some more time passes. Dustin Hoffman meets Mrs. Robinson.

Now, after the storm, the room doesn't feel as cold as the snowy maze in *The Shining*. Now it's warm, the screen is showing corduroy sofas, fur coats, and hairstyles ready for adventures, like Hoffman's.

With the clarity given by having felt your own death for the first time, it's like I'm no longer breathing just to exist, but to feel. I'm grateful to still have my head resting on his chest, his arms gently encircling me.

I breathe in his smell, the woven thread bracelets on his wrist, the rough palms of his hands (tennis, African safaris). I recover my strength little by little; my energy returns sweetly; sparks of light ignite my insides and warm me up. I'll treat myself better, I will. Patience, I'm not as old as I think.

Dustin Hoffman goes into Mrs. Robinson's room. The energy keeps growing, like an ivy climbing from my ankle to tangle through my hair.

I sit up. I look him in the eye gratefully, my renewed life on my lips. He looks at me and smiles, happy to be here, now, with me. My face smells of caipirinha.

I think of the first time I saw him, at the club, when my sweaty tits had drawn two wet half-moons on my flesh-colored T-shirt; when he pointed out the trees of unknown name with the tip of his racket and I didn't know English, and he was like Kevin Costner in *Dances with Wolves*.

I remember his playing the trumpet. Two tongues playing with an ecstasy tablet and that naked back playing the grand piano. I remember that he looked at me and smiled, and I thought I'd never dare to kiss a man like that.

Dustin Hoffman jams the church doors shut with a giant cross . . . and John and I make love. A thousand dust particles are suspended in the air, invisible. Our bodies in the dark outside the mellow glow of antique lamps. This can only be the center of the universe.

The Unexpected Happens: "Oh Happy Day!"

"Hairy . . . Do fish get water in their eyes?"

These are the words of the same child who yesterday was proudly applauding his brother's mathematical calculation of the lifespan of a toy. The same whose lower lip is now brimming with saliva, a sure sign that he's been mulling over the question for some time.

"Or do they keep them closed," he continues, "and swim like that, and when they jump out of the water, they open them, then close them again when they land back in the water?"

Shit, it's only nine o'clock in the morning. It's my day off, and I volunteered to take them on a cultural excursion to make up for my sudden disappearance last night "due to a panic attack." We're in the car, on the way there. And I think, *Do fish even have eyelids?*

"Well, Bini . . ." I stretch out my words long enough to allow one of his siblings to intervene.

"Fish don't have eyelids, Bini." Aksel is doing his best to control his annoyance. "Don't you remember what they explained at the conference on the physiology and hydrodynamics of fish at the Natural History Museum in New York?"

"He was three, Aksel. Of course he doesn't remember!" Eva is flicking through her printouts of all the shots used by Guardiola's Barça B team; she looks lovely, strands of messy blond hair escaping her ponytail to fall untidily over her slightly bulging forehead.

"But if they don't have eyelids, how do they sleep?" Bini's starting to stress out. Sometimes this happens when the question is too big and the answer takes too long in coming.

"Well, I suppose they must sleep with their eyes open, Bini," I intervene, without really thinking about it, just to calm him. "Like Mr. Satan in *Dragon Ball*, or Gandalf!"

"Did you just say Satan? Why are you talking about Satan now, Hairy? Do you mean I should ask God about it?" Bini can't quite grasp how we've ended up here. "How can you get to sleep if you don't close your eyes? You wouldn't be able to stop looking at everything!"

"Don't listen to her, Bini. Rita doesn't know what she's talking about." Aksel's on the attack, but I say nothing; I don't want a confrontation. "Who would think of explaining the discipline of ichthyology through religion or fictitious characters no one's heard of?" He makes his tone as scathing as he dares.

After my bittersweet evening yesterday, I can't afford any more slipups. I park in a vacant space outside Martin Luther King's house.

"Don't worry, Bini." Eva takes ownership of the silence, apparently unconcerned, a sign of clear emotional intelligence. "Fish have been on this planet for much longer than humans. I'm sure they know what they're doing."

Other than seeing his speech in schoolbooks and movies, until a few weeks ago, I knew next to nothing about him. So I went to the national history shelf in the house and found the official book: *The Autobiography of Martin Luther King, Jr.* And when Andrew saw me holding it in Starbucks, he said, "If you start this book, there's another you'll have to read."

"Then I won't start it," I joked.

But Andrew didn't laugh.

I read the book and steeped myself in the life of Martin Luther King. And when I told Andrew I'd finished, he stared at me, put down the pile of the *New York Times* he was carrying, and produced the book he'd been keeping behind the counter for this very moment. *The Autobiography of Malcolm X.* He held it out to me with both hands, as if consciously bearing the weight of the words he was giving me, just as serious as the day he didn't laugh.

"The future belongs to those who prepare today," he told me, and I asked if that was a dig aimed at me, who had studied for a degree for nothing, and would like to be preparing for a professional future, but still didn't know which.

But he didn't answer, and, once I had the book in my hands, he offered me something that sounded like Thai latte, his usual broad smile back in place.

I finished the book last week, simultaneously enlightened and terrified. Because of the racism Atlanta had seen, because of the dark history of the South and the rest of the country, because of what was still happening.

Suddenly, I felt the impact of living so close to where that beautiful and horrific story had taken place, and I had a terrific urge to go there. I found it incredible that we lived just fifteen minutes from his house. All the way from Antònia's cows to Martin Luther King.

I look at the house and say emotionally, *"I have a dream."* Then I look around me, and the absence of people in this fairly central neighborhood makes me wonder. Where is everyone? I pick up the book and compare the photo again to make sure we're not in the wrong place, which wouldn't surprise me.

"Why have we come here?" complains Aksel. Again. "I've already been with school!"

Perfect, we're in the right place. Aksel keeps on grumbling as he combs his curls back with his fingers. Now I see him from a distance, in full daylight, I could swear he's grown and gotten slimmer. For days, I've been wanting to give him a hug, but chances are he has a lethal syringe filled with sodium thiopental—the things I'm learning with this family!—to get rid of me once and for all.

"But you haven't been with me," I tell him.

I open the wooden door into the complex, anesthetized by the moment. I feel the weight of history beneath my new pink leather high-heeled boots, gazing at the window where the great man very possibly wrote his speech for posterity. I imagine the last time he touched this door, before that fatal morning in Memphis, the significance of the . . .

"Where's Bini?"

"What?"

"I can't see Bini." Eva's focused voice wakes me up like a sharp slap.

"What? What do you mean? He was here a moment ago!"

"He wasn't 'here a moment ago,' Rita." Aksel is angry. "You got out of the car without even watching us, or checking whether we had our jackets or anything. As usual."

"Bini? Bini!" Eva shouts, worried.

I look all around, and I can't see him. All I see is a group of junkies at the end of the street.

"Don't worry, he must be here somewhere, it's all fine . . ."

"Biniii!" Aksel starts running, nervous. He checks the car, then jogs up the stairs two at a time to look in the house.

"Bini?" I try to stay calm. I analyze the surroundings and think like a five-year-old boy. Well, no, I don't—I think like Bini. I'm shitting myself. I see a sports court, a church . . .

"Evaaaa!" Aksel shouts for his sister, who is running toward the junkies.

"Eva! *What are you doing?*"

I run after her, Aksel behind me. Eva is putting into practice all the tricks I've taught her to run as she's never run before; the momentum of her arms, the length of her strides, her drive, and, when I finally catch up, she's already chatting to the junkies.

"In the church! They say they saw him go into the church!"

I make sure Aksel and Eva are following me, and now I'm running. I sprint in my pink ankle boots like I just stole a ball from the defense in a basketball game. The junkies are shouting, "Run, Forrest, run!" No one ever catches up with me.

I climb the stairs to the white door of the church and fling it open, spreading my arms as far as I can.

My dramatic entrance makes the pastor stop short in his sermon and demands the attention of around a hundred believers in the pews (the place is jam-packed). Men in jackets and ties; women in a thousand colors of fabrics and hats, feathers and veils in front of their eyes. It's a sight to behold.

But none of that matters to me because I see Bini in the last row, alive and unharmed, listening to the service with his hands beneath his tiny ass, and he looks at me with surprise, as though he wasn't expecting to see me. As if he were the father of a family and I were a distant cousin passing through, the last person he expected to see.

"Oh, Hairy!" the little guy says with complete calm. "Shhh . . ." He tells me to be silent and calm down. "Have you finished the tour already?"

I look at him without saying a word, take him by the hand, and try to make room for myself next to him and his siblings in the most discreet pew I can find.

But the pastor doesn't seem to like the idea.

"Now listen here, young lady!" The church is silent. What is the deal with Atlantan preachers and me? The man raises his arm atop the pulpit and asks for an explanation. "What do you mean by bursting into the house of the Lord like this?" His accent is thick, southern, Black, and he's asking out of curiosity; he really wants to know. "You scared us!"

"Sorry, sorry everyone, I'd lost a child . . ."

"Well, all right then, welcome to your house."

The pastor continues with his sermon. We can't leave now; I interrupted him just as he was introducing a visiting choir from Birmingham.

"Hairy"—Bini nods toward his hand—"my haaaannnd!"

I'm not squeezing it in anger; I'm squeezing it in fear. Fear of having lost him. Because Aksel was right: I'm hopeless. If it weren't for the fact that they're extremely gifted and self-sufficient for their ages, there's every chance I would have lost them at some gas station in Alabama on the first trip to algebra class. Because, let's face it, they're the ones who take care of me.

The pastor is talking about honesty and telling an anecdote about his neighbor Kimberley, by way of example.

The choir from Birmingham is getting ready; they're all dressed in purple floor-length robes.

Trumpets, sax, and a drum. A piano starts. A young, bald man with a goatee starts to sing from the corner.

"Oh happy day . . ."

The members of the choir, arranged in three rows, gravitate in unison from right to left, with fully coordinated movements, creating a gentle, hypnotic scene. This is the first time I've seen a gospel choir sing.

"Oh happy day . . ."

The young man has a very deep voice, with such power . . . He guides the rest, maintaining a low, calm tone, until after one more "Oh happy day," he raises his voice and starts the new verse with an "eeeeeaaaa . . ." that climbs in pitch and volume.

The whole choir takes it up a notch. Explosion! They clap to the new rhythm. Another explosion! A torrent of bold, joyful voices generates a burst of energy that climbs to the ceiling and takes over the whole room, my shoulders and neck, the children's bodies, everything.

I want to shout something tacky like "Carpe diem!" but I make up the words and sing along, and feel that with every clap of my hands, I'm gaining an extra year of life.

Out of the corner of my eye, I watch Aksel, mesmerized by the swaying robes, the art of the song, the setting. Because he knows what it means to be on the stage, to make yourself vulnerable and tell a story with voice and hands.

The conductor of the band, who must be eighty, is giving tiny hops and his smile couldn't be wider, caught up in the force of the music. I see arms raised, hands on hearts, eyes closed, and people leaving their pews and spreading out to follow the rhythm with their legs. The energy is incredible, the voices echoing in my lungs, the kids can't stop laughing. Let this never end! Let time stand still! We sing with our hands and our feet and with everything we are at this moment. We sing to life, and we sing to the four of us. To being here, now, all together.

The music stops abruptly, and, despite the sudden silence, the room remains submerged in a cloud of magic. The members of the choir raise fists in the air and give us about thirty smiles brighter than the morning sun creeping through the windows of Ebenezer Baptist Church.

I look at Aksel with the feeling of having freed myself of a great weight. I grab him by the shoulders and look him in the eye.

"Aksel . . ." I get a lump in my throat; he's looking at me as though he wants to listen. "It was my fault. It was my fault that I didn't get there in time for you to see me from the stage." He lowers his head, hurt. "It isn't true that I stopped to revive a deer—"

"Oh, really?" asks Eva, disappointed.

"No . . . I'm sorry. But as I was driving like crazy, hoping to get there in time to see you, I thought that even if I wasn't there, it would all go well. That the bravery that had gotten you onto that stage was all you needed, that you didn't need anyone else to rap Bohr's theory on your own. That you didn't need me. Because you'd already done it, Aksel." He finally lifts his head. "You've already found your passion in life, and you did the hardest thing of all: You faced up to it. You're an example to everyone. To me and to your siblings, and they don't know it yet, but to your parents too. I'm so sorry, Aksel. Please forgive me."

"Yes, forgive her, Aksel," says Bini, who's hugging Eva.

Aksel gazes at me through his blond curls, without pushing them back from his face. The congregation is starting to disperse, shooting us affectionate smiles as they pass. Aksel finally yields. He ignores the unwritten rule that no prepubescent boy can show signs of affection toward his au pair, and he hugs me. He hugs me tight. I finally smell that scent of dust and vanilla from his hair, his body skinnier and taller. I close my eyes and think that I never could have imagined loving him so much.

We leave the church buzzing with the kind of jubilation you usually feel after a good concert. The community splits up into a dazzling regiment of multicolored hats.

The pastor says goodbye after confessing to Bini that he's not sure whether Satan sleeps with his eyes open or closed, and invites us to come back soon.

We find the car surrounded by buses that, by this time, are unloading a veritable flood of tourists visiting Martin Luther King's house. The children and I link hands and cross the street in a beautifully uncoordinated sprint, and as we reach the other side, as I notice a thin film of dust over my pink boots, the unexpected occurs.

"Rita?" A high, clear, Catalan voice is calling me. It's coming from a girl about my age, slim and olive skinned. I don't know who she is.

"Yes?" I reply, astounded, as though I've just met a stranger who's come through an impossible space-time portal. "Sorry, do we know each other? I'm really bad with faces . . ."

"Shit, what a surprise! I'm Elena, a friend of Alba Casamayor, do you remember?"

The space-time portal is making me feel very strange. Vila Universitària, here in Atlanta. Alba Casamayor and Martin Luther King.

"Oh! Albaaa! Yes, now I remember! I can't believe it, what a coincidence! What are you doing here?"

"You don't remember me at all, do you?"

"Yes! No, I'm sorry, I don't."

"Man, we met at the last party at the Autònoma!"

"Ah . . ."

"But you'd just eaten an *ensaïmada* stuffed with marijuana with your friend from Mallorca, and, when we were introduced, it had already started to take effect. I went with you to buy Nevados doughnuts and everything . . ."

A half year later, the enigma of who brought the Nevados doughnuts to the apartment has finally been resolved.

"Wow! Incredible! I'm stunned! And what are you doing here?"

"I'm on a stopover between Guatemala and Barcelona, and I took advantage of the fact you can get an excursion direct from the airport and . . ." She looks at me slightly strangely, but joyfully.

"Very good, very good . . ." Elena's very happy. "What . . . what's up?"

"Ohhh . . . It's just, I'm really pleased to see you . . ."

"Well . . . Yes, yes, me too . . . It's always so nice to speak in Catalan . . ."

"Yeah . . ." She laughs "But you've got Six for that, don't you?"

"What? Six? How do you know Six?"

"Didn't Alba tell you?" I don't get it at all. "Every time you send one of your emails, we all get together, all the girls from the IT class, and we read it together! We've read them all! We enjoy them so much! One day we'll get thrown out of class for it . . ."

"The emails? What emails?"

"The ones you send about your adventures here in Atlanta! I forward them to my uncle too. The emails where you talk about meeting Tek Soo, who always blushes, or when you met John at the club and were wearing a flesh-colored T-shirt with sweaty tits." Apparently, I have no filters. "But my favorite one is where the pastor caught the girls playing with that pig . . . You made that one up, right?"

"No, actually . . ." I'm bewildered. "Everything I say . . . it all happened for real . . . Perhaps I exaggerate it a little, because I'm of Andalusian descent, after all, but they're all true stories . . ."

"Shit, that's amazing!"

"Shit, you're amazing!" I shout. "I'm freaking out!"

"Well, anyway . . . Don't stop writing, Rita. You make our nanotechnology classes bearable! If I'm being honest, sometimes it's hard to understand what you write, because you don't use accents and you go on for infinite paragraphs, and sometimes you give way too much description, but they're funny . . ."

"Well, thanks very much." Someone's calling her.

"I have to go, Rita, or I'll miss the tour!"

I'm just standing there, watching the tourists merge with the colorfully dressed women. Some will make a voyage into history. Others will go home to make grits and okra.

The kids are fighting in the background about something to do with prime numbers, and suddenly, surreal and joyful in equal measure, in this untarmacked corner of the world, the unexpected appears.

Pam's neon sign. Aksel's rap. Michael's Grand Canyon.

The certainty in Yaya's eyes that sunny afternoon on the roof terrace, when everything seemed so clear. Finally, I can recognize what I've been looking for all this time. Finally, my vocation.

Six's Best Sex

Beeeep.

"Hairy," says Eva, demanding my attention from three steps below me. "What I wanted to tell you the other day is that a false nine has greater ability to move about to draw out the defender. But . . . do you think Xavi would be better at a long pass than Iniesta? I'm just not sure."

"One second, Eva."

Beeeep.

"Yes, I'll put Xavi on because, although Iniesta is more of an all-rounder, Xavi has better stats for precision. Well, Xavi's a genius, wouldn't you say?"

"Damn right . . . And Iniesta too."

Beeeep.

"Must remember: 'Play out from the back. The speed of the ball is more important than the speed of the legs.'"

"Whoa, missing person returns from the underworld!" I say, happy to hear her voice. "You okay?"

"What? Whoa yourself!"

"What do you mean? I've called you a bunch of times!" I complain.

"Rita, haven't you seen my calls? Anyway, your voicemail is full. I can't leave you any more messages."

"Not a single call, Six! I was starting to get worried! I haven't had a single call from you, although I've had about a million spam calls, presumably trying to sell me slimming belts. I got another one just before you called!"

"That was me, idiot! I didn't call you from work—that's my personal number."

"From your personal number? Are you okay? Why?"

"You don't have my personal number?" asks Six.

"No, because you always call me from work."

"Shit."

"But why have you called me from your personal phone?"

"If you get forty-nine calls, you have to eventually pick up, Rita! Even if it is someone selling fucking belts! Besides, you're a beanpole. Why do you want a slimming belt? Anyway, it doesn't matter. What are you doing? What's that infernal noise? Where are you?"

"It's the kids, Six, the kids. What do you think it is? Eva is studying her strategy for tomorrow's soccer match. It's very important. She's been preparing for months . . . She has to pass, whatever it takes."

"I know. We've known each other for months now, remember?"

"That's what I'm saying! What about you? What's up? Winter is ending! It smells like Paris Fashion Week, Wes Anderson pastels, the first beers on Plaza del Sol."

"Shut up, you deluded fool—you're from a tiny village in the Pyrenees, and you live in Atlanta."

"Christ, you sound like Voldemort. Good thing my self-esteem is robust."

"Anyway, since I couldn't get a hold of you, I called the house and spoke to Fulbright . . . You are right—he's gay."

"He so is! This morning, I finally managed to sneak into his calendar and saw that they've arranged to meet again. It didn't say where, but it said 'important PP.' I don't know, I'm intrigued. I dreamed I caught them fucking on the atrium at the Nobel Prize ceremony."

"He has to come out of the closet and soon," says Six. "No one can keep that hidden."

"Chitawas isn't just very well endowed," I continue, "but he's the complete opposite to Fulbright. He's everything he'd like to be, the reprobate he's never been."

"Keep me updated, please. I need to know."

"Sure. The other day I remembered that you never told me about Tek Soo! You said men disgusted you . . ."

"I never said men disgusted me. I said it's disgusting how easily I can get one. That night I was horny, and Tek Soo was there, like a little puppy, waiting for me."

"Poor Tek Soo . . . And what? Zero body hair and boring as a walrus?"

"Look, in most cases, it would make me want to hurl to remember it, but, Rita, I had an amazing time with Tek Soo . . ."

"Go on."

"I swear. If I were you, I'd give him a go, that guy gives some memorable cunnilingus."

"I don't believe it!"

"Believe it. Man, what a noise those lunatics make. Where are you, a park full of velociraptors?"

"I'd say it's more like a pig slaughter. But no, I'm at Eva's soccer training—she has the exam at the end of the semester. We've been training all year, but the girl is stubborn as a mule and doesn't want me to show her how to do a bicycle kick."

"What do bicycles have to do with it?"

"Doesn't matter. Can I ask why you aren't calling me from your work phone and why you're smoking menthol cigarettes at four o'clock in the afternoon, when it's your sacred post-lunch ritual?"

"How the hell do you know I'm smoking?"

"Because of the minuscule pause before you light it as you press the menthol button. It's pretty obvious."

"Freak."

"It's called being observant."

"I've quit my job." Six becomes serious.

"What? You're kidding!"

"A week ago."

"What? Why? Does that mean you can't buy gas on the company credit card anymore?"

"No, and that really made me think twice," says Six.

"And no more free entry into that nightclub?"

"Rita, that nightclub is the worst. Everything I hate about American culture is in that room full of white sofas. All those muscles, it's so disgusting."

"Yeah, but we got free Cuba libres."

"Yeah, the Cuba libres, the Cuba libres . . ."

"Come on, that's enough. You're joking about quitting, right?" Now I get serious.

"No, it's no joke."

"What?"

"I've quit my job, Rita."

"But . . . what happened?"

Silence.

"Six?"

"All . . . all right." She's embarrassed. Her pauses are very long.

"Something serious is up with you. You've barely said a curse word since I answered the phone. You haven't ranted and raved about the patriarchy or the salary gap. You haven't told me that Zuckerberg has just taken on a woman as head of operations and on her first day she realized there were no women's toilets because there's never been a female director before. Your voice is lower and sweeter. Six, this is serious."

"Rita . . ."

"You've fallen in love!"

"Pfffff . . ."

"Shit, you've fallen in love."

"Yes, it's kind of major."

"Wow. It can't be. Incredible! Impossible! How? Who is she?"

"She's a goddess, Rita. A Greek goddess with curly hair and green eyes. Our eyes locked, and it was earth-shattering. It happened in a parking lot in broad daylight. We both just stood there, frozen. Just like that. I dropped my coffee and everything . . . She has curly hair and green eyes."

"Yes, you've already mentioned the hair and the eyes. It's straight from a second-rate rom-com. What a cliché."

"No! No . . . Man, you know how angry all that stuff makes me, especially clichés. I hate clichés more than I hate corny comedy acts and musicals, more than I hate *Sesame Street*!"

"Hey, show some respect for *Sesame Street*—I found it funny even if you didn't!"

"But I'm trapped, Rita. Trapped in a spiral of pleasure and irrationality that's stopping me from seeing clearly."

"A spiral of pleasure, you say . . . Seeing what clearly?"

"Well, it's like my lens prescription has changed . . . What I'm telling you is, it's amazing. I literally froze when I saw her . . . I mean, literally, I couldn't move; she had to come over to me."

"Impossible."

"What I don't understand is why the whole of humankind isn't in love with her too. She didn't even laugh when I dropped my coffee."

"The coffee thing is true?"

"Yes."

"Holy Mother of God."

"And she came over. She told me her name is Valentina, and she gave me her card. Like that, all business. And she was only there by chance, Rita, by chance! She'd never been in that parking lot before—she hadn't even been to Atlanta before!"

"My mind is blown. Which parking lot?"

"The . . . the . . . the Murphy's one."

"Nooo! You went to Murphy's without me? What about our pact? Do you have any idea how many times I've wanted to go and couldn't because you weren't there?"

"You know I need French toast at least once a week, and it had been two. It was quick, honestly . . . After she gave me her card, she told me I had a crumb on my forehead, and I laughed and she brushed it off, and I said that . . . I said it must have been there for at least twenty minutes, and that must be why the waiter was laughing at me . . ."

I'm speechless.

"I called her fifteen minutes later. I couldn't wait any longer."

"Shit, this is serious."

"And we went out for dinner that night . . . at . . . at Murphy's."

I can't believe this.

"That was where we met! And it was incredible, in-cred-i-ble . . . I've never felt anything like it—I really mean that. And she, she's never felt anything for another woman, she hadn't even thought about it, she didn't care, it was like 'Okay, this is very pure, so let's do it' . . . She's so emotionally present, so intelligent, so beautiful and . . ."

"And . . . ?"

"I'm floating, Rita. Floating."

"Shit . . . So I see . . . Well, I'm genuinely happy for you . . . But what does she have to do with your job?"

"Okay." Six makes a guttural, guilty-sounding noise. "The thing is . . ."

"Listen, where are you? Is it raining?"

"Shit, woman! You're like Sherlock Holmes on ecstasy."

"It's raining, but no big deal, Six."

"Promise me you won't get mad."

"Hmm . . ."

"Promise me."

"Shoot."

"I've moved to Seattle."

"I'm sorry?"

"I've been in Seattle for a week now . . ."

My chest fills with an unbearable sense of betrayal. When you're so far from home, a friend like Six isn't just a friend. She's a best friend multiplied by one hundred. My eyes fill with tears. There's no one left on the soccer field. Just Eva and her folder full of strategic possibilities.

"I don't believe it."

"Rita, honestly, what I feel for Valentina is in another league."

"Yes, but you don't move to the other side of the country for that! You're practically in Alaska, you idiot!"

"But we feel this connection. It was such an overwhelming certainty that I couldn't do anything. We haven't stopped making love since that day . . . She didn't even go to the conference she'd come to Atlanta for. I missed three days of work and couldn't even invent an excuse when my boss asked me where I'd been . . . Man, I cry when I orgasm! I cry!"

I remain silent.

"Are you mad?"

"Hence the menthol."

"What?"

"You're smoking menthol, because it's lunchtime in Seattle."

"Elementary."

An extended silence.

"How could you have left without saying goodbye?"

"Well . . . it all happened so quickly, Rita, I'm sorry, I called you a thousand times . . ."

"I suppose you'll have to come back to get your stuff, won't you?"

"No . . . Thing is . . . I've already taken everything . . ."

"Amazing. Amazing! Fucking slimming belts."

"I know. It's madness—it might just be the most impulsive thing I've ever done. But I have no family, Rita. I have no home, and although being an orphan is really shitty and comes with more traumas than Charlie Sheen has STDs, the only positive is that I don't have to explain anything to anyone. I am my home."

"Whoa."

"Well, you know what I mean, I . . . and you."

Silence.

"Sorry, really I am. I couldn't say goodbye, it was agony, I even drove round Leafmore, but I didn't know which was your house, and I went to Georgia Tech, to the language school, but there was no one there."

"Yeah, it's the Christmas break . . . I'll be back tomorrow."

"When I find a job, you'll be the first person I visit. And we'll go to Murphy's together, and go partying at Hall in the Wall, and stop off at San Francisco Coffee, and shopping at Urban Outfitters; we'll repeat all our favorite rituals. I miss you already."

"Well, sure, now that you don't have a job." I'm so angry at the way she's just wiped out her personality, that self-assurance that defines her.

"I'm not worried about the job—you know my résumé is outstanding. I could sell Thai sake just as easily as gold faucets. Besides, I'm at the epicenter of global technological development! I go for coffee where Bill Gates used to go in the 1970s! Everyone here is young, has a degree, they understand me when I speak, and most of them already have an iPhone! Have you ever seen one? They don't have a keypad!"

"They don't make sake in Thailand."

"But I'd sell it to you regardless."

I stay silent.

She stays silent.

"I have to go . . ."

"Why? I didn't hear any of the kids calling for you."

Another silence.

"Rita . . ."

"What?"

"Without you, I wouldn't have been able to stand living in Atlanta."

Goddamn it, I miss her!

"I wouldn't have been able to stand selling gold faucets to Russians who spit on the floor. I wouldn't have been able to stand a routine for more than two years. I never would have lasted so long in a city, and it's because of you. Since the day I met you, I realized that when we were together, it was the closest thing I had to feeling at home . . . To having a family."

I can't find any words.

"And they say that families are our compass, our guide. They're the inspiration to achieve the most impossible of goals, our pillar when we stumble."

"You got that from some fancy detox teabag."

"No, it's a quote from the governor of Oklahoma on the back of a magazine."

"For God's sake."

"But I mean it anyway!"

Silence again.

"It's too late. We're already family, Rita. You might find it hard to believe, but I'm in Seattle today partly because of you: If I didn't know I can always count on you, I never would have dared. Because you taught me to be happy, to be ridiculously happy just because they play a song we both like in a nightclub, to eat eggs Benedict as though they were Beluga caviar, and to feel what it is to have a true friend. Do you remember that day, when we were eating brunch in San Francisco Coffee, we were crying with laughter, and a woman came up and said that she would pay to be able to laugh like that with a friend?"

"Yes . . ."

"You taught me that. You've made me feel less angry than I've ever felt in my life, Rita . . . And that's . . . that's a miracle."

"Yeah, a miracle."

"I love you, Rita."

"You're very brave, Six . . ."

"That sounded very much like a 'Thanks, I love you too.'"

"No, idiot, I do love you, too, but it'll be shit without you . . . Damn it, Six, this is brutal . . . I could kill you right now, but I'm happy for you . . . Really, honestly, I really am. Valentina must be fucking amazing."

"Perhaps now you'll have some peace to find what you want to do amid your chaos of supergifted children and Jägermeister?"

"Pfff . . ."

"Perhaps it will come to you, just like that, in a parking lot."

"Actually, it was right after watching a gospel choir, in front of Martin Luther King's house."

"What? What do you mean? You're not going to become a nun now, are you? Don't shave your head, okay? You have gorgeous hair!"

Eva's First and Last Soccer Match

Every weekend, when my brother and I had a basketball game, Yaya always came. She would fill a lunchbox with fritters, drive over in her little car, and find a seat in the Puigcerdà games hall to watch a sport she didn't entirely understand, but which made her drop a fritter every time Albert or I scored (which happened a lot; it would be false modesty to claim otherwise).

Year after year, the passion grew both on the court and among the supporters, and we essentially became local sporting heroes. (Years later, I would still occasionally bump into an old fan at the door of Trànsit and share a cigarette at seven o'clock in the morning).

The sports hall would fill up with family and onlookers who didn't have anything better to do, who would come for the afternoon and get their month's worth of gossip. It was sure to be a good show. One of the best moments was when the "juniors" arrived. An average of two years older than us and potential deflowerers, they fascinated us, and we watched them with the same cool enthusiasm that they devoted to us.

Once in a lifetime, everyone should feel the emotions that we did on that basketball court. Educational moments that reeked of sweat and permanent marker, that would make a permanent impression on a group of teenagers experiencing countless firsts under the hopeful gaze of our parents.

And that's more or less what I'm seeing today. Eva's end-of-semester soccer game is about to begin: Squirrels versus Toucans. I have to say, the parental expectations in my day were much less intimidating than this. The tension here is more like a Champions League Final between Barça and Madrid.

To any passerby, the scene would look like just another beautiful day in the capital of Georgia. As I climb the bleachers, I catch wafts of rosemary and roses. The air smells of spring already, and the sun is giving us a much-needed dose of vitamin D.

A dozen eight-year-olds hover round Eva's class coach with unkempt vitality—dregs of Gatorade trickling down their lips, their tiny socks uneven—but their infancy seems to vanish as the countdown announces the imminent start of the game. I'm focusing on the strategy. The coach's marker runs through the tactics drawn on a whiteboard, but something's happened, because this isn't the strategy that Eva and I proposed. It's all wrong.

The coach crosses herself.

The kids do the same. My God, the nerves.

The game begins.

The parents start shouting with the first kick. I look around and can't get over my amazement. It's as though they've transformed. I'm sure I see one of the fathers spitting on the ground. Pastor Paul has his eyes riveted on his daughter, Mary, and I can almost sense his invocation to Our Lord God from here. We could be at Maracanã stadium.

There's no trace of the elegance expected of an intellectual mass like this; their usual sobriety has been left at home among the books, Harvard diplomas, and landscaped backyards.

On another occasion—well, any other occasion—this panorama would have made me incredibly happy: finally, a bit of red blood, a bit of spirit! But not today. When you're on the field, the last thing you want is your parents embarrassing you. Especially when you're eight.

Luckily, Hanne and Fulbright are by no means the worst, perhaps because they're so astounded to see their daughter's face sweating on a soccer field for the first time. Equally, if this game doesn't go well, they'll be astounded when Eva gets the first fail in Bookland history, and her path toward Harvard will be tarnished with a potentially fatal black mark. This country.

When the other side scores the first goal, Eva looks at me, runs her hands through her hair, and gesticulates up and down, left to right with her arms. I don't understand a thing, but I nod in agreement. It doesn't matter so much if she doesn't win, but she needs to do more than just complain about the coach's strategy.

(Although she has good reason to. This woman doesn't seem to notice the chaos within the team. Her instructions make no sense.)

With the second goal, Eva's hair gets even more disheveled; she lets her arm drop angrily, like a dead weight. On the other side of the field, a mother is berating the referee for not blowing the whistle for a clear foul. Another parent tells her she's exaggerating. On the third goal, Eva looks at me and laughs with irony and desperation. I silently tell her to stop giving everyone instructions and to intervene: to take control of the ball and counterattack, to anticipate, to shoot at the goal, to do all the things we practiced!

But she does nothing.

Eva stands like a stone at the side of the field, looks at the touchline, and then starts crossing the field with all the caution of an adult who's just started a job with an open-ended contract. And, as if carrying the truth of the world in her pocket, she throws me one final glance and abandons the game.

One of the first times I was alone with Eva, I remember she was wearing a hand-me-down swim club T-shirt of her brother's; I also remember that she smiled at me and squeezed my waist with all the strength her little, blond-fuzzed arms would allow.

Back then, I thought it was a sincere embrace, a welcome, but days later, I realized it had been more of a plea, a hope that I would come to be the ally that Daniela had been. Not that Eva needs any kind of help, or that she doesn't get on well with her brothers, but Daniela had become like an older sister, the other girl in the house. Eva enjoyed the extra affection, the Colombian's sweet, loving words, the sisterhood that her brothers couldn't provide.

It took me a while to realize that when she was rude to me, when she got frustrated because I didn't know that the mammoths became extinct in the Paleolithic and not the Ice Age (my reference being *Ice Age* the movie), or the difference between RAM and ROM, she was actually angry because I wasn't Daniela. But little by little, before I knew it, we had worked out how to build our own little territory, different from the one she shared with Daniela, but just as nice.

Eva, like all the Booklands, has an intelligence I couldn't reasonably describe with my meager repertoire of adjectives, but perhaps more interesting than that is her ingenuity. And her inherent generosity and goodwill make her seem more than just a child. Eva is a wonder machine.

If she doesn't come on to play the second half, I think about what I'll say to her when I see her devastation. I'll focus on how proud I am at the path she's traveled since the start of the semester and tell her it's no big deal. That if she doesn't get into Harvard, it isn't the end of the world. I'll remind her where we started and how far we got.

Eva's class is losing 3–0, but, to the surprise of the rival team and the desperation of the parents, they come out of the locker room shouting and laughing. The parents glower. "They have no competitive spirit! These kids don't know what it means to struggle in life! We've made it all too easy for them!" Spit. Spit.

And then I see her. Eva is skipping onto the field, ponytail ever looser, whiteboard in hand, by the coach's side. The woman turns to look at the Booklands and me, and winks at us, as though she's doing Eva a favor. But she knows as well as I do that this eight-year-old girl is her only hope.

The Squirrels are distributed around the field according to Barça's lineup for the Champions League Final 2006. It takes them all of a minute to score the first goal. The crowd celebrates with pleased, but contained, applause—the consolation goal—aware that there's little chance of a comeback. They're still down 3–1, after all.

Eva, for her part, shows no sign of exaltation; she gestures with her fingers, confident and persuasive, giving her teammates instructions, which they follow to the letter. And for one glorious instant, Eva turns to wink at me, and I feel stratospheric.

The opponents don't know what has hit them, and the second goal comes soon after. The parents can't believe their eyes. Hanne issues the most guttural cry I've ever heard her make. Fulbright unfastens the top button of his shirt, revealing a glimpse of the hairy chest that must drive Chitawas wild (only a few days until they meet again). Aksel and Bini are standing on their seats, screeching like bolting sheep. The comeback is no longer merely a fantasy.

Ten minutes to go. The coach asks for calm, glances at the tactics Eva has drawn on the whiteboard, and issues orders to her Squirrels. The Squirrels quiet down and look at Eva. Arms stretched in the air, maximum tension. Silence on the field.

Eva shouts one word I can't make out, and, next thing, Katie launches into action and lobs the ball more beautifully than either she or anyone else would have thought her capable. The ball traces a perfect parabola. The tension is unbearable. The ball lands in the goal, a sight that will be engraved forever in the mind of little Katie, not to mention everyone else here today. Goal!

From now on, no one is responsible for their actions, or for the dark adrenaline-fueled thoughts that escape from the onlookers' mouths. It's no longer important whether the mammoths disappeared in the Paleolithic or the Ice Age, RAM or ROM. From now on, only one thing matters: winning.

A girl wallops a boy. Another falls to the ground and cries. The referee, who is just as excited as the rest of the crowd, calls for order. There's not a single person sitting; Eva drops the whiteboard to the ground. Five minutes left.

The rival team tries to shoot for the goal like Katie did . . . but they miss. It's close. Heart attack. They try again just seconds later. Even closer. Double heart attack. If Yaya were here, she would have sent her fritters flying as far as Wyoming.

The opposition attacks again. The rival goal is right there. Only two minutes left! And then the inevitable happens. A boy with bigger quads than me sends a terrific shot toward our goalkeeper, so well aimed that every Squirrel family stops breathing. Everything seems to be moving in slow motion. The spit backlit against the sun, Pastor Paul struggling to get his prayers out fast enough. Silent shouting. It can't go in. It can't.

Against all odds, Pastor Paul's prayers do the trick, and the ball hits the crossbar and rebounds with such force that it comes to stop at Mary's feet. She has been waiting at the very spot where Eva told her to stand. Mary shoots. And Mary scores the winning goal. The game is over.

This is the stuff of history, the first page of the legend. The anecdote that will be passed down through generations.

The world keeps moving in slow motion, and I see Fulbright jumping with his arms in the air and his shirt now fastened by a single button only. Hanne is hugging a random spectator and jumping up and down so much that her sandal goes flying. The pastor opens his mouth wide and looks at the sky, dropping to his knees. Bini is laughing and crying at the same time, and Aksel is shouting so hard that the veins on his neck stand out. Mary and Katie and the rest of the Squirrels run to Eva and embrace in a way they've never known until now. With a joy they've never known until now.

Eva allows herself to be embraced. She has no ponytail now, no whiteboard, nothing, and they toss her in the air, just like her inspiration, Pep Guardiola, will be tossed in the air by his team in a couple of years' time. Back on the ground, she separates from the group, jumps the fence, and starts to climb the bleachers in giant strides. And I climb down with giant strides, and we meet. She hugs me with all the strength she has left, and I'm the happiest person in the world.

I think we should all get to experience a moment like this in life. Because each and every one of us deserves it, and because after feeling such beauty and such strength, we become better people than we were before.

Always and Irrefutably, Meatballs

The generous spring light gently caresses the relics on Roberta's shelves. The portable record player, the coffee grinder, the two Aztec ass drums. I identify some new photos. Roberta standing in front of a pyramid in Egypt and another of her walking through rice paddies. Vietnam, perhaps. She doesn't look much like a tourist and always seems to be accompanied by some renowned explorer. How does she manage to travel so much?

She's sitting in her chair with an uncharacteristic lack of urgency, saying nothing. All my writing assignments are sitting on her desk, but she doesn't touch them. As if doing something significant, she opens a small wood-paneled refrigerator hidden beneath her desk and takes out a bottle of Coke. This is the first time I've been in her study and she hasn't been in a rush. Today, she seems to have all the time in the world.

Without picking up the pace, she pours the Coke haltingly. The fizzing sound of the liquid as it lands in the bottom of the glass seems to animate her. The next pour starts when the first bubbles have dissipated. Each pour seems shorter than the last. I think I must be missing something. I inspect the room from the corner of my eye. Bit by bit, Roberta pours out the last drop from the glass bottle. Then she picks up the glass, gazes at it, and finally, after a million years . . .

"How are you, Rita?"

Finally, she takes a drink.

"I'm flipping out at the Coke."

"Normally people laugh or ask on the third pour."

"Normally?"

"I did an extra couple of pours with you, but nothing. You sat through the whole charade, looking at me as though I were eating Lord Byron's underwear."

"Roberta!" She's as scandalous as an old woman with an Alp accent. More like Yaya than I'd realized.

"Rita, meatballs, please, I'm a writing teacher, not Laura Bush."

"Even so."

"How are you?"

"Fine, you've already asked me." I'm nervous. "I'm absolutely fine. Is something the matter?"

"How are you getting on with your piece for *The Georgian* competition?"

"I haven't started yet."

She puts down the glass. To hell with the bubbles and the short pours.

"There's still time, but you'd better get a move on."

"I'm still deciding on the topic."

"The topic isn't the most important thing."

"No?"

"Of course not. It's about writing something that will get you up off that chair and want to do nothing but write about it."

"Yeah . . . writing . . . The other day . . ." I get even more nervous. "The other day, I realized I want to write . . . as a job . . . as a profession." I twist my fingers, aware that I'm babbling. "But I realized because a girl told me she liked reading my emails, and I think it's a bit lame that I only realized that I want to take my writing seriously just because a stranger told me she likes what I write."

"Oh."

"I mean, couldn't I have worked it out on my own? Do other people's opinions matter so much to me?"

"But what does it matter how you came to realize? Name one single profession that doesn't need an audience. In which you don't need a pat on the back sometimes. From a routine job, like a mail carrier, to a prodigy like Michelangelo. We all need to know that what we're doing has some meaning, that someone appreciates it."

"Maybe . . . I don't know why I mentioned it . . . It must have been inculcated into me at the nuns' school. Narcissism as a sin, it's frowned upon to talk about yourself. Although it's one topic I don't have any problem with. If you do something well, why not show it off? If you deserve it . . ."

"Rita, focus. It doesn't matter how you realized. So, it was a stranger, that's fine. Meatballs."

"And it turns out the stranger was called Elena, like the city. That's a neat coincidence, don't you think?"

"Rita." She doesn't get the joke.

"All right, all right . . . meatballs."

"Meatballs?"

"You said meat . . . it doesn't matter."

"If you really want to write, you need to know that the writing life is a solitary one. And I'm not sure you're the solitary type."

"I've learned, Roberta, this year I've learned. Now and again solitude is necessary and restorative. Anyway, 'writer' seems like too important a word."

"Don't talk nonsense. Besides, in reality, being a writer or not isn't really your decision. Writing chooses you; you don't choose it."

"Ah."

"And it takes time to figure out whether it has chosen you. But if it has, if life has given you that blessing, you should know that you'll live a thrilling adventure. You'll discover that writing means crossing a never-ending desert and crossing it alone. A desert with an infinite horizon of better dunes for you to tread."

"Dunes . . . okay."

"Isolate yourself, Rita. Meatballs. Identify what moves you, what you enjoy, what changes you, and then write it."

"I'll look for inspiration."

"Insp . . . ? Inspiration?" She slams her fist down on the desk. "No! To hell with that! Inspiration is bullshit! Just like the classic idea that a writer has to be like Fitzgerald or Byron; a life of drugs, alcohol, and desperation. The phobia of the blank page, and blah, blah, blah . . . That's shit!" Her white curls, bouncing against her dark skin, seem like a poem. "That only works in the movies. You'll find a lot of sugary phrases from great writers who talk about the best way to write, but there's only one: Sit down and . . ."

"Bleed."

"Look at her, quoting Hemingway! Quoting them is fine, but it's reading them that will make you write better."

"All right."

Roberta relaxes. She looks away, and her speech slows.

"Writing . . . writing is a profession, Rita." It's as though she's just entered another dimension, as if what she has to say from now on weren't just for me. "Writing is a trade worthy of respect. Respect and the honor of the people who take this job seriously. Writing is art and beauty. If you think you want to do it, that it has chosen you, you have the duty to try."

"Uhm . . . all right."

She leans back in her chair and picks up the Coke to take a sip, but returns the glass to the table instead. She closes her eyes with a deep sigh. A moment passes, long enough to stretch out the parenthesis more than necessary. In the distance, we hear the door of the language school slamming shut. There's no one else left in the building. When she finally opens her eyes again, she gets up and walks over to her souvenirs.

"Earlier I said that the topic you write about isn't the most important thing."

She's speaking with her back to me, standing in front of a shelf slightly apart from the others.

"I was referring to the fact that . . . the themes at the heart of art are always the same . . . love, fear, hope. The artist's job is to give form to their existence. Who you are at the moment you paint, compose, sing, or write. If you write about love, it's possible that you'll talk about your family, your friends, and your country. If you write about fear, you'll mention the unforgettable pain of the first broken heart. In general, you'll write with agile, upbeat words colored by the memories you have now, from the bittersweet jubilation of being in your twenties. This is your strength, Rita, your truth."

Suddenly, Roberta's shoulders hunch. Her whole body seems to contract in front of a particular book.

"Whereas, if I'm writing about love . . ."

With a calculated gesture, she opens the book at an exact page and takes out a photograph. It's small, and I can't make out the image. She holds it very carefully and takes a quick glance at it. She moves toward the window in search of the warmth of the sun; the light makes her freckles stand out, her full lips squeeze tightly together, her eyes hidden behind her curls.

"If I write about love, I could write about what it means to give birth to a child. What it is to feel him coming out of you to breathe in the world with a cry. The moment when his huge eyes gaze up at you and change you forever. The sweet smell of warm blood, his skin against yours. Feeling like his laughter will extend your life. The joy of seeing him grow, of seeing life anew, all for the first time. The sea, watermelons, dogs, movies."

Her body is absolutely still.

"If I write about fear, I could write about what it is to lose him. To feel the most absolute terror. Like your life is being pulled out from under you. Like all colors disappear, and you start to live in darkness. Experiencing your own death, existing in a never-ending void, that each lungful of air you breathe feels unbearable."

Outside the window, a breeze dances through some seedlings planted in a forgotten pot. I stare at the first shoots of the year with my heart recoiling, searching for answers. How can this be? A woman with her vitality. She's looking at the shoots, too, the seedlings, but she doesn't see them. Then she finally lifts her chin toward the sun, remembering the dignity she had to retrieve years earlier. A worldly smile breaks through her white curls, showing me the Roberta I recognize.

"If I write about hope, I could talk about light. A small spark in the black universe. A very thin, weak crack, but a crack of light, after everything. The clarity of beauty . . ." She smiles more. "There's so much beauty in this world, Rita . . . I could write about what it is to revive in the kindness of others. About looking for it and finding it in all corners of the planet. Finding it in abundance! And finding goodness, too, in all forms of art. Because in art, my dear, you'll always find the essence of what it is to be human."

Without looking at it again, she slips the photo back into the book. She retraces her steps and returns to the study, to this afternoon. She grabs my essays from the desk and comes round to where I'm pinned to my chair, downcast, absorbed, and grateful. She crouches next to me, and with the confidence of someone who has returned from the brink, says, "Who you are right now, Rita, here and now, is a treasure that won't be repeated. Trap it and write it. Do it justice."

Then, she takes all my writing, holds it up, and rips it to shreds. Roberta, that muse, that ambassador of "carpe diem," returns to her chair, takes a long, refreshing slug of Coke, as though nothing has happened. And before I disappear through the door of this room of the spirit of time, she concludes:

"And remember, Rita, always and irrefutably, meatballs."

Gillette, the Secret Date, and Voice Messages

Springtime is advancing swiftly outside the living room window, leaving a trail of flowers and the premature aroma of warm cement and after-sun lotion. The heat is heavy in Atlanta.

I spend my time hunched over my computer keyboard, whether I'm on a bench by the pool with the kids splashing about in the background or sitting in the car waiting for them to come out of violin class.

And when I'm not writing, I'm reading. I read books—everything I can find, from Hermann Hesse to J. K. Rowling to Joan Didion, and random texts that Roberta gives me—and magazines, of course: *The New Yorker* on a drip, *The Georgian*, and *North Avenue Review*, which always has something that makes me laugh.

Afternoons with the kids soon slot into the usual rhythm of springtime, the shadow of the trees soon long enough to allow us to linger a bit longer in the stream next to the house, feeling the sun caress our faces.

And with the outdoors, of course, my friend Gillette has become a fixture once again on my bathroom shelf, keeping my hair at bay until further notice. Two days, perhaps three. I have no time to go for a wax.

The end of the semester is looming. My English course and the kids' schools. Homework is finished more quickly, the agendas are fuller, and the shouts are more excitable.

Aksel writes and rewrites verses on the pages of his Mandarin workbook; Eva profiles soccer strategies: "Play out from the back. The speed of the ball is more important than the speed of the legs," and agrees more readily to practice penalties and lobs. And Bini . . . Well, Bini's business ideas keep coming thick and fast: solar motorbikes that make you dinner, cups that change color according to your saliva, the idea of making your face a talking poop on the screen of the latest cell phones, like John's. They all sound great to me.

In the adult section of the Bookland family, things are less stable. Fulbright is behaving more uneasily than ever—the repeat Bookland-Chitawas meeting is imminent—and Hanne seems to be managing her uncertainty with a new hair color and some boots that look suspiciously similar to mine. The paradox is that when Fulbright is at the peak of his homosexuality, his wife is more gorgeous than ever.

"Chancha!" Conchi and her latest hot flash are demanding my attention from the front door.

"Comiiiing!"

"*Peluda*! Hairy! Come here!"

"I'm coming!"

"Here, two certified packages arrived for you. The first is from Au Pair in the States." Conchi raises her painted-on eyebrows expectantly.

"Yes, I know: I have to decide whether to stay for another year or go home."

"And what are you going to do?" If I didn't know better, I'd think she would like me to stay.

The second letter raises a smile. Conchi looks at the sender without scruples.

"John," I explain, "is on the presidential committee for *The Georgian*, a college magazine I'd like to know more about because there's a compe—"

"Suuuuuurre . . . And I'm the queen of England. Anyway, the pockets of Aksel's pants are full of scraps of paper with curse words that . . . well, make sure the señor and señora don't see. They already caught him once and got really mad."

"Did they?"

"Yes, when Daniela was here . . ." She can't contain a smile as she recalls her Colombian goddess. "He even got into trouble at school."

"Aksel? Trouble? I don't believe it."

"I know he writes things in private, and it's all the same to me, but don't let his parents catch him."

"Okay . . ." Well, let the show commence.

Conchi returns to the kitchen, and finally I'm left alone to open the packets in privacy. Saliva. Smile. Anything related to John seems to have that effect. What will it be? A gala night? A Dior dress in my size? Shares in Coca-Cola? Let's hope it's the shares; it doesn't cost him anything, after all. One would be enough.

Ah, it's all the homework Eva has left at his house; the mountain of papers Phillip has begged me a thousand times to take away and that he's decided to send me before he really starts to hate me. And . . . bingo: an envelope with my name written by hand.

> *Rita,*
> *Today, I was looking through my things, and I found the pen I'm writing you with. It belonged to my grandfather, and he used it to sign the papers that brought me here, to this paper, to us. Life is so ironic, sometimes, don't you think?*
>
> *I thought that, of all the people I could write to, you would be particularly excited by a note in my terrible handwriting in an ink with history.*
>
> *Good luck for tomorrow.*
>
> *I'll be there, hoping you win.*
>
> *And if you don't, we'll simply celebrate our existence.*

John

And just when you think he can't surprise you any more, John and his . . .

Shit!

A third envelope. The third envelope spells catastrophe. I see the word "Important" in red and bold, next to the printed logo of Aksel's school. I'd better open it.

Aksel's presentation is tomorrow! And the semester ends three weeks earlier than I thought! (What the hell kind of semester finishes in mid-May?)

Shiiiit!

I run to fetch Aksel.

I go outside and find the three of them at the porch table, sitting like retirees who've seen it all before, sipping from their respective glasses of milk and bowls of colored cereal as they play bridge. It's a cinematic afternoon. The lavender. The birds. The swing.

"Aksel."

"Hairy," says Bini, "I've drawn this cup that changes color when it comes into contact with your saliva. But do you think it's better for it to change color with the saliva or sweat from the hand?"

"I have to tell you something."

"Hairy," continues Aksel, "do you think I can use the power of Steamboat Geyser as a metaphor for the day when women finally achieve wage parity? It's the largest in the world."

"Hairy," Eva greets me from a new electrical circuit and offers me a strawberry, "want one?"

For a microsecond, I relive the epic of the game. That final kick, the unbridled joy. The embrace. The tangible extension of life.

"Children."

"Do you think the geyser is too forced as an analogy in just one verse? You get it, don't you? Or would you use Excelsior, from 1888, to take into account the historical factor? And, of course, I'll mix all this with my personal point of view, like Soul told me."

"Aksel, please, don't hold it against me. It isn't as bad as it seems, but when I explain, I beg of you not to tell your parents and not to get mad at me."

"I think I'll use Excelsior, which rose sixty-five feet higher than Steamboat, and I'll make an analogy about overcoming obstacles. I'll call Soul again to ask her what she thinks."

"Saliva is better than sweat, isn't it?" continues Bini. "It all depends what you're looking for, I suppose . . ."

"Kids!"

"A poisoning or a thief?"

"*Kids!* Aksel's presentation is tomorrow!"

Aksel brushes his hair back from his face.

"The teachers didn't say anything because in theory it's supposed to be a kind of surprise test that we should have prepared for at home. Shit."

"You always say the word 'shit,'" says Eva, sitting at the head of the table and sticking a pin into a new electric circuit. "I heard you say 'shit' from inside, and you've already said it three times. And now you've said it again. Four."

"Well, you'd better not read my verses, Eva . . . 'Shit' is entry level." Aksel raises his eyebrows proudly.

"Stop saying 'shit'! Both of you. The thing is, the test isn't in two weeks—it's tomorrow afternoon!"

The three Booklands look at me, their expressions indecipherable.

"Hairy . . ." replies Aksel.

"Please, don't tell your parents. They're still mad because Bini missed the choir final at church. We can resolve this."

"Hairy," insists Aksel in the tone of a constipated school principal, "don't worry, I already knew."

"But how? You don't understand—it's a secret strategy by the teachers!"

"We've been doing it since the start of the school year, Hairy," explains Eva. "Since Daniela left, we've been reading mail we shouldn't read and looking at the notes that only Mom and Dad should see, the ones slipped into the back of the agenda . . . And more so in these last few weeks, when you've been writing all day and you're on the moon."

Bini grabs his cup and sucks the handle, confused.

"And we listen to your voice messages, just in case," Eva informs me.

"Eva!" Aksel is a preteen again.

"Don't worry, they're fun. We don't entirely understand the ones from Six, because she speaks Catalan and very fast. But when she slows down a bit, we understand perfectly. In fact, we only had to look up four key words to understand everything. For example, '*cony*' and '*puta*,' which, as we suspected, does not mean 'a very tall woman.' Six says it all the time."

"Eva!" Aksel's face is about to explode, but Eva continues.

"If we hadn't done all that, we wouldn't have handed in a single assignment on time," says Eva. "But it's fine, Hairy. Honestly, you've helped us with so many other things, and without realizing it, you've made us more independent."

So, they know I hooked up with John? And Rachel? I don't know what to say. I don't know if this is good or bad.

"All right, but now show me what you've got, Aksel. We have to go through every last detail . . . everything's riding on tomorrow."

Mandarin Class

I'm making pancakes. I haven't made any for a thousand years, but making pancakes for the whole family is always a good idea.

Sitting at the kitchen bar, I stir the batter and notice how the humidity has returned to Atlanta in record time. Little by little, I'm rediscovering the green, vigorous city I encountered almost a year ago. The little yard outside the kitchen, tidy and well tended, and the glass table with an inch of pollen in which I wrote "Hello."

I pour the thick batter into the pan and am suddenly struck by the empirical and weird fact that the word "pancake" literally means a cake you make in a pan. The simplicity of the English language will never cease to amaze me. I make the first few pancakes enthusiastically, with aesthetic care. Round ones, oval ones, I even do one in the shape of a heart, all of them light and fluffy. The next batch is rather less whimsical. We're just back from Aksel's performance. The batter drops too quickly from my spoon; it's more of a splotch than a circle; the fluffiness vanishes. I see a lump and don't bother to fish it out. I couldn't give these shapes a name. One looks like a penis, but I lay them all out on the platter anyway.

I've always had great faith in the curative and pacifying powers of gastronomy. In my case, there's nothing that can't be cured by a good *llonganissa* or, in America, a good pancake. But today, bearing in mind what's about to go down, it's possible that all the heart-shaped pancakes in Georgia wouldn't be enough to sweeten the conversation.

Aksel and his parents are sitting on opposite sofas. Fulbright is doing his best to maintain a neutral tone. I can't tell whether his interest is genuine or whether he's about to shove the table against the wall. I limit myself to placing the platter of pancakes on the coffee table and helping myself to the first one.

"So, you're telling me you haven't been to Mandarin class all year?" Ful begins.

"No, I haven't been, but I've been doing all the homework. Peter has been passing it on to me."

Hanne takes a pancake and gives me a fleeting glance as if to say, *What the hell is this shit?*

Aksel swallows. His parents' silences are terribly long. He's still wearing his cap back-to-front, the exact position it was in when he was onstage, his unruly hair searching for an escape route.

"And I completed all the exercises at home alone. Dad, I got the second-best grade in the whole class! *Parrots, chambao, asedahey*!" Aksel says in what sounds like Mandarin.

"*Parrots, chambao, asedahey*?" replies Hanne.

"*Parrots, chambao, asedahey*?" adds Fulbright.

"That's the important thing, isn't it?" replies Aksel.

"Your grade is important, but not the most important," says Fulbright. The tension is killing me. "You know that what you've done is very serious." He turns to fix his gaze on me. "What you've done is very serious, Rita."

Fulbright sighs under his breath, sadly, and takes a pancake that looks like a frozen cod fritter.

"There are no words for this kind of betrayal." Hanne won't look up. "Lying for so long and so brazenly sets a terrible precedent in a family."

"Why didn't you tell us from the start? Why deceive us like this?" continues the father.

"Man! Why do you think?" Aksel is beyond indignant. His parents look up, as though they've missed something. "At least admit that, if we'd told you, if you'd been the ones to decide, I never would have been allowed to go onstage to . . ."

"To shout 'shit' and 'asshole' and . . . and *'whore*?" Hanne explodes.

"To rap!" he replies.

"You put your whole academic record on the line! All those years of hard work! Your future! All of it!" Now Fulbright is exploding.

Hanne is about to take another pancake, but it's the penis-shaped one. She shoots me another glare that says, *What the . . . ?* then gets up to look for some wine.

"But why?" Aksel asks his father. "I haven't put my future on the line! They asked me to demonstrate certain topics on the stage! There were no specifications about the format."

"The specifications about the format are dictated by a century-old school with a national reputation!" shouts Hanne.

"A reputation based on archaic and absurd protocol! I'm sure some members of the Ku Klux Klan went there . . ."

"Aksel!" shouts Fulbright.

"It's true!"

"I don't get it. You've always loved your school!"

"They're the ones who don't get it! Rap is art! Rap is the most visceral, sincere artistic discipline there is! Rap is truth! And my verses speak about injustice, feminism, racism, climate change . . . about me!"

"But you were saying 'whore'!" Hanne yanks out the cork.

(I thought these guys were Democrats?)

"So what? Every time I said 'whore,' attention increased thirty-seven percent, and it made the message even more powerful. I'm sure everyone will remember how many millions of tons of plastic are thrown into the ocean every year . . ."

"I'm still in shock . . ." The wine rises to the rim. "I'm still in shock!"

"I don't know what kind of schools you have in Barcelona or Puigcerdà," continues Ful, "or what kind of education they give you, but what happened here today isn't normal."

Aksel is holding back tears.

I think of him onstage. That incredible moment when he put on his cap, spun it round, and there was no going back. John looking at me with a proud smile, giving me goose bumps all over. The audience going wild. Life to the full.

The silence in the family living room is devastating. This conversation will mark the Booklands forever.

"Are you happy, Rita, finishing your year like this?" Fulbright speaks slowly, sadly, his hand trembling.

"Say something, Rita." Hanne's voice drifts through from the kitchen.

"First of all, I'd like to apologize for having kept this project . . . the rap, a secret. Having said that, if by 'like this' you're referring to right now, of course not, and I'm sorry that this conversation is frustrating for everyone. But if you mean the sight of Aksel on that stage"—a dramatic silence I didn't intend—"I can't think of a better ending."

"Well." Fulbright feels betrayed.

"And the truth is that, no," I continue, "I've never seen a performance like today's in either Barcelona or Puigcerdà." Collective defeat floating in the air. Aksel looks at me, and I couldn't love him more. "But I can tell you that your son is never happier than when he's writing songs."

"Oh, now you're going to tell us how happy our son is?" Hanne drains her glass.

"Sorry, I didn't mean to put it like that. But, compared with the happiness levels of people I've known in my life, I can say that Aksel's happiness is, quite frankly, huge. And finding the secret to your happiness at the age of ten isn't bad, is it? I would have liked to have known at that age. He's even happier with his verses than he is when we go to the planetary exhibition at Fernbank Museum."

"Really?" asks Fulbright, surprised.

Aksel hesitates, then nods silently.

"On the stage, in front of all those people, Aksel shone today. And despite the looks of terror, despite more than four teachers . . . Well, despite the teachers almost dislocating their jaws, he continued; he overcame it all and believed in what he was doing. He put himself out there . . ."

"Risked his academic record . . ." says Hanne.

"What I mean"—I can feel my eyelids prickling—"is that it took a whole lot of courage for him to get up there and show his vulnerability. To throw himself into the void. Aksel has suffered a lot to get this far. In fact, we all suffered with him, but more than anything, we've learned from him."

His parents are hiding their anger, but they also feel sad and guilty, the terror at having lost the way, the passionate path their son has traveled to this kitchen table, to this tray of questionable pancakes.

"Of course," I continue, "today he won't get an A or even a B. And I have no idea, but it's likely that when he goes to Harvard or Vanderbilt or whichever college it is, and he sits at the president's desk . . ."

"It's not normally a president; it's the . . ."

"Whoever it is, Aksel. The day you sit at that desk and they see a black mark on your file, you should be able to explain that the black mark taught you more than a lifetime of A's."

"Wow, so you're a coach now." Hanne is no longer laughing. "Don't get your hopes up . . ."

"And returning to your question, in Spain we didn't present our projects as raps, either at school or at college. But I wish I'd had a classmate in sixth grade who had dared to revolutionize the end-of-semester show, with his cap on backward, rapping about Bohr's theory, the wage gap, and climate change. Because that day would have turned on a light for me."

His parents sweep the table with their gazes. Three pancakes left. I don't know if they hate me more or agree with what I said; for better or worse, I've achieved the longest silence of all.

"There's a man at the door!" Bini ruins the moment with a cry from the landing, where he's been listening to the whole conversation with his sister.

"Is it Pastor Paul?" asks Hanne. "He has to drop off some documents for me."

"No . . . it isn't Pastor Paul, Mom. This man is stronger than Pastor Paul," replies Bini, intrigued.

"He looks familiar," said Eva next to him, "but I don't know where from . . . I think I've seen him on *Jerry Springer* . . ."

"This man is very strong!" Bini's voice is muffled by the fact that his face is pressed up against one of the little windows and he's openly staring at him. "And he has a tattoo of a really cute dog, and the eyes are hearts!"

Suddenly, Fulbright can't breathe. He fixes his gaze on me as though I were his last friend on earth before an unstoppable meteorite strikes us all. Indeed. We have only a few seconds to save this family.

Federico Chitawas is at the door.

There are only two pancakes left, one shaped like a heart, the other a penis.

“Total Eclipse of the Heart”

Chitawas has showered within the last hour. His wet hair is combed back, and he’s wearing a T-shirt with the American flag in glitter. He’s looking at his feet, nervous, inadvertently shaking the bunch of yellow tulips he’s brought for the occasion. His breath comes out in uneven bursts, a mixture of nerves and excitement, but he pulls it together when he sees that the person opening the door isn’t Fulbright but his wife. The rest of the Bookland family plus au pair are hovering behind her.

“Hello, can I help you?” Hanne gives him her best fake smile.

“Yes . . . Hi, good evening, I . . . I . . . I came to see Dr. Bookland.” Hanne turns to wrinkle her nose, asks Chitawas to wait outside, and closes the door.

“Who is this man, Ful?”

“Let me speak to him.” Ful raises his head.

“Rita!” Ful bares his lower teeth at me. “Take the kids to the kitchen!”

“Why?” asks Eva.

“My father has been in the government for all of four fucking months, Ful!” Hanne is so angry, she forgets we’re all listening in a circle around her.

“Mo-Mom, you said ‘fucking,’” Bini points out.

"What do you think the party would say if they found out the family was bringing home illegal immigrants? They could throw him out, damn it, Ful!"

Let's get this straight: Is she angry because Chitawas is a threat to her father or because he's Fulbright's lover? Did she already know they were lovers? Does she know that Ful is gay? I don't get it at all.

Fulbright ignores Hanne, brazenly and quite angrily. He goes outside to meet his lover and closes the door behind him. He looks both ways to make sure no neighbors have seen him and takes Chitawas into the garage.

I lean against the wall for a moment; I can't believe what's happening. Why the hell did he come to the house?

Hanne grunts like a rhinoceros—normal—and stomps downstairs to meet her husband in the bowels of the house. She opens the internal door to the garage so abruptly that she breaks the handle. The children try to follow her, and I want to follow them, but before Hanne leaves the room to launch herself at her husband's throat, she fixes me with a final glare.

"Take them to the kitchen."

The mixture of rage and sadness prompts the four of us to freeze on our respective stairs.

It's clear that this house will never be the same again after today.

The war starts with an icy calm. From our vantage point, we can see the three of them speaking, half hidden between the cars but their voices clearly audible.

"If you don't tell me what's going on, I'll call the police."

"For the love of God, Hanne, what are you saying! Let me explain. I told you to trust me." Ful's voice is trembling; he's winging it.

"Trust you? And this is how you repay me, bringing one home! To our house! I swear, I'll call the police."

"Don't talk nonsense. We both know you wouldn't be dumb enough to put your father's ass on the line." Her father, the politician.

At this point, I insist that we should stop eavesdropping and move into the kitchen. But the kids don't want to.

How will they react? When I was little, I always felt sorry for the children whose parents were divorced. I had the impression they seemed dirtier and were suddenly worse at soccer.

"Come on, kids . . . Shhh . . . Let's go into the kitchen, come on!"

"Perhaps he's an employee from the Starbucks you go to?" Eva is desperate to place him.

"No, no, Eva, you've never seen this man, believe me."

The evening light is creeping through the windows around the doorframe and distributing itself between the stairs where we're sitting. Bini runs his finger round the illuminated square on the wood, until a shadow splits the shape made by the light. Conchi inserts the key into the lock and enters the house. She's been at her tae kwon do class, and she's still wearing her dobok.

I try to summarize what's going on downstairs by opening my eyes extremely wide, but she ignores me. She doesn't seem interested in asking what we're all doing here sitting on the stairs, probably because she's suffering a sudden hot flash and all she cares about is ripping her clothes off. The yellow belt tied around her forehead soaks up the sweat in place of her nonexistent eyebrows. She lowers her pants to her ankles, stands in front of the refrigerator, and flaps the lapels of the jacket like a dragon cooling itself.

As I'm admiring this scene, I press firmly on the hinges of my jaw. I've been tensing since Chitawas appeared.

But Conchi's arrival seems to have sealed some kind of truce in the garage. The children are complaining that their parents aren't shouting anymore and they can't hear what's being said, until Hanne gives a cry of horror and the door slams.

And that's it. It's happened. Fulbright has summoned up the courage and confessed his homosexuality to his wife.

She can't possibly know. Hanne wouldn't have stayed with him knowing he was seeing other people, especially a porn star. She wouldn't have tolerated it even for the sake of her father's political career. This woman has cojones.

The three kids are staring at me, waiting for an explanation for their mother's shout, but I don't know what to say and my heart shrinks. All I can think about right now, as I stroke the tips of Eva's superconditioned hair, is that my au pair's contract is somewhere on the floor of my car, amid lollipops and dirt. I still haven't decided whether or not to leave. The kids. John. Roberta. Life here.

I wonder whether the blank spaces on that form are clean enough to fill them with my details and extend my stay for as long as I'm allowed. To spend this period here, when the kids will need me. My life across the Atlantic can wait.

The garage door opens with dramatic slowness. We scurry up to the living room. The handle Hanne broke before launching herself at her husband drops to the floor, but no one picks it up.

The drama weighs heavily on the shoulders of all three, who troop into the living room one after the other. Their marriage over, the lover between them, Fulbright, who dreams of Chitawas's muscles covered in coconut oil.

Hanne starts walking toward us, more slowly than usual, absorbed, but she doesn't stop. Behind her comes the intruder who, despite the size of his muscles, walks clumsily, scared, and needs to pause on every second step. But why the hell is he coming in? He needs to go away! Go away, damn it!

Finally, Fulbright. The shamed and liberated man walking with the adrenaline of the shock, but also with the relief of being able to live the life his heart and his scrotum ask for. To be who he's always wanted to be.

We wait for them on foot, tense. The silence is almost unbearable. The kids grab each other's hands, as if sensing what's about to happen. The verdict that will change their lives forever.

After what feels like ninety years, the three finally stop at the top of the stairs. All three, standing in a row on the landing where the little mail table and important papers are. The little table where we've all been so happy: where I pick up my Netflix DVDs and swipe *The New Yorker* before anyone else can get to it; where Hanne and Ful say goodbye to their kids before school and where they give each other an everyday, but always sweet, kiss good morning. That same landing where the Booklands took it for granted that life would always be easy, intellectual, and free from porn stars is now ready for the sentencing.

Hanne is winning points by the minute. What a woman, what laudable calm, her gaze fixed and decided, the dampness of her eyes controlled by vast reserves of American heroism. Wonder Woman. Chitawas lowers his head, even his steroid-induced musculature can't take this tension. His hands are sweating, and he interlinks his nervously fidgeting fingers. Anyone who'd seen him on the screen wouldn't recognize him now. Perhaps if he was wearing his luminous underpants or shouting, "Machu Dicchu!" it would be a different story.

Fulbright, intoxicated by his love for the actor, is showing no shame or regret. What's more, he lifts his chin proudly and drapes his arm around Chitawas's shoulder. His eyes couldn't be wider, his chin so high he almost looks crazy. But what is he doing? Or perhaps it's a deliberate strategy? Perhaps this is the best way: a clean cut.

Bookland senior gets ready to launch into a speech, but first he calls Conchi, as part of the family, to participate in this new start.

Conchi comes out of the kitchen with her head bent, trying to work out the complicated technique for tying her tae kwon do jacket, as she continues her endless repertoire of Colombian insults. "Eh, Ave Mariaaaa, this jacket is a son of a bitch." When she manages to get the belt to pass through the second eye, she looks up to realize that seven tense bodies have been waiting for her for some time.

Her eyes flit from one face to another uncomprehendingly. She looks at the children and senses the drama. She reads Hanne's wet eyes: Despite the Viking strength of this woman, the tears are about to flow. Conchi moves on to Fulbright, to whom she doesn't pay much attention . . . until her eyes come to rest on the muscular intruder.

It's all very quick. Conchi identifies something so powerful that in just one second, she ceases to be the woman we all know.

Has Conchi been watching porn on Ful's computer too? It can't be true! It's unbelievable!

Her joy is clear. Her bones stop aching. There's no more menopause or hot flashes or insults. The longing she carries inside her every day, with every step in her life, has just evaporated. Federico Chitawas doesn't look up; the shame weighs on him more than it does on Fulbright, but even so, Conchi draws closer to make sure what she's seeing is real.

What is she doing? She's so bold!

Conchi raises her arms, still draped in the sleeves of the dobok, and touches the man's cheeks with both hands.

No one says a word. No one understands or asks a thing. Now that I think about it, I'm not sure I can imagine Conchi watching porn in secret.

Chitawas finally looks up and confirms Conchi's suspicion. He knows her. But the look between them goes far beyond a look of mere acquaintances. An aura of immense warmth swims around them. Chitawas is crying.

I don't believe it! Now I understand!

"I'm here, my dear *mamá* . . ."

The Family of the Lovers and the Lovers of the Family

Their reunion is intense, the embrace so deep that if it emitted light, it would spread across the continent. Their bodies clamp together with the urgency of people at death's door, or who have found each other again after another life. The only embrace that could take place between mother and son after a torturous fifteen-year separation.

The love spreads and floods the whole house.

Hanne tries to contain herself, but the tears burst forth without restraint. Fulbright and I are no better. Conchi and Chitawas are trying to talk through the commotion of a dream come true, a happiness that could never be repeated.

But . . . come on . . . this is incredible: Conchi's son is Fulbright's lover? Conchi is Fulbright's new mother-in-law? I'm in a South American telenovela.

"I've got it!" Eva's cry cuts through the scene like a butcher's knife. The revelation: "This is the man who appears on Daddy's screen! The porn man!"

"Eva!" I pull her by the arms, and the tension swells again.

"What?" Hanne is searching for a response amid the snot and tears.

"You know?" continues Eva. "He's the one who wears those underpants that light up and—"

"Eva!" Fulbright glares at me as he tries to assimilate the notion of his eight-year-old daughter in front of his computer screen. "We'll talk about this later."

"But what does that mean?" Hanne's voice rises.

"Hanne, honestly . . ." Fulbright blushes. "I've said we'll talk about it later."

"Dad and Chitawas . . . Dad and Chitawas are lovees! Like on *Jerry Springer*!"

Bini's words, which not even he understands, drop like a nuclear bomb on the living room of 2007 Oak Paths Drive.

The mother-son reunion is razed by the announcement of a five-year-old boy who has just created an impact inversely proportional to his size. Fulbright looks like he's about to faint.

"Bini! For Christ's sake, what are you saying?"

Fulbright is very nervous. I genuinely don't know where Bini got the idea.

"Bini, why do you say that?" Hanne is searching for explanations that aren't forthcoming. "And why are you looking like that, Ful?"

"This child is crazy!" shouts Conchi. "Crazy!"

"He's not crazy," I say, intervening in Bini's defense. "I saw it." Shit.

"What?" Hanne grabs hold of the banister to stop herself from falling down the stairs.

"Yes! He's Machu Di . . ." It's crystal clear to Eva.

"What does 'porn' mean?" asks Bini.

"Rita! Explain yourself!" Hanne is looking at me desperately, but it's too late.

"Well . . ." I'm paralyzed. "I don't think I'm the one who should be explaining . . ."

"Rita! What are you saying?" Fulbright's eyes are injected with blood.

I can't take the pressure: There doesn't seem to be any way out other than the truth.

"Well, apart from the . . . the computer . . . I saw them go into the Marriott hotel together and . . ."

"My God, I need to sit down . . ." Hanne gropes the wall.

"And, honestly, I don't think it's all that serious . . ."

"Rita, what the hell are you saying? What isn't all that serious?" Fulbright's disheveled hair, his eyes, his bared teeth.

"The fact that you're lovers!"

"So, did you help him because he's your lover?" Hanne drops into a chair.

"Rita, have you gone crazy? Of course not!" Ful punches the little mail table, which cracks.

He's drawn blood. The blood trickles from his hand. Shouts. Heightened tension. And all of a sudden, silence.

I think how much I'd like to be in my town right now with a *llonganissa* sandwich. Or enjoying a vermouth in Barcelona with my friends, in Plaza del Sol. With olives and cockles and Espinaler sauce.

"Well . . ."

Fulbright leans against the wall at the top of the stairs. The tension starts to fade into defeat. Conchi tends to his wound and bandages his hand. Chitawas is freaking out.

"Please, let me explain." Fulbright is breathing heavily, mouth open, like he was taught in yoga class. He tilts his head back and launches into what is probably the most important speech of his existence. "For the last eight months, I've been arranging a way to get Federico to Atlanta to be with his mother." Silence. "But I didn't tell anyone. I kept it absolutely quiet so that I wouldn't get Conchi's hopes up and so as not to jeopardize my dear father-in-law's career. It's impossible to get a visa in this goddamn country—let's just say Federico has a few incidents on his record that our government doesn't look upon kindly. So in the end, I paid for Federico to come here illegally. Yes"—he looks at Hanne—"illegally. But a couple of weeks ago, I finally managed to get the paperwork sorted, which we signed in a room at the Marriott." He looks at me, less angry than he should be. "Yes, in the Marriott, a hotel, so that no one would recognize us . . . Particularly because this man here is indeed a fucking South American porn star."

"And in Poland and the Czech Republic too . . ." Apparently, Chitawas feels the need to make clear the international extent of his fan base.

"What does 'porn' mean?" Bini asks again. He's eating a dried-out candy and seems unconcerned when no one answers him again.

"I'm so proud of you, Son . . ." Conchi can't stop hugging him.

"And I did it all in secret," continues Ful, "to prevent exactly what just happened: my wife finding out that I helped an illegal immigrant and worrying it would harm her father's political career. The *logistica*," he says in Latin, "of the matter making it look like something it's not. But Rita, apart from being our dear au pair, also turns out to be fucking Hercule Poirot."

"I-I'm really sorry . . ." The blood is finally flowing to my head again, and I can just about articulate an apology that will never be anywhere near enough.

"My love"—Hanne gets up from her seat—"I never would have dreamed I'd be so happy for you to bring a porn star to the house."

"So," Eva begins, needing to clarify things, "Dad helped Conchi's son to enter the country so they could be together. Is that illegal? But he's her son!"

"What does that have to do with it?" Aksel is indignant but finally able to talk after an hour of multiple explosions in his brain.

"Dr. Bookland"—Conchi has returned to her euphoric happiness and is crying—"I can never repay you for what you did for me and my son. All these years dreaming of this moment, and now you've brought him here to me, in the flesh." Flesh indeed. "You gave me my life back. You've given me everything. The heavens have won! So don't suffer, because God will welcome you in his kingdom . . . even if you are gay."

When he hears the word "gay," when he realizes that all his years as a professor and imparter of knowledge aren't enough to allow him to explain himself, Fulbright gives in. He relinquishes the stability of his long, thin body and lets himself drop to the floor next to the little mail table, bloody, overpowered by a sudden fatigue. And sprawled on the floor, although he can't get the words out, he hopes his family understands that perhaps he watches porn but not Chitawas's porn. That all he wants to do right now is to pick up the biography of Carl Friedrich Gauss, the prince of mathematics, and quietly finish the chapter on geodesy. Or to play another mediocre game of tennis and pretend he cares about losing. He just wants a normal afternoon. An afternoon with no surprises, adrenaline, or clandestine activity. Because all Fulbright wanted to do was to help. To reunite a mother and son. And although it doesn't seem to matter what he has to say on the subject, he wants his family to understand that he isn't gay and he doesn't have a lover.

Lola's Dreams

Vivaldi's *The Four Seasons*, in all its glory, blasts through every window in John's house, sending the drapes flapping. Outside, an army of florists, gardeners, and landscapers is distributing summer in overflowing wheelbarrows. Phillip directs the orchestra with his back straight and the spring sun glinting off the gel that keeps his hair suspended in time and space.

I watch the show from a privileged viewpoint on the terrace. I'm drinking coffee with milk and peeling layers off a croissant that could easily have come from Rue Montorgueil in Paris. It seems unreal. All this aesthetic exuberance, the musical harmony, the butter on my fingers. I wonder why I haven't come for breakfast here more often, or why I didn't just move in that first day, when I entered barefoot, my hair held back by sweat and my legs covered in dust. A gardener starts to prune a bush using a figure printed on paper as a guide.

There are precisely twenty-four hours until *The Georgian* prize-giving. Piedmont Park meets the horizon in the distance: Tomorrow I'll be on the other side of it, waiting for literary judgment. I close my eyes and run through some of the phrases from my essay. I think it's good, but I couldn't say whether it's good enough to win. I think so. Or perhaps not. Yes, I think I could win the competition. I imagine what it would feel like to see my text published on paper, in print, the new dream. I go in search of another croissant.

There must be forty people sprucing up the gardens. They're everywhere; a couple are even tidying Lola's little parking lot, where she waits, elegant and spotless, for the next adventure. Hanne sends me a message, somewhat brusquer than usual, to tell me I don't need to fetch the kids from school today. The calm after the storm. I still have a Chitawas hangover. Dazed by guilt, but happy because, after the illegal immigration and porn and blood, we were all left with a feeling of justice and a love that eclipsed everything else.

A day off. I can't think of anywhere better to spend it. I embark on another voyage to the kitchen in search of a cappuccino with extra froth and, when I get back, the figure being sculpted into the bush seems human. At the top of the small hill, crossing the boundary of this world of wonders, John finally arrives. Jeans and T-shirt and chest hair poking above the neckline.

I look at him, and it strikes me that I'll never meet anyone who fascinates me quite as much as this man, so hermetic yet vulnerable. I look at him, and it makes me want to wear white T-shirts with no bra, to be terribly European, to smoke cigarettes dramatically in the haze of a streetlight. John is Paris and New York. He's a world of black-and-white photos of Havana, of clandestine jazz clubs, of poky, old wooden staircases that lead to the most bohemian penthouse.

He drapes an arm round the gardener's shoulders and smiles up at me.

"You wouldn't be so corny as to have a bush pruned into my shape, would you? Although, come to think of it, I can't think of a better idea."

"You'll love it." The terrace fills with aromas of wood and earth. "Will you stay for lunch?"

"And for dinner."

He kisses me on the lips for longer than I expected.

I spend the morning on the little terrace, chatting with him, reading issues of *The New Yorker* I haven't gotten round to, and watching the house, little by little, turning into a Seurat painting.

"My vichyssoise recipe is the original." Phillip is cooking, and John and I are listening to him, sitting very close together on the other side of the kitchen bar. "That is, the recipe that Louis Diat prepared at the Ritz-Carlton in New York, based on the way he and his brother chilled their leek and potato soup with cold milk. And so the soup was born in the 1940s. This is the genuine article; all other versions are fake. And he gave it that name because he was from Vichy."

John squeezes my hand, gently mocking the pride with which Phillip tells the story. When he turns away, we take the opportunity to kiss. The doorbell rings, and finally we're left alone. And like a couple of teenagers playing hooky, we kiss in a way that transports me to the Ritz-Carlton in New York and summers in France. The smell of vichyssoise mixes with the first scents of summer, which dance in with the flapping of the drapes. Phillip comes back to the kitchen, and John grabs me by the face with both hands to give me one last kiss.

"But there's something more important than Louis Diat's vichyssoise, darling," continues Phillip, as though he hasn't noticed what we were doing. "Have you decided whether or not to stay in Atlanta?"

Winning

Rows of gilded instruments rest on the shoulders of soldiers playing in unison on a perfect lawn. A group of cheerleaders performs a precise choreography that ticks yet another box on the list of clichés. Hundreds of proud families flood in from all corners of the country, tears in their eyes, to see their brilliant offspring toss their graduation caps in the air as I look on with terrible jealousy and longing.

Finally, it's our turn, the lowest of the low at Georgia Tech. The moment of truth, when one of us, from among almost two hundred participants, will manage to infiltrate the elite and occupy a page in the most prestigious publication of all: *The Georgian*.

Rows and rows of white seats are set out over the largest lawn on campus. My creative writing class is spread across five rows; Tek Soo is sitting next to me, happy and expectant. I look at him and think about how far he's come. I remember the day I met him, face like a tomato and his gaze glued to the floor, and now here he is, returning my smile confidently.

Everyone who matters is on the stage: the provost of the university, the director of the language school, Roberta, representatives of *The Georgian*, as well as from the other paper, *North Avenue Review*, which someone described as *The Georgian*'s pothead cousin.

And at one side of the stage, camouflaged in a Panama hat, him.

Trumpets. Drums. The ceremony begins.

The formal presentations are short and heartfelt, full of hopes, commitments, and futures. These inspirational spectacles always send me floating.

I look around me in the hope that Fulbright and Hanne have changed their minds and brought the children. But I can't see them.

This morning, I couldn't hide my disappointment when, although they must have gotten over the shock of hearing the word "lover" coming from my mouth by now, Mr. and Mrs. Bookland invented a cheap excuse to stay at home. I don't know if it's punishment or embarrassment, but the fact is they haven't come. And I deserve it.

So I'm alone. No Yaya, no parents or brother, no adoptive family waiting for the victory or defeat that has never meant so much to me in my life.

Roberta is the next to speak. Her speech is a compendium of poetry, adventure, and a dose of reality. Very much in keeping with her style. But mostly about adventure. Unlike all the others, she doesn't quote any American presidents, which I appreciate, and she reminds us that "writing won't make us rich, but it will make us fly higher than anything." Not rich. Flying. All right.

She finishes to the loudest applause of all and gives a smile that lights up the audience, until finally it's the moment of truth: the Champions League of amateur writing.

I scan the crowd once more for a sign of the Booklands. Nothing.

To deliver the prize, the provost and Karen Tucker, director of the language school, stand up to join Roberta. Karen speaks. I'm so nervous that the words are drowned out by a long and unintelligible "beeeeeeep." The speech is brief enough and to the point, and the announcement is imminent.

I don't hear what she says, but one thing is clear: The three pairs of eyes are looking in my direction, and Roberta is very happy.

I freeze. It can't be.

It's impossible! I knew it! Have I won? I've won! Really? But I used the phrase "Like a beaver, my girlfriend enjoys a log in her river."

Little by little, the speech becomes distinguishable again:

"For a remarkable mastery of a foreign language, for their elegance and intelligence"—elegance and intelligence?—"for their humility"—humility?—"and for demonstrating on these pages a talent that is hard to ignore, the prize for best literary text for the special issue of *The Georgian* goes to . . . Tek Soo Oh Rangman."

Badaboom.

My fall is like the first descent on a roller coaster. I plummet, stomach in my mouth, a bit of spittle landing on my forehead; I swallow my cries, and just before hitting the ground, I recover a smidgen of dignity and come back up to the surface.

I applaud, initially just because that's what everyone else is doing, but soon with conviction, because the truth is that it's great news. I stand up and clap so hard, I could be a flamenco dancer. Lola Flores, eat your heart out.

Tek Soo deserves it. His stories always echo with faraway countries and bygone times; and the characters are alive and passionate. After all, his grandfather, the one from Japan, was a ninja. And who the hell could beat a ninja grandfather? My Yaya was the goddamn queen of mambo, but I'm not sure I could do her justice on paper, make her into an engaging character . . . particularly given that she wasn't a ninja.

Tek Soo hugs me in a "First Lady" type of way and files through the audience to the stage, his face once again blazing.

He receives his prize to glorious applause, everyone standing. This moment is even more awesome than I thought.

At the edge of the stage, deliberately lurking in the background, John has been watching me for a while, full of pride; he knows perfectly well I haven't won, but he's looking at me as though I have. And I return his smile; the sun lights up my hair and produces chestnut-colored reflections, and for a moment we're equally beautiful, a black-and-white photo of Havana, dramatic backlit cigarettes in Paris.

The ceremony ends with copious embraces. Tek Soo squeezes me so tightly, he lifts me off the ground. It's such a beautiful day, complete with the sunshine and the running mascara.

I leave my seat and head for the stage to thank Roberta and look for John.

Then suddenly, I'm stopped by the touch of a tiny, tender hand I would recognize among a million hands.

Bini is hugging me tightly round the waist and smearing my blouse with chocolate. Then Eva and Aksel come over. I'm speechless, and I hug them as tightly as I can. Behind them, I see Fulbright and Hanne watching the scene happily. The hug is a long one, and I know I'll stay forever.

"Wow!" says a voice with unusual swagger. "So, these are the kids you look after?"

I spin around and see the guy who gave us the campus tour at the start of the year. He's accompanied by two preppy-looking girls.

"Yes, these are my kids," I reply, uncomprehending.

"I don't think we've been introduced." He holds out his hand. "My name is William Hernandes. And these are Anne Comenge and Clarianne Carré."

"Pleased to meet you. I'm Rita Ra—"

"Rita Racons," Anne cuts in. "We know."

"How?"

"Rita, we're the editorial team from *North Avenue Review*. We aren't as prestigious as *The Georgian*, but we're just as rigorous and a thousand times more irreverent . . . and more fun."

"Yes, yes, of course! I know . . . I always read you." The children are watching both sides of the conversation as though this were the Wimbledon final.

"Rita," William says, adopting a more serious tone, "we've read your essay, and we really like it. We'd like to ask whether you'll allow us to publish it in the next print issue of *North Avenue Review*."

The Tree House

I never imagined that, from here, I would be able to see the field of sunflowers where I ended up this morning on my bike, on my way to visit my favorite stone wall. I spent a long time in the field, lying on my back gazing at the sky, trying to figure out why at least five sunflowers seemed to be watching each other rather than the sun. I guess even being a sunflower can't be easy.

Bob Dylan's voice drifts through my bedroom window, joined by the tinkling cowbells of Antònia's herd; and I find it weird to be able to understand everything Dylan says in English, sitting here, on the roof terrace.

"Rita?" My brother sticks his head through the curtain at the doorway to the roof, feigning annoyance. "Mom's asking if you'd rather have black rice or *fideuà.* And I'm only asking because it's less than a week since you came back, but this nonsense of deciding the menu according to your tastes has gone too far."

"Black rice. And I'm happy to be back too." I pull a face like a hungover parakeet; he pulls one like a horny anteater.

"She also says to unpack your bag already, that your clothes will go rotten, and those tacky cards your Yankee friends wrote you will get wrinkled."

As I unpack the first card, my fingers get coated in glitter. And I laugh, because the most dazzling one of all is the card with a unicorn from Conchi and Chitawas, closely followed by one from Mrs. Gee, which, surprise, surprise, is an American flag that plays the national anthem when you open it.

Her card prompted one of the best moments of the party. I had only just arrived, still in a state of shock at the surprise, the cheers, the constant stream of people and sangria and other Mediterranean recipes that everyone had made for the occasion—even *llonganissa*!—in dishes laid out across half a dozen tables, stretching from the dining room to the kitchen and continuing outside, to the backyard.

The Booklands had made sure no one was missing. Needless to say, the whole of Leafmore was there: kids, parents, tennis friends, pool friends, Pastor Paul channeling his inner Michael Jackson, and everyone who, according to Ful and Hanne, "explicitly said that they wanted to come to your goodbye party in case you finally decide to leave."

That also included Miss Moore, Bini's teacher, and all my friends from Georgia Tech: the Venezuelans, the young dudes, Tek Soo . . . and, surprisingly, Karen Tucker!

Even Andrew appeared with a selection of new doughnuts from Starbucks.

Roberta arrived late, with her bags packed and passport in her pocket. "You're my first stop on the longest journey of the year," she said. "See? Being a teacher has its perks." She listed all the countries she would visit, including a couple I'd never heard of. We exchanged addresses; then she gave me a long hug and went on her way.

And I'm sure that if, in ten, twenty, or thirty years, someone asks me to recall a moment that marked my life, there's a good chance I'll remember my joy when I opened the front door and saw . . . Six.

We had agreed to meet in Barcelona in two months' time, but the girl flew five hours from Seattle to Atlanta just to see my face. And here she was, seeing it! "Besides," she said, "even this hopelessly lovestruck idiot didn't want to miss the chance to see all the Venezuelans together again . . . And apart from that, I really wanted to see you."

I couldn't believe it.

According to Aksel's space-time algorithm, there were seventy-eight of us at the peak, which I think was the moment when Mrs. Gee asked everyone to be quiet; the headline moment was approaching. She opened the card and told me it would make her really happy if I sang the national anthem of the United States.

At that point, I didn't care, because I was on an unprecedented high, so I raised the *llonganissa* I'd finally managed to get hold of and started to sing: "Oh say can you seeeee," and pam and poom, "whose broad stripes and bright staaaaaars," and padapoom, and so on and so on, until the rest of the party couldn't resist—we're talking about Americans and their national anthem, after all—and that beautiful summer's evening turned into a scene worthy of *American Pie.*

What a party!

I must have organized about fifteen surprise parties in my life and, now that I've been on the receiving end, I have to say it's an amazing experience.

But the reality is that what we were celebrating that afternoon was my leap into the void, a leap based on a new sensation that's difficult to describe, but which I felt very strongly inside me.

I wanted to write, and I knew that to learn to write well, I should do it in my own language. So I found a writing school in Barcelona, the Ateneu Barcelonès, which is internationally recognized and offered everything I wanted at that moment. But I didn't know if the rest of humankind would understand my decision to follow that desire, to write, to leave. And when I say the rest of humankind, I mean John.

John was at the party from the beginning, along with Phillip, Mike, and Samantha. They were the first guests I saw. When we got out of the car and the kids ran upstairs, I followed them, wondering at all the fuss until the door opened and the crowd burst out in a shout.

For the entire afternoon, he went as unnoticed as best he could and, at the same time, played his role as a happy and committed role-model neighbor. But in the eyes of the women of the district (and the men), his image has always been that of an *homme fatal* imbued with an oh-so-irresistible touch of mystery and promise. I overheard a couple of conversations speculating on why John was estranged from his family, resulting in some terrible hypotheses, but they always stopped short when I drew near. My decision to leave calmed the rumors about the two of us that were starting to spread, but that didn't mean we wouldn't remain good friends (is that what we were, good friends?).

The party passed quickly, too quickly. Six stayed until the end—even after the Venezuelans left—and we agreed to meet again after she'd visited all her other Atlanta friends.

I said goodbye to Prrr and Brrr, and the party ended with the remains of *pa amb tomàquet*, Spanish omelet, fritters, and paella. And, obviously, a few Mexican tacos. Meanwhile, I wandered round, soaking in the American wonder and generosity, all the love I had received, much more than I had ever imagined, and my phone didn't stop vibrating with goodbye messages that sounded truly sincere, as was each of the embraces telling me that Atlanta and Leafmore would always be my home. And just as I was finishing off a glass of cava, one message arrived that stood out over all the others:

I'm waiting for you in the garden, in the tree house.

Those casual words ran through my body like electricity. And I don't know if it was the cava, the sangria, or the irony, but instead of going into shock, I burst out laughing.

"We . . . do we have a tree house?" I shouted.

"Yes! I busted my kidneys building it," replied Ful from the kitchen, tipsy. "But as you can imagine, the kids have never set foot in the fucking thing!" Yes, Ful said "fucking" and didn't even try to hide it.

Then Fulbright and Hanne exchanged a glance. It was obvious that they'd screwed in the tree house on more than one occasion. But that day they were looking at each other because they'd finally done it: Their house had become the nerve center of the Leafmore party. And it had been a cool party. Very cool.

"You know," I lied as I let the final drops of cava yield to gravity on my tongue, "Prrr and Brrr told me they had a better time here than at John's last party."

On hearing that, Ful couldn't contain himself any longer. He hugged his wife and gave her an intense kiss, likely as intense as any he'd given her during their first weeks of courting on the Harvard campus, when they discovered Heraclitus's *Fragments* together and strolled around Cambridge holding hands, just like Oliver Barrett IV and Jennifer Cavalleri in *Love Story.*

At the bottom of the yard, beyond the boundary fence, was a little path. It was the kind of path you get in mystery novels, the kind that appears between bushes, and the trail vanishes in the dust and the passage of time. And what do we find at the end of those little paths in mystery novels? More mystery.

The unknown in this case was a little wooden house built at the top of a tree, geometrically finished with precision, and surrounded by green branches.

I stood there by the trunk, until the memory struck me:

A rope shoots out from inside the house and drops to a calculated distance from the ground, suitable only for the daring. I grasp the end with both hands, determined to scale it, and I run my gaze up the rope until I meet his eyes.

John wasn't drunk or stoned. He wasn't wearing his shirt unbuttoned at the top, nor could I see the chest hair that made me salivate. And he was wearing pants: This was serious.

Even so, he'd never looked as sexy as he did at that moment, leaning against that wooden wall that resurrected distant memories of the person I was a year ago.

"I'll wait by candlelight in the tree house of our dreams."

"Wow, strong start."

"It's cheap dendrological poetry, my dear." He showed me the quote written on one of the planks. "These Booklands can't leave a single corner without their mark on it."

"Did you know about this tree house?" I asked.

"No, but a friend of mine showed me how to poke around in other people's homes. And it's worth it. Don't you think that tree houses cast a kind of infallible spell?"

I laughed. The leaves danced through the window overlooking the stream. The light was purple, and John was barefoot.

"Here." He held out a small object wrapped in newspaper.

"What is it?"

"A gift."

I opened it. I had never seen it before, but I recognized it immediately.

"But it's the famous . . . the one that you . . . your . . . signed the Coca-Cola contract?"

"The very same," he replied, unperturbed.

"But this is national history, world history! It should be in a museum!"

"My God, you're so dramatic. It's a pen, Rita."

"You know it's highly likely that I'll lose it?"

"It's just a pen."

"Okay."

"And it writes really well too. I expect letters."

"You know you'll get them. As soon as I get to Barcelona, I'll write you."

A bird hopped nimbly to the end of the longest branch. We watched it for a long time, silent, sitting side by side, holding hands.

"You never thought I'd stay, did you?"

John laughed quietly to himself.

"Not for a moment."

"I hope you'll miss me at least."

"Every miserable second of my existence." He laughed, but he meant it.

After a long time, as the light was turning dark blue, John took out the napkin that Juanito had written on in La Boqueria all those years ago, that early morning when a dish of Palamós prawns saved John's life. And he showed it to me, not to give it to me, but to tell me that visiting La Boqueria, seeing Juanito, was something he had to do himself.

It wasn't an overly emotional goodbye. First, because I hate those, but mainly because, if anything was clear between John and me, it was that we would never say goodbye forever.

"By the way," I said, "I still don't know the name of these trees—I always heard it as 'river bitches.'"

"Rita, that's what they're called, river bitches."

The End

The entire Bookland family came with me to the Delta Airlines counter at the airport, like an unbreakable team. When the attendant saw us, she laughed but didn't ask any questions. It was as if we couldn't separate ourselves, as though the need to squeeze out our very last second close together was mutual. But the end had arrived, without mercy.

"Hairy . . ." Bini hasn't let go of my hand since we entered the building. "You know why fish don't close their eyes under the water? Well, out of the water too?"

"Tell me, Bini." And I don't want him to let go of my hand.

"Because they have no eyelids, Hairy. That's why they don't close them!"

"No! Really?"

"Yes! They don't have any! Hairy . . ."

"Yes, Bini . . ."

"When will you be back?"

"In no time at all . . ." The stabbing pain in my heart is horrific. "You won't have time to miss me before I come back, you'll see. In the meantime, look." I open my backpack. "I got you a present."

Bini unsticks his hand from mine.

"In this notebook, I've written down all your genius ideas. Since the first day I met you and you told me that police officers should double up as taxi drivers because they always have an empty car and they're almost certainly going to Rock 'n' Taco."

"And the toilet paper that lights up too?"

"That too. All of them, Bini. I wrote them all down." Bini flicks through the notebook attentively. "But, as you can see, there are still some blank pages, and I hope that by the time I come back, you will have filled them. Even if they seem like tiny or impossible ideas, it doesn't matter. Write them down, because they're all worth something."

"I have something for you, too, Eva."

Eva has been crying since she came to wake me in my room this morning with some banana-and-strawberry cookies that we ate together in bed.

After a year, I've finally mastered transatlantic logistical calculations, so I was able to perfectly anticipate the arrival of the gift I had planned for Eva (which arrived last night, phew!).

Eva rips off the paper, half grudgingly, half theatrically, and wipes her nose on her sleeve. It's an item of clothing. She doesn't like gifts of clothing, but then she discovers the surprise: a Barça shirt with her name written above the number 6, the same number as Xavi.

She's a thousand times more excited than I expected. The tears suddenly dry up, and she shouts and jumps because she can't believe she has an official shirt from the club that no eight-year-old girl knows better than her. She puts it on and performs a goal celebration she's practiced a million times, kissing the crest and sliding past the security gate on her knees. The braid I did in her hair before we left home is now a messy snake that looks prettier than ever.

"And for you, Aksel"—the emotion intensifies—"I got you this razor. You can't go to school next year without shaving. Haven't you noticed the mustache you're growing?"

The Booklands laugh, and Aksel's face explodes in embarrassment. He comes up and hugs me tight, and as I sniff the vanilla in his dry, unruly hair, I notice that he's grown even more.

I'd like to tell Hanne and Fulbright that I could have arrived at their house at age eighteen and worked it all out sooner. That their house, like all houses, is kind of chaotic in parts, but there's another, infinitely bigger part that's magic, a unique universe. I'd like to thank them for all the words they didn't say, for allowing me to find them on my own; for all the between-the-lines and the silences that got me where I needed to go. For the books, for showing me that reading is better than not reading. For the sodium thiopental, for the *Polovtsian Dances* and *Humoresques*, for Hannibal, for Parmenides and Empedocles. For this drive inside me that makes me want to learn more and better. But above all, for letting me love their children so much.

And I don't say all that, exactly, but I hug them very, very tightly.

From the air, more than a city, Atlanta is a leafy and infinite expanse of green nature. Miles and miles of trees peppered with what, from up here, look like tiny scars, hundreds of centipedes. Every cut is a street, and at the end of each is a house.

I know one of those houses. It's blue, and it sits at the end of a cul-de-sac. Apart from the squirrels climbing the trunks, there's not much activity on the street, but it doesn't matter, because in summer you can lie back on the porch with your arms open and listen to the sound of crickets as the old wood warms your back. On winter nights, the locals get home early, and you can watch life on the other side of the windows through a warm, beige-toned light.

I know one of those houses. It's blue, and inside are three children who live among encyclopedias, electric circuits, and reproductions of historic battles. They don't fit the usual mold for children their age, but if you dare to really love them, they can change your life forever.

As an exception, Hanne and Fulbright took the kids to the stationery store to choose the materials to make my goodbye card; for once, they were allowed to make something that wasn't from recycled materials. The kids chose recycled materials.

As to be expected, the resulting work was full of relevant information and contrasting historical facts. But it also included cartoons of moments we had shared: the clandestine parking lot where Soul rapped on that forbidden night; the pig and its rampant penis (and we all know that Eva was perfectly aware of what she was doing); a cartoon full of identical dogs—like Goldie—that Bini had painted. I've looked at it a hundred times, and every time I discover something new, like now, when I notice that the *T. rex* is finally living in vegetation appropriate to its historical period.

Bob Dylan is singing his final song through my bedroom window, but Antònia's cowbells have fallen silent: The nasal drawl climbs alone up the facade of the house. It's dinnertime.

I take a deep breath; the smell of washing on the line mingles with the aroma of black rice, prawns, and aioli. And when I open my eyes, ready to get up and go down to the kitchen, I realize that, in the pocket of my backpack where I stuffed all the cards, there's one I don't recognize.

I discover a white envelope sealed with dried saliva. It has my name written in a hand I would recognize in any galaxy of the universe.

A sudden flashback: It's the morning of my departure. Yaya's head is covered in curlers, and she's preparing all the Tupperware tubs for me to take to the airport. The old folk of the village are waiting outside the door to wave me goodbye. Before I leave, a phrase is tossed into the air: *And don' forget to check all the pockets!*

Alp, July 2007
The only journey I can tell you about, apart from when your father took me to see La Pantoja sing in Barcelona, was when I left my dear town, Las Casillas de Martos.

I remember it was a Tuesday (and you know what they say about Tuesdays—no vows and no getaways!), but I left just the same. It was all very quick. I didn't have time to grab any more than my Sunday bag and a handful of coins, because if my mother had caught me, she'd have killed me. I couldn't even take the photo of when I sang in Málaga. I left with nothing, nothing, nothing.

But I remember when I got on the train in Sevilla. I remember how I felt when I sat down next to a cageful of hens. When the train pulled out and I looked out of the window. You never forget that. I remember the fire I felt inside when I reached the station in Barcelona and saw the smoke and the broken glass, and all those people!

I think I felt I could fly. It was overwhelming, but I wasn't scared, because true travelers, those who travel with an open heart, aren't afraid. Their adrenaline keeps them too occupied. That day, for the first time in my life, I felt free.

I don't know whether there will be smoke when you get to where you're going, or if the station will have broken glass. I know you probably think you're scared, my love, but it's not fear you're feeling. You'll understand that in time.

I feel like a thousand winters have passed since I left my Andalusia. But every day I remember that Tuesday, and every day I thank God for that train journey. Because that train took me to my family, to your brother and to you.

Never forget what this journey makes you feel, how it makes you fly, because that memory will keep you going so many times in your life.

Enjoy the most thrilling journey of all, Rita, the one that will lead you to you.

Travel well, my dear.

All my love, Yaya.

PS: Eat the croquetas today, or they'll go bad.

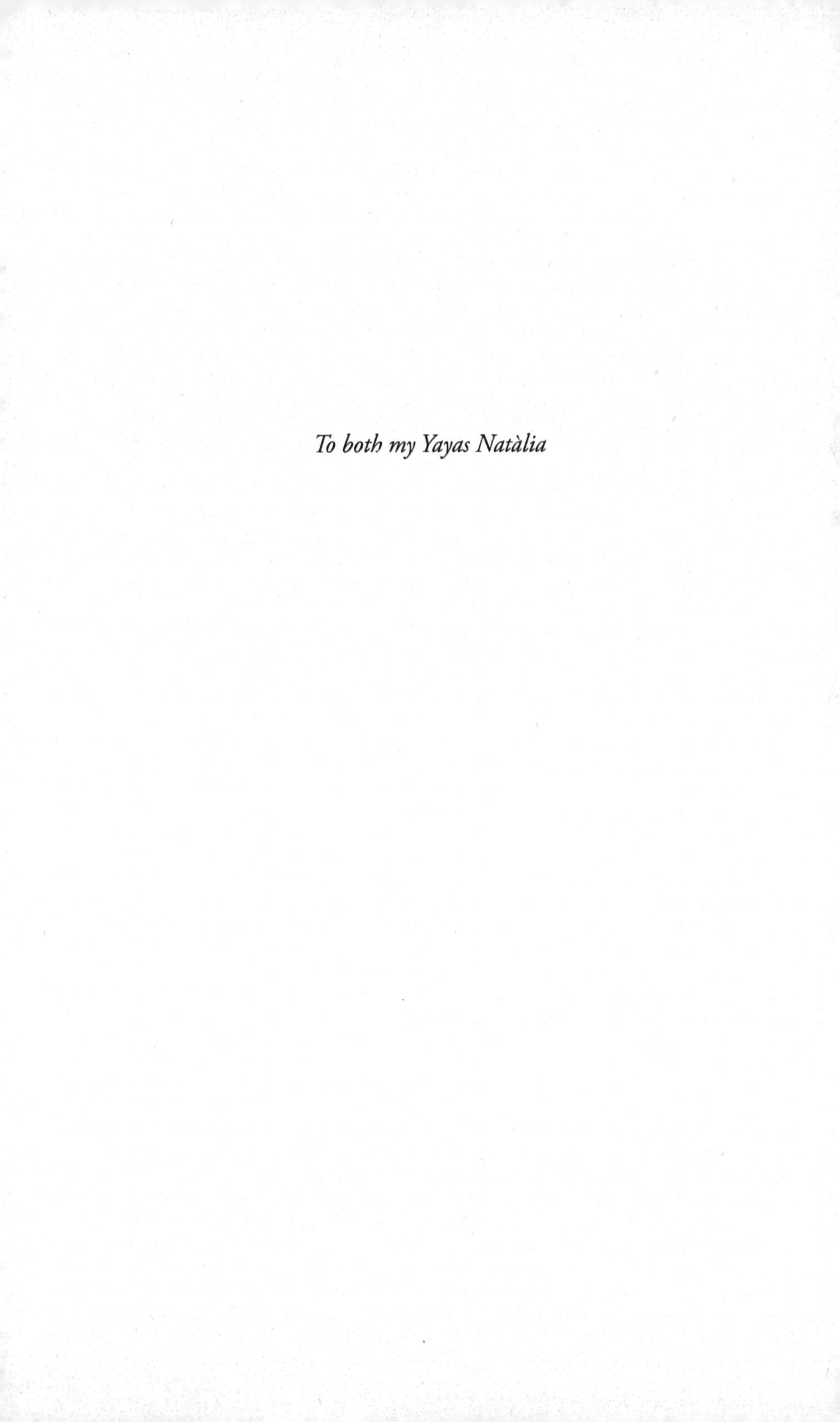

To both my Yayas Natàlia

Acknowledgments

To Esther Rebull, my Astrid, for mentioning the word "au pair" for the first time. To all the girls I met in those carpeted rooms in New York, who will never read these words. To Marta, for distracting me and bringing me *jamón*. To all the residents of Leafmore, who opened their Southern hearts and tennis courts to me. To the teachers and staff at the Language Institute of Georgia Tech, exceptional minds able to decipher even the most impossible accents, like mine. To all the friends I made there, where friendship is multiplied by a thousand. To Andre Castenell, the Starbucks barista everyone would want to have. To Alex Font, for immortalizing New York under the black and white water of Harlem's fountains. To all those who read my never-ending emails without accents, punctuation, or filters. Special thanks to Núria and Alba Casamayor and their IT classmates.

To the teachers at the Ateneu, who encouraged me to continue, especially, of course, the "esteemed" Melcior Comes. To Míriam, for the free-choice credit. To Joan Riambau, for opening unexpected emails that ended up turning into a book like this. To Anna Jolis, my editor, for sending me the email I have longed for all my life and for believing in this story.

To the incredible women at Frankie Gallo: Andrea, Judit, Pam, Anna, Cris, and Cuba, for their huge generosity. To Alba, because all journeys, at some point, take me back to those twenty-one days. To my literary sisters, Cinta and Aina, as well as Clara and Mireia. To the Chirlas, for being there.

To my whole family, for always encouraging me with overwhelming subjectivity. To my aunts and uncles for taking care of Nord while I was editing around the clock. To Antoni Bassas, for trusting in my inexperience and for the Oval anecdotes. To Duncan, for the LGBTI+ assessment; to Jay, for Bohr's theory; to Neus, for the most beautiful editing. To Ester, for waiting so long for the paper. To Blanca, wise advisor. To Edu, for the excitement.

To everyone at Betahaus, because without them I would have finished this novel five years earlier, but without experiencing some of the best years of my life and harvesting material for my second novel.

To the natives of Cerdanya.

To all my friends, I miss you.

About the Author

Photo © Guillem H. Pongiluppi

Regina Rodríguez Sirvent was born in Puigcerdà, Spain. A graduate in psychology, Regina studied screenwriting at Escola Superior de Cinema and creative writing at Ateneu Barcelonès. She has written for various newspapers and media outlets. *Singing to the Sun*, a literary sensation in Spain and winner of the L'Illa dels Llibres popular-vote award, is her first novel to be translated into English.

About the Translator

Photo © Beth Fowler

Beth Fowler has been a translator since 2009, working from Spanish and Portuguese to English. She won the Harvill Secker Young Translators' Prize in 2010, and her published translations include *Open Door* and *Paradises* by Iosi Havilio; *Ten Women* by Marcela Serrano; and *We All Loved Cowboys* by Carol Bensimon. She lives in the west of Scotland.